ATONEMENT

Ian McEwan has written two collections of stories, *First Love, Last Rites* and *In Between the Sheets*, and eight novels, *The Cement Garden*, *The Comfort of Strangers*, *The Child in Time*, *The Innocent*, *Black Dogs*, *The Daydreamer*, *Enduring Love* and *Amsterdam*, winner of the 1998 Booker Prize. He has also written several film scripts, including *The Imitation Game*, *The Ploughman's Lunch*, *Sour Sweet*, *The Good Son* and *The Innocent*.

ALSO BY IAN McEWAN

First Love, Last Rites
In Between the Sheets
The Cement Garden
The Comfort of Strangers
The Child in Time
The Innocent
Black Dogs
The Daydreamer
Enduring Love
Amsterdam

The Imitation Game
(plays for television)
Or Shall We Die?
(libretto for oratorio by Michael Berkeley)
The Ploughman's Lunch
(film script)
Sour Sweet
(film script)

Ian McEwan

ATONEMENT

V

VINTAGE

Published by Vintage 2002

4 6 8 10 9 7 5

Copyright © Ian McEwan 2001

Ian McEwan has asserted his right under the Copyright,
Designs and Patents Act 1988 to be identified as the author
of this work

This book is sold subject to the condition that it shall not
by way of trade or otherwise, be lent, resold, hired out, or
otherwise circulated without the publisher's prior consent
in any form of binding or cover other than that in which it
is published and without a similar condition including this
condition being imposed on the subsequent purchaser

Grateful acknowledgement is made to the following for
permission to reprint previously published material:
'In Memory of W. B. Yeats' from *Collected Poems* by
W. H. Auden. Used by kind permission of Faber and Faber
Ltd; 'A Shropshire Lad XVIII' by A. E. Housman. Used by
kind permission of the Society of Authors as Literary
Representatives of the Estate of A. E. Housman.

First published in Great Britain in 2001 by
Jonathan Cape

Vintage
Random House, 20 Vauxhall Bridge Road,
London SW1V 2SA

Random House Australia (Pty) Limited
20 Alfred Street, Milsons Point, Sydney,
New South Wales 2061, Australia

Random House New Zealand Limited
18 Poland Road, Glenfield, Auckland 10, New Zealand

Random House (Pty) Limited
Endulini, 5A Jubilee Road, Parktown 2193, South Africa

The Random House Group Limited Reg. No. 954009
www.randomhouse.co.uk

A CIP catalogue record for this book
is available from the British Library

ISBN 0 09 943804 6

Papers used by Random House are natural, recyclable
products made from wood grown in sustainable forests.
The manufacturing processes conform to the environ-
mental regulations of the country of origin

Printed and bound in Great Britain by
Bookmarque Ltd, Croydon, Surrey

TO ANNALENA

'Dear Miss Morland, consider the dreadful nature of the suspicions you have entertained. What have you been judging from? Remember the country and the age in which we live. Remember that we are English: that we are Christians. Consult your own understanding, your own sense of the probable, your own observation of what is passing around you. Does our education prepare us for such atrocities? Do our laws connive at them? Could they be perpetrated without being known in a country like this, where social and literary intercourse is on such a footing, where every man is surrounded by a neighbourhood of voluntary spies, and where roads and newspapers lay everything open? Dearest Miss Morland, what ideas have you been admitting?'

They had reached the end of the gallery; and with tears of shame she ran off to her own room.

Jane Austen, *Northanger Abbey*

Part One

Part One

One

The play – for which Briony had designed the posters, programmes and tickets, constructed the sales booth out of a folding screen tipped on its side, and lined the collection box in red crêpe paper – was written by her in a two-day tempest of composition, causing her to miss a breakfast and a lunch. When the preparations were complete, she had nothing to do but contemplate her finished draft and wait for the appearance of her cousins from the distant north. There would be time for only one day of rehearsal before her brother arrived. At some moments chilling, at others desperately sad, the play told a tale of the heart whose message, conveyed in a rhyming prologue, was that love which did not build a foundation on good sense was doomed. The reckless passion of the heroine, Arabella, for a wicked foreign count is punished by ill fortune when she contracts cholera during an impetuous dash towards a seaside town with her intended. Deserted by him and nearly everybody else, bed-bound in a garret, she discovers in herself a sense of humour. Fortune presents her a second chance in the form of an impoverished doctor – in fact, a prince in disguise who has elected to work among the needy. Healed by him, Arabella chooses judiciously this time, and is rewarded by reconciliation with her family and a wedding with the medical prince on 'a windy sunlit day in spring'.

Mrs Tallis read the seven pages of *The Trials of Arabella* in her bedroom, at her dressing table, with the author's arm around her shoulder the whole while. Briony studied her mother's face for every trace of shifting emotion, and Emily Tallis obliged with looks of alarm, snickers of glee and, at the end, grateful smiles and wise, affirming nods. She took her daughter in her arms, onto her lap – ah, that hot smooth little body she remembered from its infancy, and still not gone from her, not quite yet – and said that the play was 'stupendous', and agreed instantly, murmuring into the tight whorl of the girl's ear, that this word could be quoted on the poster which was to be on an easel in the entrance hall by the ticket booth.

Briony was hardly to know it then, but this was the project's highest point of fulfilment. Nothing came near it for satisfaction, all else was dreams and frustration. There were moments in the summer dusk after her light was out, burrowing in the delicious gloom of her canopy bed, when she made her heart thud with luminous, yearning fantasies, little playlets in themselves, every one of which featured Leon. In one, his big, good-natured face buckled in grief as Arabella sank in loneliness and despair. In another, there he was, cocktail in hand at some fashionable city watering hole, overheard boasting to a group of friends: Yes, my younger sister, Briony Tallis the writer, you must surely have heard of her. In a third he punched the air in exultation as the final curtain fell, although there was no curtain, there was no possibility of a curtain. Her play was not for her cousins, it was for her brother, to celebrate his return, provoke his admiration and guide him away from his careless succession of girlfriends, towards the right form of wife, the one who would persuade him to return to the countryside, the one who would sweetly request Briony's services as a bridesmaid.

She was one of those children possessed by a desire to have the world just so. Whereas her big sister's room was a stew of unclosed books, unfolded clothes, unmade bed, unemptied ashtrays, Briony's was a shrine to her controlling demon: the model farm spread across a deep window ledge consisted of the usual animals, but all facing one way – towards their owner – as if about to break into song, and even the farmyard hens were neatly corralled. In fact, Briony's was the only tidy upstairs room in the house. Her straight-backed dolls in their many-roomed mansion appeared to be under strict instructions not to touch the walls; the various thumb-sized figures to be found standing about her dressing table – cowboys, deep-sea divers, humanoid mice – suggested by their even ranks and spacing a citizen's army awaiting orders.

A taste for the miniature was one aspect of an orderly spirit. Another was a passion for secrets: in a prized varnished cabinet, a secret drawer was opened by pushing against the grain of a cleverly turned dovetail joint, and here she kept a diary locked by a clasp, and a notebook written in a code of her own invention. In a toy safe opened by six secret numbers she stored letters and postcards. An old tin petty cash box was hidden under a removable floorboard beneath her bed. In the box were treasures that dated back four years, to her ninth birthday when she began collecting: a mutant double acorn, fool's gold, a rain-making spell bought at a funfair, a squirrel's skull as light as a leaf.

But hidden drawers, lockable diaries and cryptographic systems could not conceal from Briony the simple truth: she had no secrets. Her wish for a harmonious, organised world denied her the reckless possibilities of wrongdoing. Mayhem and destruction were too chaotic for her tastes, and she did not have it in her to be cruel. Her effective status as an only child, as well as the relative isolation of the Tallis house, kept her, at least during the long summer holidays, from girlish intrigues with friends. Nothing in her life was sufficiently interesting or shameful to merit hiding; no one knew about the squirrel's skull beneath her bed, but no one wanted to know. None of this was particularly an affliction; or rather, it appeared so only in retrospect, once a solution had been found.

At the age of eleven she wrote her first story – a foolish affair, imitative of half a dozen folk tales and lacking, she realised later, that vital knowingness about the ways of the world which compels a reader's respect. But this first clumsy attempt showed her that the imagination itself was a source of secrets: once she had begun a story, no one could be told. Pretending in words was too tentative, too vulnerable, too embarrassing to let anyone know. Even writing out the *she said*s, the *and then*s, made her wince, and she felt foolish, appearing to know about the emotions of an imaginary being. Self-exposure was inevitable the moment she described a character's weakness; the reader was bound to speculate that she was describing herself. What other authority could she have? Only when a story was finished, all fates resolved and the whole matter sealed off at both ends so it resembled, at least in this one respect, every other finished story in the world, could she feel immune, and ready to punch holes in the margins, bind the chapters with pieces of string, paint or draw the cover, and take the finished work to show to her mother, or her father, when he was home.

Her efforts received encouragement. In fact, they were welcomed as the Tallises began to understand that the baby of the family possessed a strange mind and a facility with words. The long afternoons she spent browsing through dictionary and thesaurus made for constructions that were inept, but hauntingly so: the coins a villain concealed in his pocket were 'esoteric', a hoodlum caught stealing a car wept in 'shameless auto-exculpation', the heroine on her thoroughbred stallion made a 'cursory' journey through the night, the king's furrowed brow was the 'hieroglyph' of his displeasure. Briony was encouraged to read her stories aloud in the library and it surprised her parents and older sister to hear their quiet girl perform so boldly, making big gestures with her free arm, arching her eyebrows as she did the voices, and looking up from the page for seconds at a time as she read in order to gaze into one face after the other, unapologetically demanding her family's total attention as she cast her narrative spell.

Even without their attention and praise and obvious pleasure, Briony could not have been held back from her writing. In any case, she was discovering, as had many writers before her, that not all recognition is helpful. Cecilia's enthusiasm, for example, seemed a little overstated, tainted with condescension perhaps, and intrusive too; her big sister wanted each bound story catalogued and placed on the library shelves, between Rabindranath Tagore and Quintus Tertullian. If this was supposed to be a joke, Briony ignored it. She was on course now, and had found satisfaction on other levels; writing stories not only involved secrecy, it also gave her all the pleasures of miniaturisation. A world could be made in five pages, and one that was more pleasing than a model farm. The childhood of a spoiled prince could be framed within half a page, a moonlit dash through sleepy villages was one rhythmically emphatic sentence, falling in love could be achieved in a single word – a *glance*. The pages of a recently finished story seemed to vibrate in her hand with all the life they contained. Her passion for tidiness was also satisfied, for an unruly world could be made just so. A crisis in a heroine's life could be made to coincide with hailstones, gales and thunder, whereas nuptials were generally blessed with good light and soft breezes. A love of order also shaped the principles of justice, with death and marriage the main engines of housekeeping, the former being set aside exclusively for the morally dubious, the latter a reward withheld until the final page.

The play she had written for Leon's homecoming was her first excursion into drama, and she had found the transition quite effortless. It was a relief not to be writing out the *she said*s, or describing the weather or the onset of spring or her heroine's face – beauty, she had discovered, occupied a narrow band. Ugliness, on the other hand, had infinite variation. A universe reduced to what was said in it was tidiness indeed, almost to the point of nullity, and to compensate, every utterance was delivered at the extremity of some feeling or other, in the service of which the exclamation mark was indispensable. *The Trials of Arabella* may have been a melodrama, but its author had yet to hear the term. The piece was intended to inspire not laughter, but terror, relief and instruction, in that order, and the innocent intensity with which Briony set about the project – the posters, tickets, sales booth – made her particularly vulnerable to failure. She could easily have welcomed Leon with another of her stories, but it was the news that her cousins from the north were coming to stay that had prompted this leap into a new form.

That Lola, who was fifteen, and the nine-year-old twins, Jackson and Pierrot, were refugees from a bitter domestic civil war should have mattered more to Briony. She had heard her mother criticise the impulsive behaviour of her younger sister Hermione, and lament the situation of the three children, and denounce her meek, evasive brother-in-law Cecil who had fled to the safety of All Souls College, Oxford. Briony had heard her mother and sister analyse the latest twists and outrages, charges and counter charges, and she knew her cousins' visit was an open-ended one, and might even extend into term time. She had heard it said that the house could easily absorb three children, and that the Quinceys could stay as long as they liked, provided the parents, if they ever visited simultaneously, kept their quarrels away from the Tallis household. Two rooms near Briony's had been dusted down, new curtains had been hung and furniture carried in from other rooms. Normally, she would have been involved in these preparations, but they happened to coincide with her two-day writing bout and the beginnings of the front-of-house construction. She vaguely knew that divorce was an affliction, but she did not regard it as a proper subject, and gave it no thought. It was a mundane unravelling that could not be reversed, and therefore offered no opportunities to the storyteller: it belonged in the realm of disorder. Marriage was the thing, or rather, a wedding was, with its formal neatness of virtue rewarded, the thrill of its pageantry and banqueting, and dizzy promise of lifelong union. A good wedding was an unacknowledged representation of the as yet unthinkable – sexual bliss. In the aisles of country churches and grand city cathedrals, witnessed by a whole society of approving family and friends, her heroines and heroes reached their innocent climaxes and needed to go no further.

If divorce had presented itself as the dastardly antithesis of all this, it could easily have been cast onto the other pan of the scales, along with betrayal, illness, thieving, assault and mendacity. Instead it showed an unglamorous face of dull complexity and incessant wrangling. Like re-armament and the Abyssinia Question and gardening, it was simply not a subject, and when, after a long Saturday morning wait, Briony heard at last the sound of wheels on the gravel below her bedroom window, and snatched up her pages and ran down the stairs, across the hallway and out into the blinding light of midday, it was not insensitivity so much as a highly focused artistic ambition that caused her to shout to the dazed young visitors huddled together by the trap with their luggage, 'I've got your parts, all written out. First performance tomorrow! Rehearsals start in five minutes!'

Immediately, her mother and sister were there to interpose a blander timetable. The visitors – all three were ginger-haired and freckled – were shown their rooms, their cases were carried up by Hardman's son Danny, there was cordial in the kitchen, a tour of the house, a swim in the pool and lunch in the south garden, under the shade of the vines. All the while, Emily and Cecilia Tallis maintained a patter that surely robbed the guests of the ease it was supposed to confer. Briony knew that if she had travelled two hundred miles to a strange house, bright questions and jokey asides, and being told in a hundred different ways that she was free to choose, would have oppressed her. It was not generally realised that what children mostly wanted was to be left alone. However, the Quinceys worked hard at pretending to be amused or liberated, and this boded well for *The Trials of Arabella*: this trio clearly had the knack of being what they were not, even though they barely resembled the characters they were to play. Before lunch Briony slipped away to the empty rehearsal room – the nursery – and walked up and down on the painted floorboards, considering her casting options.

On the face of it, Arabella, whose hair was as dark as Briony's, was unlikely to be descended from freckled parents, or elope with a foreign freckled count, rent a garret room from a freckled innkeeper, lose her heart to a freckled prince and be married by a freckled vicar before a freckled congregation. But all this was to be so. Her cousins' colouring was too vivid – virtually fluorescent! – to be concealed. The best that could be said was that Arabella's *lack* of freckles was the sign – the hieroglyph, Briony might have written – of her distinction. Her purity of spirit would never be in doubt, though she moved through a blemished world. There was a further problem with the twins, who could not be told apart by a stranger. Was it right that the wicked count should so completely resemble the handsome prince, or that both should resemble Arabella's father *and* the vicar? What if Lola were cast as the prince? Jackson and Pierrot seemed typical eager little boys who would probably do as they were told. But would their sister play a man? She had green eyes and sharp bones in her face, and hollow cheeks, and there was something brittle in her reticence that suggested strong will and a temper easily lost. Merely floating the possibility of the role to Lola might provoke a crisis, and could Briony really hold hands with her before the altar, while Jackson intoned from the *Book of Common Prayer*?

It was not until five o'clock that afternoon that she was able to assemble her cast in the nursery. She had arranged three stools in a row, while she herself jammed her rump into an ancient baby's high-chair – a bohemian touch that gave her a tennis umpire's advantage of height. The twins had come with reluctance from the pool where they had been for three hours without a break. They were barefoot and wore singlets over trunks that dripped onto the floorboards. Water also ran down their necks from their matted hair, and both boys were shivering and jiggled their knees to keep warm. The long immersion had puckered and bleached their skin, so that in the relatively low light of the nursery their freckles appeared black. Their sister, who sat between them, with left leg balanced on right knee, was, by contrast, perfectly composed, having liberally applied perfume and changed into a green gingham frock to offset her colouring. Her sandals revealed an ankle bracelet and toenails painted vermilion. The sight of these nails gave Briony a constricting sensation around her sternum, and she knew at once that she could not ask Lola to play the prince.

Everyone was settled and the playwright was about to begin her little speech summarising the plot and evoking the excitement of performing before an adult audience tomorrow evening in the library. But it was Pierrot who spoke first.

'I hate plays and all that sort of thing.'

'I hate them too, and dressing up,' Jackson said.

It had been explained at lunch that the twins were to be distinguished by the fact that Pierrot was missing a triangle of flesh from his left ear lobe on account of a dog he had tormented when he was three.

Lola looked away. Briony said reasonably, 'How can you hate plays?'

'It's just showing off.' Pierrot shrugged as he delivered this self-evident truth.

Briony knew he had a point. This was precisely why she loved plays, or hers at least; everyone would adore her. Looking at the boys, under whose chairs water was pooling before spilling between the floorboard cracks, she knew they could never understand her ambition. Forgiveness softened her tone.

'Do you think Shakespeare was just showing off?'

Pierrot glanced across his sister's lap towards Jackson. This warlike name was faintly familiar, with its whiff of school and adult certainty, but the twins found their courage in each other.

'Everyone knows he was.'

'Definitely.'

When Lola spoke, she turned first to Pierrot and halfway through her sentence swung round to finish on Jackson. In Briony's family, Mrs Tallis never had anything to impart that needed saying simultaneously to both daughters. Now Briony saw how it was done.

'You'll be in this play, or you'll get a clout, and then I'll speak to The Parents.'

'If you clout us, *we'll* speak to The Parents.'

'You'll be in this play or I'll speak to The Parents.'

That the threat had been negotiated neatly downwards did not appear to diminish its power. Pierrot sucked on his lower lip.

'Why do we have to?' Everything was conceded in the question, and Lola tried to ruffle his sticky hair.

'Remember what The Parents said? We're guests in this house and we make ourselves – what do we make ourselves? Come on. What do we make ourselves?'

'A-menable,' the twins chorused in misery, barely stumbling over the unusual word.

Lola turned to Briony and smiled. 'Please tell us about your play.'

The Parents. Whatever institutionalised strength was locked in this plural was about to fly apart, or had already done so, but for now it could not be acknowledged, and bravery was demanded of even the youngest. Briony felt suddenly ashamed at what she had selfishly begun, for it had never occurred to her that her cousins would not want to play their parts in *The Trials of Arabella*. But they had trials, a catastrophe of their own, and now, as guests in her house, they believed themselves under an obligation. What was worse, Lola had made it clear that she too would be acting on sufferance. The vulnerable Quinceys were being coerced. And yet, Briony struggled to grasp the difficult thought, wasn't there manipulation here, wasn't Lola using the twins to express something on her behalf, something hostile or destructive? Briony felt the disadvantage of being two years younger than the other girl, of having a full two years' refinement weigh against her, and now her play seemed a miserable, embarrassing thing.

Avoiding Lola's gaze the whole while, she proceeded to outline the plot, even as its stupidity began to overwhelm her. She no longer had the heart to invent for her cousins the thrill of the first night.

As soon as she was finished Pierrot said, 'I want to be the count. I want to be a bad person.'

Jackson said simply, 'I'm a prince. I'm always a prince.'

She could have drawn them to her and kissed their little faces, but she said, 'That's all right then.'

Lola uncrossed her legs, smoothed her dress and stood, as though about to leave. She spoke through a sigh of sadness or resignation. 'I suppose that because you're the one who wrote it, you'll be Arabella . . .'

'Oh no,' Briony said. 'No. Not at all.'

She said no, but she meant yes. Of course she was taking the part of Arabella. What she was objecting to was Lola's 'because'. She was not playing Arabella because she wrote the play, she was taking the part because no other possibility had crossed her mind, because that was how Leon was to see her, because she *was* Arabella.

But she had said no, and now Lola was saying sweetly, 'In that case, do you mind if I play her? I think I could do it very well. In fact, of the two of us . . .'

She let that hang, and Briony stared at her, unable to keep the horror from her expression, and unable to speak. It was slipping away from her, she knew, but there was nothing that she could think of to say that would bring it back. Into Briony's silence, Lola pressed her advantage.

'I had a long illness last year, so I could do that part of it well too.'

Too? Briony could not keep up with the older girl. The misery of the inevitable was clouding her thoughts.

One of the twins said proudly, 'And you were in the school play.'

How could she tell them that Arabella was not a freckled person? Her skin was pale and her hair was black and her thoughts were Briony's thoughts. But how could she refuse a cousin so far from home whose family life was in ruins? Lola was reading her mind because she now played her final card, the unrefusable ace.

'Do say yes. It would be the only good thing that's happened to me in *months*.'

Yes. Unable to push her tongue against the word, Briony could only nod, and felt as she did so a sulky thrill of self-annihilating compliance spreading across her skin and ballooning outwards from it, darkening the room in throbs. She wanted to leave, she wanted to lie alone, face-down on her bed and savour the vile piquancy of the moment, and go back down the lines of branching consequences to the point before the destruction began. She needed to contemplate with eyes closed the full richness of what she had lost, what she had given away, and to anticipate the new regime. Not only Leon to consider, but what of the antique peach and cream satin dress that her mother was looking out for her, for Arabella's wedding? That would now be given to Lola. How could her mother reject the daughter who had loved her all these years? As she saw the dress make its perfect, clinging fit around her cousin and witnessed her mother's heartless smile, Briony knew her only reasonable choice then would be to run away, to live under hedges, eat berries and speak to no one, and be found by a bearded woodsman one winter's dawn, curled up at the base of a giant oak, beautiful and dead, and barefoot, or perhaps wearing the ballet pumps with the pink ribbon straps . . .

Self-pity needed her full attention, and only in solitude could she breathe life into the lacerating details, but at the instant of her assent – how the tilt of a skull could change a life! – Lola had picked up the bundle of Briony's manuscript from the floor, and the twins had slipped from their chairs to follow their sister into the space in the centre of the nursery that Briony had cleared the day before. Did she dare leave now? Lola was pacing the floorboards, one hand to her brow as she skimmed through the first pages of the play, muttering the lines from the prologue. She announced that nothing was to be lost by beginning at the beginning, and now she was casting her brothers as Arabella's parents and describing the opening to them, seeming to know all there was to know about the scene. The advance of Lola's dominion was merciless and made self-pity irrelevant. Or would it be all the more annihilatingly delicious? – for Briony had not even been cast as Arabella's mother, and now was surely the time to sidle from the room and tumble into face-down darkness on the bed. But it was Lola's briskness, her obliviousness to anything beyond her own business, and Briony's certainty that her own feelings would not even register, still less provoke guilt, which gave her the strength to resist.

In a generally pleasant and well-protected life, she had never really confronted anyone before. Now she saw: it was like diving into the swimming pool in early June; you simply had to make yourself do it. As she squeezed out of the high-chair and walked over to where her cousin stood her heart thudded inconveniently and her breath was short.

She took the play from Lola and said in a voice that was constricted and more high-pitched than usual, 'If you're Arabella, then I'll be the director, thank you very much, and I'll read the prologue.'

Lola put her speckled hand to her mouth. 'Sor-reeee!' she hooted. 'I was just trying to get things started.'

Briony was unsure how to respond, so she turned to Pierrot and said, 'You don't look much like Arabella's mother.'

The countermanding of Lola's casting decision, and the laughter in the boys it provoked, made for a shift in the balance of power. Lola made an exaggerated shrug of her bony shoulders and went to stare out of the window. Perhaps she herself was struggling with the temptation to flounce from the room.

Though the twins began a wrestling match, and their sister suspected the onset of a headache, somehow the rehearsal began. The silence into which Briony read the prologue was tense.

> This is the tale of spontaneous Arabella
> Who ran off with an extrinsic fellow.
> It grieved her parents to see their first born
> Evanesce from her home to go to Eastbourne
> Without permission . . .

His wife at his side, Arabella's father stood at the wrought-iron gates of his estate, first pleading with his daughter to reconsider her decision, then in desperation ordering her not to go. Facing him was the sad but stubborn heroine with the count beside her, and their horses, tethered to a nearby oak, were neighing and pawing the ground, impatient to be off. The father's tenderest feelings were supposed to make his voice quaver as he said,

> My darling one, you are young and lovely,
> But inexperienced, and though you think
> The world is at your feet,
> It can rise up and tread on you.

Briony positioned her cast; she herself clutched Jackson's arm, Lola and Pierrot stood several feet away, hand in hand. When the boys met each other's eye they had a giggling fit which the girls shushed at. There had been trouble enough already, but Briony began to understand the chasm that lay between an idea and its execution only when Jackson began to read from his sheet in a stricken monotone, as though each word was a name on a list of dead people, and was unable to pronounce 'inexperienced' even though it was said for him many times, and left out the last two words of his lines – 'it can rise up and tread'. As for Lola, she spoke her lines correctly but casually, and sometimes smiled inappropriately at some private thought, determined to demonstrate that her nearly adult mind was elsewhere.

And so they went on, the cousins from the north, for a full half an hour, steadily wrecking Briony's creation, and it was a mercy, therefore, when her big sister came to fetch the twins for their bath.

Two

Partly because of her youth and the glory of the day, partly because of her blossoming need for a cigarette, Cecilia Tallis half ran with her flowers along the path that went by the river, by the old diving pool with its mossy brick wall, before curving away through the oak woods. The accumulated inactivity of the summer weeks since finals also hurried her along; since coming home, her life had stood still, and a fine day like this made her impatient, almost desperate.

The cool high shade of the woods was a relief, the sculpted intricacies of the tree trunks enchanting. Once through the iron kissing gate, and past the rhododendrons beneath the ha-ha, she crossed the open parkland – sold off to a local farmer to graze his cows on – and came up behind the fountain and its retaining wall and the half-scale reproduction of Bernini's *Triton* in the Piazza Barberini in Rome.

The muscular figure, squatting so comfortably on his shell, could blow through his conch a jet only two inches high, the pressure was so feeble, and water fell back over his head, down his stone locks and along the groove of his powerful spine, leaving a glistening dark green stain. In an alien northern climate he was a long way from home, but he was beautiful in morning sunlight, and so were the four dolphins that supported the wavy-edged shell on which he sat. She looked at the improbable scales on the dolphins and on the Triton's thighs, and then towards the house. Her quickest way into the drawing room was across the lawn and terrace and through the French windows. But her childhood friend and university acquaintance, Robbie Turner, was on his knees, weeding along a rugosa hedge, and she did not feel like getting into conversation with him. Or at least, not now. Since coming down, landscape gardening was his last craze but one. Now there was talk of medical college, which after a literature degree seemed rather pretentious. And presumptuous too, since it was her father who would have to pay.

She refreshed the flowers by plunging them into the fountain's basin, which was full-scale, deep and cold, and avoided Robbie by hurrying round to the front of the house – it was an excuse, she thought, to stay outside another few minutes. Morning sunlight, or any light, could not conceal the ugliness of the Tallis home – barely forty years old, bright orange brick, squat, lead-paned baronial Gothic, to be condemned one day in an article by Pevsner, or one of his team, as a tragedy of wasted chances, and by a younger writer of the modern school as 'charmless to a fault'. An Adam-style house had stood here until destroyed by fire in the late 1880s. What remained was the artificial lake and island with its two stone bridges supporting the driveway, and, by the water's edge, a crumbling stuccoed temple. Cecilia's grandfather, who grew up over an ironmonger's shop and made the family fortune with a series of patents on padlocks, bolts, latches and hasps, had imposed on the new house his taste for all things solid, secure and functional. Still, if one turned one's back to the front entrance and glanced down the drive, ignoring the Friesians already congregating in the shade of widely spaced trees, the view was fine enough, giving an impression of timeless, unchanging calm which made her more certain than ever that she must soon be moving on.

She went indoors, quickly crossed the black and white tiled hall – how familiar her echoing steps, how annoying – and paused to catch her breath in the doorway of the drawing room. Dripping coolly onto her sandalled feet, the untidy bunch of rose-bay willow-herb and irises brought her to a better state of mind. The vase she was looking for was on an American cherry-wood table by the French windows which were slightly ajar. Their south-east aspect had permitted parallelograms of morning sunlight to advance across the powder-blue carpet. Her breathing slowed and her desire for a cigarette deepened, but still she hesitated by the door, momentarily held by the perfection of the scene – by the three faded Chesterfields grouped around the almost new Gothic fireplace in which stood a display of wintry sedge, by the unplayed, untuned harpsichord and the unused rosewood music stands, by the heavy velvet curtains, loosely restrained by an orange and blue tasselled rope, framing a partial view of cloudless sky and the yellow and grey mottled terrace where camomile and feverfew grew between the paving cracks. A set of steps led down to the lawn on whose border Robbie still worked, and which extended to the Triton fountain fifty yards away.

All this – the river and flowers, running, which was something she rarely did these days, the fine ribbing of the oak trunks, the high-ceilinged room, the geometry of light, the pulse in her ears subsiding in the stillness – all this pleased her as the familiar was transformed into a delicious strangeness. But she also felt reproved for her homebound boredom. She had returned from Cambridge with a vague notion that her family was owed an uninterrupted stretch of her company. But her father remained in town, and her mother, when she wasn't nurturing her migraines, seemed distant, even unfriendly. Cecilia had carried up trays of tea to her mother's room – as spectacularly squalid as her own – thinking some intimate conversations might develop. However, Emily Tallis wanted to share only tiny frets about the household, or she lay back against the pillows, her expression unreadable in the gloom, emptying her cup in wan silence. Briony was lost to her writing fantasies – what had seemed a passing fad was now an enveloping obsession. Cecilia had seen them on the stairs that morning, her younger sister leading the cousins, poor things, who had arrived only yesterday, up to the nursery to rehearse the play Briony wanted to put on that evening, when Leon and his friend were expected. There was so little time, and already one of the twins had been detained by Betty in the scullery for some wrongdoing or other. Cecilia was not inclined to help – it was too hot, and whatever she did, the project would end in calamity, with Briony expecting too much, and no one, especially the cousins, able to measure up to her frenetic vision.

Cecilia knew she could not go on wasting her days in the stews of her untidied room, lying on her bed in a haze of smoke, chin propped on her hand, pins and needles spreading up through her arm as she read her way through Richardson's *Clarissa*. She had made a half-hearted start on a family tree, but on the paternal side, at least until her great-grandfather opened his humble hardware shop, the ancestors were irretrievably sunk in a bog of farm labouring, with suspicious and confusing changes of surnames among the men, and common-law marriages unrecorded in the parish registers. She could not remain here, she knew she should make plans, but she did nothing. There were various possibilities, all equally unpressing. She had a little money in her account, enough to keep her modestly for a year or so. Leon repeatedly invited her to spend time with him in London. University friends were offering to help her find a job – a dull one certainly, but she would have her independence. She had interesting uncles and aunts on her mother's side who were always happy to see her, including wild Hermione, mother of Lola and the boys, who even now was over in Paris with a lover who worked in the wireless.

No one was holding Cecilia back, no one would care particularly if she left. It wasn't torpor that kept her – she was often restless to the point of irritability. She simply liked to feel that she was prevented from leaving, that she was needed. From time to time she persuaded herself she remained for Briony's sake, or to help her mother, or because this really was her last sustained period at home and she would see it through. In fact, the thought of packing a suitcase and taking the morning train did not excite her. Leaving for leaving's sake. Lingering here, bored and comfortable, was a form of self-punishment tinged with pleasure, or the expectation of it; if she went away something bad might happen or, worse, something good, something she could not afford to miss. And there was Robbie, who exasperated her with his affectation of distance, and his grand plans which he would only discuss with her father. They had known each other since they were seven, she and Robbie, and it bothered her that they were awkward when they talked. Even though she felt it was largely his fault – could his first have gone to his head? – she knew this was something she must clear up before she thought of leaving.

Through the open windows came the faint leathery scent of cow dung, always present except on the coldest days, and noticeable only to those who had been away. Robbie had put down his trowel and stood to roll a cigarette, a hangover from his Communist Party time – another abandoned fad, along with his ambitions in anthropology, and the planned hike from Calais to Istanbul. Still, her own cigarettes were two flights up, in one of several possible pockets.

She advanced into the room, and thrust the flowers into the vase. It had once belonged to her Uncle Clem, whose funeral, or re-burial, at the end of the war she remembered quite well: the gun carriage arriving at the country churchyard, the coffin draped in the regimental flag, the raised swords, the bugle at the graveside, and, most memorably for a five-year-old, her father weeping. Clem was his only sibling. The story of how he had come by the vase was told in one of the last letters the young lieutenant wrote home. He was on liaison duties in the French sector and initiated a last-minute evacuation of a small town west of Verdun before it was shelled. Perhaps fifty women, children and old people were saved. Later, the mayor and other officials led Uncle Clem back through the town to a half-destroyed museum. The vase was taken from a shattered glass case and presented in gratitude. There was no refusing, however inconvenient it might have seemed to fight a war with Meissen porcelain under one arm. A month later the vase was left for safety in a farmhouse, and Lieutenant Tallis waded across a river in spate to retrieve it, returning the same way at midnight to join his unit. In the final days of the war, he was sent on patrol duties and gave the vase to a friend for safekeeping. It slowly found its way back to the regimental headquarters, and was delivered to the Tallis home some months after Uncle Clem's burial.

There was really no point trying to arrange wild flowers. They had tumbled into their own symmetry, and it was certainly true that too even a distribution between the irises and the rose-bay willow-herb ruined the effect. She spent some minutes making adjustments in order to achieve a natural chaotic look. While she did so she wondered about going out to Robbie. It would save her from running upstairs. But she felt uncomfortable and hot, and would have liked to check her appearance in the large gilt mirror above the fireplace. But if he turned round – he was standing with his back to the house, smoking – he would see right into the room. At last she was finished and stood back again. Now her brother's friend, Paul Marshall, might believe that the flowers had simply been dropped in the vase in the same carefree spirit with which they had been picked. It made no sense, she knew, arranging flowers before the water was in – but there it was; she couldn't resist moving them around, and not everything people did could be in a correct, logical order, especially when they were alone. Her mother wanted flowers in the guest room and Cecilia was happy to oblige. The place to go for water was the kitchen. But Betty was preparing to cook tonight's meal, and was in terrorising mood. Not only the little boy, Jackson or Pierrot, would be cowering – so too would the extra help from the village. Already, even from the drawing room, it was possible to hear an occasional muffled bad-tempered shout and the clang of a saucepan hitting the hob with unnatural force. If Cecilia went in now she would have to mediate between her mother's vague instructions and Betty's forceful state of mind. It surely made more sense to go outside and fill the vase at the fountain.

Some time in her teens a friend of Cecilia's father who worked in the Victoria and Albert Museum had come to examine the vase and declared it sound. It was genuine Meissen porcelain, the work of the great artist Höroldt, who painted it in 1726. It had most certainly once been the property of King August. Even though it was reckoned to be worth more than the other pieces in the Tallis home, which were mostly junk collected by Cecilia's grandfather, Jack Tallis wanted the vase in use, in honour of his brother's memory. It was not to be imprisoned behind a glass case. If it had survived the war, the reasoning went, then it could survive the Tallises. His wife did not disagree. The truth was, whatever its great value, and beyond its association, Emily Tallis did not much like the vase. Its little painted Chinese figures gathered formally in a garden around a table, with ornate plants and implausible birds, seemed fussy and oppressive. Chinoiserie in general bored her. Cecilia herself had no particular view, though she sometimes wondered just how much it might fetch at Sotheby's. The vase was respected not for Höroldt's mastery of polychrome enamels or the blue and gold interlacing strapwork and foliage, but for Uncle Clem, and the lives he had saved, the river he had crossed at midnight, and his death just a week before the Armistice. Flowers, especially wild flowers, seemed a proper tribute.

Cecilia gripped the cool porcelain in both hands as she stood on one foot, and with the other hooked the French windows open wide. As she stepped out into the brightness, the rising scent of warmed stone was like a friendly embrace. Two swallows were making passes over the fountain, and a chiff-chaff's song was piercing the air from within the sinewy gloom of the giant Cedar of Lebanon. The flowers swung in the light breeze, tickling her face as she crossed the terrace and carefully negotiated the three crumbly steps down to the gravel path. Robbie turned suddenly at the sound of her approach.

'I was away in my thoughts,' he began to explain.

'Would you roll me one of your Bolshevik cigarettes?'

He threw his own cigarette aside, took the tin which lay on his jacket on the lawn and walked alongside her to the fountain. They were silent for a while.

'Beautiful day,' she then said through a sigh.

He was looking at her with amused suspicion. There was something between them, and even she had to acknowledge that a tame remark about the weather sounded perverse.

'How's *Clarissa*?' He was looking down at his fingers rolling the tobacco.

'Boring.'

'We mustn't say so.'

'I wish she'd get on with it.'

'She does. And it gets better.'

They slowed, then stopped so that he could put the finishing touches to her roll-up.

She said, 'I'd rather read Fielding any day.'

She felt she had said something stupid. Robbie was looking away across the park and the cows towards the oak wood that lined the river valley, the wood she had run through that morning. He might be thinking she was talking to him in code, suggestively conveying her taste for the full-blooded and sensual. That was a mistake, of course, and she was discomfited and had no idea how to put him right. She liked his eyes, she thought, the unblended mix of orange and green, made even more granular in sunlight. And she liked the fact that he was so tall. It was an interesting combination in a man, intelligence and sheer bulk. Cecilia had taken the cigarette and he was lighting it for her.

'I know what you mean,' he said as they walked the remaining few yards to the fountain. 'There's more life in Fielding, but he can be psychologically crude compared to Richardson.'

She set down the vase by the uneven steps that rose to the fountain's stone basin. The last thing she wanted was an undergraduate debate on eighteenth-century literature. She didn't think Fielding was crude at all, or that Richardson was a fine psychologist, but she wasn't going to be drawn in, defending, defining, attacking. She was tired of that, and Robbie was tenacious in argument.

Instead she said, 'Leon's coming today, did you know?'

'I heard a rumour. That's marvellous.'

'He's bringing a friend, this man Paul Marshall.'

'The chocolate millionaire. Oh no! And you're giving him flowers!'

She smiled. Was he pretending to be jealous to conceal the fact that he was? She no longer understood him. They had fallen out of touch at Cambridge. It had been too difficult to do anything else. She changed the subject.

'The Old Man says you're going to be a doctor.'

'I'm thinking about it.'

'You must love the student life.'

He looked away again, but this time for only a second or less, and when he turned to her she thought she saw a touch of irritation. Had she sounded condescending? She saw his eyes again, green and orange flecks, like a boy's marble. When he spoke he was perfectly pleasant.

'I know you never liked that sort of thing, Cee. But how else do you become a doctor?'

'That's my point. Another six years. Why do it?'

He wasn't offended. She was the one who was over-interpreting, and jittery in his presence, and she was annoyed with herself.

He was taking her question seriously. 'No one's really going to give me work as a landscape gardener. I don't want to teach, or go in for the civil service. And medicine interests me . . .' He broke off as a thought occurred to him. 'Look, I've agreed to pay your father back. That's the arrangement.'

'That's not what I meant at all.'

She was surprised that he should think she was raising the question of money. That was ungenerous of him. Her father had subsidised Robbie's education all his life. Had anyone ever objected? She had thought she was imagining it, but in fact she was right – there was something trying in Robbie's manner lately. He had a way of wrong-footing her whenever he could. Two days before he had rung the front doorbell – in itself odd, for he had always had the freedom of the house. When she was called down, he was standing outside asking in a loud, impersonal voice if he could borrow a book. As it happened, Polly was on all fours, washing the tiles in the entrance hall. Robbie made a great show of removing his boots which weren't dirty at all, and then, as an afterthought, took his socks off as well, and tiptoed with comic exaggeration across the wet floor. Everything he did was designed to distance her. He was play-acting the cleaning lady's son come to the big house on an errand. They went into the library together, and when he found his book, she asked him to stay for a coffee. It was a pretence, his dithering refusal – he was one of the most confident people she had ever met. She was being mocked, she knew. Rebuffed, she left the room and went upstairs and lay on the bed with *Clarissa*, and read without taking in a word, feeling her irritation and confusion grow. She was being mocked, or she was being punished – she did not know which was worse. Punished for being in a different circle at Cambridge, for not having a charlady for a mother; mocked for her poor degree – not that they actually awarded degrees to women anyway.

Awkwardly, for she still had her cigarette, she picked up

the vase and balanced it on the rim of the basin. It would
have made better sense to take the flowers out first, but she
was too irritable. Her hands were hot and dry and she had
to grip the porcelain all the tighter. Robbie was silent, but
she could tell from his expression – a forced, stretched smile
that did not part his lips – that he regretted what he had said.
That was no comfort either. This was what happened when
they talked these days; one or the other was always in the
wrong, trying to call back the last remark. There was no ease,
no stability in the course of their conversations, no chance to
relax. Instead, it was spikes, traps, and awkward turns that
caused her to dislike herself almost as much as she disliked
him, though she did not doubt that he was mostly to blame.
She hadn't changed, but there was no question that he had.
He was putting distance between himself and the family that
had been completely open to him and given him everything.
For this reason alone – expectation of his refusal, and her own
displeasure in advance – she had not invited him to dinner
that night. If he wanted distance, then let him have it.

Of the four dolphins whose tails supported the shell on
which the Triton squatted, the one nearest to Cecilia had its
wide-open mouth stopped with moss and algae. Its spherical
stone eyeballs, as big as apples, were iridescent green. The
whole statue had acquired around its northerly surfaces a
bluish-green patina, so that from certain approaches, and in
low light, the muscle-bound Triton really seemed a hundred
leagues under the sea. Bernini's intention must have been for
the water to trickle musically from the wide shell with its
irregular edges into the basin below. But the pressure was
too weak, so that instead the water slid soundlessly down
the underside of the shell where opportunistic slime hung in
dripping points, like stalactites in a limestone cave. The basin
itself was over three feet deep and clear. The bottom was
of a pale, creamy stone over which undulating white-edged
rectangles of refracted sunlight divided and overlapped.

Her idea was to lean over the parapet and hold the flowers

in the vase while she lowered it on its side into the water, but it was at this point that Robbie, wanting to make amends, tried to be helpful.

'Let me take that,' he said, stretching out a hand. 'I'll fill it for you, and you take the flowers.'

'I can manage, thanks.' She was already holding the vase over the basin.

But he said, 'Look, I've got it.' And he had, tightly between forefinger and thumb. 'Your cigarette will get wet. Take the flowers.'

This was a command on which he tried to confer urgent masculine authority. The effect on Cecilia was to cause her to tighten her grip. She had no time, and certainly no inclination, to explain that plunging vase and flowers into the water would help with the natural look she wanted in the arrangement. She tightened her hold and twisted her body away from him. He was not so easily shaken off. With a sound like a dry twig snapping, a section of the lip of the vase came away in his hand, and split into two triangular pieces which dropped into the water and tumbled to the bottom in a synchronous, see-sawing motion, and lay there, several inches apart, writhing in the broken light.

Cecilia and Robbie froze in the attitude of their struggle. Their eyes met, and what she saw in the bilious mélange of green and orange was not shock, or guilt, but a form of challenge, or even triumph. She had the presence of mind to set the ruined vase back down on the step before letting herself confront the significance of the accident. It was irresistible, she knew, even delicious, for the graver it was, the worse it would be for Robbie. Her dead uncle, her father's dear brother, the wasteful war, the treacherous crossing of the river, the preciousness beyond money, the heroism and goodness, all the years backed up behind the history of the vase reaching back to the genius of Horoldt, and beyond him to the mastery of the arcanists who had re-invented porcelain.

'You idiot! Look what you've done.'

29

He looked into the water, then he looked at back at her, and simply shook his head as he raised a hand to cover his mouth. By this gesture he assumed full responsibility, but at that moment, she hated him for the inadequacy of the response. He glanced towards the basin and sighed. For a moment he thought she was about to step backwards onto the vase, and he raised his hand and pointed, though he said nothing. Instead he began to unbutton his shirt. Immediately she knew what he was about. Intolerable. He had come to the house and removed his shoes and socks – well, she would show him then. She kicked off her sandals, unbuttoned her blouse and removed it, unfastened her skirt and stepped out of it and went to the basin wall. He stood with hands on his hips and stared as she climbed into the water in her underwear. Denying his help, any possibility of making amends, was his punishment. The unexpectedly freezing water that caused her to gasp was his punishment. She held her breath, and sank, leaving her hair fanned out across the surface. Drowning herself would be his punishment.

When she emerged a few seconds later with a piece of pottery in each hand, he knew better than to offer to help her out of the water. The frail white nymph, from whom water cascaded far more successfully than it did from the beefy Triton, carefully placed the pieces by the vase. She dressed quickly, turning her wet arms with difficulty through her silk sleeves, and tucking the unfastened blouse into the skirt. She picked up her sandals and thrust them under her arm, put the fragments in the pocket of her skirt and took up the vase. Her movements were savage, and she would not meet his eye. He did not exist, he was banished, and this was also the punishment. He stood there dumbly as she walked away from him, barefoot across the lawn, and he watched her darkened hair swing heavily across her shoulders, drenching her blouse. Then he turned and looked into the water in case there was a piece she had missed. It was difficult to see because the roiling surface had yet to recover its tranquillity, and the turbulence was driven by the lingering spirit of her fury. He put his hand flat upon the surface, as though to quell it. She, meanwhile, had disappeared into the house.

Three

According to the poster in the hallway, the date of the first performance of *The Trials of Arabella* was only one day after the first rehearsal. However, it was not easy for the writer-director to find clear time for concentrated work. As on the preceding afternoon, the trouble lay in assembling the cast. During the night Arabella's disapproving father, Jackson, had wet the bed, as troubled small boys far from home will, and was obliged by current theory to carry his sheets and pyjamas down to the laundry and wash them himself, by hand, under the supervision of Betty who had been instructed to be distant and firm. This was not represented to the boy as a punishment, the idea being to instruct his unconscious that future lapses would entail inconvenience and hard work; but he was bound to feel it as reproof as he stood at the vast stone sink which rose level to his chest, suds creeping up his bare arms to soak his rolled-up shirt sleeves, the wet sheets as heavy as a dead dog and a general sense of calamity numbing his will. Briony came down at intervals to check on his progress. She was forbidden to help, and Jackson, of course, had never laundered a thing in his life; the two washes, countless rinses and the sustained two-handed grappling with the mangle, as well as the fifteen trembling minutes he had afterwards at the kitchen table with bread and butter and a glass of water, took up two hours' rehearsal time.

Betty told Hardman when he came in from the morning heat for his pint of ale that it was enough that she was having to prepare a special roast dinner in such weather, and that she personally thought the treatment too harsh, and would have administered several sharp smacks to the buttocks and washed the sheets herself. This would have suited Briony, for the morning was slipping away. When her mother came down to see for herself that the task was done, it was inevitable that a feeling of release should settle on the participants, and in Mrs Tallis's mind a degree of unacknowledged guilt, so that when Jackson asked in a small voice if he might please now be allowed a swim in the pool and could his brother come too, his wish was immediately granted, and Briony's objections generously brushed aside, as though she were the one who was imposing unpleasant ordeals on a helpless little fellow. So there was swimming, and then there had to be lunch.

Rehearsals had continued without Jackson, but it was undermining not to have the important first scene, Arabella's leave-taking, brought to perfection, and Pierrot was too nervous about the fate of his brother down in the bowels of the house to be much in the way of a dastardly foreign count; whatever happened to Jackson would be Pierrot's future too. He made frequent trips to the lavatory at the end of the corridor.

When Briony returned from one of her visits to the laundry, he asked her, 'Has he had the spanking?'

'Not as yet.'

Like his brother, Pierrot had the knack of depriving his lines of any sense. He intoned a roll-call of words: 'Do-you-think-you-can-escape-from-my-clutches?' All present and correct.

'It's a question,' Briony cut in. 'Don't you see? It goes up at the end.'

'What do you mean?'

'There. You just did it. You start low and end high. It's a *question*.'

He swallowed hard, drew a breath and made another

attempt, producing this time a roll-call on a rising chromatic scale.

'At the end. It goes up at the end!'

Now came a roll-call on the old monotone, with a break of register, a yodel, on the final syllable.

Lola had come to the nursery that morning in the guise of the adult she considered herself at heart to be. She wore pleated flannel trousers that ballooned at the hips and flared at the ankle, and a short-sleeved sweater made of cashmere. Other tokens of maturity included a velvet choker of tiny pearls, the ginger tresses gathered at the nape and secured with an emerald clasp, three loose silver bracelets around a freckled wrist, and the fact that whenever she moved, the air about her tasted of rose water. Her condescension, being wholly restrained, was all the more potent. She was coolly responsive to Briony's suggestions, spoke her lines, which she seemed to have learned overnight, with sufficient expression, and was gently encouraging to her little brother, without encroaching at all on the director's authority. It was as if Cecilia, or even their mother, had agreed to spend some time with the little ones by taking on a role in the play, and was determined not to let a trace of boredom show. What was missing was any demonstration of ragged, childish enthusiasm. When Briony had shown her cousins the sales booth and the collection box the evening before, the twins had fought each other for the best front-of-house roles, but Lola had crossed her arms and paid decorous, grown-up compliments through a half smile that was too opaque for the detection of irony.

'How marvellous. How awfully clever of you, Briony, to think of that. Did you really make it all by yourself?'

Briony suspected that behind her older cousin's perfect manners was a destructive intent. Perhaps Lola was relying on the twins to wreck the play innocently, and needed only to stand back and observe.

These unprovable suspicions, Jackson's detainment in the

laundry, Pierrot's wretched delivery and the morning's colossal heat were oppressive to Briony. It bothered her too when
she noticed Danny Hardman watching from the doorway. He
had to be asked to leave. She could not penetrate Lola's
detachment or coax from Pierrot the common inflections of
everyday speech. What a relief, then, suddenly to find herself
alone in the nursery. Lola had said she needed to reconsider
her hair, and her brother had wandered off down the corridor,
to the lavatory, or beyond.

Briony sat on the floor with her back to one of the tall
built-in toy cupboards and fanned her face with the pages of
her play. The silence in the house was complete – no voices or
footfalls downstairs, no murmurs from the plumbing; in the
space between one of the open sash windows a trapped fly
had abandoned its struggle, and outside, the liquid birdsong
had evaporated in the heat. She pushed her knees out straight
before her and let the folds of her white muslin dress and the
familiar, endearing, pucker of skin about her knees fill her
view. She should have changed her dress this morning. She
thought how she should take more care of her appearance,
like Lola. It was childish not to. But what an effort it was. The
silence hissed in her ears and her vision was faintly distorted –
her hands in her lap appeared unusually large and at the same
time remote, as though viewed across an immense distance.
She raised one hand and flexed its fingers and wondered, as
she had sometimes before, how this thing, this machine for
gripping, this fleshy spider on the end of her arm, came to be
hers, entirely at her command. Or did it have some little life of
its own? She bent her finger and straightened it. The mystery
was in the instant before it moved, the dividing moment
between not moving and moving, when her intention took
effect. It was like a wave breaking. If she could only find
herself at the crest, she thought, she might find the secret of
herself, that part of her that was really in charge. She brought
her forefinger closer to her face and stared at it, urging it to
move. It remained still because she was pretending, she was

not entirely serious, and because willing it to move, or being about to move it, was not the same as actually moving it. And when she did crook it finally, the action seemed to start in the finger itself, not in some part of her mind. When did it know to move, when did she know to move it? There was no catching herself out. It was either-or. There was no stitching, no seam, and yet she knew that behind the smooth continuous fabric was the real self – was it her soul? – which took the decision to cease pretending, and gave the final command.

These thoughts were as familiar to her, and as comforting, as the precise configuration of her knees, their matching but competing, symmetrical and reversible, look. A second thought always followed the first, one mystery bred another: was everyone else really as alive as she was? For example, did her sister really matter to herself, was she as valuable to herself as Briony was? Was being Cecilia just as vivid an affair as being Briony? Did her sister also have a real self concealed behind a breaking wave, and did she spend time thinking about it, with a finger held up to her face. Did everybody, including her father, Betty, Hardman? If the answer was yes, then the world, the social world, was unbearably complicated, with two billion voices, and everyone's thoughts striving in equal importance and everyone's claim on life as intense, and everyone thinking they were unique, when no one was. One could drown in irrelevance. But if the answer was no, then Briony was surrounded by machines, intelligent and pleasant enough on the outside, but lacking the bright and private *inside* feeling she had. This was sinister and lonely, as well as unlikely. For, though it offended her sense of order, she knew it was overwhelmingly probable that everyone else had thoughts like hers. She knew this, but only in a rather arid way; she didn't really feel it.

The rehearsals also offended her sense of order. The self-contained world she had drawn with clear and perfect lines had been defaced with the scribble of other minds, other needs; and time itself, so easily sectioned on paper into acts and scenes, was even now dribbling uncontrollably away. Perhaps she wouldn't get Jackson back until after lunch. Leon and his friend were arriving in the early evening, or even sooner, and the performance was set for seven o'clock. And still there had been no proper rehearsal, and the twins could not act, or even speak, and Lola had stolen Briony's rightful role, and nothing could be managed, and it was hot, ludicrously hot. The girl squirmed in her oppression and stood. Dust from along the skirting board had dirtied her hands and the back of her dress. Away in her thoughts, she wiped her palms down her front as she went towards the window. The simplest way to have impressed Leon would have been to write him a story and put it in his hands herself, and watch as he read it. The title lettering, the illustrated cover, the pages *bound* – in that word alone she felt the attraction of the neat, limited and controllable form she had left behind when she decided to write a play. A story was direct and simple, allowing nothing to come between herself and her reader – no intermediaries with their private ambitions or incompetence, no pressures of time, no limits on resources. In a story you only had to wish, you only had to write it down and you could have the world; in a play you had to make do with what was available: no horses, no village streets, no seaside. No curtain. It seemed so obvious now that it was too late: a story was a form of telepathy. By means of inking symbols onto a page, she was able to send thoughts and feelings from her mind to her reader's. It was a magical process, so commonplace that no one stopped to wonder at it. Reading a sentence and understanding it were the same thing; as with the crooking of a finger, nothing lay between them. There was no gap during which the symbols were unravelled. You saw the word *castle*, and it was there, seen from some distance, with woods in high summer spread before it, the air bluish and soft with smoke rising from the blacksmith's forge, and a cobbled road twisting away into the green shade . . .

She had arrived at one of the nursery's wide-open windows

and must have seen what lay before her some seconds before she registered it. It was a scene that could easily have accommodated, in the distance at least, a medieval castle. Some miles beyond the Tallises' land rose the Surrey Hills and their motionless crowds of thick crested oaks, their greens softened by a milky heat haze. Then, nearer, the estate's open parkland, which today had a dry and savage look, roasting like a savannah, where isolated trees threw harsh stumpy shadows and the long grass was already stalked by the leonine yellow of high summer. Closer, within the boundaries of the balustrade, were the rose gardens and, nearer still, the Triton fountain and standing by the basin's retaining wall was her sister, and right before her was Robbie Turner. There was something rather formal about the way he stood, feet apart, head held back. A proposal of marriage. Briony would not have been surprised. She herself had written a tale in which a humble woodcutter saved a princess from drowning and ended by marrying her. What was presented here fitted well. Robbie Turner, only son of a humble cleaning lady and of no known father, Robbie who had been subsidised by Briony's father through school and university, had wanted to be a landscape gardener, and now wanted to take up medicine, had the boldness of ambition to ask for Cecilia's hand. It made perfect sense. Such leaps across boundaries were the stuff of daily romance.

What was less comprehensible, however, was how Robbie imperiously raised his hand now, as though issuing a command which Cecilia dared not disobey. It was extraordinary that she was unable to resist him. At his insistence she was removing her clothes, and at such speed. She was out of her blouse, now she had let her skirt drop to the ground and was stepping out of it, while he looked on impatiently, hands on hips. What strange power did he have over her. Blackmail? Threats? Briony raised two hands to her face and stepped back a little way from the window. She should shut her eyes, she thought, and spare herself the sight of her sister's shame.

But that was impossible, because there were further surprises. Cecilia, mercifully still in her underwear, was climbing into the pond, was standing waist deep in the water, was pinching her nose – and then she was gone. There was only Robbie, and the clothes on the gravel, and beyond, the silent park and the distant, blue hills.

The sequence was illogical – the drowning scene, followed by a rescue, should have preceded the marriage proposal. Such was Briony's last thought before she accepted that she did not understand, and that she must simply watch. Unseen, from two storeys up, with the benefit of unambiguous sunlight, she had privileged access across the years to adult behaviour, to rites and conventions she knew nothing about, as yet. Clearly, these were the kinds of things that happened. Even as her sister's head broke the surface – thank God! – Briony had her first, weak intimation that for her now it could no longer be fairy-tale castles and princesses, but the strangeness of the here and now, of what passed between people, the ordinary people that she knew, and what power one could have over the other, and how easy it was to get everything wrong, completely wrong. Cecilia had climbed out of the pond and was fixing her skirt, and with difficulty pulling her blouse on over her wet skin. She turned abruptly and picked up from the deep shade of the fountain's wall a vase of flowers Briony had not noticed before, and set off with it towards the house. No words were exchanged with Robbie, not a glance in his direction. He was now staring into the water, and then he too was striding away, no doubt satisfied, round the side of the house. Suddenly the scene was empty; the wet patch on the ground where Cecilia had got out of the pond was the only evidence that anything had happened at all.

Briony leaned back against a wall and stared unseeingly down the nursery's length. It was a temptation for her to be magical and dramatic, and to regard what she had witnessed as a tableau mounted for her alone, a special moral for her wrapped in a mystery. But she knew very well that if she had not stood when she did, the scene would still have happened, for it was not about her at all. Only chance had brought her to the window. This was not a fairy tale, this was the real, the adult world in which frogs did not address princesses, and the only messages were the ones that people sent. It was also a temptation to run to Cecilia's room and demand an explanation. Briony resisted because she wanted to chase in solitude the faint thrill of possibility she had felt before, the elusive excitement at a prospect she was coming close to defining, at least emotionally. The definition would refine itself over the years. She was to concede that she may have attributed more deliberation than was feasible to her thirteen-year-old self. At the time there may have been no precise form of words; in fact, she may have experienced nothing more than impatience to begin writing again.

As she stood in the nursery waiting for her cousins' return she sensed she could write a scene like the one by the fountain and she could include a hidden observer like herself. She could imagine herself hurrying down now to her bedroom, to a clean block of lined paper and her marbled, Bakelite fountain pen. She could see the simple sentences, the accumulating telepathic symbols, unfurling at the nib's end. She could write the scene three times over, from three points of view; her excitement was in the prospect of freedom, of being delivered from the cumbrous struggle between good and bad, heroes and villains. None of these three was bad, nor were they particularly good. She need not judge. There did not have to be a moral. She need only show separate minds, as alive as her own, struggling with the idea that other minds were equally alive. It wasn't only wickedness and scheming that made people unhappy, it was confusion and misunderstanding; above all, it was the failure to grasp the simple truth that other people are as real as you. And only in a story could you enter these different minds and show how they had an equal value. That was the only moral a story need have.

Six decades later she would describe how at the age of thirteen she had written her way through a whole history of literature, beginning with stories derived from the European tradition of folk tales, through drama with simple moral intent, to arrive at an impartial psychological realism which she had discovered for herself, one special morning during a heat wave in 1935. She would be well aware of the extent of her self-mythologising, and she gave her account a self-mocking, or mock-heroic tone. Her fiction was known for its amorality, and like all authors pressed by a repeated question, she felt obliged to produce a story line, a plot of her development that contained the moment when she became recognisably herself. She knew that it was not correct to refer to her dramas in the plural, that her mockery distanced her from the earnest, reflective child, and that it was not the long-ago morning she was recalling so much as her subsequent accounts of it. It was possible that the contemplation of a crooked finger, the unbearable idea of other minds and the superiority of stories over plays were thoughts she had had on other days. She also knew that whatever actually happened drew its significance from her published work and would not have been remembered without it.

However, she could not betray herself completely; there could be no doubt that some kind of revelation occurred. When the young girl went back to the window and looked down, the damp patch on the gravel had evaporated. Now there was nothing left of the dumb show by the fountain beyond what survived in memory, in three separate and overlapping memories. The truth had become as ghostly as invention. She could begin now, setting it down as she had seen it, meeting the challenge by refusing to condemn her sister's shocking near-nakedness, in daylight, right by the house. Then the scene could be recast, through Cecilia's eyes, and then Robbie's. But now was not the time to begin. Briony's sense of obligation, as well as her instinct for order, were powerful; she must complete what she had initiated, there was a rehearsal in progress, Leon was on his way, the household was expecting a performance tonight. She should go down once more to the laundry to see whether the trials of Jackson were at an end. The writing could wait until she was free.

Four

It was not until the late afternoon that Cecilia judged the vase repaired. It had baked all afternoon on a table by a south-facing window in the library, and now three fine meandering lines in the glaze, converging like rivers in an atlas, were all that showed. No one would ever know. As she crossed the library with the vase in both hands, she heard what she thought was the sound of bare feet on the hallway tiles outside the library door. Having passed many hours deliberately not thinking about Robbie Turner, it seemed an outrage to her that he should be back in the house, once again without his socks. She stepped out into the hallway, determined to face down his insolence, or his mockery, and was confronted instead by her sister, clearly in distress. Her eyelids were swollen and pink, and she was pinching on her lower lip with forefinger and thumb, an old sign with Briony that some serious weeping was to be done.

'Darling! What's up?'

Her eyes in fact were dry, and they lowered fractionally to take in the vase, then she pushed on past, to where the easel stood supporting the poster with the merry, multicoloured title, and a Chagall-like montage of highlights from her play in water-colour scattered around the lettering – the tearful parents waving, the moon-lit ride to the coast, the heroine on her sickbed, a wedding. She paused before it, and then, with one violent, diagonal stroke, ripped away more than half of it and let it fall to the floor. Cecilia put the vase down and hurried over, and knelt down to retrieve the fragment before her sister began to trample on it. This would not be the first time she had rescued Briony from self-destruction.

'Little Sis. Is it the cousins?'

She wanted to comfort her sister, for Cecilia had always loved to cuddle the baby of the family. When she was small and prone to nightmares – those terrible screams in the night – Cecilia used to go to her room and wake her. *Come back*, she used to whisper. *It's only a dream. Come back.* And then she would carry her into her own bed. She wanted to put her arm round Briony's shoulder now, but she was no longer tugging on her lip, and had moved away to the front door and was resting one hand on the great brass lion's-head handle that Mrs Turner had polished that afternoon.

'The cousins are stupid. But it's not only that. It's . . .' She trailed away, doubtful whether she should confide her recent revelation.

Cecilia smoothed the jagged triangle of paper and thought how her little sister was changing. It would have suited her better had Briony wept and allowed herself to be comforted on the silk chaise longue in the drawing room. Such stroking and soothing murmurs would have been a release for Cecilia after a frustrating day whose various cross-currents of feeling she had preferred not to examine. Addressing Briony's problems with kind words and caresses would have restored a sense of control. However, there was an element of autonomy in the younger girl's unhappiness. She had turned her back and was opening the door wide.

'But what is it then?' Cecilia could hear the neediness in her own voice.

Beyond her sister, far beyond the lake, the driveway curved across the park, narrowed and converged over rising ground to a point where a tiny shape, made formless by the warping heat, was growing, and then flickered and seemed to recede. It would be Hardman, who said he was too old to learn to drive a car, bringing the visitors in the trap.

Briony changed her mind and faced her sister. 'The whole thing's a mistake. It's the wrong . . .' She snatched a breath and glanced away, a signal, Cecilia sensed, of a dictionary word about to have its first outing. 'It's the wrong genre!' She pronounced it, as she thought, in the French way, monosyllabically, but without quite getting her tongue round the 'r'.

'*Jean?*' Cecilia called after her. 'What are you talking about?'

But Briony was hobbling away on soft white soles across the fiery gravel.

Cecilia went to the kitchen to fill the vase, and carried it up to her bedroom to retrieve the flowers from the handbasin. When she dropped them in they once again refused to fall into the artful disorder she preferred, and instead swung round in the water into a wilful neatness, with the taller stalks evenly distributed around the rim. She lifted the flowers and let them drop again, and they fell into another orderly pattern. Still, it hardly mattered. It was difficult to imagine this Mr Marshall complaining that the flowers by his bedside were too symmetrically displayed. She took the arrangement up to the second floor, along the creaking corridor to what was known as Auntie Venus's room, and set the vase on a chest of drawers by a four-poster bed, thus completing the little commission her mother had set her that morning, eight hours before.

However, she did not immediately leave, for the room was pleasingly uncluttered by personal possessions – in fact, apart from Briony's, it was the only tidy bedroom. And it was cool here, now that the sun had moved round the house. Every drawer was empty, every bare surface without so much as a fingerprint. Under the chintz counterpane the sheets would be starchily pure. She had an impulse to slip her hand between the covers to feel them, but instead she moved deeper into Mr Marshall's room. At the foot of the four-poster, the seat of a Chippendale sofa had been so carefully straightened that sitting down would have seemed a desecration. The air was smooth with the scent of wax, and in the honeyed light, the gleaming surfaces of the furniture seemed to ripple and breathe. As her approach altered her angle of view, the revellers on the lid of an ancient trousseau chest writhed into dance steps. Mrs Turner must have passed through that morning. Cecilia shrugged away the association with Robbie. Being here was a kind of trespass, with the room's future occupant just a few hundred yards away from the house.

From where she had arrived by the window she could see that Briony had crossed the bridge to the island, and was walking down the grassy bank, and beginning to disappear among the lakeshore trees that surrounded the island temple. Further off, Cecilia could just make out the two hatted figures sitting up on the bench behind Hardman. Now she saw a third figure whom she had not noticed before, striding along the driveway towards the trap. Surely it was Robbie Turner on his way home. He stopped, and as the visitors approached, his outline seemed to fuse with that of the visitors. She could imagine the scene – the manly punches to the shoulder, the horseplay. She was annoyed that her brother could not know that Robbie was in disgrace, and she turned from the window with a sound of exasperation, and set off for her room in search of a cigarette.

She had one packet remaining, and only after several minutes of irritable raking through her mess did she find it in the pocket of a blue silk dressing gown on her bathroom floor. She lit up as she descended the stairs to the hall, knowing that she would not have dared had her father been at home. He had precise ideas about where and when a woman should be seen smoking: not in the street, or any other public place, not on entering a room, not standing up, and only when offered, never from her own supply – notions as self-evident to him as natural justice. Three years among the sophisticates of Girton had not provided her with the courage to confront him. The light-hearted ironies she might have deployed among her friends deserted her in his presence, and she heard her own voice become thin when she attempted some docile contradiction. In fact, being at odds with her father about anything at all, even an insignificant domestic detail, made her uncomfortable, and nothing that great literature might have done to modify her sensibilities, none of the lessons of practical criticism, could quite deliver her from obedience. Smoking on the stairway when her father was installed in his Whitehall ministry was all the revolt her education would allow, and still it cost her some effort.

As she reached the broad landing that dominated the hall-way, Leon was showing Paul Marshall through the wide-open front entrance. Danny Hardman was behind them with their luggage. Old Hardman was just in view outside, gazing mutely at the five-pound note in his hand. The indirect afternoon light, reflected from the gravel and filtered through the fanlight, filled the entrance hall with the yellowish-orange tones of a sepia print. The men had removed their hats and stood waiting for her, smiling. Cecilia wondered, as she sometimes did when she met a man for the first time, if this was the one she was going to marry, and whether it was this particular moment she would remember for the rest of her life – with gratitude, or profound and particular regret.

'Sis-Celia!' Leon called. When they embraced she felt against her collar-bone through the fabric of his jacket a thick fountain pen, and smelled pipe smoke in the folds of his clothes, prompting a moment's nostalgia for afternoon tea visits to rooms in men's colleges, rather polite and anodyne occasions mostly, but cheery too, especially in winter.

Paul Marshall shook her hand and made a faint bow. There was something comically brooding about his face. His opener was conventionally dull.

'I've heard an awful lot about you.'

'And me you.' What she could remember was a telephone conversation with her brother some months before, during which they had discussed whether they had ever eaten, or would ever eat, an Amo bar.

'Emily's lying down.'

It was hardly necessary to say it. As children they claimed to be able to tell from across the far side of the park whenever their mother had a migraine by a certain darkening at the windows.

'And the Old Man's staying in town?'

'He might come later.'

Cecilia was aware that Paul Marshall was staring at her, but before she could look at him she needed to prepare something to say.

'The children were putting on a play, but it rather looks like it's fallen apart.'

Marshall said, 'That might have been your sister I saw down by the lake. She was giving the nettles a good thrashing.'

Leon stepped aside to let Hardman's boy through with the bags. 'Where are we putting Paul?'

'On the second floor.' Cecilia had inclined her head to direct these words at the young Hardman. He had reached the foot of the stairs and now stopped and turned, a leather suitcase in each hand, to face them where they were grouped, in the centre of the chequered, tiled expanse. His expression was of tranquil incomprehension. She had noticed him hanging around the children lately. Perhaps he was interested in Lola. He was sixteen, and certainly no boy. The roundness she remembered in his cheeks had gone, and the childish bow of his lips had become elongated and innocently cruel. Across his brow a constellation of acne had a new-minted look, its garishness softened by the sepia light. All day long, she realised, she had been feeling strange, and seeing strangely, as though everything was already long in the past, made more vivid by posthumous ironies she could not quite grasp.

She said to him patiently, 'The big room past the nursery.'

'Auntie Venus's room,' Leon said.

Auntie Venus had been for almost half a century a vital

nursing presence across a swathe of the Northern Territories in Canada. She was no one's aunt particularly, or rather, she was Mr Tallis's dead second cousin's aunt, but no one questioned her right, after her retirement, to the room on the second floor where, for most of their childhoods, she had been a sweet-natured, bedridden invalid who withered away to an uncomplaining death when Cecilia was ten. A week later Briony was born.

Cecilia led the visitors into the drawing room, through the French windows, past the roses towards the swimming pool, which was behind the stable block and was surrounded on four sides by a high thicket of bamboo, with a tunnel-like gap for an entrance. They walked through, bending their heads under low canes, and emerged onto a terrace of dazzling white stone from which the heat rose in a blast. In deep shadow, set well back from the water's edge, was a white-painted tin table with a pitcher of iced punch under a square of cheesecloth. Leon unfolded the canvas chairs and they sat with their glasses in a shallow circle facing the pool. From his position between Leon and Cecilia, Marshall took control of the conversation with a ten-minute monologue. He told them how wonderful it was, to be away from town, in tranquillity, in the country air; for nine months, for every waking minute of every day, enslaved to a vision, he had shuttled between headquarters, his boardroom and the factory floor. He had bought a large house on Clapham Common and hardly had time to visit it. The launch of Rainbow Amo had been a triumph, but only after various distribution catastrophes which had now been set right; the advertising campaign had offended some elderly bishops so another was devised; then came the problems of success itself, unbelievable sales, new production quotas, and disputes about overtime rates, and the search for a site for a second factory about which the four unions involved had been generally sullen and had needed to be charmed and coaxed like children; and now, when all had been brought to fruition, there loomed the greater challenge yet of Army

Amo, the khaki bar with the Pass the Amo! slogan; the concept rested on an assumption that spending on the Armed Forces must go on increasing if Mr Hitler did not pipe down; there was even a chance that the bar could become part of the standard-issue ration pack; in that case, if there were to be a general conscription, a further five factories would be needed; there were some on the board who were convinced there should and would be an accommodation with Germany and that Army Amo was a dead duck; one member was even accusing Marshall of being a warmonger; but, exhausted as he was, and maligned, he would not be turned away from his purpose, his vision. He ended by repeating that it was wonderful to find oneself 'way out here' where one could, as it were, catch one's breath.

Watching him during the first several minutes of his delivery, Cecilia felt a pleasant sinking sensation in her stomach as she contemplated how deliciously self-destructive it would be, almost erotic, to be married to a man so nearly handsome, so hugely rich, so unfathomably stupid. He would fill her with his big-faced children, all of them loud, bone-headed boys with a passion for guns and football and aeroplanes. She watched him in profile as he turned his head towards Leon. A long muscle twitched above the line of his jaw as he spoke. A few thick black hairs curled free of his eyebrow, and from his earholes there sprouted the same black growth, comically kinked like pubic hair. He should instruct his barber.

The smallest shift in her gaze brought her Leon's face, but he was staring politely at his friend and seemed determined not to meet her eye. As children they used to torment each other with 'the look' at the Sunday lunches their parents gave for elderly relatives. These were awesome occasions worthy of the ancient silver service; the venerable great-uncles and aunts and grandparents were Victorians, from their mother's side of the family, a baffled and severe folk, a lost tribe who arrived at the house in black cloaks having wandered peevishly for two decades in an alien, frivolous century. They terrified the ten-year-old Cecilia and her twelve-year-old brother, and a giggling fit was always just a breath away. The one who caught the look was helpless, the one who bestowed it, immune. Mostly, the power was with Leon whose look was mock-solemn, and consisted of drawing the corners of his mouth downwards while rolling his eyes. He might ask Cecilia in the most innocent voice for the salt to be passed, and though she averted her gaze as she handed it to him, though she turned her head and inhaled deeply, it could be enough simply to know that he was doing his look to consign her to ninety minutes of quaking torture. Meanwhile, Leon would be free, needing only to top her up occasionally if he thought she was beginning to recover. Only rarely had she reduced him with an expression of haughty pouting. Since the children were sometimes seated between adults, giving the look had its dangers – making faces at table could bring down disgrace and an early bedtime. The trick was to make the attempt while passing between, say, licking one's lips and smiling broadly, and at the same time catch the other's eye. On one occasion they had looked up and delivered their looks simultaneously, causing Leon to spray soup from his nostrils onto the wrist of a great-aunt. Both children were banished to their rooms for the rest of the day.

Cecilia longed to take her brother aside and tell him that Mr Marshall had pubic hair growing from his ears. He was describing the boardroom confrontation with the man who called him a warmonger. She half raised her arm as though to smooth her hair. Automatically, Leon's attention was drawn by the motion, and in that instant she delivered the look he had not seen in more than ten years. He pursed his lips and turned away, and found something of interest to stare at near his shoe. As Marshall turned to Cecilia, Leon raised a cupped hand to shield his face, but could not disguise from his sister the tremor along his shoulders. Fortunately for him, Marshall was reaching his conclusion.

'. . . where one can, as it were, catch one's breath.'

Immediately, Leon was on his feet. He walked to the edge
of the pool and contemplated a sodden red towel left near the
diving board. Then he strolled back to them, hands in pockets,
quite recovered.

He said to Cecilia, 'Guess who we met on the way in.'

'Robbie.'

'I told him to join us tonight.'

'Leon! You didn't!'

He was in a teasing mood. Revenge perhaps. He said to
his friend, 'So the cleaning lady's son gets a scholarship to
the local grammar, gets a scholarship to Cambridge, goes up
the same time as Cee – and she hardly speaks to him in three
years! She wouldn't let him *near* her Roedean chums.'

'You should have asked me first.'

She was genuinely annoyed, and observing this, Marshall
said placatingly, 'I knew some grammar school types at Oxford
and some of them were damned clever. But they could be
resentful, which was a bit rich, I thought.'

She said, 'Have you got a cigarette?'

He offered her one from a silver case, threw one to Leon
and took one for himself. They were all standing now, and
as Cecilia leaned towards Marshall's lighter, Leon said, 'He's
got a first-rate mind, so I don't know what the hell he's doing,
messing about in the flower beds.'

She went to sit on the diving board and tried to give the
appearance of relaxing, but her tone was strained. 'He's
wondering about a medical degree. Leon, I wish you hadn't
asked him.'

'The Old Man's said yes?'

She shrugged. 'Look, I think you ought to go round to the
bungalow now and ask him not to come.'

Leon had walked to the shallow end and stood facing her
across the gently rocking sheet of oily blue water.

'How can I possibly do that?'

'I don't care how you do it. Make an excuse.'

'Something's happened between you.'

'No, it hasn't.'

'Is he bothering you?'

'For God's sake!'

She got up irritably and walked away, towards the swimming pool pavilion, an open structure supported by three fluted pillars. She stood, leaning against the central pillar, smoking and watching her brother. Two minutes before, they had been in league and now they were at odds – childhood revisited indeed. Paul Marshall stood halfway between them, turning his head this way and that when they spoke, as though at a tennis match. He had a neutral, vaguely inquisitive air, and seemed untroubled by this sibling squabble. That at least, Cecilia thought, was in his favour.

Her brother said, 'You think he can't hold a knife and fork.'

'Leon, stop it. You had no business inviting him.'

'What rot!'

The silence that followed was partly mitigated by the drone of the filtration pump. There was nothing she could do, nothing she could make Leon do, and she suddenly felt the pointlessness of argument. She lolled against the warm stone, lazily finishing her cigarette and contemplating the scene before her – the foreshortened slab of chlorinated water, the black inner tube of a tractor tyre propped against a deck chair, the two men in cream linen suits of infinitesimally different hues, bluish-grey smoke rising against the bamboo green. It looked carved, fixed, and again, she felt it: it had happened a long time ago, and all outcomes, on all scales – from the tiniest to the most colossal – were already in place. Whatever happened in the future, however superficially strange or shocking, would also have an unsurprising, familiar quality, inviting her to say, but only to herself, Oh yes, of course. That. I should have known.

She said lightly, 'D'you know what I think?'

'What's that?'

'We should go indoors, and you should mix us a fancy kind of drink.'

Paul Marshall banged his hands together and the sound ricocheted between the columns and the back wall of the pavilion. 'There's something I do rather well,' he called. 'With crushed ice, rum and melted dark chocolate.'

The suggestion prompted an exchange of glances between Cecilia and her brother, and thus their discord was resolved. Leon was already moving away, and as Cecilia and Paul Marshall followed him and converged on the gap in the thicket she said, 'I'd rather have something bitter. Or even sour.'

He smiled, and since he had reached the gap first, he paused to hand her through, as though it were a drawing room doorway, and as she passed she felt him touch her lightly on her forearm.

Or it may have been a leaf.

Five

Neither the twins nor Lola knew precisely what led Briony to abandon the rehearsals. At the time, they did not even know she had. They were doing the sickbed scene, the one in which bed-bound Arabella first receives into her garret the prince disguised as the good doctor, and it was going well enough, or no worse than usual, with the twins speaking their lines no more ineptly than before. As for Lola, she didn't wish to dirty her cashmere by lying on the floor, and instead slumped in a chair, and the director could hardly object to that. The older girl entered so fully into the spirit of her own aloof compliance that she felt beyond reproach. One moment, Briony was giving patient instructions to Jackson, then she paused, and frowned, as if about to correct herself, and then she was gone. There was no pivotal moment of creative difference, no storming or flouncing out. She turned away, and simply drifted out, as though on her way to the lavatory. The others waited, unaware that the whole project was at an end. The twins thought they had been trying hard, and Jackson in particular, feeling he was still in disgrace in the Tallis household, thought he might begin to rehabilitate himself by pleasing Briony.

While they waited, the boys played football with a wooden brick and their sister gazed out the window, humming softly to herself. After an immeasurable period of time, she went out into the corridor and along to the end where there was an open door to an unused bedroom. From here she had a view of the driveway and the lake across which lay a column of shimmering phosphorescence, white hot from the fierce late afternoon heat. Against this column she could just make out Briony beyond the island temple, standing right by the water's edge. In fact, she may even have been standing in the water – against such light it was difficult to tell. She did not look as if she was about to come back. On her way out of the room, Lola noticed by the bed a masculine-looking suitcase of tan leather and heavy straps and faded steamer labels. It reminded her vaguely of her father, and she paused by it, and caught the faint sooty scent of a railway carriage. She put her thumb against one of the locks and slid it. The polished metal was cool, and her touch left little patches of shrinking condensation. The clasp startled her as it sprang up with a loud chunky sound. She pushed it back and hurried from the room.

There followed more formless time for the cousins. Lola sent the twins down to see if the pool was free – they felt uneasy being there when adults were present. The twins returned to report that Cecilia was there with two other grown-ups, but by now Lola was not in the nursery. She was in her tiny bedroom, arranging her hair in front of a hand mirror propped against the window-sill. The boys lay on her narrow bed, and tickled each other, and wrestled, and made loud howling noises. She could not be bothered to send them to their own room. Now there was no play, and the pool was not available, unstructured time oppressed them. Homesickness fell upon them when Pierrot said he was hungry – dinner was hours away, and it would not be proper to go down now and ask for food. Besides, the boys would not go in the kitchen because they were terrified of Betty whom they had seen on the stairs grimly carrying red rubber sheets towards their room.

A little later the three found themselves back in the nursery which, apart from the bedrooms, was the only room they felt they had a right to be in. The scuffed blue brick was where they had left it, and everything was as before.

They stood about and Jackson said, 'I don't like it here.'

The simplicity of the remark unhinged his brother who went by a wall and found something of interest in the skirting board which he worried with the tip of his shoe.

Lola put her arm across his shoulder and said, 'It's all right. We'll be going home soon.' Her arm was much thinner and lighter than his mother's and Pierrot began to sob, but quietly, still mindful of being in a strange house where politeness was all.

Jackson was tearful too, but he was still capable of speech. 'It won't be soon. You're just saying that. We can't go home anyway . . .' He paused to gather his courage. 'It's a divorce!'

Pierrot and Lola froze. The word had never been used in front of the children, and never uttered by them. The soft consonants suggested an unthinkable obscenity, the sibilant ending whispered the family's shame. Jackson himself looked distraught as the word left him, but no wishing could bring it back now, and for all he could tell, saying it out loud was as great a crime as the act itself, whatever that was. None of them, including Lola, quite knew. She was advancing on him, her green eyes narrowed like a cat's.

'How *dare* you say that.'

''S true,' he mumbled and looked away. He knew that he was in trouble, that he deserved to be in trouble, and he was about to run for it when she seized him by an ear and put her face close to his.

'If you hit me,' he said quickly, 'I'll tell The Parents.' But he himself had made the invocation useless, a ruined totem of a lost golden age.

'You will never *ever* use that word again. D'you hear me?'

Full of shame, he nodded, and she let him go.

The boys had been shocked out of tears, and now Pierrot,

as usual eager to repair a bad situation, said brightly, 'What shall we do now?'

'I'm always asking myself that.'

The tall man in a white suit standing in the doorway may have been there many minutes, long enough to have heard Jackson speak the word, and it was this thought, rather than the shock of his presence, that prevented even Lola from making a response. Did he know about their family? They could only stare and wait to find out. He came towards them and extended his hand.

'Paul Marshall.'

Pierrot, who was the nearest, took the hand in silence, as did his brother. When it was the girl's turn she said, 'Lola Quincey. This is Jackson and that's Pierrot.'

'What marvellous names you all have. But how am I supposed to tell you two apart?'

'I'm generally considered more pleasant,' Pierrot said. It was a family joke, a line devised by their father which usually made strangers laugh when they put the question. But this man did not even smile as he said, 'You must be the cousins from the north.'

They waited tensely to hear what else he knew, and watched as he walked the length of the nursery's bare boards and stooped to retrieve the brick which he tossed in the air and caught smartly with a snap of wood against skin.

'I'm staying in a room along the corridor.'

'I know,' Lola said. 'Auntie Venus's room.'

'Exactly so. Her old room.'

Paul Marshall lowered himself into the armchair lately used by the stricken Arabella. It really was a curious face, with the features scrunched up around the eyebrows, and a big empty chin like Desperate Dan's. It was a cruel face, but his manner was pleasant, and this was an attractive combination, Lola thought. He settled his trouser creases as he looked from Quincey to Quincey. Lola's attention was drawn to the black and white leather of his brogues, and he was aware of her admiring them and waggled one foot to a rhythm in his head.

'I'm sorry to hear about your play.'

The twins moved closer together, prompted from below the threshold of awareness to close ranks by the consideration that if he knew more than they did about the rehearsals, he must know a great deal besides. Jackson spoke from the heart of their concern.

'Do you know our parents?'

'Mr and Mrs Quincey?'

'Yes!'

'I've read about them in the paper.'

The boys stared at him as they absorbed this and could not speak, for they knew that the business of newspapers was momentous: earthquakes and train crashes, what the government and nations did from day to day, and whether more money should be spent on guns in case Hitler attacked England. They were awed, but not completely surprised, that their own disaster should rank with these godly affairs. This had the ring of confirming truth.

To steady herself, Lola put her hands on her hips. Her heart was beating painfully hard and she could not trust herself to speak, even though she knew she had to. She thought a game was being played which she did not understand, but she was certain there had been an impropriety, or even an insult. Her voice gave out when she began, and she was obliged to clear her throat and start again.

'What have you read about them?'

He raised his eyebrows, which were thick and fused together, and blew a dismissive, blubbery sound through his lips. 'Oh, I don't know. Nothing at all. Silly things.'

'Then I'll thank you not to talk about them in front of the children.'

It was a construction she must have once overheard, and she had uttered it in blind faith, like an apprentice mouthing the incantation of a magus.

It appeared to work. Marshall winced in acknowledgment of his error, and leaned towards the twins. 'Now you two listen carefully to me. It's clear to everybody that your parents are absolutely wonderful people who love you very much and think about you all the time.'

Jackson and Pierrot nodded in solemn agreement. Job done, Marshall turned his attention back to Lola. After two strong gin cocktails in the drawing room with Leon and his sister, Marshall had come upstairs to find his room, unpack and change for dinner. Without removing his shoes, he had stretched out on the enormous four-poster and, soothed by the country silence, the drinks and the early evening warmth, dropped away into a light sleep in which his young sisters had appeared, all four of them, standing around his bedside, prattling and touching and pulling at his clothes. He woke, hot across his chest and throat, uncomfortably aroused, and briefly confused about his surroundings. It was while he was sitting on the edge of his bed, drinking water, that he heard the voices that must have prompted his dream. When he went along the creaky corridor and entered the nursery, he had seen three children. Now he saw that the girl was almost a young woman, poised and imperious, quite the little Pre-Raphaelite princess with her bangles and tresses, her painted nails and velvet choker.

He said to her, 'You've jolly good taste in clothes. Those trousers suit you especially well, I think.'

She was pleased rather than embarrassed and her fingers lightly brushed the fabric where it ballooned out across her narrow hips. 'We got them in Liberty's when my mother brought me to London to see a show.'

'And what did you see?'

'*Hamlet*.' They had in fact seen a matinée pantomime at the London Palladium during which Lola had spilled a strawberry drink down her frock, and Liberty's was right across the street.

'One of my favourites,' Paul said. It was fortunate for

her that he too had neither read nor seen the play, having studied chemistry. But he was able to say musingly, 'To be or not to be.'

'That is the question,' she agreed. 'And I like your shoes.'

He tilted his foot to examine the craftsmanship. 'Yes. Ducker's in The Turl. They make a wooden thingy of your foot and keep it on a shelf for ever. Thousands of them down in a basement room, and most of the people are long dead.'

'How simply awful.'

'I'm hungry,' Pierrot said again.

'Ah well,' Paul Marshall said, patting his pocket. 'I've got something to show you if you can guess what I do for a living.'

'You're a singer,' Lola said. 'At least, you have a nice voice.'

'Kind but wrong. D'you know, you remind me of my favourite sister . . .'

Jackson interrupted. 'You make chocolates in a factory.'

Before too much glory could be heaped upon his brother, Pierrot added, 'We heard you talking at the pool.'

'Not a guess then.'

He drew from his pocket a rectangular bar wrapped in greaseproof paper and measuring about four inches by one. He placed it on his lap and carefully unwrapped it and held it up for their inspection. Politely, they moved nearer. It had a smooth shell of drab green against which he clicked his fingernail.

'Sugar casing, see? Milk chocolate inside. Good for any conditions, even if it melts.'

He held his hand higher and tightened his grip, and they could see the tremor in his fingers exaggerated by the bar.

'There'll be one of these inside the kitbag of every soldier in the land. Standard issue.'

The twins looked at each other. They knew that an adult had no business with sweets. Pierrot said, 'Soldiers don't eat chocolate.'

His brother added, 'They like cigarettes.'

'And anyway, why should they all get free sweets and not the children?'

'Because they'll be fighting for their country.'

'Our dad says there isn't going to be a war.'

'Well, he's wrong.'

Marshall sounded a little testy, and Lola said reassuringly, 'Perhaps there will be one.'

He smiled up at her. 'We're calling it the Army Amo.'

'Amo amas amat,' she said.

'Exactly.'

Jackson said, 'I don't see why everything you buy has to end in o.'

'It's really boring,' Pierrot said. 'Like Polo and Aero.'

'And Oxo and Brillo.'

'I think what they're trying to tell me,' Paul Marshall said to Lola as he presented her the bar, 'is that they don't want any.'

She took it solemnly, and then for the twins, gave a serves-you-right look. They knew this was so. They could hardly plead for Amo now. They watched her tongue turn green as it curled around the edges of the candy casing. Paul Marshall sat back in the armchair, watching her closely over the steeple he made with his hands in front of his face.

He crossed and uncrossed his legs. Then he took a deep breath. 'Bite it,' he said softly. 'You've got to bite it.'

It cracked loudly as it yielded to her unblemished incisors, and there was revealed the white edge of the sugar shell, and the dark chocolate beneath it. It was then that they heard a woman calling up the stairs from the floor below, and then she called again, more insistently, from just along the corridor, and this time the twins recognised the voice and a look of sudden bewilderment passed between them.

Lola was laughing through her mouthful of Amo. 'There's Betty looking for you. Bath time! Run along now. Run along.'

Six

Not long after lunch, once she was assured that her sister's children and Briony had eaten sensibly and would keep their promise to stay away from the pool for at least two hours, Emily Tallis had withdrawn from the white glare of the afternoon's heat to a cool and darkened bedroom. She was not in pain, not yet, but she was retreating before its threat. There were illuminated points in her vision, little pinpricks, as though the worn fabric of the visible world was being held up against a far brighter light. She felt in the top right corner of her brain a heaviness, the inert body weight of some curled and sleeping animal; but when she touched her head and pressed, the presence disappeared from the co-ordinates of actual space. Now it was in the top right corner of her mind, and in her imagination she could stand on tiptoe and raise her right hand to it. It was important, however, not to provoke it; once this lazy creature moved from the peripheries to the centre, then the knifing pains would obliterate all thought, and there would be no chance of dining with Leon and the family tonight. It bore her no malice, this animal, it was indifferent to her misery. It would move as a caged panther might: because it was awake, out of boredom, for the sake of movement itself, or for no reason at all, and with no awareness. She lay supine on her bed without a pillow, a glass of water within easy reach and, at her side, a book she knew she could not read. A long, blurred strip of daylight reflected on the ceiling above the pelmet was all that broke the darkness. She lay rigidly apprehensive, held at knife-point, knowing that fear would not let her sleep and that her only hope was in keeping still.

She thought of the vast heat that rose above the house and park, and lay across the Home Counties like smoke, suffocating the farms and towns, and she thought of the baking railway tracks that were bringing Leon and his friend, and the roasting black-roofed carriage in which they would sit by an open window. She had ordered a roast for this evening and it would be too stifling to eat. She heard the house creak as it expanded. Or were the rafters and posts drying out and contracting against the masonry? Shrinking, everything was shrinking. Leon's prospects, for example, diminishing by the year as he refused the offer of a leg-up from his father, the chance of something decent in the civil service, preferring instead to be the humblest soul in a private bank, and living for the weekends and his rowing eight. She could be angrier with him if he were not so sweet-natured and content and surrounded by successful friends. Too handsome, too popular, no sting of unhappiness and ambition. One day he might bring home a friend for Cecilia to marry, if three years at Girton had not made her an impossible prospect, with her pretensions to solitude, and smoking in the bedroom, and her improbable nostalgia for a time barely concluded and for those fat girls in glasses from New Zealand with whom she had shared a set, or was it a gyp? The cosy jargon of Cecilia's Cambridge – the Halls, the Maids' Dancing, the Little-Go, and all the self-adoring slumming, the knickers drying before the electric fire and two to a hairbrush, made Emily Tallis a little cross, though not remotely jealous. She had been educated at home until the age of sixteen, and was sent to Switzerland for two years which were shortened to one for economy, and she knew for a fact that the whole performance, women at the

'Varsity, was childish really, at best an innocent lark, like the girls' rowing eight, a little posturing alongside their brothers dressed up in the solemnity of social progress. They weren't even awarding girls proper degrees. When Cecilia came home in July with her finals' result – the nerve of the girl to be disappointed with it! – she had no job or skill and still had a husband to find and motherhood to confront, and what would her bluestocking teachers – the ones with silly nicknames and 'fearsome' reputations – have to tell her about that? Those self-important women gained local immortality for the blandest, the most timid of eccentricities – walking a cat on a dog's lead, riding about on a man's bike, being seen with a sandwich in the street. A generation later these silly, ignorant ladies would be long dead and still revered at High Table and spoken of in lowered voices.

Feeling the black-furred creature begin to stir, Emily let her thoughts move away from her eldest daughter and sent the tendrils of a worrying disposition out towards her youngest. Poor darling Briony, the softest little thing, doing her all to entertain her hard-bitten wiry cousins with the play she had written from her heart. To love her was to be soothed. But how to protect her against failure, against that Lola, the incarnation of Emily's youngest sister who had been just as precocious and scheming at that age, and who had recently plotted her way out of a marriage, into what she wanted everyone to call a nervous breakdown. She could not afford to let Hermione into her thoughts. Instead, Emily, breathing quietly in the darkness, gauged the state of the household by straining to listen. In her condition, this was the only contribution she could make. She rested her palm against her forehead, and heard another tick as the building shrank tighter. From far below came a metallic clang, a falling saucepan lid perhaps; the pointless roast dinner was in the earliest stages of preparation. From upstairs, the thud of feet on floorboards and children's voices, two or three at least, talking at once, rising, falling, and rising again, perhaps in dissent, perhaps excited agreement. The nursery was on the floor above, and only one room along. *The Trials of Arabella*. If she were not so ill, she would go up now and supervise or help, for it was too much for them, she knew. Illness had stopped her giving her children all a mother should. Sensing this, they had always called her by her first name. Cecilia should lend a hand, but she was too wrapped up in herself, too much the intellectual to bother with children . . . Emily successfully resisted the pursuit of this line, and seemed to drift away then, not quite into sleep, but out of thought into invalid nullity, and many minutes passed until she heard in the hallway outside her bedroom footfalls on the stairs, and by the muffled sound of them thought they must be barefoot and therefore Briony's. The girl would not wear her shoes in the hot weather. Minutes later, from the nursery again, energetic scuffling and something hard rattling across the floorboards. The rehearsals had disintegrated, Briony had retreated in a sulk, the twins were fooling about, and Lola, if she was as much like her mother as Emily believed, would be tranquil and triumphant.

Habitual fretting about her children, her husband, her sister, the help, had rubbed her senses raw; migraine, mother-love and, over the years, many hours of lying still on her bed, had distilled from this sensitivity a sixth sense, a tentacular awareness that reached out from the dimness and moved through the house, unseen and all-knowing. Only the truth came back to her, for what she knew, she knew. The indistinct murmur of voices heard through a carpeted floor surpassed in clarity a typed-up transcript; a conversation that penetrated a wall or, better, two walls, came stripped of all but its essential twists and nuances. What to others would have been a muffling was to her alert senses, which were fine-tuned like the cat's whiskers of a old wireless, an almost unbearable amplification. She lay in the dark and knew everything. The less she was able to do, the more she was aware. But though she sometimes longed to rise up and intervene, especially if she thought Briony was in need of her, the fear of pain kept her in place. At worst, unrestrained, a matching set of sharpened kitchen knives would be drawn across her optic nerve, and then again, with a greater downward pressure, and she would be entirely shut in and alone. Even groaning increased the agony.

And so she lay there as the late afternoon slipped by. The front door had opened and closed. Briony would have gone out with her mood, probably to be by water, by the pool, or the lake, or perhaps she had gone as far as the river. Emily heard a careful tread on the stairs – Cecilia at last taking the flowers up to the guest's room, a simple errand she had been asked many times that day to perform. Then later, Betty calling to Danny, and the sound of the trap on the gravel, and Cecilia going down to meet the visitors, and soon, spreading through the gloom, the faintest tang of a cigarette – she had been asked a thousand times not to smoke on the stairs, but she would be wanting to impress Leon's friend, and that in itself might not be a bad thing. Voices echoing in the hall, Danny struggling up with the luggage, and coming down again, and silence – Cecilia would have taken Leon and Mr Marshall to the pool to drink the punch that Emily herself had made that morning. She heard the scampering of a four-legged creature coming down the stairs – the twins, wanting the pool and about to be disappointed that it had been taken over.

She tumbled away into a doze, and was woken by the drone of a man's voice in the nursery, and children answering. Surely not Leon, who would be inseparable from his sister now they were re-united. It would be Mr Marshall whose room was just along from the nursery, and he was talking to the twins, she decided, rather than Lola. Emily wondered if they were being impertinent, for each twin seemed to behave as though his social obligations were halved. Now Betty was coming up the stairs, calling to them as she came, a little too harshly perhaps, given Jackson's ordeal of the morning.

Bathtime, teatime, bedtime – the hinge of the day: these childhood sacraments of water, food and sleep had all but vanished from the daily round. Briony's late and unexpected appearance had kept them alive in the household well into Emily's forties, and how soothing, how fixing they had been; the lanolin soap and thick white bath sheet, the girlish prattle echoing in the steamy bathroom acoustic; enfolding her in the towel, trapping her arms and taking her onto her lap for a moment of babyish helplessness that Briony had revelled in not so long ago; but now baby and bath water had vanished behind a locked door, though that was rare enough, for the girl always looked in need of a wash and a change of clothes. She had vanished into an intact inner world of which the writing was no more than the visible surface, the protective crust which even, or especially, a loving mother could not penetrate. Her daughter was always off and away in her mind, grappling with some unspoken, self-imposed problem, as though the weary, self-evident world could be re-invented by a child. Useless to ask Briony what she was thinking. There was a time one would have received a bright and intricate response that would in turn have unfolded silly and weighty questions to which Emily gave her best answers; and while the meandering hypotheses they indulged were hard to recall in detail now, she knew she never spoke so well as she had to her eleven-year-old last-born. No dinner table, no shaded margin of a tennis court ever heard her so easily and richly associative. Now the demons of self-consciousness and talent had struck her daughter dumb, and though Briony was no less loving – at breakfast she had sidled up and locked fingers with her – Emily mourned the passing of an age of eloquence. She would never again speak like that to anyone, and this was what it meant to want another child. Soon she would be forty-seven.

The muted thunder of the plumbing – she had not noticed it begin – ceased with a judder that shook the air. Now Hermione's boys would be in the bathroom, their narrow, bony little bodies at each end of the tub, and the same folded white towels would be on the faded blue wicker chair, and underfoot, the giant cork mat with a corner chewed away by a dog long-dead; but instead of prattle, dread silence, and no mother, only Betty whose kindly heart no child would ever discover. How could Hermione have a nervous breakdown – the generally preferred term for her friend who worked in the wireless – how could she choose silence and fear and sorrow in her children? Emily supposed that she herself should be overseeing this bathtime. But she knew that even if the knives were not poised above her optic nerve, she would attend to her nephews only out of duty. They were not her own. It was as simple as that. And they were little boys, therefore fundamentally uncommunicative, with no gift for intimacy, and worse, they had diluted their identities, for she had never found this missing triangle of flesh. One could only know them generally.

She eased herself onto an elbow and brought the glass of water to her lips. It was beginning to fade, the presence of her animal tormentor, and now she was able to arrange two pillows against the headboard in order to sit up. This was a slow and awkward manoeuvre because she was fearful of sudden movement, and thus the creaking of the bedsprings was prolonged, and half obscured the sound of a man's voice. Propped on her side, she froze, with the corner of a pillow clenched in one hand, and beamed her raw attention into every recess of the house. There was nothing, and then, like a lamp turned on and off in total darkness, there was a little squeal of laughter abruptly smothered. Lola then, in the nursery with Marshall. She continued to settle herself, and lay back at last, and sipped her lukewarm water. This wealthy young entrepreneur might not be such a bad sort, if he was prepared to pass the time of day entertaining children. Soon she would be able to risk turning on the bedside lamp, and within twenty minutes she might be able to rejoin the household and pursue the various lines of her anxiety. Most urgent was a sortie into the kitchen to discover whether it was not too late to convert the roast into cold cuts and salads, and then she must greet her son and appraise his friend and make him welcome. As soon as this was accomplished, she would satisfy herself that the twins were properly taken care of, and perhaps allow them some sort of compensating treat. Then it would be time to make the telephone call to Jack who would have forgotten to tell her he was not coming home. She would talk herself past the terse woman on the switchboard, and the pompous young fellow in the outer office, and she would reassure her husband that there was no need to feel guilt. She would track down Cecilia and make sure she had arranged the flowers as instructed, and that she should jolly well make an effort for the evening by taking on some of the responsibilities of a hostess and that she wore something pretty and didn't smoke in every room. And then, most important of all, she should set off in search of Briony because the collapse of the play was a terrible blow and the child would need all the comfort a mother could give. Finding her would mean exposure to unadulterated sunlight, and even the diminishing rays of early evening could provoke an attack. The sunglasses would have to be found then, and this, rather than the kitchen, would have to be the priority, because they were somewhere in this room, in a drawer, between a book, in a pocket, and it would be a bother to come upstairs again for them. She should also put on some flat-soled shoes in case Briony had gone all the way to the river . . .

And so Emily lay back against the pillows for another several minutes, her creature having slunk away, and patiently planned, and revised her plans, and refined an order for them. She would soothe the household, which seemed to her, from the sickly dimness of the bedroom, like a troubled and sparsely populated continent from whose forested vastness competing elements made claims and counter-claims upon her restless attention. She had no illusions: old plans, if one could ever remember them, the plans that time had overtaken, tended to have a febrile and over-optimistic grip on events. She could send her tendrils into every room of the house, but she could not send them into the future. She also knew that, ultimately, it was her own peace of mind she strove for; self-interest and kindness were best not separated. Gently, she pushed herself upright and swung her feet to the floor and wriggled them into her slippers. Rather than risk drawing the curtains just yet, she turned on the reading light, and tentatively began the hunt for her dark glasses. She had already decided where to look first.

Seven

The island temple, built in the style of Nicholas Revett in the late 1780s, was intended as a point of interest, an eye-catching feature to enhance the pastoral ideal, and had of course no religious purpose at all. It was near enough to the water's edge, raised upon a projecting bank, to cast an interesting reflection in the lake, and from most perspectives the row of pillars and the pediment above them were charmingly half obscured by the elms and oaks that had grown up around. Closer to, the temple had a sorrier look: moisture rising through a damaged damp-course had caused chunks of stucco to fall away. Sometime in the late nineteenth century clumsy repairs were made with unpainted cement which had turned brown and gave the building a mottled, diseased appearance. Elsewhere, the exposed laths, themselves rotting away, showed through like the ribs of a starving animal. The double doors that opened onto a circular chamber with a domed roof, had long ago been removed, and the stone floor was thickly covered in leaves and leaf mould and the droppings of various birds and animals that wandered in and out. All the panes were gone from the pretty, Georgian windows, smashed by Leon and his friends in the late twenties. The tall niches that had once contained statuary were empty but for the filthy ruins of spider webs. The only furniture was a bench carried in from the village cricket pitch – again, the youthful Leon and his terrible friends from school. The legs had been kicked away and used to break the windows, and were lying outside, softly crumbling into the earth among the nettles and the incorruptible shards of glass.

Just as the swimming pool pavilion behind the stable block imitated features of the temple, so the temple was supposed to embody references to the original Adam house, though nobody in the Tallis family knew what they were. Perhaps it was the style of column, or the pediment, or the proportions of the windows. At different times, but most often at Christmas, when moods were expansive, family members strolling over the bridges promised to research the matter, but no one cared to set aside the time when the busy new year began. More than the dilapidation, it was this connection, this lost memory of the temple's grander relation, which gave the useless little building its sorry air. The temple was the orphan of a grand society lady, and now, with no one to care for it, no one to look up to, the child had grown old before its time, and let itself go. There was a tapering soot stain as high as a man on an outside wall where two tramps had once, outrageously, lit a bonfire to roast a carp that was not theirs. For a long time there had been a shrivelled boot lying exposed on grass kept trim by rabbits. But when Briony looked today, the boot had vanished, as everything would in the end. The idea that the temple, wearing its own black band, grieved for the burned-down mansion, that it yearned for a grand and invisible presence, bestowed a faintly religious ambience. Tragedy had rescued the temple from being entirely a fake.

It is hard to slash at nettles for long without a story imposing itself, and Briony was soon absorbed and grimly content, even though she appeared to the world like a girl in the grip of a terrible mood. She had found a slender hazel branch and stripped it clean. There was work to do, and she set about it. A tall nettle with a preening look, its head coyly drooping and its middle leaves turned outwards like hands protesting innocence – this was Lola, and though she whimpered for mercy, the singing arc of a three-foot switch cut her down at the knees and sent her worthless torso flying. This was too satisfying to let go, and the next several nettles were Lola too; this one, leaning across to whisper in the ear of its neighbour, was cut down with an outrageous lie on her lips; here she was again, standing apart from the others, head cocked in poisonous scheming; over there she lorded it among a clump of young admirers and was spreading rumours about Briony. It was regrettable, but the admirers had to die with her. Then she rose again, brazen with her various sins – pride, gluttony, avarice, unco-operativeness – and for each she paid with a life. Her final act of spite was to fall at Briony's feet and sting her toes. When Lola had died enough, three pairs of young nettles were sacrificed for the incompetence of the twins – retribution was indifferent and granted no special favours to children. Then play writing itself became a nettle, became several in fact; the shallowness, the wasted time, the messiness of other minds, the hopelessness of pretending – in the garden of the arts, it was a weed and had to die.

No longer a playwright and feeling all the more refreshed for that, and watching out for broken glass, she moved further round the temple, working along the fringe where the nibbled grass met the disorderly undergrowth that spilled out from among the trees. Flaying the nettles was becoming a self-purification, and it was childhood she set about now, having no further need for it. One spindly specimen stood in for everything she had been up until this moment. But that was not enough. Planting her feet firmly in the grass, she disposed of her old self year by year in thirteen strokes. She severed the sickly dependency of infancy and early childhood, and the schoolgirl eager to show off and be praised, and the eleven-year-old's silly pride in her first stories and her reliance on her mother's good opinion. They flew over her left shoulder and lay at her feet. The slender tip of the switch made a two-tone sound as it sliced the air. No more! she made it say. Enough! Take that!

Soon, it was the action itself that absorbed her, and the newspaper report which she revised to the rhythm of her swipes. No one in the world could do this better than Briony Tallis who would be representing her country next year at the Berlin Olympics and was certain to win the gold. People studied her closely and marvelled at her technique, her preference for bare feet because it improved her balance – so important in this demanding sport – with every toe playing its part; the manner in which she led with the wrist and snapped the hand round only at the end of her stroke, the way she distributed her weight and used the rotation in her hips to gain extra power, her distinctive habit of extending the fingers of her free hand – no one came near her. Self-taught, the youngest daughter of a senior civil servant. Look at the concentration in her face, judging the angle, never fudging a shot, taking each nettle with inhuman precision. To reach this level required a lifetime's dedication. And how close she had come to wasting that life as a playwright!

She was suddenly aware of the trap behind her, clattering over the first bridge. Leon at last. She felt his eyes upon her. Was this the kid sister he had last seen on Waterloo Station only three months ago, and now a member of an international elite? Perversely, she would not allow herself to turn and acknowledge him; he must learn that she was independent now of other people's opinion, even his. She was a grand master, lost to the intricacies of her art. Besides, he was bound to stop the trap and come running down the bank, and she would have to suffer the interruption with good grace.

The sound of wheels and hooves receding over the second bridge proved, she supposed, that her brother knew the meaning of distance and professional respect. All the same, a little sadness was settling on her as she kept hacking away, moving further round the island temple until she was out of sight of the road. A ragged line of chopped nettles on the grass marked her progress, as did the stinging white bumps on her feet and ankles. The tip of the hazel switch sang through its arc, leaves and stems flew apart, but the cheers of the crowds were harder to summon. The colours were ebbing from her fantasy, her self-loving pleasures in movement and balance were fading, her arm was aching. She was becoming a solitary girl swiping nettles with a stick, and at last she stopped and tossed it towards the trees and looked around her.

The cost of oblivious daydreaming was always this moment of return, the realignment with what had been before and now seemed a little worse. Her reverie, once rich in plausible details, had become a passing silliness before the hard mass of the actual. It was difficult to come back. *Come back*, her sister used to whisper when she woke her from a bad dream. Briony had lost her godly power of creation, but it was only at this moment of return that the loss became evident; part of a daydream's enticement was the illusion that she was helpless before its logic: forced by international rivalry to compete at the highest level among the world's finest and to accept the challenges that came with pre-eminence in her field – her field of nettle slashing – driven to push beyond her limits to assuage the roaring crowd, and to be the best, and, most importantly, unique. But of course, it had all been her – by her and about her, and now she was back in the world, not one she could make, but the one that had made her, and she felt herself shrinking under the early evening sky. She was weary of being outdoors, but she was not ready to go in. Was that really all there was in life, indoors or out? Wasn't there somewhere else for people to go? She turned her back on the island temple and wandered slowly over the perfect lawn the rabbits had made, towards the bridge. In front of her, illuminated by the lowering sun, was a cloud of insects, each one bobbing randomly, as though fixed on an invisible elastic string – a mysterious courtship dance, or sheer insect exuberance that defied her to find a meaning. In a spirit of mutinous resistance, she climbed the steep grassy slope to the bridge, and when she stood on the driveway, she decided she would stay there and wait until something significant happened to her. This was the challenge she was putting to existence – she would not stir, not for dinner, not even for her mother calling her in. She would simply wait on the bridge, calm and obstinate, until events, real events, not her own fantasies, rose to her challenge, and dispelled her insignificance.

Eight

In the early evening, high-altitude clouds in the western sky formed a thin yellow wash which became richer over the hour, and then thickened until a filtered orange glow hung above the giant crests of parkland trees; the leaves became nutty brown, the branches glimpsed among the foliage oily black, and the desiccated grasses took on the colours of the sky. A Fauvist dedicated to improbable colour might have imagined a landscape this way, especially once sky and ground took on a reddish bloom and the swollen trunks of elderly oaks became so black they began to look blue. Though the sun was weakening as it dropped, the temperature seemed to rise because the breeze that had brought faint relief all day had faded, and now the air was still and heavy.

The scene, or a tiny portion of it, was visible to Robbie Turner through a sealed skylight window if he cared to stand up from his bath, bend his knees and twist his neck. All day long his small bedroom, his bathroom and the cubicle wedged between them he called his study, had baked under the southern slope of the bungalow's roof. For over an hour after returning from work he lay in a tepid bath while his blood and, so it seemed, his thoughts, warmed the water. Above him the framed rectangle of sky slowly shifted through its limited segment of the spectrum, yellow to orange, as he sifted unfamiliar feelings and returned to certain memories again and again. Nothing palled. Now and then, an inch below the water's surface, the muscles of his stomach tightened involuntarily as he recalled another detail. A drop of water on her upper arm. Wet. An embroidered flower, a simple daisy, sewn between the cups of her bra. Her breasts wide apart and small. On her back, a mole half covered by a strap. When she climbed out of the pond, a glimpse of the triangular darkness her knickers were supposed to conceal. Wet. He saw it, he made himself see it again. The way her pelvic bones stretched the material clear of her skin, the deep curve of her waist, her startling whiteness. When she reached for her skirt, a carelessly raised foot revealed a patch of soil on each pad of her sweetly diminishing toes. Another mole the size of a farthing on her thigh and something purplish on her calf – a strawberry mark, a scar. Not blemishes. Adornments.

He had known her since they were children, and he had never looked at her. At Cambridge she came to his rooms once with a New Zealand girl in glasses and someone from her school, when there was a friend of his from Downing there. They idled away an hour with nervous jokes, and handed cigarettes about. Occasionally, they passed in the street and smiled. She always seemed to find it awkward – That's our cleaning lady's son, she might have been whispering to her friends as she walked on. He liked people to know he didn't care – there goes my mother's employer's daughter, he once said to a friend. He had his politics to protect him, and his scientifically based theories of class, and his own rather forced self-certainty. I am what I am. She was like a sister, almost invisible. That long, narrow face, the small mouth – if he had ever thought about her at all, he might have said she was a little horsey in appearance. Now he saw it was a strange beauty – something carved and still about the face, especially around the inclined planes of her cheekbones, with a wild flare to the nostrils, and a full, glistening rosebud mouth. Her eyes were dark and contemplative. It was a statuesque look, but her movements were quick and impatient – that vase would still be in one piece if she had not jerked it so suddenly from his hands. She was restless, that was clear, bored and confined by the Tallis household, and soon she would be gone.

He would have to speak to her soon. He stood up at last from his bath, shivering, in no doubt that a great change was coming over him. He walked naked through his study into the bedroom. The unmade bed, the mess of discarded clothes, a towel on the floor, the room's equatorial warmth were disablingly sensual. He stretched out on the bed, face down into his pillow and groaned. The sweetness of her, the delicacy, his childhood friend, and now in danger of becoming unreachable. To strip off like that – yes, her endearing attempt to seem eccentric, her stab at being bold had an exaggerated, homemade quality. Now she would be in agonies of regret, and could not know what she had done to him. And all of this would be very well, it would be rescuable, if she was not so angry with him over a broken vase that had come apart in his hands. But he loved her fury too. He rolled onto his side, eyes fixed and unseeing, and indulged a cinema fantasy: she pounded against his lapels before yielding with a little sob to the safe enclosure of his arms and letting herself be kissed; she didn't forgive him, she simply gave up. He watched this several times before he returned to what was real: she was angry with him, and she would be angrier still when she knew he was to be one of the dinner guests. Out there, in the fierce light, he hadn't thought quickly enough to refuse Leon's invitation. Automatically, he had bleated out his yes, and now he would face her irritation. He groaned again, and didn't care if he were heard downstairs, at the memory of how she had taken off her clothes in front of him – so indifferently, as though he were an infant. Of course. He saw it clearly now. The idea was to humiliate him. There it stood, the undeniable fact. Humiliation. She wanted it for him. She was not mere sweetness, and he could not afford to condescend to her, for she was a force, she could drive him out of his depth and push him under.

But perhaps – he had rolled onto his back – he should not believe in her outrage. Wasn't it too theatrical? Surely she must have meant something better, even in her anger. Even in her anger, she had wanted to show him just how beautiful she was and bind him to her. How could he trust such a self-serving idea derived from hope and desire? He had to. He crossed his legs, clasped his hands behind his head, feeling his skin cool as it dried. What might Freud say? How about: she hid the unconscious desire to expose herself to him behind a show of temper. Pathetic hope! It was an emasculation, a sentence, and this – what he was feeling now – this torture was his punishment for breaking her ridiculous vase. He should never see her again. He had to see her tonight. He had no choice anyway – he was going. She would despise him for coming. He should have refused Leon's invitation, but the moment it was made his pulse had leaped and his bleated yes had left his mouth. He'd be in a room with her tonight, and the body he had seen, the moles, the pallor, the strawberry mark, would be concealed inside her clothes. He alone would know, and Emily of course. But only he would be thinking of them. And Cecilia would not speak to him or look at him. Even that would be better than lying here groaning. No, it wouldn't. It would be worse, but he still wanted it. He had to have it. He wanted it to be worse.

At last he rose, half dressed and went into his study and sat at his typewriter, wondering what kind of letter he should write to her. Like the bedroom and bathroom, the study was squashed under the apex of the bungalow's roof, and was little more than a corridor between the two, barely six feet long and five feet wide. As in the two other rooms, there was a skylight framed in rough pine. Piled in a corner, his hiking gear – boots, alpenstock, leather knapsack. A knife-scarred kitchen table took up most of the space. He tilted back his chair and surveyed his desk as one might a life. At one end, heaped high against the sloping ceiling were the folders and exercise books from the last months of his preparations for finals. He had no further use for his notes, but too much work, too much success was bound up with them and he could not bring himself to throw them out yet. Lying partly across them were some of his hiking maps, of North Wales, Hampshire and Surrey and of the abandoned hike to Istanbul. There was a compass with slitted sighting mirror he had once used to walk without maps to Lulworth Cove.

Beyond the compass were his copies of Auden's *Poems* and Housman's *A Shropshire Lad*. At the other end of the table were various histories, theoretical treatises and practical handbooks on landscape gardening. Ten typed-up poems lay beneath a printed rejection slip from *Criterion* magazine, initialled by Mr Eliot himself. Closest to where Robbie sat were the books of his new interest. *Gray's Anatomy* was open by a folio pad of his own drawings. He had set himself the task of drawing and committing to memory the bones of the hand. He tried to distract himself by running through some of them now, murmuring their names: capitate, hamate, triquetral, lunate . . . His best drawing so far, done in ink and coloured pencils and showing a cross-section of the oesophageal tract and the airways, was tacked to a rafter above the table. A pewter tankard with its handle missing held all the pencils and pens. The typewriter was a fairly recent Olympia, given to him on his twenty-first by Jack Tallis at a lunchtime party held in the library. Leon had made a speech as well as his father, and Cecilia had been there surely. But Robbie could not remember a single thing they might have said to each other. Was that why she was angry now, because he had ignored her for years? Another pathetic hope.

At the outer reaches of the desk, various photographs: the cast of *Twelfth Night* on the college lawn, himself as Malvolio, cross-gartered. How apt. There was another group shot, of himself and the thirty French kids he had taught in a boarding school near Lille. In a *belle époque* metal frame tinged with verdigris was a photograph of his parents, Grace and Ernest, three days after their wedding. Behind them, just poking into the picture, was the front wing of a car – certainly not theirs, and further off, an oast house looming over a brick wall. It was a good honeymoon, Grace always said, two weeks picking hops with her husband's family, and sleeping in a gypsy caravan parked in a farmyard. His father wore a collarless shirt. The neck-scarf and the rope belt around his flannel trousers may have been playful Romany touches. His head and face were round, but the effect was not exactly jovial, for his smile for the camera was not wholehearted enough to part his lips, and rather than hold the hand of his young bride, he had folded his arms. She, by contrast, was leaning into his side, nestling her head on his shoulder and holding onto his shirt at the elbow awkwardly with both hands. Grace, always game and good-natured, was doing the smiling for two. But willing hands and a kind spirit would not be enough. It looked as though Ernest's mind was already elsewhere, already drifting seven summers ahead to the evening when he would walk away from his job as the Tallises' gardener, away from the bungalow, without luggage, without even a farewell note on the kitchen table, leaving his wife and their six-year-old son to wonder about him for the rest of their lives.

Elsewhere, strewn between the revision notes, landscape gardening and anatomy piles, were various letters and cards: unpaid battels, letters from tutors and friends congratulating him on his first, which he still took pleasure in re-reading, and others mildly querying his next step. The most recent, scribbled in brownish ink on Whitehall departmental notepaper, was a message from Jack Tallis agreeing to help with fees at medical school. There were application forms, twenty pages long, and thick, densely printed admission handbooks from Edinburgh and London whose methodical, exacting prose seemed to be a foretaste of a new kind of academic rigour. But today they suggested to him, not adventure and a fresh beginning, but exile. He saw it in prospect – the dull terraced street far from here, a floral wallpapered box with a louring wardrobe and candlewick bedspread, the earnest new friends mostly younger than himself, the formaldehyde vats, the echoing lecture room – every element devoid of her.

From among the landscape books he took the volume on Versailles he had borrowed from the Tallis library. That was the day he first noticed his awkwardness in her presence. Kneeling to remove his work shoes by the front door, he had become aware of the state of his socks – holed at toe and heel and, for all he knew, odorous – and on impulse had removed them. What an idiot he had then felt, padding behind her across the hall and entering the library barefoot. His only thought was to leave as soon as he could. He had escaped through the kitchen and had to get Danny Hardman to go round the front of the house to collect his shoes and socks.

She probably would not have read this treatise on the hydraulics of Versailles by an eighteenth-century Dane who extolled in Latin the genius of Le Nôtre. With the help of a dictionary, Robbie had read five pages in a morning and then given up and made do with the illustrations instead. It would not be her kind of book, or anyone's really, but she had handed it to him from the library steps and somewhere on its leather surface were her fingerprints. Willing himself not to, he raised the book to his nostrils and inhaled. Dust, old paper, the scent of soap on his hands, but nothing of her. How had it crept up on him, this advanced stage of fetishising the love object? Surely Freud had something to say about that in *Three Essays on Sexuality*. And so did Keats, Shakespeare and Petrarch, and all the rest, and it was in the *Romaunt of the Rose*. He had spent three years dryly studying the symptoms, which had seemed no more than literary conventions, and now, in solitude, like some ruffed and plumed courtier come to the edge of the forest to contemplate a discarded token, he was worshipping her traces – not a handkerchief, but fingerprints! – while he languished in his lady's scorn.

For all that, when he fed a sheet of paper into the typewriter he did not forget the carbon. He typed the date and salutation and plunged straight into a conventional apology for his 'clumsy and inconsiderate behaviour'. Then he paused. Was he going to make any show of feeling at all, and if so, at what level?

'If it's any excuse, I've noticed just lately that I'm rather light-headed in your presence. I mean, I've never gone bare-foot into someone's house before. It must be the heat!'

How thin it looked, this self-protective levity. He was like a man with advanced TB pretending to have a cold. He flicked the return lever twice and re-wrote: 'It's hardly an excuse, I know, but lately I seem to be awfully light-headed around you. What was I doing, walking barefoot into your house? And have I ever snapped off the rim of an antique vase before?' He rested his hands on the keys while he confronted the urge to type her name again. 'Cee, I don't think I can blame the heat!' Now jokiness had made way for melodrama, or plaintiveness. The rhetorical questions had a clammy air; the exclamation mark was the first resort of those who shout to make themselves clearer. He forgave this punctuation only in his mother's letters where a row of five indicated a jolly good joke. He turned the drum and typed an 'x'. 'Cecilia, I don't think I can blame the heat.' Now the humour was removed, and an element of self-pity had crept in. The exclamation mark would have to be reinstated. Volume was obviously not its only business.

He tinkered with his draft for a further quarter of an hour, then threaded in new sheets and typed up a fair copy. The crucial lines now read: 'You'd be forgiven for thinking me mad – wandering into your house barefoot, or snapping your antique vase. The truth is, I feel rather light-headed and foolish in your presence, Cee, and I don't think I can blame the heat! Will you forgive me? Robbie.' Then, after a few moments' reverie, tilted back on his chair, during which time he thought about the page at which his *Anatomy* tended to fall open these days, he dropped forwards and typed before he could stop himself, 'In my dreams I kiss your cunt, your sweet wet cunt. In my thoughts I make love to you all day long.'

There it was – ruined. The draft was ruined. He pulled the sheet clear of the typewriter, set it aside, and wrote his letter out in longhand, confident that the personal touch fitted the occasion. As he looked at his watch he remembered that before setting out he should polish his shoes. He stood up from his desk, careful not to thump his head on the rafter.

He was without social unease – inappropriately so, in the view of many. At a dinner in Cambridge once, during a sudden silence round the table, someone who disliked Robbie asked loudly about his parents. Robbie held the man's eye and answered pleasantly that his father had walked out long ago and that his mother was a charlady who supplemented her income as an occasional clairvoyant. His tone was of easy-going tolerance of his questioner's ignorance. Robbie elaborated upon his circumstances, then ended by asking politely about the parents of the other fellow. Some said that it was innocence, or ignorance of the world, that protected Robbie from being harmed by it, that he was a kind of holy fool who could step across the drawing room equivalent of hot coals without harm. The truth, as Cecilia knew, was simpler. He had spent his childhood moving freely between the bungalow and the main house. Jack Tallis was his patron, Leon and Cecilia were his best friends, at least until grammar school. At university, where Robbie discovered that he was cleverer than many of the people he met, his liberation was complete. Even his arrogance need not be on display.

Grace Turner was happy to take care of his laundry – how else, beyond hot meals, to show mother love when her only baby was twenty-three? – but Robbie preferred to shine his own shoes. In a white singlet and the trousers of his suit, he went down the short straight run of stairs in his stockinged feet carrying a pair of black brogues. By the living room door was a narrow space that ended in the frosted glass door of the front entrance through which a diffused blood-orange light embossed the beige and olive wallpaper in fiery honeycomb patterns. He paused, one hand on the doorknob, surprised by the transformation, then he entered. The air in the room felt moist and warm, and faintly salty. A session must have just ended. His mother was on the sofa with her feet up and her carpet slippers dangling from her toes.

'Molly was here,' she said, and moved herself upright to be sociable. 'And I'm glad to tell you she's going to be all right.'

Robbie fetched the shoeshine box from the kitchen, sat down in the armchair nearest his mother and spread out a page of a three-day-old *Daily Sketch* on the carpet.

'Well done you,' he said. 'I heard you at it and went up for a bath.'

He knew he should be leaving soon, he should be polishing his shoes, but instead he leaned back in the chair, stretched his great length and yawned.

'Weeding! What am I doing with my life?'

There was more humour than anguish in his tone. He folded his arms and stared at the ceiling while massaging the instep of one foot with the big toe of the other.

His mother was staring at the space above his head. 'Now come on. Something's up. What's wrong with you. And don't say "Nothing".'

Grace Turner became the Tallises' cleaner the week after Ernest walked away. Jack Tallis did not have it in him to turn out a young woman and her child. In the village he found a replacement gardener and handyman who was not in need of a tied cottage. At the time it was assumed Grace would keep the bungalow for a year or two before moving on or remarrying. Her good nature and her knack with the polishing – her dedication to the surface of things, was the family joke – made her popular, but it was the adoration she aroused in the six-year-old Cecilia and her eight-year-old brother Leon that was the saving of her, and the making of Robbie. In the school holidays Grace was allowed to bring her own six-year-old along. Robbie grew up with the run of the nursery and those other parts of the house the children were permitted, as well as the grounds. His tree-climbing pal was Leon, Cecilia was the little sister who trustingly held his hand and made him feel immensely wise. A few years later, when Robbie won his scholarship to the local grammar, Jack Tallis took the first step in an enduring patronage by paying for the uniform and textbooks. This was the year Briony was born. The difficult birth was followed by Emily's long illness. Grace's helpfulness secured her position: on Christmas day that year – 1922 – Leon dressed in top hat and riding breeches, walked through the snow to the bungalow with a green envelope from his father. A solicitor's letter informed her that the freehold of the bungalow was now hers, irrespective of the position she held with the Tallises. But she had stayed on, returning to housework as the children grew older, with responsibilities for the special polishing.

Her theory about Ernest was that he had got himself sent to the Front under another name, and never returned. Otherwise, his lack of curiosity about his son was inhuman. Often, in the minutes she had to herself each day as she walked from the bungalow to the house, she would reflect on the benign accidents of her life. She had always been a little frightened of Ernest. Perhaps they would not have been so happy together as she had been living alone with her darling genius son in her own tiny house. If Mr Tallis had been a different kind of man . . . Some of the women who came for a shilling's glimpse of the future had been left by their husbands, even more had husbands killed at the Front. It was a pinched life the women led, and it easily could have been hers.

'Nothing,' he said in answer to her question. 'There's nothing up with me at all.' As he took up a brush and a tin of blacking, he said, 'So the future's looking bright for Molly.'

'She's going to remarry within five years. And she'll be very happy. Someone from the north with qualifications.'

'She deserves no less.'

They sat in comfortable silence while she watched him buffing his brogues with a yellow duster. By his handsome cheekbones the muscles twitched with the movement, and along his forearms they fanned and shifted in complicated re-arrangements under the skin. There must have been something right with Ernest to have given her a boy like this.

'So you're off out.'

'Leon was just arriving as I was coming away. He had his friend with him, you know, the chocolate magnate. They persuaded me to join them for dinner tonight.'

'Oh, and there was me all afternoon, on the silver. And doing out his room.'

He picked up his shoes and stood. 'When I look for my face in my spoon, I'll see only you.'

'Get on. Your shirts are hanging in the kitchen.'

He packed up the shoeshine box and carried it out, and chose a cream linen shirt from the three on the airer. He came back through and was on his way out, but she wanted to keep him a little longer.

'And those Quincey children. That boy wetting his bed and all. The poor little lambs.'

He lingered in the doorway and shrugged. He had looked in and seen them round the pool, screaming and laughing through the late-morning heat. They would have run his wheelbarrow into the deep end if he had not gone across. Danny Hardman was there too, leering at their sister when he should have been at work.

'They'll survive,' he said.

Impatient to be out, he skipped up the stairs three at a time. Back in his bedroom he finished dressing hurriedly, whistling tunelessly as he stooped to grease and comb his hair before the mirror inside his wardrobe. He had no ear for music at all, and found it impossible to tell if one note was higher or lower than another. Now he was committed to the evening, he felt excited and, strangely, free. It couldn't be worse than it already was. Methodically, and with pleasure in his own efficiency, as though preparing for some hazardous journey or military exploit, he accomplished the familiar little chores – located his keys, found a ten-shilling note inside his wallet, brushed his teeth, smelled his breath against a cupped hand, from the desk snatched up his letter and folded it into an envelope, loaded his cigarette case and checked his lighter. One last time, he braced himself in front of the mirror. He bared his gums, and turned to present his profile and looked across his shoulder at his image. Finally, he patted his pockets, then loped down the stairs, three at a time again, called a farewell to his mother, and stepped out onto the narrow brick path which led between the flower beds to a gate in the picket fence.

In the years to come he would often think back to this time, when he walked along the footpath that made a shortcut through a corner of the oak woods and joined the main drive where it curved towards the lake and the house. He was not late, and yet he found it difficult to slow his pace. Many immediate and other less proximal pleasures mingled in the richness of these minutes: the fading, reddish dusk, the warm, still air saturated with the scents of dried grasses and baked earth, his limbs loosened by the day's work in the gardens, his skin smooth from his bath, the feel of his shirt and of this, his only suit. The anticipation and dread he felt at seeing her was also a kind of sensual pleasure, and surrounding it, like an embrace, was a general elation – it might hurt, it was horribly inconvenient, no good might come of it, but he had found out for himself what it was to be in love, and it thrilled him. Other tributaries swelled his happiness; he still derived satisfaction from the thought of his first – the best in his year he was told. And now there was confirmation from Jack Tallis of his continuing support. A fresh adventure ahead, not an exile at all, he was suddenly certain. It was right and good that he should study medicine. He could not have explained his optimism – he was happy and therefore bound to succeed.

One word contained everything he felt, and explained why he was to dwell on this moment later. Freedom. In his life as in his limbs. Long ago, before he had even heard of grammar schools, he was entered for an exam that led him to one. Cambridge, much as he enjoyed it, was the choice of his ambitious headmaster. Even his subject was effectively chosen for him by a charismatic teacher. Now, finally, with the exercise of will, his adult life had begun. There was a story he was plotting with himself as the hero, and already its opening had caused a little shock among his friends. Landscape gardening was no more than a bohemian fantasy, as well as a lame ambition – so he had analysed it with the help of Freud – to replace or surpass his absent father. Schoolmastering – in fifteen years' time, Head of English, Mr R. Turner, MA Cantab – was not in the story either, nor was teaching at a university. Despite his first, the study of English literature seemed in retrospect an absorbing parlour game, and reading books and having opinions about them, the desirable adjunct to a civilised existence. But it was not the core, whatever Dr Leavis said in his lectures. It was not the necessary priesthood, nor the most vital pursuit of an enquiring mind, nor the first and last defence against a barbarian horde, any more than the study of painting or music, history or science. At various talks in his final year Robbie had heard a psychoanalyst, a Communist trade union official and a physicist each declare for his own field as passionately, as convincingly, as Leavis had for his own. Such claims were probably made for medicine, but for Robbie the matter was simpler and more personal: his practical nature and his frustrated scientific aspirations would find an outlet, he would have skills far more elaborate than the ones he had acquired in practical criticism, and above all he would have made his own decision. He would take lodgings in a strange town – and begin.

He had emerged from the trees and reached the point where the path joined the drive. The falling light magnified the dusky expanse of the park, and the soft yellow glow at the windows on the far side of the lake made the house seem almost grand and beautiful. She was in there, perhaps in her bedroom, preparing for dinner – out of view, at the back of the building on the second floor. Facing over the fountain. He pushed away these vivid, daylight thoughts of her, not wanting to arrive feeling deranged. The hard soles of his shoes rapped loudly on the metalled road like a giant clock, and he made himself think about time, about his great hoard, the luxury of an unspent fortune. He had never before felt so self-consciously young, nor experienced such appetite, such impatience for the story to begin. There were men at Cambridge who were mentally agile as teachers, and still played a decent game of tennis, still rowed, who were twenty years older than him. Twenty years at least in which to unfold his story at roughly this level of physical well-being – almost as long as he had already lived. Twenty years would sweep him forward to the futuristic date of 1955. What of importance would he know then that was obscure now? Might there be for him another thirty years beyond that time, to be lived out at some more thoughtful pace?

He thought of himself in 1962, at fifty, when he would be old, but not quite old enough to be useless, and of the weathered, knowing doctor he would be by then, with the secret stories, the tragedies and successes stacked behind him. Also stacked would be books by the thousand, for there would be a study, vast and gloomy, richly crammed with the trophies of a lifetime's travel and thought – rare rain-forest herbs, poisoned arrows, failed electrical inventions, soapstone figurines, shrunken skulls, aboriginal art. On the shelves, medical reference and meditations, certainly, but also the books that now filled the cubby hole in the bungalow attic – the eighteenth-century poetry that had almost persuaded him he should be a landscape gardener, his third-edition Jane Austen, his Eliot and Lawrence and Wilfred Owen, the complete set of Conrad, the priceless 1783 edition of Crabbe's

The Village, his Housman, the autographed copy of Auden's *The Dance of Death*. For this was the point, surely: he would be a better doctor for having read literature. What deep readings his modified sensibility might make of human suffering, of the self-destructive folly or sheer bad luck that drive men towards ill-health! Birth, death, and frailty in between. Rise and fall – this was the doctor's business, and it was literature's too. He was thinking of the nineteenth-century novel. Broad tolerance and the long view, an inconspicuously warm heart and cool judgment; his kind of doctor would be alive to the monstrous patterns of fate, and to the vain and comic denial of the inevitable; he would press the enfeebled pulse, hear the expiring breath, feel the fevered hand begin to cool and reflect, in the manner that only literature and religion teach, on the puniness and nobility of mankind . . .

His footsteps quickened in the still summer evening to the rhythm of his exultant thoughts. Ahead of him, about a hundred yards away, was the bridge, and on it, he thought, picked out against the darkness of the road, was a white shape which seemed at first to be part of the pale stone of the parapet. Staring at it dissolved its outlines, but within a few paces it had taken on a vaguely human form. At this distance he was not able to tell whether it faced away or towards him. It was motionless and he assumed he was being watched. He tried for a second or two to entertain himself with the idea of a ghost, but he had no belief in the supernatural, not even in the supremely undemanding being that presided over the Norman church in the village. It was a child, he saw now, and therefore it must be Briony, in the white dress he had seen her wearing earlier in the day. He could see her clearly now and he raised his hand and called out to her, and said, 'It's me, Robbie,' but still she did not move.

As he approached it occurred to him that it might be preferable for his letter to precede him into the house. Otherwise he might have to pass it to Cecilia in company, watched perhaps by her mother who had been rather cool towards him since he came down. Or he might be unable to give the letter to Cecilia at all because she would be keeping her distance. If Briony gave it to her, she would have time to read it and reflect in private. The few extra minutes might soften her.

'I was wondering if you'd do me a favour,' he said as he came up to her.

She nodded and waited.

'Will you run ahead and give this note to Cee?'

He put the envelope into her hand as he spoke, and she took it without a word.

'I'll be there in a few minutes,' he started to say, but she had already turned and was running across the bridge. He leaned back against the parapet and took out a cigarette as he watched her bobbing and receding form fade into the dusk. It was an awkward age in a girl, he thought contentedly. Twelve, or was it thirteen? He lost sight of her for a second or two, then saw her as she crossed the island, highlighted against the darker mass of trees. Then he lost her again, and it was only when she reappeared, on the far side of the second bridge, and was leaving the drive to take a shortcut across the grass that he stood suddenly, seized by horror and absolute certainty. An involuntary, wordless shout left him as he took a few hurried steps along the drive, faltered, ran on, then stopped again, knowing that pursuit was pointless. He could no longer see her as he cupped his hands around his mouth and bellowed Briony's name. That was pointless too. He stood there, straining his eyes to see her – as if that would help – and straining his memory too, desperate to believe that he was mistaken. But there was no mistake. The handwritten letter he had rested on the open copy of *Gray's Anatomy*, Splanchnology section, page 1546, the vagina. The typed page, left by him near the typewriter, was the one he had taken and folded into the envelope. No need for Freudian smart-aleckry – the explanation was simple and mechanical – the innocuous letter was lying across figure 1236, with its bold spread and rakish crown of pubic hair, while his obscene draft was on the table, within easy reach. He bellowed Briony's name again, though he knew she must be by the front entrance by now. Sure enough, within seconds, a distant rhombus of ochre light containing her outline widened, paused, then narrowed to nothing as she entered the house and the door was closed behind her.

Nine

On two occasions within half an hour, Cecilia stepped out of her bedroom, caught sight of herself in the gilt-frame mirror at the top of the stairs and, immediately dissatisfied, returned to her wardrobe to reconsider. Her first resort was a black crêpe de Chine dress which, according to the dressing-table mirror, bestowed by means of clever cutting a certain severity of form. Its air of invulnerability was heightened by the darkness of her eyes. Rather than offset the effect with a string of pearls, she reached in a moment's inspiration for a necklace of pure jet. The lipstick's bow had been perfect at first application. Various tilts of the head to catch perspectives in triptych reassured her that her face was not too long, or not this evening. She was expected in the kitchen on behalf of her mother, and Leon was waiting for her, she knew, in the drawing room. Still, she found time, as she was about to leave, to return to the dressing table and apply her perfume to the points of her elbows, a playful touch in accord with her mood as she closed the door of her bedroom behind her.

But the public gaze of the stairway mirror as she hurried towards it revealed a woman on her way to a funeral, an austere, joyless woman moreover, whose black carapace had affinities with some form of matchbox-dwelling insect. A stag beetle! It was her future self, at eighty-five, in widow's weeds. She did not linger – she turned on her heel, which was also black, and returned to her room.

She was sceptical, because she knew the tricks the mind could play. At the same time, her mind was – in every sense – where she was to spend the evening, and she had to be at ease with herself. She stepped out of the black crêpe dress where it fell to the floor, and stood in her heels and underwear, surveying the possibilities on the wardrobe racks, mindful of the passing minutes. She hated the thought of appearing austere. Relaxed was how she wanted to feel, and, at the same time, self-contained. Above all, she wanted to look as though she had not given the matter a moment's thought, and that would take time. Downstairs the knot of impatience would be tightening in the kitchen, while the minutes she was planning to spend alone with her brother were running out. Soon her mother would appear and want to discuss the table placings, Paul Marshall would come down from his room and be in need of company, and then Robbie would be at the door. How was she to think straight?

She ran a hand along the few feet of personal history, her brief chronicle of taste. Here were the flapper dresses of her teenage years, ludicrous, limp, sexless things they looked now, and though one bore wine stains and another a burn hole from her first cigarette, she could not bring herself to turn them out. Here was a dress with the first timid hint of shoulder pads, and others followed more assertively, muscular older sisters throwing off the boyish years, rediscovering waistlines and curves, dropping their hemlines with self-sufficient disregard for the hopes of men. Her latest and best piece, bought to celebrate the end of finals, before she knew about her miserable third, was the figure-hugging dark green bias-cut backless evening gown with a halter neck. Too dressy to have its first outing at home. She ran her hand further back and brought out a moiré silk dress with a pleated bodice and scalloped hem – a safe choice since the pink was muted and musty enough for evening wear. The triple mirror thought so too. She changed her shoes, swapped her jet for the pearls, retouched her make-up, rearranged her hair, applied a little perfume to the base of her throat, more of which was now exposed, and was back out in the corridor in less than fifteen minutes.

Earlier in the day she had seen old Hardman going about the house with a wicker basket, replacing electric bulbs. Perhaps there was now a harsher light at the top of the stairs, for she had never had this difficulty with the mirror there before. Even as she approached from a distance of forty feet, she saw that it was not going to let her pass; the pink was in fact innocently pale, the waistline was too high, the dress flared like an eight-year-old's party frock. All it needed was rabbit buttons. As she drew nearer, an irregularity in the surface of the ancient glass foreshortened her image and she confronted the child of fifteen years before. She stopped and experimentally raised her hands to the side of her head and gripped her hair in bunches. This same mirror must have seen her descend the stairs like this on dozens of occasions, on her way to one more friend's afternoon birthday bash. It would not help her state of mind, to go down looking like, or believing she looked like, Shirley Temple.

More in resignation than irritation or panic, she returned to her room. There was no confusion in her mind: these too-vivid, untrustworthy impressions, her self-doubt, the intrusive visual clarity and eerie differences that had wrapped themselves around the familiar were no more than continuations, variations of how she had been seeing and feeling all day. Feeling, but preferring not to think. Besides, she knew what she had to do and she had known it all along. She owned only one outfit that she genuinely liked, and that was the one she should wear. She let the pink dress fall on top of the black and, stepping contemptuously through the pile, reached for the gown, her green backless post-finals gown. As she pulled it on she approved of the firm caress of the bias-cut through the silk of her petticoat, and she felt sleekly impregnable, slippery and secure; it was a mermaid who rose to meet her in her own full-length mirror. She left the pearls in place, changed back into the black high-heel shoes, once more retouched her hair and make-up, forwent another dab of scent and then, as she opened the door, gave out a shriek of terror. Inches from her was a face and a raised fist. Her immediate, reeling perception was of a radical, Picasso-like perspective in which tears, rimmed and bloated eyes, wet lips and raw, unblown nose blended in a crimson moistness of grief. She recovered herself, placed her hands on the bony shoulders and gently turned the whole body so she could see the left ear. This was Jackson, about to knock on her door. In his other hand there was a grey sock. As she stepped back she noticed he was in ironed grey shorts and white shirt, but was otherwise barefoot.

'Little fellow! What's the matter?'

For the moment, he could not trust himself to speak. Instead, he held up his sock and with it gestured along the corridor. Cecilia leaned out and saw Pierrot some distance off, also barefoot, also holding a sock, and watching.

'You've got a sock each then.'

The boy nodded and swallowed, and then at last he was able to say, 'Miss Betty says we'll get a smack if we don't go down now and have our tea, but there's only one pair of socks.'

'And you've been fighting over it.'

Jackson shook his head emphatically.

As she went along the corridor with the boys to their room, first one then the other put his hand in hers and she was surprised to find herself so gratified. She could not help thinking about her dress.

'Didn't you ask your sister to help you?'

'She's not talking to us at the moment.'

'Why ever not?'

'She *hates* us.'

Their room was a pitiful mess of clothes, wet towels, orange peel, torn-up pieces of a comic arranged around a sheet of paper, upended chairs partly covered by blankets and the mattresses at a slew. Between the beds was a broad damp stain on the carpet in the centre of which lay a bar of soap and damp wads of lavatory paper. One of the curtains hung at a tilt below the pelmet, and though the windows were open, the air was dank, as though exhaled many times. All the drawers in the clothes chest stood open and empty. The impression was of closeted boredom punctuated by contests and schemes – jumping between the beds, building a camp, half devising a board game, then giving up. No one in the Tallis household was looking after the Quincey twins, and to conceal her guilt she said brightly, 'We'll never find anything with the room in this state.'

She began restoring order, remaking the beds, kicking off her high heels to mount a chair to fix the curtain, and setting the twins small achievable tasks. They were obedient to the letter, but they were quiet and hunched as they went about the work, as though it were retribution rather than deliverance, a scolding rather than kindness, she intended. They were ashamed of their room. Standing on the chair in her clinging dark green dress, watching the bright ginger heads bobbing and bending to their chores, the simple thought came to her, how hopeless and terrifying it was for them to be without love, to construct an existence out of nothing in a strange house.

With difficulty, for she could not bend her knees very far, she stepped down and sat on the edge of a bed and patted a space on each side of her. However, the boys remained standing, watching her expectantly. She used the faintly sing-song tones of a nursery school teacher she had once admired.

'We don't need to cry over lost socks, do we?'

Pierrot said, 'Actually, we'd prefer to go home.'

Chastened, she resumed the tones of adult conversation. 'That's impossible at the moment. Your mother's in Paris with – having a little holiday, and your father's busy in college, so you'll have to be here for a bit. I'm sorry you've been neglected. But you did have a jolly time in the pool . . .'

Jackson said, 'We wanted to be in the play and then Briony walked off and still hasn't come back.'

'Are you sure?' Someone else to worry about. Briony should have returned long ago. This in turn reminded her of the people downstairs waiting: her mother, the cook, Leon, the visitor, Robbie. Even the warmth of the evening filling the room through the open windows at her back imposed responsibilities; this was the kind of summer's evening one dreamed of all year, and now here it was at last with its heavy fragrance, its burden of pleasures, and she was too distracted by demands and minor distress to respond. But she simply had to. It was wrong not to. It would be paradise outside on the terrace drinking gin and tonics with Leon. It was hardly her fault that Aunt Hermione had run off with some toad who delivered fireside sermons on the wireless every week. Enough sadness. Cecilia stood up and clapped her hands.

'Yes, it's too bad about the play, but there's nothing we can do. Let's find you some socks and get on.'

A search revealed that the socks they had arrived in were being washed, and that in the obliterating thrill of passion, Aunt Hermione had omitted to pack more than one extra pair. Cecilia went to Briony's bedroom and rummaged in a drawer for the least girlish design – white, ankle length, with red and green strawberries around the tops. She assumed there would be a fight now for the grey socks, but the opposite was the case, and to avoid further sorrow she was obliged to return to Briony's room for another pair. This time she paused to peer out of the window at the dusk and wonder where her sister was. Drowned in the lake, ravished by gypsies, struck by a passing motor car, she thought ritually, a sound principle being that nothing was ever as one imagined it, and this was an efficient means of excluding the worst.

Back with the boys, she tidied Jackson's hair with a comb dipped in water from a vase of flowers, holding his chin tightly between forefinger and thumb as she carved across his scalp a fine, straight parting. Pierrot patiently waited his turn, then without a word they ran off downstairs together to face Betty.

Cecilia followed at a slow pace, passing the critical mirror with a glance and completely satisfied with what she saw. Or rather, she cared less, for her mood had shifted since being with the twins, and her thoughts had broadened to include a vague resolution which took shape without any particular content and prompted no specific plan; she had to get away. The thought was calming and pleasurable, and not desperate at all. She reached the first-floor landing and paused. Downstairs, her mother, guilt-stricken by her absence from the family, would be spreading anxiety and confusion all about her. To this mix must be added the news, if it was the case, that Briony was missing. Time and worry would be expended before she was found. There would be a phone call from the department to say that Mr Tallis had to work late and would stay up in town. Leon, who had the pure gift of avoiding responsibility, would not assume his father's role. Nominally, it would pass to Mrs Tallis, but ultimately the success of the evening would be in Cecilia's care. All this was clear and not worth struggling against – she would not be abandoning herself to a luscious summer's night, there would be no long session with Leon, she would not be walking barefoot across the lawns under the midnight stars. She felt under her hand the black-stained varnished pine of the bannisters, vaguely neo-Gothic, immovably solid and sham. Above her head there hung by three chains a great cast-iron chandelier which had never been lit in her lifetime. One depended instead on a pair of tasselled wall lights shaded by a quarter-circle of fake parchment. By their soupy yellow glow she moved quietly across the landing to look towards her mother's room. The half-open door, the column of light across the corridor carpet, confirmed that Emily Tallis had risen from her daybed. Cecilia returned to the stairs and hesitated again, reluctant to go down. But there was no choice.

There was nothing new in the arrangements and she was not distressed. Two years ago her father disappeared into the preparation of mysterious consultation documents for the Home Office. Her mother had always lived in an invalid's shadow land, Briony had always required mothering from her older sister, and Leon had always floated free, and she had always loved him for it. She had not thought it would be so easy to slip into the old roles. Cambridge had changed her fundamentally and she thought she was immune. No one in her family, however, noticed the transformation in her, and she was not able to resist the power of their habitual expectations. She blamed no one, but she had hung about the house all summer, encouraged by a vague notion she was re-establishing an important connection with her family. But the connections had never been broken, she now saw, and anyway her parents were absent in their different ways, Briony was lost to her fantasies and Leon was in town. Now it was time for her to move on. She needed an adventure. There was an invitation from an uncle and aunt to accompany them to New York. Aunt Hermione was in Paris. She could go to London and find a job – it was what her father expected of her. It was excitement she felt, not restlessness, and she would not allow this evening to frustrate her. There would be other evenings like this, and to enjoy them she would have to be elsewhere.

Animated by this new certainty – choosing the right dress had surely helped – she crossed the hallway, pushed through the baize door and strode along the chequered tiled corridor to the kitchen. She entered a cloud in which disembodied faces hung at different heights, like studies in an artist's sketch-book, and all eyes were turned down to a display upon the kitchen table, obscured to Cecilia by Betty's broad back. The blurred red glow at ankle level was the coal fire of the double range whose door was kicked shut just then with a great clang and an irritable shout. The steam rose thickly from a vat of boiling water which no one was attending. The cook's help, Doll, a thin girl from the village with her hair in an austere bun, was at the sink making a bad-tempered clatter scouring the saucepan lids, but she too was half turned to see what Betty had set upon the table. One of the faces was Emily Tallis's, another was Danny Hardman's, a third was his father's. Floating above the rest, standing on stools perhaps, were Jackson and Pierrot, their expressions solemn. Cecilia felt the gaze of the young Hardman on her. She returned it fiercely, and was gratified when he turned away. The labour in the kitchen had been long and hard all day in the heat, and the residue was everywhere: the flagstone floor was slick with the spilt grease of roasted meat and trodden-in peel; sodden tea towels, tributes to heroic forgotten labours, drooped above the range like decaying regimental banners in church; nudging Cecilia's shin, an overflowing basket of vegetable trimmings which Betty would take home to feed to her Gloucester Old Spot, fattening for December. The cook glanced over her shoulder to take in the newcomer, and before she turned away there was time to see the fury in eyes that cheek fat had narrowed to gelatinous slices.

'Take it orf!' she yelled. No doubting that the irritation was directed at Mrs Tallis. Doll sprang from sink to range, skidded and almost slipped, and picked up two rags to drag the cauldron off the heat. The improving visibility revealed Polly, the chambermaid who everyone said was simple, and who stayed on late whenever there was a do. Her wide and trusting eyes were also fixed upon the kitchen table. Cecilia moved round behind Betty to see what everyone else could see – a huge blackened tray recently pulled from the oven bearing a quantity of roast potatoes that still sizzled mildly. There were perhaps a hundred in all, in ragged rows of pale gold down which Betty's metal spatula dug and scraped and turned. The undersides held a stickier yellow glow, and here and there a gleaming edge was picked out in nacreous brown, and the occasional filigree lacework that blossomed around a ruptured skin. They were, or would be, perfect.

The last row was turned and Betty said, 'You want these, Ma'am, in a potato salad?'

'Exactly so. Cut the burnt bits away, wipe off the fat, put them in the big Tuscan bowl and give them a good dousing in olive oil and then . . .' Emily gestured vaguely towards a display of fruit by the larder door where there may or may not have been a lemon.

Betty addressed the ceiling. 'Will you be wanting a Brussels sprouts salad?'

'Really, Betty.'

'A cauliflower gratin salad? A horseradish sauce salad?'

'You're making a great fuss about nothing.'

'A bread and butter pudding salad?'

One of the twins snorted.

Even as Cecilia guessed what would come next, it began to happen. Betty turned to her, gripped her arm, and made her appeal. 'Miss Cee, it was a roast what was ordered and we've been at it all day in temperatures above the boiling point of *blood*.'

The scene was novel, the spectators were an unusual element, but the dilemma was familiar enough: how to keep the peace and not humiliate her mother. Also, Cecilia had resolved afresh to be with her brother on the terrace; it was therefore important to be with the winning faction and push to a quick conclusion. She took her mother aside, and Betty, who knew the form well enough, ordered everyone back to their business. Emily and Cecilia Tallis stood by the open door that led to the kitchen garden.

'Darling, there's a heatwave and I'm not going to be talked out of a salad.'

'Emily, I know it's far too hot, but Leon's absolutely dying for one of Betty's roasts. He goes on about them all the time. I heard him boasting about them to Mr Marshall.'

'Oh my God,' Emily said.

'I'm with you. I don't want a roast. Best thing is to give everyone a choice. Send Polly out to cut some lettuces. There's beetroot in the larder. Betty can do some new potatoes and let them cool.'

'Darling, you're right. You know, I'd hate to let little Leon down.'

And so it was resolved and the roast was saved. With tactful good grace, Betty set Doll to scrubbing new potatoes, and Polly went outside with a knife.

As they came away from the kitchen Emily put on her dark glasses and said, 'I'm glad that's settled because what's really bothering me is Briony. I know she's upset. She's moping around outside and I'm going to bring her in.'

'Good idea. I was worried about her too,' Cecilia said. She was not inclined to dissuade her mother from wandering far away from the terrace.

The drawing room which had transfixed Cecilia that morning with its parallelograms of light was now in gloom, lit by a single lamp near the fireplace. The open French windows framed a greenish sky, and against that, in silhouette at some distance, the familiar head and shoulders of her brother. As she made her way across the room she heard the tinkle of ice cubes against his glass, and as she stepped out she smelled the pennyroyal, camomile and feverfew crushed underfoot, and headier now than in the morning. No one remembered the name, or even the appearance, of the temporary gardener who made it his project some years back to plant up the cracks between the paving stones. At the time, no one understood what he had in mind. Perhaps that was why he was sacked.

'Sis! I've been out here forty minutes and I'm half stewed.'

'Sorry. Where's my drink?'

On a low wooden table set against the wall of the house was a paraffin globe lamp and ranged around it a rudimentary bar. At last the gin and tonic was in her hand. She lit a cigarette from his and they chinked glasses.

'I like the frock.'

'Can you see it?'

'Turn round. Gorgeous. I'd forgotten about that mole.'

'How's the bank?'

'Dull and perfectly pleasant. We live for the evenings and weekends. When are you going to come?'

They wandered off the terrace onto the gravel path between the roses. The Triton pond rose before them, an inky mass whose complicated outline was honed against a sky turning greener as the light fell. They could hear the trickle of water, and Cecilia thought she could smell it too, silvery and sharp. It may have been the drink in her hand.

She said after a pause, 'I am going a little mad here.'

'Being everyone's mother again. D'you know, there are girls getting all sorts of jobs now. Even taking the Civil Service exams. That would please the Old Man.'

'They'd never have me with a third.'

'Once your life gets going you'll find that stuff doesn't mean a thing.'

They reached the fountain and turned to face the house, and remained in silence for a while, leaning against the parapet, at the site of her disgrace. Reckless, ridiculous, and above all shaming. Only time, a prudish veil of hours, prevented her brother from seeing her as she had been. But she had no such protection from Robbie. He had seen her, he would always be able to see her, even as time smoothed out the memory to a bar-room tale. She was still irritated with her brother about the invitation, but she needed him, she wanted a share in his freedom. Solicitously, she prompted him to give her his news.

In Leon's life, or rather, in his account of his life, no one was mean-spirited, no one schemed or lied or betrayed. Everyone was celebrated at least in some degree, as though it was a cause for wonder that anyone existed at all. He remembered all his friends' best lines. The effect of one of Leon's anecdotes was to make his listener warm to humankind and its failings. Everyone was, at a minimal estimate, 'a good egg' or 'a decent sort', and motivation was never judged to be at variance with outward show. If there was mystery or contradiction in a friend, Leon took the long view and found a benign explanation. Literature and politics, science and religion did not bore him – they simply had no place in his world, and nor did any matter about which people seriously disagreed. He had taken a degree in law and was happy to have forgotten the whole experience. It was hard to imagine him ever lonely, or bored or despondent; his equanimity was bottomless, as was his lack of ambition, and he assumed that everyone else was much like him. Despite all this, his blandness was perfectly tolerable, even soothing.

He talked first of his rowing club. He had been stroke for the second eight recently, and though everyone had been kind, he thought he was happier taking the pace from someone else. Likewise, at the bank there had been mention of promotion and when nothing came of it he was somewhat relieved. Then the girls: the actress Mary, who had been so wonderful in *Private Lives*, had suddenly removed herself without explanation to Glasgow and no one knew why. He suspected she was tending a dying relative. Francine, who spoke beautiful French and had outraged the world by wearing a monocle, had gone with him to a Gilbert and Sullivan last week and in the interval they had seen the King who had seemed to glance in their direction. The sweet, dependable, well-connected Barbara whom Jack and Emily thought he should marry had invited him to spend a week at her parents' castle in the Highlands. He thought it would be churlish not to go.

Whenever he seemed about to dry up, Cecilia prodded him with another question. Inexplicably, his rent at the Albany had gone down. An old friend had got a girl with a lisp pregnant, had married her and was jolly happy. Another was buying a motorbike. The father of a chum had bought a vacuum cleaner factory and said it was a licence to print money. Someone's grandmother was a brave old stick for walking half a mile on a broken leg. As sweet as the evening air, this talk moved through and round her, conjuring a world of good intentions and pleasant outcomes. Shoulder to shoulder, half standing, half sitting, they faced their childhood home whose architecturally confused medieval references seemed now to be whimsically light-hearted; their mother's migraine was a comic interlude in a light opera, the sadness of the twins a sentimental extravagance, the incident in the kitchen no more than the merry jostling of lively spirits.

When it was her turn to give an account of recent months, it was impossible not to be influenced by Leon's tone, though her version of it came through, helplessly, as mockery. She ridiculed her own attempts at genealogy; the family tree was wintry and bare, as well as rootless. Grandfather Harry Tallis was the son of a farm labourer who, for some reason, had changed his name from Cartwright and whose birth and marriage were not recorded. As for *Clarissa* – all those daylight hours curled up on the bed with pins and needles in her arm – it surely proved the case of *Paradise Lost* in reverse – the heroine became more loathsome as her death-fixated virtue was revealed. Leon nodded and pursed his lips; he would not pretend to know what she was talking about, nor would he interrupt. She gave a farcical hue to her weeks of boredom and solitude, of how she had come to be with the family, and make amends for being away, and had found her parents and sister absent in their different ways. Encouraged by her brother's generous near-laughter, she attempted comic sketches based on her daily need for more cigarettes, on Briony tearing down her poster, on the twins outside her room with a sock each, and on their mother's desire for a miracle at the feast – roast potatoes into potato salad. Leon did not take the biblical reference here. There was desperation in all she said, an emptiness at its core, or something excluded or unnamed that made her talk faster, and exaggerate with less conviction. The agreeable nullity of Leon's life was a polished artefact, its ease deceptive, its limitations achieved by invisible hard work and the accidents of character, none of which she could hope to rival. She linked her arm with his and squeezed. That was another thing about Leon: soft and charming in company, but through his jacket his arm had the consistency of tropical hardwood. She felt soft at every level, and transparent. He was looking at her fondly.

'What's up, Cee?'

'Nothing. Nothing at all.'

'You really ought to come and stay with me and look around.'

There was a figure moving about on the terrace, and lights were coming on in the drawing room. Briony called out to her brother and sister.

Leon called back. 'We're over here.'

'We should go in,' Cecilia said, and still arm in arm, they began to walk towards the house. As they passed the roses she wondered if there really was anything she wanted to tell him. Confessing to her behaviour this morning was certainly not possible.

'I'd love to come up to town.' Even as she said the words she imagined herself being dragged back, incapable of packing her bag or of making the train. Perhaps she didn't want to go at all, but she repeated herself a little more emphatically.

'I'd love to come.'

Briony was waiting impatiently on the terrace to greet her brother. Someone addressed her from inside the drawing room and she spoke over her shoulder in reply. As Cecilia and Leon approached, they heard the voice again – it was their mother trying to be stern.

'I'm only saying it one more time. You will go up now and wash and change.'

With a lingering look in their direction, Briony moved towards the French windows. There was something in her hand.

Leon said, 'We could set you up in no time at all.'

When they stepped into the room, into the light of several lamps, Briony was still there, still barefoot and in her filthy white dress, and her mother was standing by the door on the far side of the room, smiling indulgently. Leon stretched out his arms and did the comic Cockney voice he reserved for her.

'An' if it ain't my li'le Sis!'

As she hurried past, Briony pushed into Cecilia's hand a piece of paper folded twice and then she squealed her brother's name and leaped into his embrace.

Conscious of her mother watching her, Cecilia adopted an expression of amused curiosity as she unfolded the sheet. Commendably, it was a look she was able to maintain as she took in the small block of typewriting and in a glance absorbed it whole – a unit of meaning whose force and colour was derived from the single repeated word. At her elbow, Briony was telling Leon about the play she had written for him, and lamenting her failure to stage it. *The Trials of Arabella*, she kept repeating. *The Trials of Arabella*. Never had she appeared so animated, so weirdly excited. She still had her arms about his neck, and was standing on tiptoe to nuzzle her cheek against his.

Initially, a simple phrase chased round and round in Cecilia's thoughts: *Of course, of course*. How had she not seen it? Everything was explained. The whole day, the weeks before, her childhood. A lifetime. It was clear to her now. Why else take so long to choose a dress, or fight over a vase, or find everything so different, or be unable to leave? What had made her so blind, so obtuse? Many seconds had passed, and it was no longer plausible to be staring fixedly at the sheet of paper. The act of folding it away brought her to an obvious realisation: it could not have been sent unsealed. She turned to look at her sister.

Leon was saying to her, 'How about this? I'm good at voices, you're even better. We'll read it aloud together.'

Cecilia moved round him, into Briony's view.

'Briony? Briony, did you read this?'

But Briony, engaged in a shrill response to her brother's suggestion, writhed in his arms and turned her face from her sister and half buried it in Leon's jacket.

From across the room Emily said soothingly, 'Calmly now.'

Again, Cecilia shifted her position so that she was on the other side of her brother. 'Where's the envelope?'

Briony turned her face away again and laughed wildly at something Leon was telling her.

Then Cecilia was aware of another figure in their presence, at the edge of vision, moving behind her, and when she turned she confronted Paul Marshall. In one hand he held a silver tray on which stood five cocktail glasses, each one half filled with a viscous brown substance. He lifted a glass and presented it to her.

'I insist you try it.'

Ten

The very complexity of her feelings confirmed Briony in her view that she was entering an arena of adult emotion and dissembling from which her writing was bound to benefit. What fairy tale ever held so much by way of contradiction? A savage and thoughtless curiosity prompted her to rip the letter from its envelope – she read it in the hall after Polly had let her in – and though the shock of the message vindicated her completely, this did not prevent her from feeling guilty. It was wrong to open people's letters, but it was right, it was essential, for her to know everything. She had been delighted to see her brother again, but that did not prevent her from exaggerating her feelings to avoid her sister's accusing question. And afterwards she had only pretended to be eagerly obedient to her mother's command by running up to her room; as well as wanting to escape Cecilia, she needed to be alone to consider Robbie afresh, and to frame the opening paragraph of a story shot through with real life. No more princesses! The scene by the fountain, its air of ugly threat, and at the end, when both had gone their separate ways, the luminous absence shimmering above the wetness on the gravel – all this would have to be reconsidered. With the letter, something elemental, brutal, perhaps even criminal had been introduced, some principle of darkness, and even in her excitement over the possibilities, she did not doubt that her sister was in some way threatened and would need her help.

The word: she tried to prevent it sounding in her thoughts, and yet it danced through them obscenely, a typographical demon, juggling vague, insinuating anagrams – an uncle and a nut, the Latin for next, an Old English king attempting to turn back the tide. Rhyming words took their form from children's books – the smallest pig in the litter, the hounds pursuing the fox, the flat-bottomed boats on the Cam by Grantchester meadow. Naturally, she had never heard the word spoken, or seen it in print, or come across it in asterisks. No one in her presence had ever referred to the word's existence, and what was more, no one, not even her mother, had ever referred to the existence of that part of her to which – Briony was certain – the word referred. She had no doubt that that was what it was. The context helped, but more than that, the word was at one with its meaning, and was almost onomatopoeic. The smooth-hollowed, partly enclosed forms of its first three letters were as clear as a set of anatomical drawings. Three figures huddling at the foot of the cross. That the word had been written by a man confessing to an image in his mind, confiding a lonely preoccupation, disgusted her profoundly.

She had read the note standing shamelessly in the centre of the entrance hall, immediately sensing the danger contained by such crudity. Something irreducibly human, or male, threatened the order of their household, and Briony knew that unless she helped her sister, they would all suffer. It was also clear that she would have to be helped in a delicate, tactful manner. Otherwise, as Briony knew from experience, Cecilia would turn on her.

These thoughts preoccupied her as she washed her hands and face and chose a clean dress. The socks she wanted to wear were not to be found, but she wasted no time in hunting. She put on some others, strapped on her shoes and sat at her desk. Downstairs, they were drinking cocktails and she would have at least twenty minutes to herself. She could brush her hair on the way out. Outside her open window a cricket was singing. A sheaf of foolscap from her father's office was before her, the desk light threw down its comforting yellow patch, the fountain pen was in her hand. The orderly troupe of farm animals lined along the window-sill and the strait-laced dolls poised in the various rooms of their open-sided mansion waited for the gem of her first sentence. At that moment, the urge to be writing was stronger than any notion she had of what she might write. What she wanted was to be lost to the unfolding of an irresistible idea, to see the black thread spooling out from the end of her scratchy silver nib and coiling into words. But how to do justice to the changes that had made her into a real writer at last, and to her chaotic swarm of impressions, and to the disgust and fascination she felt? Order must be imposed. She should begin, as she had decided earlier, with a simple account of what she had seen at the fountain. But that episode in the sunlight was not quite so interesting as the dusk, the idle minutes on the bridge lost to daydreaming, and then Robbie appearing in the semi-darkness, calling to her, holding in his hand the little white square that contained the letter that contained the word. And what did the word contain?

She wrote, 'There was an old lady who swallowed a fly.'

Surely it was not too childish to say there had to be a story; and this was the story of a man whom everybody liked, but about whom the heroine always had her doubts, and finally she was able to reveal that he was the incarnation of evil. But wasn't she – that was, Briony the writer – supposed to be so worldly now as to be above such nursery-tale ideas as good and evil? There must be some lofty, god-like place from which all people could be judged alike, not pitted against each other, as in some lifelong hockey match, but seen noisily jostling together in all their glorious imperfection. If such a place existed, she was not worthy of it. She could never forgive Robbie his disgusting mind.

Trapped between the urge to write a simple diary account of her day's experiences, and the ambition to make something greater of them that would be polished, self-contained and obscure, she sat for many minutes frowning at her sheet of paper and its infantile quotation and did not write another word. Actions she thought she could describe well enough, and she had the hang of dialogue. She could do the woods in winter, and the grimness of a castle wall. But how to do feelings? All very well to write, *She felt sad*, or describe what a sad person might do, but what of sadness itself, how was that put across so it could be felt in all its lowering immediacy? Even harder was the threat, or the confusion of feeling contradictory things. Pen in hand, she stared across the room towards her hard-faced dolls, the estranged companions of a childhood she considered closed. It was a chilly sensation, growing up. She would never sit on Emily's or Cecilia's lap again, or only as a joke. Two summers ago, on her eleventh birthday, her parents, brother and sister and a fifth person she could not remember had taken her out onto the lawn and tossed her in a blanket eleven times, and then once for luck. Could she trust it now, the hilarious freedom of the upward flight, the blind trust in the kindly grip of adult wrists, when the fifth person could so easily have been Robbie?

At the sound of the soft clearing of a female throat, she looked up, startled. It was Lola. She was leaning apologetically into the room, and as soon as their eyes met she tapped the door gently with her knuckles.

'Can I come in?'

She came in anyway, her movements somewhat restricted by the blue satin sheath dress she wore. Her hair was loose and she was barefoot. As she approached, Briony put away her pen and covered her sentence with the corner of a book. Lola sat herself down on the edge of the bed and blew dramatically through her cheeks. It was as though they had always had a sisterly end-of-day chat.

'I've had the most appalling evening.'

When Briony was obliged by her cousin's fierce stare to raise an eyebrow, she continued, 'The twins have been torturing me.'

She thought it was a figure of speech until Lola twisted her shoulder to reveal, high on her arm, a long scratch.

'How awful!'

She held out her wrists. Round each were blotchy bands of chafing.

'Chinese burns!'

'Exactly.'

'I'll get some antiseptic for your arm.'

'I've done all that myself.'

It was true, the womanly tang of Lola's perfume could not conceal a childish whiff of Germolene. The least Briony could do was to leave her desk and go to sit beside her cousin.

'You poor thing!'

Briony's compassion made Lola's eyes fill, and her voice went husky.

'Everybody thinks they're angels just because they look alike, but they're little *brutes*.'

She held back a sob, seeming to bite it down with a tremor along her jaw, and then inhaled deeply several times through flared nostrils. Briony took her hand and thought she could see how one might begin to love Lola. Then she went to her chest of drawers and took out a hankie, unfolded it and gave it to her. Lola was about to use it, but the sight of its gaily printed motif of cowgirls and lariats caused her to give out a gentle hooting sound on a rising note, the kind of noise children make to imitate ghosts. Downstairs the doorbell rang, and moments later, just discernible, the rapid tick of high heels on the tiled floor of the hallway. It would be Robbie, and Cecilia was going to the door herself. Worried that Lola's crying could be heard downstairs, Briony got to her feet again and pushed the bedroom door closed. Her cousin's distress produced in her a state of restlessness, an agitation that was close to joy. She went back to the bed and put her arm round Lola who raised her hands to her face and began to cry. That a girl so brittle and domineering should be brought this low by a couple of nine-year-old boys seemed wondrous to Briony, and it gave her a sense of her own power. It was what lay behind this near-joyful feeling. Perhaps she was not as weak as she always assumed; finally, you had to measure yourself by other people – there really was nothing else. Every now and then, quite unintentionally, someone taught you something about yourself. At a loss for words, she gently rubbed her cousin's shoulder and reflected that Jackson and Pierrot alone could not be responsible for such grief; she remembered there was other sorrow in Lola's life. The family home in the north – Briony imagined streets of blackened mills, and grim men trudging to work with sandwiches in tin boxes. The Quincey home was closed up and might never open again.

Lola was beginning to recover. Briony asked softly, 'What happened.'

The older girl blew her nose and thought for a moment. 'I was getting ready for a bath. They came bursting in and pounced on me. They got me down on the floor . . .' At this memory she paused to fight another rising sob.

'But why would they do that?'

She took a deep breath and composed herself. She stared unseeingly across the room. 'They want to go home. I said they couldn't. They think I'm the one who's keeping them here.'

The twins unreasonably venting their frustration on their sister – all this made sense to Briony. But what was troubling her organised spirit now was the thought that soon the call would come to go downstairs and her cousin would need to be in possession of herself.

'They just don't understand,' Briony said wisely as she went to the handbasin and filled it with hot water. 'They're just little kids who've taken a bad knock.'

Full of sadness, Lola lowered her head and nodded in such a way that Briony felt a rush of tenderness for her. She guided Lola to the basin and put a flannel in her hands. And then, from a mixture of motives – a practical need to change the subject, the desire to share a secret and show the older girl that she too had worldly experiences, but above all because she warmed to Lola and wanted to draw her closer – Briony told her about meeting Robbie on the bridge, and the letter, and how she had opened it, and what was in it. Rather than say the word out loud, which was unthinkable, she spelled it out for her, backwards. The effect on Lola was gratifying. She raised her dripping face from the basin and let her mouth fall open. Briony passed her a towel. Some seconds passed while Lola pretended to find her words. She was hamming it up a bit, but that was fine, and so was her hoarse whisper.

'Thinking about it *all the time*?'

Briony nodded and faced away, as though grappling with tragedy. She could learn to be a little more expressive from her cousin whose turn it now was to put a comforting hand on Briony's shoulder.

'How appalling for you. The man's a maniac.'

A maniac. The word had refinement, and the weight of medical diagnosis. All these years she had known him and that was what he had been. When she was little he used to carry her on his back and pretend to be a beast. She had been alone with him many times at the swimming hole where he taught her one summer how to tread water and do the breast stroke. Now his condition was named she felt a certain consolation, though the mystery of the fountain episode deepened. She had already decided not to tell that story, suspecting that the explanation was simple and that it would be better not to expose her ignorance.

'What's your sister going to do?'

'I just don't know.' Again, she did not mention that she dreaded her next meeting with Cecilia.

'D'you know, on our first afternoon I thought he was a monster when I heard him shouting at the twins by the swimming pool.'

Briony tried to recall similar moments when the symptoms

of mania might have been observed. She said, 'He's always pretended to be rather nice. He's deceived us for years.'

The change of subject had worked the trick, for the area around Lola's eyes which had been inflamed was freckly and pale once more and she was very much her old self. She took Briony's hand. 'I think the police should know about him.'

The constable in the village was a kindly man with a waxed moustache whose wife kept hens and delivered fresh eggs on her bicycle. Communicating the letter and its word, even spelling it out backwards for him, was inconceivable. She went to move her hand away but Lola tightened her grip and seemed to read the younger girl's mind.

'We just need to show them the letter.'

'She might not agree to it.'

'I bet she will. Maniacs can attack anyone.'

Lola looked suddenly thoughtful and seemed about to tell her cousin something new. But instead she sprang away and took up Briony's hairbrush and stood in front of the mirror vigorously brushing out her hair. She had barely started when they heard Mrs Tallis calling them down to dinner. Lola was immediately petulant, and Briony assumed that these rapid changes of mood were part of her recent upset.

'It's hopeless. I'm nowhere near ready,' she said, close to tears again. 'I haven't even started on my face.'

'I'll go down now,' Briony soothed her. 'I'll tell them you'll be a little while yet.' But Lola was already on her way out the room and did not seem to hear.

After Briony tidied her hair she remained in front of the mirror, studying her own face, wondering what she might do when she came to 'start' on it, which she knew she must one day soon. Another demand on her time. At least she had no freckles to conceal or soften, and that surely saved labour. Long ago, at the age of ten, she decided that lipstick made her seem clownish. That notion was due for revision. But not yet, when there was so much else to consider. She stood by the desk and absently replaced the top of her fountain pen.

Writing a story was a hopeless, puny enterprise when such powerful and chaotic forces were turning about her, and when all day long successive events had absorbed or transformed what had gone before. There was an old lady who swallowed a fly. She wondered whether she had made a terrible mistake by confiding in her cousin – Cecilia would hardly be pleased if excitable Lola started flaunting her knowledge of Robbie's note. And how was it possible to go downstairs now and be at table with a maniac? If the police made an arrest, she, Briony, might be made to appear in court, and say the word aloud, in proof.

Reluctantly, she left her room and made her way along the gloomy panelled corridor to the head of the stairs where she paused to listen. The voices were still in the drawing room – she heard her mother's and Mr Marshall's, and then, separately, the twins talking to each other. No Cecilia then, no maniac. Briony felt her heart rate rise as she began her unwilling descent. Her life had ceased to be simple. Only three days ago she was finishing off *The Trials of Arabella* and waiting for her cousins. She had wanted everything to be different, and here it was; and not only was it bad, it was about to get worse. She stopped again on the first landing to consolidate a scheme; she would keep well clear of her skittish cousin, not even catch her eye – she could not afford to be drawn into a conspiracy, nor did she wish to prompt a disastrous outburst. And Cecilia, whom she ought to protect, she dared not go near. Robbie, obviously, she should avoid for safety's sake. Her mother with her fussing would not be helpful. It would be impossible to think straight in her presence. It was the twins she should go for – they would be her refuge. She would stay close and look after them. These summer dinners always started so late – it was past ten o'clock – and the boys would be tired. And otherwise she should be sociable with Mr Marshall and ask him about sweets – who thought them up, how they got made. It was a coward's plan but she could think of no other. With dinner about to be served, this was hardly the moment to be summoning PC Vockins from the village.

She continued down the stairs. She should have advised Lola to change in order to conceal the scratch on her arm. Being asked about it might start her crying again. But then, it would probably have been impossible to talk her out of a dress that made it so difficult to walk. Attaining adulthood was all about the eager acceptance of such impediments. She herself was taking them on. It wasn't her scratch, but she felt responsible for it, and for everything that was about to happen. When her father was home, the household settled around a fixed point. He organised nothing, he didn't go about the house worrying on other people's behalf, he rarely told anyone what to do – in fact, he mostly sat in the library. But his presence imposed order and allowed freedom. Burdens were lifted. When he was there, it no longer mattered that her mother retreated to her bedroom; it was enough that he was downstairs with a book on his lap. When he took his place at the dining table, calm, affable, utterly certain, a crisis in the kitchen became no more than a humorous sketch; without him, it was a drama that clutched the heart. He knew most things worth knowing, and when he didn't know, he had a good idea which authority to consult, and would take her into the library to help him find it. If he had not been, as he described it, a slave to the Ministry, and to Eventuality Planning, if he had been at home, sending Hardman down for the wines, steering the conversation, deciding without appearing to when it was time to 'go through', she would not be crossing the hallway now with such heaviness in her step.

It was these thoughts of him that made her slow as she passed the library door which, unusually, was closed. She stopped to listen. From the kitchen, the chink of metal against porcelain, from the drawing room her mother talking softly, and closer by, one of the twins saying in a high, clear voice, 'It's got a "u" in it, actually,' and his brother replying, 'I don't care. Put it in the envelope.' And then, from behind the library door, a scraping noise followed by a thump and a murmur that could have been a man's or a woman's. In memory – and Briony later gave this matter some thought – she had no particular expectations as she placed her hand on the brass handle and turned it. But she had seen Robbie's letter, she had cast herself as her sister's protector, and she had been instructed by her cousin: what she saw must have been shaped in part by what she already knew, or believed she knew.

At first, when she pushed open the door and stepped in, she saw nothing at all. The only light was from a single green-glass desk lamp which illuminated little more than the tooled leather surface on which it stood. When she took another few steps she saw them, dark shapes in the furthest corner. Though they were immobile, her immediate understanding was that she had interrupted an attack, a hand-to-hand fight. The scene was so entirely a realisation of her worst fears that she sensed that her over-anxious imagination had projected the figures onto the packed spines of books. This illusion, or hope of one, was dispelled as her eyes adjusted to the gloom. No one moved. Briony stared past Robbie's shoulder into the terrified eyes of her sister. He had turned to look back at the intruder, but he did not let Cecilia go. He had pushed his body against hers, pushing her dress right up above her knee and had trapped her where the shelves met at right angles. His left hand was behind her neck, gripping her hair, and with his right he held her forearm which was raised in protest, or self-defence.

He looked so huge and wild, and Cecilia with her bare shoulders and thin arms so frail that Briony had no idea what she could achieve as she started to go towards them. She wanted to shout, but she could not catch her breath, and her tongue was slow and heavy. Robbie moved in such a way that her view of her sister was completely obscured. Then Cecilia was struggling free, and he was letting her go. Briony stopped and said her sister's name. When she pushed past

Briony there was no sign in Cecilia of gratitude or relief. Her face was expressionless, almost composed, and she looked right ahead to the door she was about to leave by. Then she was gone, and Briony was left alone with him. He too would not meet her eye. Instead he faced into the corner, and busied himself straightening his jacket and arranging his tie. Warily, she moved backwards away from him, but he made no move to attack her, and did not even look up. So she turned and ran from the room to find Cecilia. But the hallway was empty, and it was not clear which way she had gone.

Eleven

Despite the late addition of chopped fresh mint to a blend of melted chocolate, egg yolk, coconut milk, rum, gin, crushed banana and icing sugar, the cocktail was not particularly refreshing. Appetites already cloyed by the night's heat were further diminished. Nearly all the adults entering the airless dining room were nauseated by the prospect of a roast dinner, or even roast meat with salad, and would have been content with a glass of cool water. But water was available only to the children, while the rest were to revive themselves with a dessert wine at room temperature. Three bottles stood ready opened on the table – in Jack Tallis's absence Betty usually made an inspired guess. None of the three tall windows would open because their frames had warped long ago, and an aroma of warmed dust from the Persian carpet rose to meet the diners as they entered. One comfort was that the fishmonger's van bringing the first course of dressed crab had broken down.

The effect of suffocation was heightened by the dark-stained panelling reaching from the floor and covering the ceiling, and by the room's only painting, a vast canvas that hung above a fireplace unlit since its construction – a fault in the architectural drawings had left no provision for a flue or chimney. The portrait, in the style of Gainsborough, showed an aristocratic family – parents, two teenage girls and an infant, all thin-lipped, and pale as ghouls – posed before a vaguely Tuscan landscape. No one knew who these people were, but it was likely that Harry Tallis thought they would lend an impression of solidity to his household.

Emily stood at the head of the table placing the diners as they came in. She put Leon on her right, and Paul Marshall on her left. To his right Leon had Briony and the twins, while Marshall had Cecilia on his left, then Robbie, then Lola. Robbie stood behind his chair, gripping it for support, amazed that no one appeared to hear his still-thudding heart. He had escaped the cocktail, but he too had no appetite. He turned slightly to face away from Cecilia, and as the others took their places noted with relief that he was seated down among the children.

Prompted by a nod from his mother, Leon muttered a short suspended grace – For what we are about to receive – to which the scrape of chairs was the amen. The silence that followed as they settled and unfolded their napkins would easily have been dispersed by Jack Tallis introducing some barely interesting topic while Betty went around with the beef. Instead, the diners watched and listened to her as she stooped murmuring at each place, scraping the serving spoon and fork across the silver platter. What else could they attend to, when the only other business in the room was their own silence? Emily Tallis had always been incapable of small talk and didn't much care. Leon, entirely at one with himself, lolled in his chair, wine bottle in hand, studying its label. Cecilia was lost to the events of ten minutes before and could not have composed a simple sentence. Robbie was familiar with the household and would have started something off, but he too was in turmoil. It was enough that he could pretend to ignore Cecilia's bare arm at his side – he could feel its heat – and the hostile gaze of Briony who sat diagonally across from him. And even if it had been considered proper for children to introduce a topic, they too would have been incapable:

Briony could think only of what she had witnessed, Lola was subdued both by the shock of physical assault and an array of contradictory emotions, and the twins were absorbed in a plan.

It was Paul Marshall who broke more than three minutes of asphyxiating silence. He moved back in his chair to speak behind Cecilia's head to Robbie.

'I say, are we still on for tennis tomorrow?'

There was a two-inch scratch, Robbie noticed, from the corner of Marshall's eye, running parallel to his nose, drawing attention to the way his features were set high up in his face, bunched up under the eyes. Only fractions of an inch kept him from cruel good looks. Instead, his appearance was absurd – the empty tract of his chin was at the expense of a worried, over-populated forehead. Out of politeness, Robbie too had moved back in his seat to hear the remark, but even in his state he flinched. It was inappropriate, at the beginning of the meal, for Marshall to turn away from his hostess and begin a private conversation.

Robbie said tersely, 'I suppose we are,' and then, to make amends for him, added for general consideration, 'Has England ever been hotter?'

Leaning away from the field of Cecilia's body warmth, and averting his eyes from Briony's, he found himself pitching the end of his question into the frightened gaze of Pierrot diagonally to his left. The boy gaped, and struggled, as he might in the classroom, with a test in history. Or was it geography? Or science?

Briony leaned over Jackson to touch Pierrot's shoulder, all the while keeping her eyes on Robbie. 'Please leave him alone,' she said in a forceful whisper, and then to the little boy, softly, 'You don't have to answer.'

Emily spoke up from her end of the table. 'Briony, it was a perfectly bland remark about the weather. You'll apologise, or go now to your room.'

Whenever Mrs Tallis exercised authority in the absence of

her husband, the children felt obliged to protect her from seeming ineffectual. Briony, who in any case would not have left her sister undefended, lowered her head and said to the tablecloth, 'I'm very sorry. I wish I hadn't said it.'

The vegetables in lidded serving dishes, or on platters of faded Spode, were passed up and down, and such was the collective inattention or the polite desire to conceal a lack of appetite, that most ended with roast potatoes and potato salad, Brussels sprouts and beetroot, and lettuce leaves foundering in gravy.

'The Old Man's not going to be too pleased,' Leon said as he got to his feet. 'It's a 1921 Barsac, but it's open now.' He filled his mother's glass, then his sister's and Marshall's, and when he was standing by Robbie he said, 'And a healing draught for the good doctor. I want to hear about this new plan.'

But he did not wait for a reply. On his way back to his seat he said, 'I love England in a heat wave. It's a different country. All the rules change.'

Emily Tallis picked up her knife and fork and everyone did likewise.

Paul Marshall said, 'Nonsense. Name a single rule that changes.'

'All right. At the club the only place one's allowed to remove one's jacket is the billiard room. But if the temperature reaches ninety degrees before three o'clock, then jackets can be taken off in the upstairs bar the following day.'

'The following day! A different country indeed.'

'You know what I mean. People are more at ease – a couple of days' sunshine and we become Italians. Last week in Charlotte Street they were eating dinner at pavement tables.'

'It was always the view of my parents,' Emily said, 'that hot weather encouraged loose morals among young people. Fewer layers of clothing, a thousand more places to meet. Out of doors, out of control. Your grandmother especially was uneasy when it was summer. She would dream up a thousand reasons to keep my sisters and me in the house.'

'Well then,' Leon said. 'What do you think, Cee? Have you behaved even worse than usual today?'

All eyes were on her, and the brotherly banter was relentless.

'Good heavens, you're blushing. The answer must be yes.'

Sensing that he should step in for her, Robbie started to say, 'Actually . . .'

But Cecilia spoke up. 'I'm awfully hot, that's all. And the answer is yes. I behaved very badly. I persuaded Emily against her will that we should have a roast in your honour, regardless of the weather. Now you're sticking to salad while the rest of us are suffering because of you. So pass him the vegetables, Briony, and perhaps he'll pipe down.'

Robbie thought he heard a tremor in her voice.

'Good old Cee. Top form,' Leon said.

Marshall said, 'That's put you in your place.'

'I suppose I'd better pick on someone smaller.' Leon smiled at Briony by his side. 'Have you done something bad today on account of the terrible heat? Have you broken the rules? Please tell us you have.' He took her hand in mock-beseeching, but she pulled it away.

She was still a child, Robbie thought, not beyond confessing or blurting out that she had read his note, which in turn could lead her to describe what she had interrupted. He was watching her closely as she played for time, taking her napkin, dabbing her lips, but he felt no particular dread. If it had to, let it happen. However appalling, the dinner would not last for ever, and he would find a way to be with Cecilia again that night, and together they would confront the extraordinary new fact in their lives – their changed lives – and resume. At the thought, his stomach plunged. Until that time, everything was shadowy irrelevance and he was afraid of nothing. He took a deep pull of the sugary lukewarm wine and waited.

Briony said, 'It's boring of me, but I've done nothing wrong today.'

He had underestimated her. The emphasis could only have been intended for him and her sister.

Jackson at her elbow spoke out. 'Oh yes you have. You wouldn't let there be a play. We wanted to be in the play.' The boy looked around the table, his green eyes shining with the grievance. 'And you said you wanted us to.'

His brother was nodding. 'Yes. You wanted us to be in it.' No one could know the extent of their disappointment.

'There, you see,' Leon said. 'Briony's hot-headed decision. On a cooler day we'd be in the library watching the theatricals now.'

These harmless inanities, far preferable to silence, allowed Robbie to retreat behind a mask of amused attention. Cecilia's left hand was cupped above her cheek, presumably to exclude him from her peripheral vision. By appearing to listen to Leon who was now recounting his glimpse of the King in a West End theatre, Robbie was able to contemplate her bare arm and shoulder, and while he did so he thought she could feel his breath on her skin, an idea which stirred him. At the top of her shoulder was a little dent, scalloped in the bone, or suspended between two bones, with a fuzz of shadow along its rim. His tongue would soon trace the oval of this rim and push into the hollow. His excitement was close to pain and sharpened by the pressure of contradictions: she was familiar like a sister, she was exotic like a lover; he had always known her, he knew nothing about her; she was plain, she was beautiful; she was capable – how easily she protected herself against her brother – and twenty minutes ago she had wept; his stupid letter repelled her but it unlocked her. He regretted it, and he exulted in his mistake. They would be alone together soon, with more contradictions – hilarity and sensuousness, desire and fear at their recklessness, awe and impatience to begin. In an unused room somewhere on the second floor, or far from the house, beneath the trees by the river. Which? Mrs Tallis's mother was no fool. Outdoors. They would wrap themselves in the satin darkness and begin again. And this was no fantasy, this was real, this was his near future, both desirable and unavoidable. But that was what wretched Malvolio thought whose part he had played once on the college lawn – 'nothing that can be can come between me and the full prospect of my hopes'.

Half an hour before there had been no hope at all. After Briony had disappeared into the house with his letter, he kept on walking, agonising about turning back. Even when he reached the front door, his mind was not made up, and he loitered several minutes under the porch lamp and its single faithful moth, trying to choose the less disastrous of two poor options. It came down to this: go in now and face her anger and disgust, give an explanation which would not be accepted, and most likely be turned away – unbearable humiliation; or go home now without a word, leaving the impression that the letter was what he intended, be tortured all night and for days to come by brooding, knowing nothing of her reaction – even more unbearable. And spineless. He went over it again and it looked the same. There was no way out, he would have to speak to her. He put his hand over the bell push. Still, it remained tempting to walk away. He could write her an apology from the safety of his study. Coward! The cool porcelain was under the tip of his forefinger, and before the arguments could start around again, he made himself press it. He stood back from the door feeling like a man who had just swallowed a suicide pill – nothing to do but wait. From inside he heard steps, staccato female steps across the hall.

When she opened the door he saw the folded note in her hand. For several seconds they continued to stare at each other and neither spoke. For all his hesitation he had prepared nothing to say. His only thought was that she was even more beautiful than his fantasies of her. The silk dress she wore seemed to worship every curve and dip of her lithe body, but the small sensual mouth was held tight in disapproval, or perhaps even disgust. The house lights behind her were strong in his eyes, making it hard to read her precise expression.

Finally he said, 'Cee, it was a mistake.'

'A mistake?'

Voices reached him across the hallway through the open door of the drawing room. He heard Leon's voice, then Marshall's. It may have been fear of interruption that caused her to step back and open the door wider for him. He followed her across the hall into the library which was in darkness, and waited by the door while she searched for the switch of a desk lamp. When it came on he pushed the door closed behind him. He guessed that in a few minutes he would be walking back across the park towards the bungalow.

'It wasn't the version I intended to send.'

'No.'

'I put the wrong one in the envelope.'

'Yes.'

He could gauge nothing by these terse replies and he was still unable to see her expression clearly. She moved beyond the light, down past the shelves. He stepped further into the room, not quite following her, but unwilling to let her out of close range. She could have sent him packing from the front door and now there was a chance of giving an explanation before he left.

She said, 'Briony read it.'

'Oh God. I'm sorry.'

He had been about to conjure for her a private moment of exuberance, a passing impatience with convention, a memory of reading the Orioli edition of *Lady Chatterley's Lover*, which he had bought under the counter in Soho. But this new element – the innocent child – put his lapse beyond mitigation. It would have been frivolous to go on. He could only repeat himself, this time in a whisper.

'I'm sorry . . .'

She was moving further away, towards the corner, into deeper shadow. Even though he thought she was recoiling from him, he took another couple of steps in her direction.

'It was a stupid thing. You were never meant to read it. No one was.'

Still she shrank away. One elbow was resting on the shelves, and she seemed to slide along them, as though about to disappear between the books. He heard a soft, wet sound, the kind that is made when one is about to speak and the tongue unglues from the roof of the mouth. But she said nothing. It was only then that it occurred to him that she might not be shrinking from him, but drawing him with her deeper into the gloom. From the moment he had pressed the bell he had nothing to lose. So he walked towards her slowly as she slipped back, until she was in the corner where she stopped and watched him approach. He too stopped, less than four feet away. He was close enough now, and there was just enough light, to see she was tearful and trying to speak. For the moment it was not possible and she shook her head to indicate that he should wait. She turned aside and made a steeple of her hands to enclose her nose and mouth and pressed her fingers into the corners of her eyes.

She brought herself under control and said, 'It's been there for weeks . . .' Her throat constricted and she had to pause. Instantly, he had an idea what she meant, but he pushed it away. She drew a deep breath, then continued more reflectively, 'Perhaps it's months. I don't know. But today . . . all day it's been strange. I mean, I've been seeing strangely, as if for the first time. Everything has looked different – too sharp, too real. Even my own hands looked different. At other times I seem to be watching events as if they happened long ago. And all day I've been furious with you – and with myself. I thought that I'd be perfectly happy never seeing you or speaking to you again. I thought you'd go off to medical school and I'd be happy. I was so angry with you. I suppose it's been a way of not thinking about it. Rather convenient really . . .'

She gave a tense little laugh.

He said, 'It?'

Until now, her gaze had been lowered. When she spoke

again she looked at him. He saw only the glimmer of the whites of her eyes.

'You knew before me. Something has happened, hasn't it? And you knew before me. It's like being close up to something so large you don't even see it. Even now, I'm not sure I can. But I know it's there.'

She looked down and he waited.

'I know it's there because it made me behave ridiculously. And you, of course . . . But this morning, I've never done anything like that before. Afterwards I was so angry about it. Even as it was happening. I told myself I'd given you a weapon to use against me. Then, this evening, when I began to understand – well, how could I have been so ignorant about myself? And so stupid?' She started, seized by an unpleasant idea. 'You do know what I'm talking about. Tell me you do.' She was afraid that there was nothing shared at all, that all her assumptions were wrong and that with her words she had isolated herself further, and he would think she was a fool.

He moved nearer. 'I do. I know it exactly. But why are you crying? Is there something else?'

He thought she was about to broach an impossible obstacle and he meant, of course, *someone*, but she didn't understand. She didn't know how to answer and she looked at him, quite flummoxed. Why was she crying? How could she begin to tell him when so much emotion, so many emotions, simply engulfed her? He in turn felt that his question was unfair, inappropriate, and he struggled to think of a way of putting it right. They stared at each other in confusion, unable to speak, sensing that something delicately established might slip from them. That they were old friends who had shared a childhood was now a barrier – they were embarrassed before their former selves. Their friendship had become vague and even constrained in recent years, but it was still an old habit, and to break it now in order to become strangers on intimate terms required a clarity of purpose which had temporarily deserted them. For the moment, there seemed no way out with words.

He put his hands on her shoulders, and her bare skin was cool to the touch. As their faces drew closer he was uncertain enough to think she might spring away, or hit him, movie-style, across the cheek with her open hand. Her mouth tasted of lipstick and salt. They drew away for a second, he put his arms around her and they kissed again with greater confidence. Daringly, they touched the tips of their tongues, and it was then she made the falling, sighing sound which, he realised later, marked a transformation. Until that moment, there was still something ludicrous about having a familiar face so close to one's own. They felt watched by their bemused childhood selves. But the contact of tongues, alive and slippery muscle, moist flesh on flesh, and the strange sound it drew from her, changed that. This sound seemed to enter him, pierce him down his length so that his whole body opened up and he was able to step out of himself and kiss her freely. What had been self-conscious was now impersonal, almost abstract. The sighing noise she made was greedy and made him greedy too. He pushed her hard into the corner, between the books. As they kissed she was pulling at his clothes, plucking ineffectually at his shirt, his waistband. Their heads rolled and turned against one another as their kissing became a gnawing. She bit him on the cheek, not quite playfully. He pulled away, then moved back and she bit him hard on his lower lip. He kissed her throat, forcing back her head against the shelves, she pulled his hair and pushed his face down against her breasts. There was some inexpert fumbling until he found her nipple, tiny and hard, and put his mouth around it. Her spine went rigid, then juddered along its length. For a moment he thought she had passed out. Her arms were looped around his head and when she tightened her grip he rose through it, desperate to breathe, up to his full height and enfolded her, crushing her head against his chest. She bit him again and pulled at his shirt. When they heard a button ping against the floorboards, they had to suppress their grins and look away. Comedy would have destroyed them. She trapped his nipple between her teeth. The sensation was unbearable. He tilted her face up, and trapping her against his ribs, kissed her eyes and parted her lips with his tongue. Her helplessness drew from her again the sound like a sigh of disappointment.

At last they were strangers, their pasts were forgotten. They were also strangers to themselves who had forgotten who or where they were. The library door was thick and none of the ordinary sounds that might have reminded them, might have held them back, could reach them. They were beyond the present, outside time, with no memories and no future. There was nothing but obliterating sensation, thrilling and swelling, and the sound of fabric on fabric and skin on fabric as their limbs slid across each other in this restless, sensuous wrestling. His experience was limited and he knew only at second hand that they need not lie down. As for her, beyond all the films she had seen, and all the novels and lyrical poems she had read, she had no experience at all. Despite these limitations, it did not surprise them how clearly they knew their own needs. They were kissing again, her arms were clasped behind his head. She was licking his ear, then biting his ear lobe. Cumulatively, these bites aroused him and enraged him, goaded him. Under her dress he felt for her buttocks and squeezed hard, and half turned her to give her a retaliatory slap, but there wasn't quite the space. Keeping her eyes fixed on his, she reached down to remove her shoes. There was more fumbling now, with buttons and positioning of legs and arms. She had no experience at all. Without speaking, he guided her foot onto the lowest shelf. They were clumsy, but too selfless now to be embarrassed. When he lifted the clinging, silky dress again he thought her look of uncertainty mirrored his own. But there was only one inevitable end, and there was nothing they could do but go towards it.

Supported against the corner by his weight, she once again

clasped her hands behind his neck, and rested her elbows on his shoulder and continued to kiss his face. The moment itself was easy. They held their breath before the membrane parted, and when it did she turned away quickly, but made no sound – it seemed to be a point of pride. They moved closer, deeper and then, for seconds on end, everything stopped. Instead of an ecstatic frenzy, there was stillness. They were stilled not by the astonishing fact of arrival, but by an awed sense of return – they were face to face in the gloom, staring into what little they could see of each other's eyes, and now it was the impersonal that dropped away. Of course, there was nothing abstract about a face. The son of Grace and Ernest Turner, the daughter of Emily and Jack Tallis, the childhood friends, the university acquaintances, in a state of expansive, tranquil joy, confronted the momentous change they had achieved. The closeness of a familiar face was not ludicrous, it was wondrous. Robbie stared at the woman, the girl he had always known, thinking the change was entirely in himself, and was as fundamental, as fundamentally biological, as birth. Nothing as singular or as important had happened since the day of his birth. She returned his gaze, struck by the sense of her own transformation, and overwhelmed by the beauty in a face which a lifetime's habit had taught her to ignore. She whispered his name with the deliberation of a child trying out the distinct sounds. When he replied with her name, it sounded like a new word – the syllables remained the same, the meaning was different. Finally he spoke the three simple words that no amount of bad art or bad faith can ever quite cheapen. She repeated them, with exactly the same slight emphasis on the second word, as though she were the one to say them first. He had no religious belief, but it was impossible not to think of an invisible presence or witness in the room, and that these words spoken aloud were like signatures on an unseen contract.

They had been motionless for perhaps as long as half a minute. Longer would have required the mastery of some

formidable tantric art. They began to make love against the
library shelves which creaked with their movement. It is
common enough at such times to fantasize arriving in a
remote and high place. He imagined himself strolling on
a smooth, rounded mountain summit, suspended between
two higher peaks. He was in an unhurried, reconnoitring
mood, with time to go to a rocky edge and take a glimpse
of the near-vertical scree down which he would shortly have
to throw himself. It was a temptation to leap into clear space
now, but he was a man of the world and he could walk away,
and wait. It was not easy, for he was being drawn back and
he had to resist. As long as he did not think of the edge,
he would not go near it, and would not be tempted. He
forced himself to remember the dullest things he knew –
boot black, an application form, a wet towel on his bedroom
floor. There was also an upturned dustbin lid with an inch
of rain-water inside, and the incomplete tea-ring stain on the
cover of his Housman poems. This precious inventory was
interrupted by the sound of her voice. She was calling to
him, inviting him, murmuring in his ear. Exactly so. They
would jump together. He was with her now, peering into an
abyss, and they saw how the scree plunged down through
the cloud cover. Hand in hand, they would fall backwards.
She repeated herself, mumbling in his ear, and this time he
heard her clearly.

'Someone's come in.'

He opened his eyes. It was a library, in a house, in total
silence. He was wearing his best suit. Yes, it all came back to
him with relative ease. He strained to look over his shoulder
and saw only the dimly illuminated desk, there as before, as
though remembered from a dream. From where they were in
their corner, it was not possible to see the door. But there was
no sound, not a thing. She was mistaken, he was desperate
for her to be mistaken and she actually was. He turned back
to her, and was about to tell her so, when she tightened her
grip on his arm and he looked back once more. Briony moved

slowly into their view, stopped by the desk and saw them. She stood there stupidly, staring at them, her arms hanging loose at her sides, like a gunslinger in a Western showdown. In that shrinking moment he discovered that he had never hated anyone until now. It was a feeling as pure as love, but dispassionate and icily rational. There was nothing personal about it, for he would have hated anyone who came in. There were drinks in the drawing room or on the terrace, and that was where Briony was supposed to be – with her mother, and the brother she adored, and the little cousins. There was no good reason why she should be in the library, except to find him and deny him what was his. He saw it clearly, how it had happened: she had opened a sealed envelope to read his note and been disgusted, and in her obscure way felt betrayed. She had come looking for her sister – no doubt with the exhilarated notion of protecting her, or admonishing her, and had heard a noise from behind the closed library door. Propelled from the depths of her ignorance, silly imagining and girlish rectitude, she had come to call a halt. And she hardly had to do that – of their own accord, they had moved apart and turned away, and now both were discreetly straightening their clothes. It was over.

The main course plates had long been cleared away and Betty had returned with the bread and butter pudding. Was it imagining on his part, Robbie wondered, or malign intent on hers, that made the adults' portions appear twice the size of the children's? Leon was pouring from the third bottle of Barsac. He had removed his jacket, thus allowing the other two men to do the same. There was a soft tapping on the window panes as various flying creatures of the night threw themselves against the glass. Mrs Tallis dabbed at her face with a napkin and looked fondly at the twins. Pierrot was whispering in Jackson's ear.

'No secrets at the dinner table, boys. We'd all like to hear, if you don't mind.'

Jackson, the delegated voice, swallowed hard. His brother stared at his lap.

'We'd like to be excused, Aunt Emily. Please can we go to the lavatory?'

'Of course. But it's may, not can. And there's no need to be quite so specific.'

The twins slipped from their chairs. As they reached the door, Briony squealed and pointed.

'My socks! They're wearing my strawberry socks!'

The boys halted and turned, and looked in shame from their ankles to their aunt. Briony was half standing. Robbie assumed that powerful emotions in the girl were finding release.

'You went in my room and took them from my drawer.'

Cecilia spoke for only the second time during the meal. She too was venting deeper feelings.

'Shut up, for goodness' sake! You really are a tiresome little prima donna. The boys had no clean socks so I took some of yours.'

Briony stared at her, amazed. Attacked, betrayed, by the one she only longed to protect. Jackson and Pierrot were still looking towards their aunt who dismissed them now with a quizzical tilt of her head and a faint nod. They closed the door behind them with exaggerated, perhaps even satirical, care, and at the moment they released the handle Emily picked up her spoon and the company followed her.

She said mildly, 'You could be a little less expressive towards your sister.'

As Cecilia turned towards her mother Robbie caught a whiff of underarm perspiration, which put him in mind of freshly cut grass. Soon they would be outside. Briefly, he closed his eyes. A two-pint jug of custard was placed beside him, and he wondered that he had the strength to lift it.

'I'm sorry, Emily. But she has been quite over the top all day long.'

Briony spoke with adult calm. 'That's pretty strong, coming from you.'

'Meaning what?'

That, Robbie knew, was not the question to ask. At this stage in her life Briony inhabited an ill-defined transitional space between the nursery and adult worlds which she crossed and recrossed unpredictably. In the present situation she was less dangerous as an indignant little girl.

In fact, Briony herself had no clear idea of what she meant, but Robbie could not know this as he moved in quickly to change the subject. He turned to Lola on his left, and said in a way that was intended to include the whole table, 'They're nice lads, your brothers.'

'Hah!' Briony was savage, and did not give her cousin time to speak. 'That shows what little you know.'

Emily put down her spoon. 'Darling, if this continues, I must ask you to leave the table.'

'But look what they did to her. Scratched her face, and gave her a Chinese burn!'

All eyes were on Lola. Her complexion pulsed darker beneath her freckles, making her scratch appear less vivid.

Robbie said, 'It doesn't look too bad.'

Briony glared at him. Her mother said, 'Little boys' fingernails. We should get you some ointment.'

Lola appeared brave. 'Actually, I've put some on. It's feeling a lot better already.'

Paul Marshall cleared his throat. 'I saw it myself – had to break it up and pull them off her. I have to say, I was surprised, little fellows like that. They went for her all right . . .'

Emily had left her chair. She came to Lola's side and lifted her hands in hers. 'Look at your arms! It's not just chafing. You're bruised up to your elbows. How on earth did they do that?'

'I don't know, Aunt Emily.'

Once again, Marshall tilted back in his seat. He spoke behind Cecilia and Robbie's head to the young girl who

141

stared at him as her eyes filled with tears. 'There's no shame in making a fuss, you know. You're awfully brave, but you have taken a bad knock.'

Lola was making an effort not to cry. Emily drew her niece towards her midriff and stroked her head.

Marshall said to Robbie, 'You're right, they're nice lads. But I suppose they've been through a lot lately.'

Robbie wanted to know why Marshall had not mentioned the matter before if Lola had been so badly harmed, but the table was now in commotion. Leon called across to his mother, 'Do you want me to phone a doctor?' Cecilia was rising from the table. Robbie touched her arm and she turned, and for the first time since the library, their eyes met. There was no time to establish anything beyond the connection itself, then she hurried round to be by her mother who began to give instructions for a cold compress. Emily murmured comforting words to the top of her niece's head. Marshall remained in his seat and filled his glass. Briony also stood up, and as she did so, gave another of her penetrating girlish cries. She took from Jackson's seat an envelope and held it up to show them.

'A letter!'

She was about to open it. Robbie could not prevent himself asking, 'Who's it addressed to?'

'It says, To everyone.'

Lola disengaged from her aunt and wiped her face with her napkin. Emily drew on a surprising new source of authority. 'You will not open it. You will do as you are told and bring it to me.'

Briony caught the unusual tone in her mother's voice and meekly walked round the table with the envelope. Emily took one step away from Lola as she pulled a scrap of lined paper clear. When she read it, Robbie and Cecilia were able to read it too.

We are gong to run away becase Lola and Betty are horid to us and we want to go home. Sory we took some frute And there was'nt a play.

They had each signed their first names with zigzag flourishes. There was silence after Emily had read it aloud. Lola stood up and took a couple of steps towards a window, then changed her mind and walked back towards the end of the table. She was looking from left to right in a distracted manner and murmuring over and over, 'Oh hell, oh hell . . .'

Marshall came and put his hand on her arm. 'It's going to be all right. We'll make up some search parties and find them in no time.'

'Absolutely,' Leon said. 'They've only been gone a few minutes.'

But Lola was not listening and seemed to have made up her mind. As she strode towards the door she said, 'Mummy will kill me.'

When Leon tried to take her by her shoulder she shrugged away, and then she was through the door. They heard her running across the hall.

Leon turned to his sister. 'Cee, you and I will go together.'

Marshall said, 'There's no moon. It's pretty dark out there.'

The group was moving towards the door and Emily was saying, 'Someone ought to wait here and that might as well be me.'

Cecilia said, 'There are torches behind the cellar door.'

Leon said to his mother, 'I think you ought to phone the constable.'

Robbie was the last to leave the dining room and the last, he thought, to adjust to the new situation. His first reaction, which did not fade when he stepped into the relative coolness of the hallway, was that he had been cheated. He could not believe that the twins were in danger. The cows would scare them home. The vastness of the night beyond the house, the dark trees, the welcoming shadows, the cool new-mown grass – all this had been reserved, he had designated it as belonging exclusively to himself and Cecilia. It was waiting for them, theirs to use and claim. Tomorrow, or any time other than now, would not do. But suddenly the house had spilled its contents into a night which now belonged to a half-comic domestic crisis. They would be out there for hours, hallooing and waving their torches, the twins would eventually be found, tired and dirty, Lola would be calmed down, and after some self-congratulation over nightcaps, the evening would be over. Within days, or even hours, it would have become an amusing memory to be wheeled out on family occasions: the night the twins ran away.

The search parties were setting off as he reached the front door. Cecilia had linked arms with her brother and as they set off she glanced back and saw him standing in the light. She gave him a look, a shrug, which said – there's nothing we can do for now. Before he could enact for her some gesture of loving acceptance, she turned, and she and Leon marched on, calling out the boys' names. Marshall was even further ahead, making his way down the main drive, visible only by the torch he held. Lola was not in sight. Briony was walking around the side of the house. She, of course, would not want to be in Robbie's company, and that was some relief, for he had already decided: if he could not be with Cecilia, if he could not have her to himself, then he too, like Briony, would go out searching alone. This decision, as he was to acknowledge many times, transformed his life.

Twelve

However elegant the old Adam-style building had been, however beautifully it once commanded the parkland, the walls could not have been as sturdy as those of the baronial structure that replaced it, and its rooms could never have possessed the same quality of stubborn silence that occasionally smothered the Tallis home. Emily felt its squat presence now as she closed the front door on the search parties and turned to cross the hallway. She assumed that Betty and her helpers were still eating dessert in the kitchen and would not know that the dining room was deserted. There was no sound. The walls, the panelling, the pervasive heaviness of nearly new fixtures, the colossal fire dogs, the walk-in fireplaces of bright new stone referred back through the centuries to a time of lonely castles in mute forests. Her father-in-law's intention, she supposed, was to create an ambience of solidity and family tradition. A man who spent a lifetime devising iron bolts and locks understood the value of privacy. Noise from outside the house was excluded completely, and even homelier indoor sounds were muffled, and sometimes even eliminated somehow.

Emily sighed, failed to hear herself quite, and sighed again. She was by the telephone which stood on a semicircular wrought-iron table by the library door, and her hand rested upon the receiver. To speak to PC Vockins, she would first have to talk to his wife, a garrulous woman who liked to chat about eggs and related matters – the price of chicken feed, the foxes, the frailty of the modern paper bag. Her husband refused to display the deference one might expect from a policeman. He had a sincere way with a platitude which he made resonate like hard-won wisdom in his tight-buttoned chest: it never rained but it poured, the devil made work for idle hands, one rotten apple spoiled the barrel. The rumour in the village was that before he joined the Force and grew his moustache, he was a trade unionist. There was a sighting of him, back in the days of the General Strike, carrying pamphlets on a train.

Besides, what would she ask of the village constable? By the time he had told her that boys would be boys and raised a search party of half a dozen local men from their beds, an hour would have passed, and the twins would have come back on their own, scared into their senses by the immensity of the world at night. In fact, it was not the boys who were on her mind, but their mother, her sister, or rather her incarnation within the wiry frame of Lola. When Emily rose from the dining table to comfort the girl, she was surprised by a feeling of resentment. The more she felt it, the more she fussed over Lola to hide it. The scratch on her face was undeniable, the bruising on her arm really rather shocking, given that it was inflicted by little boys. But an old antagonism afflicted Emily. It was her sister Hermione she was soothing, – Hermione, stealer of scenes, little mistress of histrionics, whom she pressed against her breasts. As of old, the more Emily seethed, the more attentive she became. And when poor Briony found the boys' letter, it was the same antagonism that had made Emily turn on her with unusual sharpness. How unfair! But the prospect of her daughter, of any girl younger than herself, opening the envelope, and raising the tension by doing it just a little too slowly, and then reading aloud to the company, breaking the news and making herself the centre of the drama, called up old memories and ungenerous thoughts.

Hermione had lisped and pranced and pirouetted through their childhoods, showing off at every available moment with no thought – so her scowling, silent older sister believed – for how ludicrous and desperate she appeared. There were always adults available to encourage this relentless preening. And when, famously, the eleven-year-old Emily had shocked a roomful of visitors by running into a French window and cutting her hand so badly that a spray of blood had made a scarlet bouquet on the white muslin dress of a nearby child, it was the nine-year-old Hermione who took centre stage with a screaming attack. While Emily lay in obscurity on the floor, in the shadow of a sofa, with a medical uncle applying an expert tourniquet, a dozen relatives worked to calm her sister. And now she was in Paris frolicking with a man who worked in the wireless while Emily cared for her children. *Plus ça change*, PC Vockins might have said.

And Lola, like her mother, would not be held back. As soon as the letter was read, she upstaged her runaway brothers with her own dramatic exit. Mummy will kill me indeed. But it was Mummy whose spirit she was keeping alive. When the twins came back, it was a certain bet that Lola would still have to be found. Bound by an iron principle of self-love, she would stay out longer in the darkness, wrapping herself in some fabricated misfortune, so that the general relief when she appeared would be all the more intense, and all the attention would be hers. That afternoon, without stirring from her daybed, Emily had guessed that Lola was undermining Briony's play, a suspicion confirmed by the diagonally ripped poster on the easel. And just as she predicted, Briony had been outside somewhere, sulking and impossible to find. How like Hermione Lola was, to remain guiltless while others destroyed themselves at her prompting.

Emily stood irresolutely in the hall, wishing to be in no particular room, straining for the voices of the searchers outside and – if she was honest with herself – relieved she could hear nothing. It was a drama about nothing, the missing boys; it was Hermione's life imposed upon her own. There was no reason to worry about the twins. They were unlikely to go near the river. Surely, they would tire and come home. She was ringed by thick walls of silence which hissed in her ears, rising and falling in volume to some pattern of its own. She took her hand from the phone and massaged her forehead – no trace of the beast migraine, and thank God for that – and went towards the drawing room. Another reason not to dial PC Vockins was that soon Jack would phone with his apologies. The call would be placed through the Ministry operator; then she would hear the young assistant with the nasal, whinnying voice, and finally her husband's from behind his desk, resonating in the enormous room with the coffered ceiling. That he worked late she did not doubt, but she knew he did not sleep at his club, and he knew that she knew this. But there was nothing to say. Or rather, there was too much. They resembled each other in their dread of conflict, and the regularity of his evening calls, however much she disbelieved them, was a comfort to them both. If this sham was conventional hypocrisy, she had to concede that it had its uses. She had sources of contentment in her life – the house, the park, above all, the children – and she intended to preserve them by not challenging Jack. And she did not miss his presence so much as his voice on the phone. Even being lied to constantly, though hardly like love, was sustained attention; he must care about her to fabricate so elaborately and over such a long stretch of time. His deceit was a form of tribute to the importance of their marriage.

Wronged child, wronged wife. But she was not as unhappy as she should be. One role had prepared her for the other. She paused in the entrance to the drawing room and observed that the chocolate-smeared cocktail glasses had yet to be cleared away, and that the doors into the garden still stood open. Now the faintest stirring of a breeze rustled the display of sedge that stood before the fireplace. Two or three stout-bodied moths circled the lamp that stood upon the harpsichord. When would anyone ever play it again? That night creatures were drawn to lights where they could be most easily eaten by other creatures was one of those mysteries that gave her modest pleasure. She preferred not to have it explained away. At a formal dinner once a professor of some science or other, wanting to make small-talk, had pointed out a few insects gyrating above a candelabra. He had told her that it was the visual impression of an even deeper darkness beyond the light that drew them in. Even though they might be eaten, they had to obey the instinct that made them seek out the darkest place, on the far side of the light – and in this case it was an illusion. It sounded to her like sophistry, or an explanation for its own sake. How could anyone presume to know the world through the eyes of an insect? Not everything had a cause, and pretending otherwise was an interference in the workings of the world that was futile, and could even lead to grief. Some things were simply so.

She did not wish to know why Jack spent so many consecutive nights in London. Or rather, she did not wish to be told. Nor did she wish to know more about the work that kept him late at the Ministry. Months ago, not long after Christmas, she went into the library to wake him from an afternoon sleep and saw a file open upon the desk. It was only the mildest wifely curiosity that prompted her to peep, for she had little interest in civic administration. On one page she saw a list of headings: exchange controls, rationing, the mass evacuation of large towns, the conscription of labour. The facing page was handwritten. A series of arithmetical calculations was interspersed by blocks of text. Jack's straight-backed, brown-ink copperplate told her to assume a multiplier of fifty. For every one ton of explosive dropped, assume fifty casualties. Assume 100,000 tons of bombs dropped in two weeks. Result: five million casualties. She had not yet woken him and his soft, whistling exhalations blended with winter birdsong that came from somewhere beyond the lawn. Aqueous sunlight rippled over the spines of books and the smell of warm dust was everywhere. She went to the window and stared out, trying to spot the bird among bare oak branches that stood out black against a broken sky of grey and palest blue. She knew well there had to be such forms of bureaucratic supposition. And yes, there were precautions administrators took to indemnify themselves against all eventualities. But these extravagant numbers were surely a form of self-aggrandisement, and reckless to the point of irresponsibility. Jack, the household's protector, its guarantor of tranquillity, was relied on to take the long view. But this was silly. When she woke him he grunted and leaned forward with a sudden movement to close the files, and then, still seated, pulled her hand to his mouth and kissed it dryly.

She decided against closing the French windows, and sat down at one end of the Chesterfield. She was not exactly waiting, she felt. No one else she knew had her knack of keeping still, without even a book on her lap, of moving gently through her thoughts, as one might explore a new garden. She had learned her patience through years of side-stepping migraine. Fretting, concentrated thought, reading, looking, wanting – all were to be avoided in favour of a slow drift of association, while the minutes accumulated like banked snow and the silence deepened around her. Sitting here now she felt the night air tickle the hem of her dress against her shin. Her childhood was as tangible as the shot silk – a taste, a sound, a smell, all of these, blended into an entity that was surely more than a mood. There was a presence in the room, her aggrieved, overlooked ten-year-old self, a girl even quieter than Briony, who used to wonder at the massive emptiness of time, and marvel that the nineteenth century was about to end. How like her, to sit in the room like this, not 'joining in'. This ghost had been summoned not by Lola imitating Hermione, or the inscrutable twins disappearing into the night. It was the slow retraction, the retreat into autonomy which signalled the approaching end of Briony's childhood. It was haunting Emily once more. Briony was her last, and nothing between now and the grave would be as elementally important or pleasurable as the care of a child. She wasn't a fool. She knew it was self-pity, this mellow expansiveness as she contemplated what looked like her own ruin: Briony would surely go off to her sister's college, Girton, and she, Emily, would grow stiffer in the limbs and more irrelevant by the day; age and weariness would return Jack to her, and nothing would be said, or needed to be said. And here was the ghost of her childhood, diffused throughout the room, to remind her of the limited arc of existence. How quickly the story was over. Not massive and empty at all, but headlong. Ruthless.

Her spirits were not particularly lowered by these common-place reflections. She floated above them, gazing down neutrally, absently braiding them with other preoccupations. She planned to plant a clump of ceanothus along the approach to the swimming pool. Robbie was wanting to persuade her to erect a pergola and train along it a slow-growing wisteria whose flower and scent he liked. But she and Jack would be long buried before the full effect was achieved. The story would be over. She thought of Robbie at dinner when there had been something manic and glazed in his look. Might he be smoking the reefers she had read about in a magazine, these cigarettes that drove young men of bohemian inclination across the borders of insanity? She liked him well enough, and was pleased for Grace Turner that he had turned out to be bright. But really, he was a hobby of Jack's, living proof of some levelling principle he had pursued through the years. When he spoke about Robbie, which wasn't often, it was with a touch of self-righteous vindication. Something had been established which Emily took to be a criticism of herself. She had opposed Jack when he proposed paying for the boy's education, which smacked of meddling to her, and unfair on Leon and the girls. She did not consider herself proved wrong simply because Robbie had come away from Cambridge with a first. In fact, it had made things harder for Cecilia with her third, though it was preposterous of her to pretend to be disappointed. Robbie's elevation. 'Nothing good will come of it' was the phrase she often used, to which Jack would respond smugly that plenty of good had come already.

For all that, Briony had been thoroughly improper at dinner to speak that way to Robbie. If she had resentments of her own, Emily sympathised. It was to be expected. But to express them was undignified. Thinking of the dinner again – how artfully Mr Marshall had put everyone at ease. Was he suitable? It was a pity about his looks, with one half of his face looking like an over-furnished bedroom. Perhaps in time it would come to seem rugged, this chin like a wedge of cheese. Or chocolate. If he really were to supply the whole of the British Army with Amo bars he could become immensely rich. But Cecilia, having learned modern forms of snobbery at Cambridge, considered a man with a degree in chemistry incomplete as a human being. Her very words. She had lolled about for three years at Girton with the kind of books she could equally have read at home – Jane Austen, Dickens, Conrad, all in the library downstairs, in complete sets. How had that pursuit, reading the novels that others took as their leisure, let her think she was superior to anyone else? Even a chemist had his uses. And this one had found a way of making chocolate out of sugar, chemicals, brown colouring and vegetable oil. And no cocoa butter. To produce a ton of the stuff, he had explained over his astonishing cocktail, cost next to nothing. He could undercut his competitors *and* increase his profit margin. Vulgarly put, but what comfort, what untroubled years might flow from these cheap vats.

More than thirty minutes passed unnoticed as these scraps – memories, judgments, vague resolutions, questions – uncoiled quietly before her, while she barely shifted her position and did not hear the clock strike the quarter hours. She was aware of the breeze strengthening, pushing one French window closed, before dying down once more. She was disturbed later by Betty and her helpers clearing the dining room, then those sounds also subsided and, again, Emily was far out along the branching roads of her reveries, drifting by association, and with the expertise born of a thousand headaches, avoiding all things sudden or harsh. When at last the phone rang she rose immediately, without any start of surprise, and went back out into the hallway, lifted the receiver and called out as she always did on a rising note of a question,

'Tallises?'

There came the switchboard, the nasal assistant, a pause and the crackle of the long-distance line, then Jack's neutral tone.

'Dearest. Later than usual. I'm terribly sorry.'

It was eleven thirty. But she did not mind, for he would be back at the weekend, and one day he would be home for ever and not an unkind word would be spoken.

She said, 'It's perfectly all right.'

'It's the revisions to the Statement Relating to Defence. There's to be a second printing. And then one thing and another.'

'Rearmament,' she said soothingly.

'I'm afraid so.'

'You know, everyone's against it.'

He chuckled. 'Not in this office.'

'And I am.'

'Well, my dear. I hope to persuade you one day.'

'And I you.'

The exchange held a trace of affection, and its familiarity was comfort. As usual, he asked for an account of her day. She told him of the great heat, the collapse of Briony's play, and the arrival of Leon with his friend of whom she said, 'He's in your camp. But he wants more soldiers so that he can sell the government his chocolate bar.'

'I see. Ploughshares into tinfoil.'

She described the dinner, and Robbie's wild look at the table. 'Do we really need to be putting him through medical college?'

'We do. It's a bold move. Typical of him. I know he'll make a go of it.'

Then she gave an account of how the dinner ended with the twins' note, and the search parties going off into the grounds.

'Little scallywags. And where were they after all?'

'I don't know. I'm still waiting to hear.'

There was silence down the line, broken only by distant mechanical clicking. When the senior Civil Servant spoke at last he had already made his decisions. The rare use of her first name conveyed his seriousness.

'I'm going to put the telephone down now, Emily, because I'm going to call the police.'

'Is it really necessary? By the time they get here . . .'

'If you hear any news you'll let me know straight away.'

'Wait . . .'

At a sound she had turned. Leon was coming through the main door. Close behind him was Cecilia whose look was one of mute bewilderment. Then came Briony with an arm round her cousin's shoulders. Lola's face was so white and rigid, like a clay mask, that Emily, unable to read an expression there, instantly knew the worst. Where were the twins?

Leon crossed the hall towards her, his hand outstretched for the phone. There was a streak of dirt from his trouser cuffs to the knees. Mud, and in such dry weather. His breathing was heavy from exertion, and a greasy lank of hair swung over his face as he snatched the receiver from her and turned his back.

'Is that you, Daddy? Yes. Look, I think you'd better come down. No, we haven't, and there's worse. No, no, I can't tell you now. If you can, tonight. We'll have to phone them anyway. Best you do it.'

She put her hand over her heart and took a couple of paces back to where Cecilia and the girls stood watching. Leon had lowered his voice and was muttering quickly into the cupped receiver. Emily couldn't hear a word, and did not want to.

She would have preferred to retreat upstairs to her room, but Leon finished the call with an echoing rattle of the Bakelite and turned to her. His eyes were tight and hard, and she wondered if it was anger that she saw. He was trying to take deeper breaths, and he stretched his lips across his teeth in a strange grimace.

He said, 'We'll go in the drawing room where we can sit down.'

She caught his meaning precisely. He wouldn't tell her now, he wouldn't have her collapsing on the tiles and cracking her skull. She stared at him, but she did not move.

'Come on, Emily,' he said.

Her son's hand was hot and heavy on her shoulder, and she felt its dampness through the silk. Helplessly, she let herself be guided towards the drawing room, all her terror concentrated on the simple fact that he wanted her seated before he broke his news.

Thirteen

Within the half hour Briony would commit her crime. Conscious that she was sharing the night expanse with a maniac, she kept close to the shadowed walls of the house at first, and ducked low beneath the sills whenever she passed in front of a lighted window. She knew he would be heading off down the main drive because that was the way her sister had gone with Leon. As soon as she thought a safe distance had opened up, Briony swung out boldly from the house in a wide arc that took her towards the stable block and the swimming pool. It made sense, surely, to see if the twins were there, fooling about with the hoses, or floating face-down in death, indistinguishable to the last. She thought how she might describe it, the way they bobbed on the illuminated water's gentle swell, and how their hair spread like tendrils and their clothed bodies softly collided and drifted apart. The dry night air slipped between the fabric of her dress and her skin, and she felt smooth and agile in the dark. There was nothing she could not describe: the gentle pad of a maniac's tread moving sinuously along the drive, keeping to the verge to muffle his approach. But her brother was with Cecilia, and that was a burden lifted. She could describe this delicious air too, the grasses giving off their sweet cattle smell, the hard-fired earth which still held the embers of the day's heat and exhaled the mineral odour of clay, and the faint breeze carrying from the lake a flavour of green and silver.

She broke into a loping run across the grass and thought she could go on all night, knifing through the silky air, sprung forwards by the steely coil of the hard ground under her feet, and by the way darkness doubled the impression of speed. She had dreams in which she ran like this, then tilted forward, spread her arms and, yielding to faith – the only difficult part, but easy enough in sleep – left the ground by simply stepping off it, and swooped low over hedges and gates and roofs, then hurtled upwards and hovered exultantly below the cloud base, above the fields, before diving down again. She sensed now how this might be achieved, through desire alone; the world she ran through loved her and would give her what she wanted and would let it happen. And then, when it did, she would describe it. Wasn't writing a kind of soaring, an achievable form of flight, of fancy, of the imagination?

But there was a maniac treading through the night with a dark, unfulfilled heart – she had frustrated him once already – and she needed to be earthbound to describe him too. She must first protect her sister against him, and then find ways of conjuring him safely on paper. Briony slowed to a walking pace, and thought how he must hate her for interrupting him in the library. And though it horrified her, it was another entry, a moment of coming into being, another first: to be hated by an adult. Children hated generously, capriciously. It hardly mattered. But to be the object of adult hatred was an initiation into a solemn new world. It was promotion. He might have doubled back, and be waiting for her with murderous thoughts behind the stable block. But she was trying not to be afraid. She had held his gaze there in the library while her sister had slipped past her, giving no outward acknowledgment of her deliverance. It was not about thanks, she knew that, it was not about rewards. In matters of selfless love, nothing needed to be said, and she would protect her sister, even if Cecilia failed to acknowledge her debt. And Briony could not be afraid now of Robbie; better by far to let him become the object of her detestation and disgust. They had provided for all manner of pleasant things for him, the Tallis family: the very home he had grown up in, countless trips to France, and his grammar school uniform and books, and then Cambridge – and in return he had used a terrible word against her sister and, in a fantastic abuse of hospitality, used his strength against her too, and sat insolently at their dining table pretending that nothing was different. The pretence, and how she ached to expose it! Real life, her life now beginning, had sent her a villain in the form of an old family friend with strong, awkward limbs and a rugged friendly face who used to carry her on his back, and swim with her in the river, holding her against the current. That seemed about right – truth was strange and deceptive, it had to be struggled for, against the flow of the everyday. This was exactly what no one would have expected, and of course – villains were not announced with hisses or soliloquies, they did not come cloaked in black, with ugly expressions. Across the other side of the house, walking away from her, were Leon and Cecilia. She might be telling him about the assault. If she was, he would have his arm around her shoulders. Together, the Tallis children would see this brute off, see him safely out of their lives. They would have to confront and convert their father, and comfort him in his rage and disappointment. That his protégé should turn out to be a maniac! Lola's word stirred the dust of other words around it – man, mad, axe, attack, accuse – and confirmed the diagnosis.

She made her way round the stable block and stopped under the arched entrance, beneath the clock tower. She called out the twins' names, and heard in reply only the stir and scuff of hooves, and the thump of a heavy body pressing against a stall. She was glad she had never fallen for a horse or pony, for she would surely be neglecting it by this stage of her life. She did not approach the animals now, even though they sensed her presence. In their terms, a genius, a god, was loitering on the periphery of their world and they were straining for her attention. But she turned and continued towards the swimming pool. She wondered whether having final responsibility for someone, even a creature like a horse or a dog, was fundamentally opposed to the wild and inward journey of writing. Protective worrying, engaging with another's mind as one entered it, taking the dominant role as one guided another's fate, was hardly mental freedom. Perhaps she might become one of those women – pitied or envied – who chose not to have children. She followed the brick path that led round the outside of the stable block. Like the earth, the sandy bricks radiated the day's trapped heat. She felt it on her cheek and down her bare calf as she passed along. She stumbled as she hurried through the darkness of the bamboo tunnel, and emerged onto the reassuring geometry of the paving stones.

The underwater lights, installed that spring, were still a novelty. The upward bluish gleam gave everything around the pool a colourless, moonlit look, like a photograph. A glass jug, two tumblers and a piece of cloth stood on the old tin table. A third tumbler containing pieces of soft fruit stood poised at the end of the diving board. There were no bodies in the pool, no giggling from the darkness of the pavilion, no shushing from the shadows of the bamboo thickets. She took a slow turn around the pool, no longer searching, but drawn to the glow and glassy stillness of the water. For all the threat the maniac posed to her sister, it was delightful to be out so late, with permission. She did not really think the twins were in danger. Even if they had seen the framed map of the area in the library and were clever enough to read it, and were intending to leave the grounds and walk north all night, they would have to follow the drive into the woods along by the railway line. At this time of year, when the tree canopy was thick over the road, the way was in total blackness. The only other route out was through the kissing gate, down towards the river. But here too there would be no light, no way of keeping to the path or ducking the branches that hung low over it, or dodging the nettles that grew thickly on either side. They would not be bold enough to put themselves in danger.

They were safe, Cecilia was with Leon, and she, Briony, was free to wander in the dark and contemplate her extraordinary day. Her childhood had ended, she decided now as she came away from the swimming pool, the moment she tore down her poster. The fairy stories were behind her, and in the space of a few hours she had witnessed mysteries, seen an unspeakable word, interrupted brutal behaviour, and by incurring the hatred of an adult whom everyone had trusted, she had become a participant in the drama of life beyond the nursery. All she had to do now was discover the stories, not just the subjects, but a way of unfolding them, that would do justice to her new knowledge. Or did she mean, her wiser grasp of her own ignorance?

Staring at water for minutes on end had put her in mind of the lake. Perhaps the boys were hiding in the island temple. It was obscure, but not too cut off from the house, a friendly little place with the consolation of water and not too many shadows. The others might have gone straight across the bridge without looking down there. She decided to keep to her route and reach the lake by circling round the back of the house.

Two minutes later she was crossing the rose beds and the gravel path in front of the Triton fountain, scene of another mystery that clearly foretold the later brutalities. As she passed it she thought she heard a faint shout, and thought she saw from the corner of her eye a point of light flash on and off. She stopped, and strained to hear over the sound of trickling water. The shout and the light had come from the woods by the river, a few hundred yards away. She walked in that direction for half a minute, and stopped to listen again. But there was nothing, nothing but the tumbling dark mass of the woods just discernible against the greyish-blue of the western sky. After waiting a while she decided to turn back. In order to pick up her path she was walking directly towards the house, towards the terrace where a paraffin globe lamp shone among glasses, bottles, and an ice bucket. The drawing-room French windows still stood wide open to the night. She could see right into the room. And by the light of a single lamp she could see, partially obscured by the hang of a velvet curtain, one end of a sofa across which there lay at a peculiar angle a cylindrical object that seemed to hover. It was only after she had covered another fifty yards that she understood that she was looking at a disembodied human leg. Closer still, and she grasped the perspectives; it was her mother's of course, and she would be waiting for the twins. She was mostly obscured by the drapes, and one stockinged leg was supported by the knee of the other, which gave it its curious, slanting and levitated appearance.

Briony moved to a window on her left as she came right up to the house in order to be clear of Emily's sight line. She was positioned too far behind her mother to see her eyes. She could make out only the dip in her cheekbone of her eye socket. Briony was certain her eyes would be closed. Her head was tilted back, and her hands lay lightly clasped in her lap. Her right shoulder rose and fell faintly with her breathing. Briony could not see her mouth, but she knew its downward curve, easily mistaken for the sign – the hieroglyph – of reproach. But it was not so, because her mother was endlessly kind and sweet and good. Looking at her sitting alone, late at night, was sad, but pleasantly so. Briony indulged herself by looking through the window in a spirit of farewell. Her mother was forty-six, dispiritingly old. One day she would die. There would be a funeral in the village at which Briony's dignified reticence would hint at the vastness of her sorrow. As her friends came up to murmur their condolences they would feel awed by the scale of her tragedy. She saw herself standing alone in a great arena, within a towering colosseum, watched not only by all the people she knew, but all those she would ever know, the whole cast of her life, assembled to love her in her loss. And at the churchyard, in what they called the grandparents' corner, she and Leon and Cecilia would stand in an interminable embrace in the long grass by the new headstone, again watched. It had to be witnessed. It was the pity of these well-wishers that pricked her eyes.

She could have gone in to her mother then and snuggled close beside her and begun a résumé of the day. If she had she would not have committed her crime. So much would not have happened, nothing would have happened, and the smoothing hand of time would have made the evening barely memorable: the night the twins ran away. Was it 'thirty-four, or five or six? But for no particular reason, apart from the vague obligation of the search and the pleasure of being out so late, she came away, and as she did so her shoulder caught an edge of one of the open French windows, knocking it shut. The sound was sharp – seasoned pine on hardwood – and rang out like a rebuke. To stay she would have to explain herself, so she slipped away into the darkness, tiptoeing quickly over the slabs of stone and the scented herbs that grew between them. Then she was on the lawn between the rose beds where it was possible to run soundlessly. She came round the side of the house to the front, onto the gravel she had hobbled across barefoot that afternoon.

Here she slowed as she turned down the driveway towards the bridge. She was back at her starting point and thought she was bound to see the others, or hear their calls. But there was no one. The dark shapes of the widely spaced trees across the park made her hesitate. Someone hated her, that had to be remembered, and he was unpredictable and violent. Leon, Cecilia and Mr Marshall would be a long way off now. The nearer trees, or at least their trunks, had a human form. Or could conceal one. Even a man standing in front of a tree trunk would not be visible to her. For the first time, she was aware of the breeze pouring through the tops of the trees, and this familiar sound unsettled her. Millions of separate and precise agitations bombarded her senses. When the wind picked up briefly and died, the sound moved away from her, travelling out across the darkened park like a living thing. She stopped and wondered whether she had the courage to keep on to the bridge, cross it, and leave it to go down the steep bank to the island temple. Especially when there really was not much at stake – just a hunch of hers that the boys may have wandered down there. Unlike the adults, she had no torch. Nothing was expected of her, she was a child after all in their eyes. The twins were not in danger.

She remained on the gravel for a minute or two, not quite frightened enough to turn back, nor confident enough to go on. She could return to her mother and keep her company in the drawing room while she waited. She could take a safer route, along the driveway and back, before it entered the woods – and still give the impression of a serious search. Then, precisely because the day had proved to her that she was not a child, and that she was now a figure in a richer story and had to prove herself worthy of it, she forced herself to walk on and cross the bridge. From beneath her, amplified by the stone arch, came the hiss of the breeze disturbing the sedge, and a sudden beating of wings against water which subsided abruptly. These were everyday sounds magnified by darkness. And darkness was nothing – it was not a substance, it was not a presence, it was no more than an absence of light. The bridge led to nothing more than an artificial island in an artificial lake. It had been there two hundred years almost, and its detachment marked it out from the rest of the land, and it belonged to her more than to anyone else. She was the only one who ever came here. To the others it was no more than a corridor to and from home, a bridge between the bridges, an ornament so familiar as to be invisible. Hardman came with his son twice a year to scythe the grass around the temple. The tramps had passed through. Stray migrating geese sometimes honoured the little grassy shore. Otherwise it was a lonely kingdom of rabbits, water birds and water rats.

So it should have been a simple matter, to pick her way down the bank and go across the grass towards the temple. But again, she hesitated, and simply looked, without even calling out to the twins. The building's indistinct pallor shimmered in the dark. When she stared at it directly it dissolved completely. It stood about a hundred feet away, and nearer, in the centre of the grassy stretch, there was a shrub she did not remember. Or rather, she remembered it being closer to the shore. The trees were not right either, what she could see of them. The oak was too bulbous, the elm too straggly, and in their strangeness they seemed in league. As she put her hand out to touch the parapet of the bridge, a duck startled her with a high, unpleasant call, almost human in its breathy downward note. It was the steepness of the bank, of course, which held her back, and the idea of descent, and the fact that there was not much point. But she had made her decision. She went down backwards, steadying herself on clumps of grass, and at the bottom paused only to wipe her hands on her dress.

She walked directly towards the temple, and had gone seven or eight steps, and was about to call out the names of the twins, when the bush that lay directly in her path – the one she thought should be closer to the shore – began to break up in front of her, or double itself, or waver, and then fork. It was changing its shape in a complicated way, thinning at the base as a vertical column rose five or six feet. She would have stopped immediately had she not still been so completely bound to the notion that this was a bush, and that she was witnessing some trick of darkness and perspective. Another second or two, another couple of steps, and she saw that this was not so. Then she stopped. The vertical mass was a figure, a person who was now backing away from her and beginning to fade into the darker background of the trees. The remaining darker patch on the ground was also a person, changing shape again as it sat up and called her name.

'Briony?'

She heard the helplessness in Lola's voice – it was the sound she had thought belonged to a duck – and in an instant, Briony understood completely. She was nauseous with disgust and fear. Now the larger figure reappeared, circling right round the edge of the clearing and heading for the bank down which she had just come. She knew she should attend to Lola, but she could not help watching as he mounted the slope quickly and without effort, and disappeared onto the roadway. She heard his footsteps as he strode towards the house. She had no doubt. She could describe him. There was nothing she could not describe. She knelt down beside her cousin.

'Lola. Are you all right?'

Briony touched her shoulder, and was groping for her hand without success. Lola was sitting forward, with her arms crossed around her chest, hugging herself and rocking slightly. The voice was faint and distorted, as though impeded by something like a bubble, some mucus in her throat. She needed to clear her throat. She said, vaguely, 'I'm sorry, I didn't, I'm sorry . . .'

Briony whispered, 'Who was it?' and before that could be answered, she added, with all the calm she was capable of, 'I saw him. I *saw* him.'

Meekly, Lola said, 'Yes.'

For the second time that evening, Briony felt a flowering of tenderness for her cousin. Together they faced real terrors. She and her cousin were close. Briony was on her knees, trying to put her arms round Lola and gather her to her, but the body was bony and unyielding, wrapped tight about itself like a seashell. A winkle. Lola hugged herself and rocked.

Briony said, 'It was him, wasn't it?'

She felt against her chest, rather than saw, her cousin nod, slowly, reflectively. Perhaps it was exhaustion.

After many seconds Lola said in the same weak, submissive voice, 'Yes. It was him.'

Suddenly, Briony wanted her to say his name. To seal the crime, frame it with the victim's curse, close his fate with the magic of naming.

'Lola,' she whispered, and could not deny the strange elation she felt. 'Lola. Who was it?'

The rocking stopped. The island became very still. Without quite shifting her position, Lola seemed to move away, or to move her shoulders, half shrug, half sway, to free herself of Briony's sympathetic touch. She turned her head away and looked out across the emptiness where the lake was. She may have been about to speak, she may have been about to embark upon a long confession in which she would find her feelings as she spoke them and lead herself out of her numbness towards something that resembled both terror and joy. Turning away may well have been not a distancing, but an act of intimacy, a way of gathering herself to begin to speak her feelings to the only person she thought, so far from home, she could trust herself to talk to. Perhaps she had already drawn breath and parted her lips. But it did not matter because Briony was about to cut her off and the opportunity would be lost. So many seconds had passed – thirty? forty-five? – and the younger girl could no longer hold herself back. Everything connected. It was her own discovery. It was her story, the one that was writing itself around her.

'It was Robbie, wasn't it?'

The maniac. She wanted to say the word.

Lola said nothing and did not move.

Briony said it again, this time without the trace of a question. It was a statement of fact. 'It was Robbie.'

Though she had not turned, or moved at all, it was clear that something was changing in Lola, a warmth rising from her skin and a sound of dry swallowing, a heaving convulsion of muscle in her throat that was audible as a series of sinewy clicks.

Briony said it again. Simply. 'Robbie.'

From far out in the lake came the fat, rounded plop of a fish jumping, a precise and solitary sound, for the breeze had dropped away completely. Nothing scary in the treetops or among the sedge now. At last Lola turned slowly to face her.

She said, 'You saw him.'

'How could he,' Briony moaned. 'How dare he.'

Lola placed her hand on her bare forearm and gripped. Her mild words were widely spaced. 'You saw him.'

Briony drew nearer to her and covered Lola's hand with her own. 'You don't even know yet what happened in the library, before dinner, just after we were talking. He was attacking my sister. If I hadn't come in, I don't know what he would have done . . .'

However close they were, it was not possible to read expressions. The dark disc of Lola's face showed nothing at all, but Briony sensed she was only half listening, and this was confirmed when she cut in to repeat, 'But you saw him. You actually saw him.'

'Of course I did. Plain as day. It was him.'

Despite the warmth of the night, Lola was beginning to shiver and Briony longed for something she could take off and place round her shoulders.

Lola said, 'He came up behind me, you see. He knocked me to the ground . . . and then . . . he pushed my head back and his hand was over my eyes. I couldn't actually, I wasn't able . . .'

'Oh Lola.' Briony put out her hand to touch her cousin's face and found her cheek. It was dry, but it wouldn't be, she knew it wouldn't be for long. 'Listen to me. I couldn't mistake him. I've known him all my life. I saw him.'

'Because I couldn't say for sure. I mean, I thought it might be him by his voice.'

'What did he say?'

'Nothing. I mean, it was the sound of his voice, breathing, noises. But I couldn't see. I couldn't say for sure.'

'Well I can. And I will.'

And so their respective positions, which were to find public expression in the weeks and months to come, and then be pursued as demons in private for many years afterwards, were established in these moments by the lake, with Briony's certainty rising whenever her cousin appeared to doubt herself. Nothing much was ever required of Lola after that, for she was able to retreat behind an air of wounded confusion, and as treasured patient, recovering victim, lost child, let herself be bathed in the concern and guilt of the adults in her life. How could we have let this happen to a child? Lola could not, and did not need to, help them. Briony offered her a chance, and she seized it instinctively; less than that – she simply let it settle over her. She had little more to do than remain silent behind her cousin's zeal. Lola did not need to lie, to look her supposed attacker in the eye and summon the courage to accuse him, because all that work was done for her, innocently, and without guile by the younger girl. Lola was required only to remain silent about the truth, banish it and forget it entirely, and persuade herself not of some contrary tale, but simply of her own uncertainty. She couldn't see, his hand was over her eyes, she was terrified, she couldn't say for sure.

Briony was there to help her at every stage. As far as she was concerned, everything fitted; the terrible present fulfilled the recent past. Events she herself witnessed foretold her cousin's calamity. If only she, Briony, had been less innocent, less stupid. Now she saw, the affair was too consistent, too symmetrical to be anything other than what she said it was. She blamed herself for her childish assumption that Robbie would limit his attentions to Cecilia. What was she thinking of? He was a maniac after all. Anyone would do. And he was bound to go for the most vulnerable – a spindly girl, stumbling about in the dark in an unfamiliar place, bravely searching around the island temple for her brothers. Just as Briony herself had been about to do. That his victim could easily have been her increased Briony's outrage and fervour. If her poor cousin was not able to command the truth, then she would do it for her. *I can. And I will.*

As early as the week that followed, the glazed surface of conviction was not without its blemishes and hairline cracks. Whenever she was conscious of them, which was not often, she was driven back, with a little swooping sensation in her stomach, to the understanding that what she knew was not literally, or not only, based on the visible. It was not simply her eyes that told her the truth. It was too dark for that. Even Lola's face at eighteen inches was an empty oval, and this figure was many feet away, and turned from her as it moved back around the clearing. But nor was this figure invisible, and its size and manner of moving were familiar to her. Her eyes confirmed the sum of all she knew and had recently experienced. The truth was in the symmetry, which was to say, it was founded in common sense. The truth instructed her eyes. So when she said, over and again, I saw him, she meant it, and was perfectly honest, as well as passionate. What she meant was rather more complex than what everyone else so eagerly understood, and her moments of unease came when she felt that she could not express these nuances. She did not even seriously try. There were no opportunities, no time, no permission. Within a couple of days, no, within a matter of hours, a process was moving fast and well beyond her control. Her words summoned awful powers from the familiar and picturesque local town. It was as if these terrifying authorities, these uniformed agents, had been lying in wait behind the façades of pretty buildings for a disaster they knew must come. They knew their own minds, they knew what they wanted and how to proceed. She was asked again and again, and as she repeated herself, the burden of consistency was pressed upon her. What she had said she must say again. Minor deviations earned her little frowns on wise brows, or a degree of frostiness and withdrawal of sympathy. She became anxious to please, and learned quickly that the minor qualifications she might have added would disrupt the process that she herself had set in train.

She was like a bride-to-be who begins to feel her sickening qualms as the day approaches, and dares not speak her mind because so many preparations have been made on her behalf. The happiness and convenience of so many good people would be put at risk. These are fleeting moments of private disquiet, only dispelled by abandoning herself to the joy and excitement of those around her. So many decent people could not be wrong, and doubts like hers, she's been told, are to be expected. Briony did not wish to cancel the whole arrangement. She did not think she had the courage, after all her initial certainty and two or three days of patient, kindly interviewing, to withdraw her evidence. However, she would have preferred to qualify, or complicate, her use of the word 'saw'. Less like seeing, more like knowing. Then she could have left it to her interrogators to decide whether they would proceed together in the name of this kind of vision. They were impassive whenever she wavered, and firmly recalled her to her earliest statements. Was she a silly girl, their manner implied, who had wasted everybody's time? And they took an austere view of the visual. There was enough light, it was established, from stars, and from the cloud base reflecting street lights from the nearest town. Either she saw, or she did not see. There lay nothing in between; they did not say as much, but their brusqueness implied it. It was in those moments, when she felt their coolness, that she reached back to revive her first ardour and said it again. I saw him. I know it was him. Then it was comforting to feel she was confirming what they already knew.

She would never be able to console herself that she was pressured or bullied. She never was. She trapped herself, she marched into the labyrinth of her own construction, and was too young, too awestruck, too keen to please, to insist on making her own way back. She was not endowed with, or old enough to possess, such independence of spirit. An imposing congregation had massed itself around her first certainties, and now it was waiting and she could not disappoint it at the altar. Her doubts could be neutralised only by plunging in deeper. By clinging tightly to what she believed she knew, narrowing her thoughts, reiterating her testimony, she was able to keep from mind the damage she only dimly sensed she was doing. When the matter was closed, when the sentence was passed and the congregation dispersed, a ruthless youthful forgetting, a wilful erasing, protected her well into her teens.

'Well I can. And I will.'

They sat in silence for a while, and Lola's shivering began to subside. Briony supposed she should get her cousin home, but she was reluctant to break this closeness for the moment – she had her arms around the older girl's shoulders and she seemed to yield now to Briony's touch. They saw far beyond the lake a bobbing pinprick of light – a torch being carried along the drive – but they did not comment on it. When at last Lola spoke her tone was reflective, as though she were pondering subtle currents of counter-arguments.

'But it doesn't make sense. He's such a close friend of your family. It might not have been him.'

Briony murmured, 'You wouldn't be saying that if you'd been with me in the library.'

Lola sighed and shook her head slowly, as though trying to reconcile herself to the unacceptable truth.

They were silent again and they might have sat longer had it not been for the damp – not quite yet dew – that was beginning to settle on the grass as the clouds cleared and the temperature dropped.

When Briony whispered to her cousin, 'Do you think you can walk?' she nodded bravely. Briony helped her to stand, and arm in arm at first, and then with Lola's weight on Briony's shoulder, they made their way across the clearing towards the bridge. They reached the bottom of the slope and it was here that Lola finally began to cry.

'I can't go up there,' she had several attempts at saying. 'I'm just too weak.' It would be better, Briony decided, for her to run to the house and fetch help, and she was just about to explain this to Lola and settle her on the ground when they heard voices from the road above, and then torchlight was in their eyes. It was a miracle, Briony thought, when she heard her brother's voice. Like the true hero he was, he came down the bank in several easy strides and without even asking what the trouble was, took Lola into his arms and picked her up as though she were a small child. Cecilia was calling down in a voice that sounded hoarse with concern. No one answered her. Leon was already making his way up the incline at such a pace it was an effort to keep up with him. Even so, before they reached the driveway, before he had the chance to set Lola down, Briony was beginning to tell him what had happened, exactly as she had seen it.

Fourteen

Her memories of the interrogation and signed statements and testimony, or of her awe outside the courtroom from which her youth excluded her, would not trouble her so much in the years to come as her fragmented recollection of that late night and summer dawn. How guilt refined the methods of self-torture, threading the beads of detail into an eternal loop, a rosary to be fingered for a lifetime.

Back in the house at last, there began a dreamlike time of grave arrivals, tears and subdued voices and urgent footsteps across the hallway, and her own vile excitement that kept her drowsiness at bay. Of course, Briony was old enough to know that the moment was entirely Lola's, but she was soon led away by sympathetic womanly hands to her bedroom to await the doctor and his examination. Briony watched from the foot of the stairs as Lola ascended, sobbing loudly and flanked by Emily and Betty, and followed by Polly who carried a basin and towels. Her cousin's removal left Briony centre stage – there was no sign yet of Robbie – and the way she was listened to, deferred to and gently prompted seemed at one with her new maturity.

It must have been about this time that a Humber stopped outside the house and two police inspectors and two con- stables were shown in. Briony was their only source, and she made herself speak calmly. Her vital role fuelled her certainty. This was in the unstructured time before formal interviews, when she was standing facing the officers in the hallway, with Leon on one side of her and her mother on the other. But how had her mother materialised so quickly from Lola's bedside? The senior inspector had a heavy face, rich in seams, as though carved from folded granite. Briony was fearful of him as she told her story to this watchful unmoving mask; as she did so she felt a weight lifting from her and a warm submissive feeling spread from her stomach to her limbs. It was like love, a sudden love for this watchful man who stood unquestioningly for the cause of goodness, who came out at all hours to do battle in its name, and who was backed by all the human powers and wisdom that existed. Under his neutral gaze her throat constricted and her voice began to buckle. She wanted the inspector to embrace her and comfort her and forgive her, however guiltless she was. But he would only look at her and listen. *It was him. I saw him.* Her tears were further proof of the truth she felt and spoke, and when her mother's hand caressed her nape, she broke down completely and was led towards the drawing room.

But if she was there being consoled by her mother on the Chesterfield, how did she come to remember the arrival of Dr McLaren in his black waistcoat and his old-fashioned raised shirt collar, carrying the Gladstone bag that had been witness to the three births and all the childhood illnesses of the Tallis household? Leon conferred with the doctor, leaning towards him to murmur a manly summary of events. Where was Leon's carefree lightness now? This quiet consultation was typical of the hours to come. Each fresh arrival was briefed in this way; people – police, doctor, family members, servants – stood in knots that unravelled and reformed in corners of rooms, the hallway and the terrace outside the French windows. Nothing was brought together, or formulated in public. Everyone knew the terrible facts of a violation, but it remained everyone's secret, shared in whispers among shifting groups that broke away self-importantly to new business. Even more serious, potentially, was the matter of the missing children. But the general view, constantly reiterated like a magic spell, was that they were safely asleep somewhere in the park. In this way attention remained mostly fixed on the plight of the girl upstairs.

Paul Marshall came in from searching and learned the news from the inspectors. He walked up and down the terrace with them, one on each side, and on the turn offered them cigarettes from a gold case. When their conversation was over, he patted the senior man on the shoulder and seemed to send them on their way. Then he came inside to confer with Emily Tallis. Leon led the doctor upstairs who descended some while later intangibly enlarged by his professional encounter with the core of all their concerns. He too stood in lengthy conference with the two plainclothes men, and then with Leon, and finally with Leon and Mrs Tallis. Not long before his departure, the doctor came and placed his familiar small dry hand on Briony's forehead, fingered her pulse and was satisfied. He took up his bag, but before he was gone there was a final muttered interview by the front door.

Where was Cecilia? She hovered on the peripheries, speaking to no one, always smoking, raising the cigarette to her lips with a rapid, hungry movement, and pulling it away in agitated disgust. At other times she twisted a handkerchief in her hand as she paced the hallway. Normally, she would have taken control of a situation like this, directing the care of Lola, reassuring her mother, listening to the doctor's advice, consulting with Leon. Briony was close by when her brother came over to talk to Cecilia, who turned away, unable to help, or even speak. As for their mother, untypically she rose to the crisis, free of migraine and the need to be alone. She actually grew as her older daughter shrank into private misery. There were times when Briony, called on again to give her account, or some detail of it, saw her sister approach within earshot and look on with a smouldering impenetrable gaze. Briony became nervous of her and kept close to her mother's side. Cecilia's eyes were bloodshot. While others stood murmuring in groups, she moved restlessly up and down the room, or from one room to another, or, on at least two occasions, went to stand outside the front door. Nervously, she transferred the hankie from one hand to the other, coiled it between her fingers, unwound it, squeezed it in a ball, took it in the other hand, lit another cigarette. When Betty and Polly brought round tea, Cecilia would not touch it.

Word came down that Lola, sedated by the doctor, was at last asleep, and the news provided temporary relief. Unusually, everyone had gathered in the drawing room where tea was taken in exhausted silence. Nobody said it, but they were waiting for Robbie. Also, Mr Tallis was expected from London at any moment. Leon and Marshall were leaning over a map they were drawing of the grounds for the inspector's benefit. He took it, studied it and passed it to his assistant. The two constables had been sent out to join those looking for Pierrot and Jackson, and more policemen were supposed to be on their way down to the bungalow in case Robbie had gone there. Like Marshall, Cecilia sat apart, on the harpsichord stool. At one point she rose to get a light from her brother, but it was the chief inspector who obliged her with his own lighter. Briony was next to her mother on the sofa, and Betty and Polly took round the tray. Briony was to have no memory of what suddenly prompted her. An idea of great clarity and persuasiveness came from nowhere, and she did not need to announce her intentions, or ask her sister's permission. Clinching evidence, cleanly independent of her own version. Verification. Or even another, separate crime. She startled the room with her gasp of inspiration, and almost knocked her mother's tea from her lap as she stood.

They all watched as she hurried from the room, but no one questioned her, such was the general fatigue. She, on the other hand, was taking the stairs two at a time, energised now by a sense of doing and being good, on the point of springing a surprise that could only earn her praise. It was rather like that Christmas morning sensation of being about to give a present that was bound to cause delight, a joyful feeling of blameless self-love.

She ran along the second-floor corridor to Cecilia's room. What squalor and disorder her sister lived in! Both wardrobe doors hung wide open. Various dresses were skewed out of their rows and some were half off their hangers. On the floor two dresses, one black, one pink, silky expensive-looking things, lay in a tangle, and round this pile lay kicked-off shoes on their sides. Briony stepped over and around the mess to get to the dressing table. What was the impulse that prevented Cecilia from replacing the caps and lids and screwtops of her make-up and perfumes? Why did she never empty her stinking ash-tray? Or make her bed, or open a window to let in the fresh air? The first drawer she tried opened only a couple of inches – it was jammed, crammed full of bottles and a cardboard package. Cecilia might have been ten years older, but there really was something quite hopeless and helpless about her. Even though Briony was fearful of the wild look her sister had downstairs, it was right, the younger girl thought as she pulled open another drawer, that she was there for her, thinking clearly, on her behalf.

Five minutes later, when she re-entered the drawing room in triumph, no one paid her any attention, and everything was exactly the same – tired, miserable adults sipping tea and smoking in silence. In her excitement she had not considered who it was she should give the letter to; a trick of her imagination had everyone reading it at once. She decided Leon should have it. She crossed the room towards her brother, but when she arrived in front of the three men she changed her mind and put the folded sheet of paper into the hands of the policeman with the face of granite. If he had an expression, it did not change as he took the letter nor when he read it, which he did at great speed, almost at a glance. His eyes met hers, then shifted to take in Cecilia who was facing away. With the slightest movement of his wrist he indicated that the other policeman should take the letter. When he was finished it was passed on to Leon who read it, folded it and returned it to the senior inspector. Briony was impressed by the muted response – such was the three men's worldliness. It was only now that Emily Tallis became aware of the focus of their interest. In answer to her unemphatic query Leon said, 'It's just a letter.'

'I'll read it.'

For the second time that evening Emily was obliged to assert her rights over written messages passing through her household. Feeling that nothing more was required of her, Briony went to sit on the Chesterfield and watched from her mother's perspective the chivalrous unease that shifted between Leon and the policemen.

'I'll read it.'

Ominously, she did not vary her tone. Leon shrugged and forced an apologetic smile – what possible objection could he have? – and Emily's mild gaze settled on the two inspectors. She belonged to a generation that treated policemen as menials, whatever their rank. Obedient to the nod from his superior, the younger inspector crossed the room and presented the letter to her. At last Cecilia, who must have been a long way off in her thoughts, was taking an interest. Then the letter lay exposed on her mother's lap, and Cecilia was on her feet, then moving towards them from the harpsichord stool.

'How dare you! How dare you all!'

Leon stood too and made a calming gesture with his palms. 'Cee . . .'

When she made a lunge to snatch the letter from her mother, she found not only her brother but the two policemen in her way. Marshall was standing too, but not interfering.

'It belongs to me,' she shouted. 'You have absolutely no right!'

Emily did not even look up from her reading, and she gave herself time to read the letter several times over. When she was done she met her daughter's fury with her own colder version.

'If you had done the right thing, young lady, with all your education, and come to me with this, then something could have been done in time and your cousin would have been spared her nightmare.'

For a moment Cecilia stood alone in the centre of the room, fluttering the fingers of her right hand, staring at them each in turn, unable to believe her association with such people, unable to begin to tell them what she knew. And though Briony felt vindicated by the reaction of the adults, and was experiencing the onset of a sweet and inward rapture, she was also pleased to be down on the sofa with her mother, partially screened by the standing men from her sister's red-eyed contempt. She held them in its grip for several seconds before she turned and walked out of the room. As she went across the hallway she gave out a cry of sheer vexation which was amplified by the raw acoustic of the bare floor tiles. In the drawing room there was a sense of relief, of relaxation almost, as they heard her go up the stairs. When Briony next remembered to look, the letter was in Marshall's hands and he was passing it back to the inspector who placed it unfolded into a binder which the younger policeman was holding open for him.

The hours of the night spun away from her and she remained untired. It occurred to no one to send her to her bed. Some immeasurable time after Cecilia had gone to her room, Briony went with her mother to the library to have the first of her formal interviews with the police. Mrs Tallis remained standing, while Briony sat on one side of the writing desk and the inspectors sat on the other. The one with the face of ancient rock, who was the one who asked the questions, turned out to be infinitely kind, speaking his unhurried questions in a gruff voice that was both gentle and sad. Since she was able to show them the precise location of Robbie's attack on Cecilia, they all wandered into that corner of the bookshelves to take a closer look. Briony wedged herself in, with her back to the books to show them how her sister was positioned, and saw the first mid-blue touches of dawn in the panes of the library's high windows. She stepped out and turned around to demonstrate the attacker's stance and showed where she herself had stood.

Emily said, 'But why didn't you tell me?'

The policemen looked at Briony and waited. It was a good question, but it would never have occurred to her to trouble her mother. Nothing but migraine would have come of it.

'We were called into dinner, then the twins ran off.'

She explained how she came by the letter, on the bridge at dusk. What led her to open it? Difficult to describe the impulsive moment, when she had not permitted herself to think of the consequences before acting, or how the writer she had only that day become needed to know, to understand everything that came her way.

She said, 'I don't know. I was being horribly nosey. I hated myself.'

It was about this time that a constable put his head round the door to give news that seemed at one with the calamity of the night. Mr Tallis's driver had rung from a phone box near Croydon airport. The departmental car, made available at short notice through the kindness of the minister, had broken down in the suburbs. Jack Tallis was asleep under a rug on the back seat and would probably have to continue by the first morning train. Once these facts had been absorbed and lamented, Briony was gently returned to the scene itself, to the events on the lake island. At this early stage, the inspector was careful not to oppress the young girl with probing questions, and within this sensitively created space she was able to build and shape her narrative in her own words and establish the key facts: there was just sufficient light for her to recognise a familiar face; when he shrank away from her and circled the clearing, his movements and height were familiar to her as well.

'You saw him then.'

'I know it was him.'

'Let's forget what you know. You're saying you saw him.'

'Yes, I saw him.'

'Just as you see me.'

'Yes.'

'You saw him with your own eyes.'

'Yes. I saw him. I saw him.'

Thus her first formal interview concluded. While she sat in the drawing room, feeling her tiredness at last, but unwilling to go to bed, her mother was questioned, then Leon and Paul Marshall. Old Hardman and his son Danny were brought in for interview. Briony heard Betty say that Danny was at home all evening with his father who was able to vouch for him. Various constables came to the front door from searching for the twins and were shown through to the kitchen. In the confused and unmemorable time of that early dawn, Briony gathered that Cecilia was refusing to leave her room, refusing to come down to be interviewed. In the days to come she would be given no choice and when she finally yielded up her own account of what happened in the library – in its way, far more shocking than Briony's, however consensual the encounter had been – it merely confirmed the general view that had formed: Mr Turner was a dangerous man. Cecilia's repeated suggestion that it was Danny Hardman they should be talking to was heard in silence. It was understandable, though poor form, that this young woman should be covering for her friend by casting suspicion on an innocent boy.

Some time after five, when there was talk of breakfast being prepared, at least for the constables, for no one else was hungry, the word flashed through the household that a figure who might be Robbie was approaching across the park. Perhaps someone had been watching from an upstairs window. Briony did not know how the decision was made that they should all go outside to wait for him. Suddenly, they were all there, family, Paul Marshall, Betty and her helpers, the policemen, a reception party grouped tightly around the front entrance. Only Lola in a drugged coma and Cecilia with her fury remained upstairs. It might have been that Mrs Tallis did not want the polluting presence to step inside her house. The inspector may have feared violence which was more easily dealt with outdoors where there was more space to make an arrest. All the magic of dawn had gone now, and in its place was a grey early morning, distinguished only by a summer's mist which was sure to burn off soon.

At first they saw nothing, though Briony thought she could make out the tread of shoes along the drive. Then everyone could hear it, and there was a collective murmur and shifting of weight as they caught sight of an indefinable shape, no more than a greyish smudge against the white, almost a hundred yards away. As the shape took form the waiting group fell silent again. No one could quite believe what was emerging. Surely it was a trick of the mist and light. No one in this age of telephones and motor cars could believe that giants seven or eight feet high existed in crowded Surrey. But here it was, an apparition as inhuman as it was purposeful. The thing was impossible and undeniable, and heading their way. Betty, who was known to be a Catholic, crossed herself as the little crowd huddled closer to the entrance. Only the senior inspector took a couple of paces forwards, and as he did so everything became clear. The clue was a second, tiny shape that bobbed alongside the first. Then it was obvious – this was Robbie, with one boy sitting up on his shoulders and the other holding his hand and trailing a little behind. When he was less than thirty feet away, Robbie stopped, and seemed about to speak, but waited instead as the inspector and the other policemen approached. The boy on his shoulders appeared to be asleep. The other boy let his head loll against Robbie's waist and drew the man's hand across his chest for protection or warmth.

Briony's immediate feeling was one of relief that the boys were safe. But as she looked at Robbie waiting calmly, she experienced a flash of outrage. Did he believe he could conceal his crime behind an apparent kindness, behind this show of being the good shepherd? This was surely a cynical attempt to win forgiveness for what could never be forgiven. She was confirmed again in her view that evil was complicated and misleading. Suddenly, her mother's hands were pressing firmly on her shoulders and turning her towards the house, delivering her into Betty's care. Emily wanted her daughter well away from Robbie Turner. It was bedtime at last. Betty took a firm grip of her hand and was leading her in as her mother and brother went forward to collect the twins. Briony's last glimpse back over her shoulder as she was pulled away showed her Robbie raising two hands, as though in surrender. He lifted the boy clear of his head and placed him gently on the ground.

An hour later she was lying on her canopy bed in the clean white cotton nightdress which Betty had found for her. The curtains were drawn, but the daylight gleam around their edges was strong, and for all her spinning sensations of tiredness, she could not sleep. Voices and images were ranged around her bedside, agitated, nagging presences, jostling and merging, resisting her attempts to set them in order. Were they all really bounded by a single day, by one period of unbroken wakefulness, from the innocent rehearsals of her play to the emergence of the giant from the mist? All that lay between was too clamorous, too fluid to understand, though she sensed she had succeeded, even triumphed. She kicked the sheet clear of her legs and turned the pillow to find a cooler patch for her cheeks. In her dizzy state she was not able to say exactly what her success had been; if it was to have gained a new maturity, she could hardly feel it now when she was so helpless, so childish even, through lack of sleep, to the point where she thought she could easily make herself cry. If it was brave to have identified a throughly bad person, then it was wrong of him to turn up with the twins like that, and she felt cheated. Who would believe her now, with Robbie posing as the kindly rescuer of lost children? All her work, all her courage and clear-headedness, all she had done to bring Lola home – for nothing. They would turn their backs on her, her mother, the policemen, her brother, and go off with Robbie Turner to indulge some adult cabal. She wanted her mother, she wanted to put her arms round her mother's neck and pull her lovely face close to hers, but her mother wouldn't come now, no one would come to Briony, no one would talk to her now. She turned her face into the pillow and let her tears drain into it, and felt that yet more was lost, when there was no witness to her sorrow.

She had been lying in the semi-darkness nursing this palatable sadness for half an hour when she heard the sound of the police car parked below her window starting up. It rolled across the gravel, then stopped. There were voices and the crunch of several footsteps. She got up and parted the curtains. The mist was still there, but it was brighter, as though illuminated from within, and she half closed her eyes while they adjusted to the glare. All four doors of the police Humber were wide open, and three constables were waiting by it. The voices came from a group directly below her, by the front door, just out of sight. Then came the sound of footsteps again, and they emerged, the two inspectors, with Robbie between them. And handcuffed! She saw how his arms were forced in front of him, and from her vantage point she saw the silver glint of steel below his shirt cuff. The disgrace of it horrified her. It was further confirmation of his guilt, and the beginning of his punishment. It had the look of eternal damnation.

They reached the car and stopped. Robbie half turned, but she could not read his expression. He stood erect, several inches higher than the inspector, with his head lifted up. Perhaps he was proud of what he had done. One of the constables got in the driver's seat. The junior inspector was walking round to the rear door on the far side and his chief was about to guide Robbie into the back seat. There was the sound of a commotion directly below Briony's window, and of Emily Tallis's voice calling sharply, and suddenly a figure was running towards the car as fast as was possible in a tight dress. Cecilia slowed as she approached. Robbie turned and took half a pace towards her and, surprisingly, the inspector stepped back. The handcuffs were in full view, but Robbie did not appear ashamed or even aware of them as he faced Cecilia and listened gravely to what she was saying. The impassive policemen looked on. If she was delivering the bitter indictment Robbie deserved to hear, it did not show on his face. Though Cecilia was facing away from her, Briony thought she was speaking with very little animation. Her accusations would be all the more powerful for being muttered. They had moved closer, and now Robbie spoke briefly, and half raised his locked hands and let them fall. She touched them with her own, and fingered his lapel, and then gripped it and shook it gently. It seemed a kindly gesture and Briony was touched by her sister's capacity for forgiveness, if this was what it was. Forgiveness. The word had never meant a thing before, though Briony had heard it exulted at a thousand school and church occasions. And all the time, her sister had understood. There was, of course, much that she did not know about Cecilia. But there would be time, for this tragedy was bound to bring them closer.

The kindly inspector with the granite face must have thought he had been indulgent enough, for he stepped forward to brush away Cecilia's hand and interpose himself. Robbie said something to her quickly over the officer's shoulder, and turned towards the car. Considerately, the inspector raised his own hand to Robbie's head and pressed down hard on it, so that he did not bang it as he stooped to climb into the back seat. The two inspectors wedged themselves on each side of their prisoner. The doors slammed, and the one constable left behind touched his helmet in salute as the car moved forwards. Cecilia remained where she was, facing down the drive, tranquilly watching the car as it receded, but the tremors along the line of her shoulders confided she was crying, and Briony knew she had never loved her sister more than now.

It should have ended there, this seamless day that had wrapped itself around a summer's night, it should have concluded then with the Humber disappearing down the drive. But there remained a final confrontation. The car had gone no more than twenty yards when it began to slow. A figure Briony had not noticed was coming down the centre of the drive and showed no intention of standing to one side. It was a woman, rather short, with a rolling walk, wearing a floral print dress and gripping what looked at first like a stick but was in fact a man's umbrella with a goose's head. The car stopped and the horn sounded as the woman came up and stood right against the radiator grill. It was Robbie's mother, Grace Turner. She raised the umbrella and shouted. The policeman in the front passenger seat had got out and was speaking to her, and then took her by the elbow. The other constable, the one who had saluted, was hurrying over. Mrs Turner shook her arm free, raised the umbrella again, this time with two hands, and brought it down, goose head first, with a crack like a pistol shot, onto the Humber's shiny bonnet. As the constables half pushed, half carried her to the edge of the drive, she began to shout a single word so loudly that Briony could hear it from her bedroom.

'Liars! Liars! Liars!' Mrs Turner roared.

With its front door wide open, the car moved past her slowly and stopped to let the policeman get back in. On his own, his colleague was having difficulty restraining her. She managed another swipe with her umbrella but the blow glanced off the car's roof. He wrestled the umbrella from her and tossed it over his shoulder onto the grass.

'Liars! Liars!' Grace Turner shouted again, and took a few hopeless steps after the retreating car, and then stopped, hands on hips, to watch as it went over the first bridge, crossed the island and then the second bridge, and finally vanished into the whiteness.

Part Two

There were horrors enough, but it was the unexpected detail that threw him and afterwards would not let him go. When they reached the level crossing, after a three-mile walk along a narrow road, he saw the path he was looking for meandering off to the right, then dipping and rising towards a copse that covered a low hill to the north-west. They stopped so that he could consult the map. But it wasn't where he thought it should be. It wasn't in his pocket, or tucked into his belt. Had he dropped it, or put it down at the last stop? He let his greatcoat fall on the ground and was reaching inside his jacket when he realised. The map was in his left hand and must have been there for over an hour. He glanced across at the other two but they were facing away from him, standing apart, smoking silently. It was still in his hand. He had prised it from the fingers of a captain in the West Kents lying in a ditch outside – outside where? These rear-area maps were rare. He also took the dead captain's revolver. He wasn't trying to impersonate an officer. He had lost his rifle and simply intended to survive.

The path he was interested in started down the side of a bombed house, fairly new, perhaps a railwayman's cottage rebuilt after the last time. There were animal tracks in the mud surrounding a puddle in a tyre rut. Probably goats.

Scattered around were shreds of striped cloth with blackened edges, remains of curtains or clothing, and a smashed-in window-frame draped across a bush, and everywhere, the smell of damp soot. This was their path, their shortcut. He folded the map away, and as he straightened from picking up the coat and was slinging it around his shoulders, he saw it. The others, sensing his movement, turned round, and followed his gaze. It was a leg in a tree. A mature plane tree, only just in leaf. The leg was twenty feet up, wedged in the first forking of the trunk, bare, severed cleanly above the knee. From where they stood there was no sign of blood or torn flesh. It was a perfect leg, pale, smooth, small enough to be a child's. The way it was angled in the fork, it seemed to be on display, for their benefit or enlightenment: this is a leg.

The two corporals made a dismissive sound of disgust and picked up their stuff. They refused to be drawn in. In the past few days they had seen enough.

Nettle, the lorry driver, took out another cigarette and said, 'So, which way, Guv'nor?'

They called him that to settle the difficult matter of rank. He set off down the path in a hurry, almost at a half run. He wanted to get ahead, out of sight, so that he could throw up, or crap, he didn't know which. Behind a barn, by a pile of broken slates, his body chose the first option for him. He was so thirsty, he couldn't afford to lose the fluid. He drank from his canteen, and walked around the barn. He made use of this moment alone to look at his wound. It was on his right side, just below his rib cage, about the size of a half crown. It wasn't looking so bad after he washed away the dried blood yesterday. Though the skin around it was red, there wasn't much swelling. But there was something in there. He could feel it move when he walked. A piece of shrapnel perhaps.

By the time the corporals caught up, he had tucked his shirt back in and was pretending to study the map. In their company the map was his only privacy.

'What's the hurry?'

'He's seen some crumpet.'

'It's the map. He's having his fucking *doubts* again.'

'No doubts, gentlemen. This is our path.'

He took out a cigarette and Corporal Mace lit it for him. Then, to conceal the trembling in his hands, Robbie Turner walked on, and they followed him, as they had followed him for two days now. Or was it three? He was lower in rank, but they followed and did everything he suggested, and to preserve their dignity, they teased him. When they tramped the roads or cut across the fields and he was silent for too long, Mace would say, 'Guv'nor, are you thinking about crumpet again?' And Nettle would chant, 'He fucking is, he fucking is.' They were townies who disliked the countryside and were lost in it. The compass points meant nothing to them. That part of basic training had passed them by. They had decided that to reach the coast, they needed him. It was difficult for them. He acted like an officer, but he didn't even have a single stripe. On the first night, when they were sheltering in the bike shed of a burned-out school, Corporal Nettle said, 'What's a private soldier like you doing talking like a toff?'

He didn't owe them explanations. He intended to survive, he had one good reason to survive, and he didn't care whether they tagged along or not. Both men had hung onto their rifles. That was something at least, and Mace was a big man, strong across the shoulders, and with hands that could have spanned one and a half octaves of the pub piano he said he played. Nor did Turner mind about the taunts. All he wanted now as they followed the path away from the road was to forget about the leg. Their path joined a track which ran between two stone walls and dropped down into a valley that had not been visible from the road. At the bottom was a brown stream which they crossed on stepping stones set deep in a carpet of what looked like miniature water parsley.

Their route swung to the west as they rose out of the valley, still between the ancient walls. Ahead of them the sky was beginning to clear a little and glowed like a promise. Everywhere else was grey. As they approached the top through a copse of chestnut trees, the lowering sun dropped below the cloud cover and caught the scene, dazzling the three soldiers as they rose into it. How fine it might have been, to end a day's ramble in the French countryside, walking into the setting sun. Always a hopeful act.

As they came out of the copse they heard bombers, so they went back in and smoked while they waited under the trees. From where they were they could not see the planes, but the view was fine. These were hardly hills that spread so expansively before them. They were ripples in the landscape, faint echoes of vast upheavals elsewhere. Each successive ridge was paler than the one before. He saw a receding wash of grey and blue fading in a haze towards the setting sun, like something oriental on a dinner plate.

Half an hour later they were making a long traverse across a deeper slope that edged further to the north and delivered them at last to another valley, another little stream. This one had a more confident flow and they crossed it by a stone bridge thick with cow dung. The corporals, who were not as tired as he was, had a lark, pretending to be revolted. One of them threw a dried lump of dung at his back. Turner did not look round. The scraps of cloth, he was beginning to think, may have been a child's pyjamas. A boy's. The dive bombers sometimes came over not long after dawn. He was trying to push it away, but it would not let him go. A French boy asleep in his bed. Turner wanted to put more distance between himself and that bombed cottage. It was not only the German army and air force pursuing him now. If there had been a moon he would have been happy walking all night. The corporals wouldn't like it. Perhaps it was time to shake them off.

Downstream of the bridge was a line of poplars whose tops fluttered brilliantly in the last of the light. The soldiers turned in the other direction and soon the track was a path again and was leaving the stream. They wound and squeezed their way through bushes with fat shiny leaves. There were also stunted oaks, barely in leaf. The vegetation underfoot smelled sweet and damp, and he thought there must be something wrong with the place to make it so different from anything they had seen.

Ahead of them was the hum of machinery. It grew louder, angrier, and suggested the high-velocity spin of flywheels or electric turbines turning at impossible speed. They were entering a great hall of sound and power.

'Bees!' he called out. He had to turn and say it again before they heard him. The air was already darker. He knew the lore well enough. If one stuck in your hair and stung you, it sent out a chemical message as it died and all who received it were compelled to come and sting and die at the same place. General conscription! After all the danger, this was a kind of insult. They lifted their great coats over their heads and ran on through the swarm. Still among the bees, they reached a stinking ditch of slurry which they crossed by a wobbling plank. They came up behind a barn where it was suddenly peaceful. Beyond it was a farmyard. As soon as they were in it, dogs were barking and an old woman was running towards them flapping her hands at them, as though they were hens she could shoo away. The corporals depended on Turner's French. He went forward and waited for her to reach him. There were stories of civilians selling bottles of water for ten francs, but he had never seen it. The French he had met were generous, or otherwise lost to their own miseries. The woman was frail and energetic. She had a gnarled, man-in-the-moon face and a wild look. Her voice was sharp.

'C'est impossible, M'sieu. Vous ne pouvez pas rester ici.'

'We'll be staying in the barn. We need water, wine, bread, cheese and anything else you can spare.'

'Impossible!'

He said to her softly, 'We've been fighting for France.'

'You can't stay here.'

'We'll be gone at dawn. The Germans are still . . .'

'It's not the Germans, M'sieu. It's my sons. They are animals. And they'll be back soon.'

Turner pushed past the woman and went to the pump which was in the corner of the yard, near the kitchen. Nettle and Mace followed him. While he drank, a girl of about ten and an infant brother holding her hand watched him from the doorway. When he finished and had filled his canteen he smiled at them and they fled. The corporals were under the pump together, drinking simultaneously. The woman was suddenly behind him, clutching at his elbow. Before she could start again he said, 'Please bring us what I asked for or we'll come in and get it for ourselves.'

'My sons are brutes. They'll kill me.'

He would have preferred to say, So be it, but instead he walked away and called over his shoulder, 'I'll talk to them.'

'And then, M'sieu, they will kill you. They will tear you to shreds.'

Corporal Mace was a cook in the same RASC unit as Corporal Nettle. Before he joined he was a warehouseman at Heal's in the Tottenham Court Road. He said he knew a thing or two about comfort, and in the barn he set about arranging their quarters. Turner would have thrown himself down on the straw. Mace found a heap of sacks and with Nettle's help stuffed them to make up three mattresses. He made headboards out of hay bales which he lifted down with a single hand. He set up a door on brick piles for a table. He took out half a candle from his pocket.

'Might as well be comfy,' he kept saying under his breath. It was the first time they had moved much beyond sexual innuendo. The three men lay on their beds, smoking and waiting. Now they were no longer thirsty their thoughts were on the food they were about to get and they heard each other's stomachs rumbling and squirting in the gloom, and it made them laugh. Turner told them about his conversation with the old woman and what she had said about her sons.

'Fifth columnists, they would be,' Nettle said. He only looked small alongside his friend, but he had a small man's sharp features and a friendly, rodent look, heightened by his way of resting the teeth of his upper jaw on his lower lip.

'Or French Nazis. German sympathisers. Like we got Mosley,' Mace said.

They were silent for a while, then Mace added, 'Or like they all are in the country, bonkers from marrying too close.'

'Whatever it is,' Turner said, 'I think you should check your weapons now and have them handy.'

They did as they were told. Mace lit the candle, and they went through the routines. Turner checked his pistol and put it within reach. When the corporals were finished, they propped the Lee-Enfields against a wooden crate and lay down on their beds again. Presently the girl came with a basket. She set it down by the barn door and ran away. Nettle fetched the basket and they spread out what they had on their table. A round loaf of brown bread, a small piece of soft cheese, an onion and a bottle of wine. The bread was hard to cut and tasted of mould. The cheese was good, but it was gone in seconds. They passed the bottle around and soon that was gone too. So they chewed on the musty bread and ate the onion.

Nettle said, 'I wouldn't give this to my fucking dog.'

'I'll go across,' Turner said, 'and get something better.'

'We'll come too.'

But for a while they lay back on their beds in silence. No one felt like confronting the old lady just yet.

Then, at the sound of footsteps, they turned and saw two men standing in the entrance. They each held something in their hands, a club perhaps, or a shotgun. In the fading light it was not possible to tell. Nor could they see the faces of the French brothers.

The voice was soft. 'Bonsoir, Messieurs.'

'Bonsoir.'

As Turner got up from his straw bed he took the revolver. The corporals reached for their rifles. 'Go easy,' he whispered.

'Anglais? Belges?'

'Anglais.'

'We have something for you.'

'What sort of thing?'

'What's he saying?' one of the corporals said.

'He says they've got something for us.'

'Fucking hell.'

The men came a couple of steps closer and raised what was in their hands. Shotguns, surely. Turner released his safety catch. He heard Mace and Nettle do the same. 'Easy,' he murmured.

'Put away your guns, Messieurs.'

'Put away yours.'

'Wait a little moment.'

The figure who spoke was reaching into his pocket. He brought out a torch and shone it not at the soldiers, but at his brother, at what was in his hand. A French loaf. And at what was in the other hand, a canvas bag. Then he showed them the two baguettes he himself was holding.

'And we have olives, cheese, pâté, tomatoes and ham. And naturally, wine. Vive l'Angleterre.'

'Er, Vive la France.'

They sat at Mace's table, which the Frenchmen, Henri and Jean-Marie Bonnet, politely admired, along with the mattresses. They were short, stocky men in their fifties. Henri wore glasses, which Nettle said looked odd on a farmer. Turner did not translate. As well as wine, they brought glass tumblers. The five men raised them in toasts to the French and British armies, and to the crushing of Germany. The brothers watched the soldiers eat. Through Turner, Mace said that he had never tasted, never even heard of, goose liver pâté, and from now on, he would eat nothing else. The Frenchmen smiled, but their manner was constrained and they seemed in no mood to get drunk. They said they had driven all the way to a hamlet near Arras in their flat-bed farm truck to look for a young cousin and her children. A great battle had been fought for the town but they had no idea who was taking it, who was defending it or who had the upper hand. They drove on the back roads to avoid the chaos of refugees. They saw farmhouses burning, and then they came across a dozen or so dead English soldiers in the road. They had to get out and drag the men aside to avoid running over them. But a couple of the bodies were almost cut in half. It must have been a big machine-gun attack, perhaps from the air, perhaps an ambush. Back in the lorry, Henri was sick in the cab, and Jean-Marie, who was at the wheel, got into a panic and drove into a ditch. They walked to a village, borrowed two horses from a farmer and pulled the Renault free. That took two hours. On the road again, they saw burned-out tanks and armoured cars, German as well as British and French. But they saw no soldiers. The battle had moved on.

By the time they reached the hamlet, it was late afternoon. The place had been completely destroyed and was deserted. Their cousin's house was smashed up, with bullet holes all over the walls, but it still had its roof. They went in every room and were relieved to find no one there. She must have taken the children and joined the thousands of people on the roads. Afraid of driving back at night, they parked in a wood and tried to sleep in the cab. All night long they heard the artillery pounding Arras. It seemed impossible that anyone, or anything, could survive there. They drove back by another route, a much greater distance, to avoid passing the dead soldiers. Now, Henri explained, he and his brother were very tired. When they shut their eyes, they saw those mutilated bodies.

Jean-Marie refilled the glasses. The account, with Turner's running translation, had taken almost an hour. All the food was eaten. He thought about telling them of his own single, haunting detail. But he didn't want to add to the horror, and nor did he want to give life to the image while it remained at a distance, held there by wine and companionship. Instead, he told them how he was separated from his unit at the beginning of the retreat, during a Stuka attack. He didn't mention his injury because he didn't want the corporals to know about it. Instead he explained how they were walking cross-country to Dunkirk to avoid the air-raids along the main roads.

Jean-Marie said, 'So it's true what they're saying. You're leaving.'

'We'll be back.' He said this, but he didn't believe it.

The wine was taking hold of Corporal Nettle. He began a rambling eulogy of what he called 'Frog crumpet' – how plentiful, how available, how delicious. It was all fantasy. The brothers looked at Turner.

'He says French women are the most beautiful in the world.'

They nodded solemnly and raised their glasses.

They were all silent for a while. Their evening was almost at an end. They listened to the night sounds they had grown used to – the rumble of artillery, stray shots in the distance, a booming far-off explosion – probably sappers blowing a bridge in the retreat.

'Ask them about their mum,' Corporal Mace suggested. 'Let's get that one cleared up.'

'We were three brothers,' Henri explained. 'The eldest, Paul, her first-born, died near Verdun in 1915. A direct hit from a shell. There was nothing to bury apart from his helmet. Us two, we were lucky. We came through without a scratch. Since then, she's always hated soldiers. But now she's eighty-three and losing her mind, it's an obsession with her. French, English, Belgian, German. She makes no distinction. You're all the same to her. We worry that when the Germans come, she'll go at them with a pitchfork and they'll shoot her.'

Wearily, the brothers got to their feet. The soldiers did the same.

Jean-Marie said, 'We would offer you hospitality at our kitchen table. But to do that, we would have to lock her in her room.'

'But this has been a magnificent feast,' Turner said.

Nettle was whispering in Mace's ear and he was nodding. Nettle took from his bag two cartons of cigarettes. Of course, it was the right thing to do. The Frenchmen made a polite show of refusing, but Nettle came round the table and shoved the gifts into their arms. He wanted Turner to translate.

'You should have seen it, when the order came through to destroy the stores. Twenty thousand cigarettes. We took whatever we wanted.'

A whole army was fleeing to the coast, armed with cigarettes to keep the hunger away.

The Frenchmen gave courteous thanks, complimented Turner on his French, then bent over the table to pack the empty bottles and glasses into the canvas bag. There was no pretending that they would meet again.

'We'll be gone at first light,' Turner said. 'So we'll say goodbye.'

They shook hands.

Henri Bonnet said, 'All that fighting we did twenty-five years ago. All those dead. Now the Germans back in France. In two days they'll be here, taking everything we have. Who would have believed it?'

Turner felt, for the first time, the full ignominy of the retreat. He was ashamed. He said, with even less conviction than before, 'We'll be back to throw them out, I promise you.'

The brothers nodded and, with final smiles of farewell, left the dim circle of the candle's glow and crossed the darkness towards the open barn door, the glasses chinking against the bottles as they went.

For a long time he lay on his back smoking, staring into the blackness of the cavernous roof. The corporals' snores rose and fell in counterpoint. He was exhausted, but not sleepy. The wound throbbed uncomfortably, each beat precise and tight. Whatever was in there was sharp and close to the surface, and he wanted to touch it with a fingertip. Exhaustion made him vulnerable to the thoughts he wanted least. He was thinking about the French boy asleep in his bed, and about the indifference with which men could lob shells into a landscape. Or empty their bomb bays over a sleeping cottage by a railway, without knowing or caring who was there. It was an industrial process. He had seen their own RA units at work, tightly knit groups, working all hours, proud of the speed with which they could set up a line, and proud of their discipline, drills, training, teamwork. They need never see the end result – a vanished boy. Vanished. As he formed the word in his thoughts, sleep snatched him under, but only for seconds. Then he was awake, on his bed, on his back, staring at the darkness in his cell. He could feel he was back there. He could smell the concrete floor, and the piss in the bucket, and the gloss paint on the walls, and hear the snores of the men along the row. Three and a half years of nights like these, unable to sleep, thinking of another vanished boy, another vanished life that was once his own, and waiting for dawn, and slop-out and another wasted day. He did not know how he survived the daily stupidity of it. The stupidity and claustrophobia. The hand squeezing on his throat. Being here, sheltering in a barn, with an army in rout, where a child's limb in a tree was something that ordinary men could ignore, where a whole country, a whole civilisation was about to fall, was better than being there, on a narrow bed under a dim electric light, waiting for nothing. Here there were wooded valleys, streams, sunlight on the poplars which they could not take away unless they killed him. And there was hope. *I'll wait for you. Come back.* There was a chance, just a chance, of getting back. He had her last letter in his pocket and her new address. This was why he had to survive, and use his cunning to stay off the main roads where the circling dive-bombers waited like raptors.

Later, he got up from under his greatcoat, pulled on his boots and groped his way through the barn to relieve himself outside. He was dizzy with fatigue, but he was still not ready for sleep. Ignoring the snarling farm dogs, he found his way along a track to a grassy rise to watch the flashes in the southern sky. This was the approaching storm of German armour. He touched his top pocket where the poem she sent was enfolded in her letter. *In the nightmare of the dark, All the dogs of Europe bark.* The rest of her letters were buttoned into the inside pocket of his greatcoat. By standing on the wheel of an abandoned trailer he was able to see other parts of the sky. The gun flashes were everywhere but the north. The defeated army was running up a corridor that was bound to narrow, and soon must be cut off. There would be no chance of escape for the stragglers. At best, it would be prison again. Prison camp. This time, he wouldn't last. When France fell there would be no end of the war in sight. No letters from her, and no way back. No bargaining an early release in return for joining the infantry. The hand on his throat again. The prospect would be of a thousand, or thousands of incarcerated nights, sleeplessly turning over the past, waiting for his life to resume, wondering if it ever would. Perhaps it would make sense to leave now before it was too late, and keep going, all night, all day until he reached the Channel. Slip away, leave the corporals to their fate. He turned and began to make his way back down the slope and thought better of it. He could barely see the ground in front of him. He would make no progress in the dark and could easily break a leg. And perhaps the corporals weren't such complete dolts – Mace with his straw mattresses, Nettle with his gift for the brothers.

Guided by their snores, he shuffled back to his bed. But

still sleep would not come, or came only in quick plunges from which he emerged, giddy with thoughts he could not choose or direct. They pursued him, the old themes. Here it was again, his only meeting with her. Six days out of prison, one day before he reported for duty near Aldershot. When they arranged to meet at Joe Lyons tea house in the Strand in 1939, they had not seen each other for three and a half years. He was at the café early and took a corner seat with a view of the door. Freedom was still a novelty. The pace and clatter, the colours of coats, jackets and skirts, the bright, loud conversations of West End shoppers, the friendliness of the girl who served him, the spacious lack of threat – he sat back and enjoyed the embrace of the everyday. It had a beauty he alone could appreciate.

During his time inside, the only female visitor he was permitted was his mother. In case he was inflamed, they said. Cecilia wrote every week. In love with her, willing himself to stay sane for her, he was naturally in love with her words. When he wrote back, he pretended to be his old self, he lied his way into sanity. For fear of his psychiatrist who was also their censor, they could never be sensual, or even emotional. His was considered a modern, enlightened prison, despite its Victorian chill. He had been diagnosed, with clinical precision, as morbidly over-sexed, and in need of help as well as correction. He was not to be stimulated. Some letters – both his and hers – were confiscated for some timid expression of affection. So they wrote about literature, and used characters as codes. At Cambridge, they had passed each other by in the street. All those books, those happy or tragic couples they had never met to discuss! Tristan and Isolde, the Duke Orsino and Olivia (and Malvolio too), Troilus and Criseyde, Mr Knightley and Emma, Venus and Adonis. Turner and Tallis. Once, in despair, he referred to Prometheus, chained to a rock, his liver devoured daily by a vulture. Sometimes she was patient Griselde. Mention of 'a quiet corner in a library' was a code for sexual ecstasy.

They charted the daily round too, in boring, loving detail. He described the prison routine in every aspect, but he never told her of its stupidity. That was plain enough. He never told her that he feared he might go under. That too was clear. She never wrote that she loved him, though she would have if she thought it would get through. But he knew it.

She told him she had cut herself off from her family. She would never speak to her parents, brother or sister again. He followed closely all her steps along the way towards her nurse's qualification. When she wrote, 'I went to the library today to get the anatomy book I told you about. I found a quiet corner and pretended to read', he knew she was feeding on the same memories that consumed him every night, beneath thin prison blankets.

When she entered the cafe, wearing her nurse's cape, startling him from a pleasant daze, he stood too quickly and knocked his tea. He was conscious of the oversized suit his mother had saved for. The jacket did not seem to touch his shoulders at any point. They sat down, looked at each other, smiled and looked away. Robbie and Cecilia had been making love for years – by post. In their coded exchanges they had drawn close, but how artificial that closeness seemed now as they embarked on their small-talk, their helpless catechism of polite query and response. As the distance opened up between them, they understood how far they had run ahead of themselves in their letters. This moment had been imagined and desired for too long, and could not measure up. He had been out of the world, and lacked the confidence to step back and reach for the larger thought. *I love you, and you saved my life*. He asked about her lodgings. She told him.

'And do you get along all right with your landlady?'

He could think of nothing better, and feared the silence that might come down, and the awkwardness that would be a prelude to her telling him that it had been nice to meet up again. Now she must be getting back to work. Everything they had, rested on a few minutes in a library years ago. Was it too frail? She could easily slip back into being a kind of sister. Was she disappointed? He had lost weight. He had shrunk in every sense. Prison made him despise himself, while she looked as adorable as he remembered her, especially in a nurse's uniform. But she was miserably nervous too, incapable of stepping around the inanities. Instead, she was trying to be light-hearted about her landlady's temper. After a few more such exchanges, she really was looking at the little watch that hung above her left breast, and telling him that her lunch break would soon be over. They had had half an hour.

He walked with her to Whitehall, towards the bus stop. In the precious final minutes he wrote out his address for her, a bleak sequence of acronyms and numbers. He explained that he would have no leave until his basic training was over. After that, he was granted two weeks. She was looking at him, shaking her head in some exasperation, and then, at last, he took her hand and squeezed. The gesture had to carry all that had not been said, and she answered it with pressure from her own hand. Her bus came, and she did not let go. They were standing face to face. He kissed her, lightly at first, but they drew closer, and when their tongues touched, a disembodied part of himself was abjectly grateful, for he knew he now had a memory in the bank and would be drawing on it for months to come. He was drawing on it now, in a French barn, in the small hours. They tightened their embrace and went on kissing while people edged past them in the queue. Some card squawked in his ear. She was crying onto his cheek, and her sorrow stretched her lips against his. Another bus arrived. She pulled away, squeezed his wrist, and got on without a word and didn't look back. He watched her find her seat, and as the bus began to move realised he should have gone with her, all the way to the hospital. He had thrown away minutes in her company. He must learn again how to think and act for himself. He began to run along Whitehall, hoping to catch up with her at the next stop. But her bus was far ahead, and soon disappearing towards Parliament Square.

Throughout his training, they continued to write. Liberated from censorship and the need to be inventive, they proceeded cautiously. Impatient with living on the page, mindful of the difficulties, they were wary of getting ahead of the touch of hands and a single bus-stop kiss. They said they loved each other, used 'darling' and 'dearest', and knew their future was together, but they held back from wilder intimacies. Their business now was to remain connected until those two weeks. Through a Girton friend she found a cottage in Wiltshire they could borrow, and though they thought of little else in their moments of free time, they tried not to dream it away in their letters. Instead, they spoke of their routines. She was now on the maternity ward, and every day brought commonplace miracles, as well as moments of drama or hilarity. There were tragedies too, against which their own troubles faded to nothing: stillborn babies, mothers who died, young men weeping in the corridors, dazed mothers in their teens discarded by their families, infant deformities that evoked shame and love in confusing measure. When she described a happy outcome, that moment when the battle was over and an exhausted mother took the child in her arms for the first time, and gazed in rapture into a new face, it was the unspoken call to Cecilia's own future, the one she would share with him, which gave the writing its simple power, though in truth, his thoughts dwelled less on birth than conception.

He in turn described the parade ground, the rifle range, the drills, the 'bull', the barracks. He was not eligible for officer training, which was as well, for sooner or later he would have met someone in an officers' mess who knew about his past. In the ranks he was anonymous, and it turned out that to have been inside conferred a certain status. He discovered he was already well adapted to an army regime, to the terrors of kit inspection and the folding of blankets into precise squares, with the labels lined up. Unlike his fellows, he thought the food not bad at all. The days, though tiring, seemed rich in variety. The cross-country marches gave him a pleasure that he dared not express to the other recruits. He was gaining in weight and strength. His education and age marked him down, but his past made up for that and no one gave him trouble. Instead, he was regarded as a wise old bird who knew the ways of 'them', and who was handy when it came to filling out a form. Like her, he confined his letters to the daily round, interrupted by the funny or alarming anecdote: the recruit who came on parade with a boot missing; the sheep that ran amok in the barracks and could not be chased out, the sergeant instructor almost hit by a bullet on the range.

But there was one external development, one shadow that he had to refer to. After Munich last year, he was certain, like everyone else, that there would be a war. Their training was being streamlined and accelerated, a new camp was being enlarged to take more recruits. His anxiety was not for the fighting he might have to do, but the threat to their Wiltshire dream. She mirrored his fears with descriptions of contingency arrangements at the hospital – more beds, special courses, emergency drills. But for both of them there was also something fantastical about it all, remote even though likely. Surely not again, was what many people were saying. And so they continued to cling to their hopes.

There was another, closer matter that troubled him. Cecilia had not spoken to her parents, brother or sister since November 1935 when Robbie was sentenced. She would not write to them, nor would she let them know her address. Letters reached her through his mother who had sold the bungalow and moved to another village. It was through Grace that she let her family know she was well and did not wish to be contacted. Leon had come to the hospital once, but she would not speak to him. He waited outside the gates all afternoon. When she saw him, she retreated inside until he went away. The following morning he was outside the nurses' hostel. She pushed past him and would not even look in his direction. He took her elbow, but she wrenched her arm free and walked on, outwardly unmoved by his pleading.

Robbie knew better than anyone how she loved her brother, how close she was to her family, and how much the house and the park meant to her. He could never return, but it troubled him to think that she was destroying a part of herself for his sake. A month into his training he told her what was on his mind. It wasn't the first time they had been through this, but the issue had become clearer.

She wrote in reply, 'They turned on you, all of them, even my father. When they wrecked your life they wrecked mine. They chose to believe the evidence of a silly, hysterical little girl. In fact, they encouraged her by giving her no room to turn back. She was a young thirteen, I know, but I never want to speak to her again. As for the rest of them, I can never forgive what they did. Now that I've broken away, I'm beginning to understand the snobbery that lay behind their stupidity. My mother never forgave you your first. My father preferred to lose himself in his work. Leon turned out to be a grinning, spineless idiot who went along with everyone else. When Hardman decided to cover for Danny, no one in my family wanted the police to ask him the obvious questions. The police had you to prosecute. They didn't want their case messed up. I know I sound bitter, but my darling, I don't want to be. I'm honestly happy with my new life and my new friends. I feel I can breathe now. Most of all, I have you to live for. Realistically, there had to be a choice – you or them. How could it be both? I've never had a moment's doubt. I love you. I believe in you completely. You are my dearest one, my reason for life. Cee.'

He knew these last lines by heart and mouthed them now in the darkness. My reason for life. Not living, but life. That was the touch. And she was his reason for life, and why he must survive. He lay on his side, staring at where he thought the barn's entrance was, waiting for the first signs of light. He was too restless for sleep now. He wanted only to be walking to the coast.

There was no cottage in Wiltshire for them. Three weeks before his training ended, war was declared. The military response was automatic, like the reflexes of a clam. All leave was cancelled. Some time later, it was redefined as postponed. A date was given, changed, cancelled. Then, with twenty-four hours' notice, railway passes were issued. They had four days before reporting back for duty with their new regiment. The rumour was they would be on the move. She had tried to rearrange her holiday dates, and partly succeeded. When she tried again she could not be accommodated. By the time his card arrived, telling her of his arrival, she was on her way to Liverpool for a course in severe trauma nursing at the Alder Hey hospital. The day after he reached London he set out to follow her north, but the trains were impossibly slow. Priority was for military traffic moving southwards. At Birmingham New Street station he missed a connection and the next train was cancelled. He would have to wait until the following morning. He paced the platforms for half an hour in a turmoil of indecision. Finally, he chose to turn back. Reporting late for duty was a serious matter.

By the time she returned from Liverpool, he was disembarking at Cherbourg and the dullest winter of his life lay before him. The distress of course was shared between them, but she felt it her duty to be positive and soothing. 'I'm not going to go away,' she wrote in her first letter after Liverpool. 'I'll wait for you. Come back.' She was quoting herself. She knew he would remember. From that time on, this was how she ended every one of her letters to Robbie in France, right through to the last, which arrived just before the order came to fall back on Dunkirk.

It was a long bitter winter for the British Expeditionary Force in northern France. Nothing much happened. They dug trenches, secured supply lines and were sent out on night exercises that were farcical for the infantrymen because the purpose was never explained and there was a shortage of weapons. Off-duty, every man was a general. Even the lowliest private soldier had decided that the war would not be fought in the trenches again. But the anti-tank weapons that were expected never arrived. In fact, they had little heavy weaponry at all. It was a time of boredom and football matches against other units, and day-long marches along country roads with full pack, and nothing to do for hours on end but to keep in step and daydream to the beat of boots on asphalt. He would lose himself in thoughts of her, and plan his next letter, refining the phrases, trying to find comedy in the dullness.

It may have been the first touches of green along the French lanes, and the haze of bluebells glimpsed through the woods that made him feel the need for reconciliation and fresh beginnings. He decided he should try again to persuade her to make contact with her parents. She needn't forgive them, or go back over the old arguments. She should just write a short and simple letter, letting them know where and how she was. Who could tell what changes might follow over the years to come? He knew that if she did not make her peace with her parents before one of them died, her remorse would be endless. He would never forgive himself if he did not encourage her.

So he wrote in April, and her reply did not reach him until mid-May, when they were already falling back through their own lines, not long before the order came to retreat all the way to the Channel. There had been no contact with enemy fire. The letter was in his top pocket now. It was her last to reach him before the post delivery system broke down.

. . . I wasn't going to tell you about this now. I still don't know what to think and I wanted to wait until we're together. Now I have your letter, it doesn't make sense not to tell you. The first surprise is that Briony isn't at Cambridge. She didn't go up last autumn, she didn't take her place. I was amazed because I'd heard from Dr Hall that she was expected. The other surprise is that she's doing nurse's training at my old hospital. Can you imagine Briony with a bedpan? I suppose they all said the same thing about me. But she's such a fantasist, as we know to our cost. I pity the patient who receives an injection from her. Her letter is confused and confusing. She wants to meet. She's beginning to get the full grasp of what she did and what it has meant. Clearly, not going up has something to do with it. She's saying that she wants to be useful in a practical way. But I get the impression she's taken on nursing as a sort of penance. She wants to come and see me and talk. I might have this wrong, and that's why I was going to wait and go through this with you face to face, but I think she wants to recant. I think she wants to change her evidence and do it officially or legally. This might not even be possible, given that your appeal was dismissed. We need to know more about the law. Perhaps I should see a solicitor. I don't want us to get our hopes up for nothing. She might not mean what I think she does, or she might not be prepared to see it through. Remember what a dreamer she is.

I'll do nothing until I've heard from you. I wouldn't have told you any of this, but when you wrote to tell me again that I should be in touch with my parents (I admire your generous spirit), I had to let you know because the situation could change. If it's not legally possible for Briony to go before a judge and tell him she's had second thoughts, then she can at least go and tell our parents. Then they can decide what they want to do. If they can bring themselves to write a proper apology to you, then perhaps we may have the beginning of a new start.

I keep thinking of her. To go into nursing, to cut herself off from her background, is a bigger step for her than it was for me. I had my three years at Cambridge at least, and I had an obvious reason to reject my family. She must have her reasons too. I can't deny that I'm curious to find out. But I'm waiting for you, my darling, to tell me your thoughts. Yes, and by the way, she also said she's had a piece of writing turned down by Cyril Connolly at *Horizon*. So at least someone can see through her wretched fantasies.

Do you remember those premature twins I told you about? The smaller one died. It happened in the night, when I was on. The mother took it very badly indeed. We'd heard that the father was a bricklayer's mate, and I suppose we were expecting some cheeky little chap with a fag stuck on his lower lip. He'd been in East Anglia with contractors seconded to the army, building coastal defences, which was why he was so late coming to the hospital. He turned out to be a very handsome fellow, nineteen years old, more than six feet tall, with blond hair that flopped over his forehead. He has a club foot like Byron, which was why he hadn't joined up. Jenny said he looked like a Greek god. He was so sweet and gentle and patient comforting his young wife. We were all touched by it. The saddest part was that he was just getting somewhere, calming her down, when visiting time ended and Sister came through and made him leave along with everyone else. That left us to pick up the pieces. Poor girl. But four o'clock, and rules are rules.

I'm going to rush down with this to the Balham sorting office in the hope that it will be across the Channel before the weekend. But I don't want to end on a sad note. I'm actually very excited by this news about my sister and what it could mean for us. I enjoyed your story about the sergeants' latrines. I read that bit to the girls and they laughed like lunatics. I'm so glad the liaison officer has discovered your French and given you a job that makes use of it. Why did they take so long to find out about you? Did you hang back? You're right about French bread – ten minutes later and you're hungry again. All air and no substance. Balham isn't as bad as I said it was, but more about that next time. I'm enclosing a poem by Auden on the death of Yeats cut out from an old *London Mercury* from last year. I'm going down to see Grace at the weekend and I'll look in the boxes for your Housman. Must dash. You're in my thoughts every minute. I love you. I'll wait for you. Come back. Cee.

H e was woken by a boot nudging the small of his back. 'C'mon, Guv'nor. Rise and shine.'

He sat up and looked at his watch. The barn entrance was a rectangle of bluish-black. He had been asleep, he reckoned, for less than forty-five minutes. Mace diligently emptied the straw from the sacks and dismantled his table. They sat in silence on the hay bales smoking the first cigarette of the day. When they stepped outside they found a clay pot with a heavy wooden lid. Inside, wrapped in muslin cloth, was a loaf and a wedge of cheese. Turner divided the provisions right there with a bowie knife.

'In case we're separated,' he murmured.

A light was on already in the farmhouse and the dogs were in a frenzy as they walked away. They climbed a gate and began to cross a field in a northerly direction. After an hour they stopped in a coppiced wood to drink from their canteens and smoke. Turner studied the map. Already, the first bombers were high overhead, a formation of about fifty Heinkels, heading the same way to the coast. The sun was coming up and there was little cloud. A perfect day for the Luftwaffe. They walked in silence for another hour. There was no path, so he made a route by the compass, through fields of cows and sheep, turnips and young wheat. They were not as safe as he thought, away from the road. One field of cattle had a dozen shell craters, and fragments of flesh, bone and brindled skin had been blasted across a hundred-yard stretch. But each man was folded into his thoughts and no one spoke. Turner was troubled by the map. He guessed they were twenty-five miles from Dunkirk. The closer they came, the harder it would be to stay off the roads. Everything converged. There were rivers and canals to cross. When they headed for the bridges they would only lose time if they cut away across country again.

Just after ten they stopped for another rest. They had

climbed a fence to reach a track, but he could not find it on the map. It ran in the right direction anyway, over flat, almost treeless land. They had gone another half hour when they heard anti-aircraft fire a couple of miles ahead where they could see the spire of a church. He stopped to consult the map again.

Corporal Nettle said, 'It don't show crumpet, that map.'

'Ssh. He's having his doubts.'

Turner leaned his weight against a fence post. His side hurt whenever he put his right foot down. The sharp thing seemed to be protruding and snagging on his shirt. Impossible to resist probing with a forefinger. But he felt only tender, ruptured flesh. After last night, it wasn't right he should have to listen to the corporals' taunts again. Tiredness and pain were making him irritable, but he said nothing and tried to concentrate. He found the village on the map, but not the track, though it surely led there. It was just as he had thought. They would join the road, and they would need to stay on it all the way to the defence line at the Bergues-Furnes canal. There was no other route. The corporals' banter was continuing. He folded the map and walked on.

'What's the plan, Guv'nor?'

He did not reply.

'Oh, oh. Now you've offended her.'

Beyond the ack-ack, they heard artillery fire, their own, some way further to the west. As they approached the village they heard the sound of slow-moving lorries. Then they saw them, stretching in a line to the north, travelling at walking pace. It was going to be tempting to hitch a ride, but he knew from experience what an easy target they would be from the air. On foot you could see and hear what was coming.

Their track joined the road where it turned a right-angled corner to leave the village. They rested their feet for ten minutes, sitting on the rim of a stone water trough. Three- and ten-ton lorries, half-tracks and ambulances were grinding round the narrow turn at less than one mile an hour, and moving away from the village down a long straight road whose left side was flanked by plane trees. The road led directly north, towards a black cloud of burning oil that stood above the horizon, marking out Dunkirk. No need for a compass now. Dotted along the way were disabled military vehicles. Nothing was to be left for enemy use. From the backs of receding lorries the conscious wounded stared out blankly. There were also armoured cars, staff cars, Bren-gun carriers and motorbikes. Mixed in with them and stuffed or piled high with household gear and suitcases were civilian cars, buses, farm trucks and carts pushed by men and women or pulled by horses. The air was grey with diesel fumes, and straggling wearily through the stench, and for the moment moving faster than the traffic, were hundreds of soldiers, most of them carrying their rifles and their awkward greatcoats – a burden in the morning's growing warmth.

Walking with the soldiers were families hauling suitcases, bundles, babies, or holding the hands of children. The only human sound Turner heard, piercing the din of engines, was the crying of babies. There were old people walking singly. One old man in a fresh lawn suit, bow tie and carpet slippers shuffled by with the help of two sticks, advancing so slowly that even the traffic was passing him. He was panting hard. Wherever he was going he surely would not make it. On the far side of the road, right on the corner, was a shoe shop open for business. Turner saw a woman with a little girl at her side talking to a shop assistant who displayed a different shoe in the palm of each hand. The three paid no attention to the procession behind them. Moving against the flow, and now trying to edge round this same corner, was a column of armoured cars, the paintwork untouched by battle, heading south into the German advance. All they could hope to achieve against a Panzer division was an extra hour or two for the retreating soldiers.

Turner stood up, drank from his canteen and stepped into

the procession, slipping in behind a couple of Highland Light
Infantry men. The corporals followed him. He no longer felt
responsible for them now they had joined the main body of the
retreat. His lack of sleep exaggerated his hostility. Today their
teasing needled him and seemed to betray the comradeship
of the night before. In fact, he felt hostile to everyone around
him. His thoughts had shrunk to the small hard point of his
own survival.

Wanting to shake the corporals off, he quickened his pace,
overtook the Scotsmen and pushed his way past a group of
nuns shepherding a couple of dozen children in blue tunics.
They looked like the rump of a boarding school, like the one
he had taught at near Lille in the summer before he went up
to Cambridge. It seemed another man's life to him now. A
dead civilisation. First his own life ruined, then everybody
else's. He strode on angrily, knowing it was a pace he could
not maintain for long. He had been in a column like this before,
on the first day, and he knew what he was looking for. To his
immediate right was a ditch, but it was shallow and exposed.
The line of trees was on the other side. He slipped across, in
front of a Renault saloon. As he did so the driver leaned on
his horn. The shrill klaxon startled Turner into a sudden fury.
Enough! He leaped back to the driver's door and wrenched
it open. Inside was a trim little fellow in a grey suit and
fedora, with leather suitcases piled at his side and his family
jammed in the back seat. Turner grabbed the man by his tie
and was ready to smack his stupid face with an open right
hand, but another hand, one of some great strength, closed
about his wrist.

'That ain't the enemy, Guv'nor.'

Without releasing his grip, Corporal Mace pulled him away.
Nettle, who was just behind, kicked the Renault door shut
with such ferocity that the wing mirror fell off. The children
in blue tunics cheered and clapped.

The three crossed to the other side and walked on under the
line of trees. The sun was well up now and it was warm, but

the shade was not yet over the road. Some of the vehicles lying across the ditches had been shot up in air attacks. Around the abandoned lorries they passed, supplies had been scattered by troops looking for food or drink or petrol. Turner and the corporals tramped through typewriter ribbon spools spilling from their boxes, double-entry ledgers, consignments of tin desks and swivel chairs, cooking utensils and engine parts, saddles, stirrups and harnesses, sewing machines, football trophy cups, stackable chairs, and a film projector and petrol generator, both of which someone had wrecked with the crowbar that was lying nearby. They passed an ambulance, half in the ditch with one wheel removed. A brass plaque on the door said, 'This ambulance is a gift of the British residents of Brazil.'

It was possible, Turner found, to fall asleep while walking. The roar of lorry engines would be suddenly cut, then his neck muscles relaxed, his head drooped, and he would wake with a start and a swerve to his step. Nettle and Mace were for getting a lift. But he had already told them the day before what he had seen in that first column – twenty men in the back of a three-ton lorry killed with a single bomb. Meanwhile he had cowered in a ditch with his head in a culvert and caught the shrapnel in his side.

'You go ahead,' he said. 'I'm sticking here.'

So the matter was dropped. They wouldn't go without him – he was their lucky ticket.

They came up behind some more HLI men. One of them was playing the bagpipes, prompting the corporals to begin their own nasal whining parodies. Turner made as if to cross the road.

'If you start a fight, I'm not with you.'

Already a couple of Scots had turned and were muttering to each other.

'It's a braw bricht moonlicht nicht the nicht,' Nettle called out in Cockney. Something awkward might have developed then if they had not heard a pistol shot from up ahead. As they drew level the bagpipes fell silent. In a wide-open field the French cavalry had assembled in force and dismounted to form a long line. At the head stood an officer dispatching each horse with a shot to the head, and then moving on to the next. Each man stood to attention by his mount, holding his cap ceremonially against his chest. The horses patiently waited their turn.

This enactment of defeat depressed everyone's spirits further. The corporals had no heart for a tangle with the Scotsmen, who could no longer be bothered with them. Minutes later they passed five bodies in a ditch, three women, two children. Their suitcases lay around them. One of the women wore carpet slippers, like the man in the lawn suit. Turner looked away, determined not to be drawn in. If he was going to survive, he had to keep a watch on the sky. He was so tired, he kept forgetting. And it was hot now. Some men were letting their greatcoats drop to the ground. A glorious day. In another time this was what would have been called a glorious day. Their road was on a long slow rise, enough to be a drag on the legs and increase the pain in his side. Each step was a conscious decision. A blister was swelling on his left heel which forced him to walk on the edge of his boot. Without stopping, he took the bread and cheese from his bag, but he was too thirsty to chew. He lit another cigarette to curb his hunger and tried to reduce his task to the basics: you walked across the land until you came to the sea. What could be simpler, once the social element was removed? He was the only man on earth and his purpose was clear. He was walking across the land until he came to the sea. The reality was all too social, he knew; other men were pursuing him, but he had comfort in a pretence, and a rhythm at least for his feet. He walked / across /the land / until / he came / to the sea. A hexameter. Five iambs and an anapaest was the beat he tramped to now.

Another twenty minutes and the road began to level out. Glancing over his shoulder he saw the convoy stretching back down the hill for a mile. Ahead, he could not see the end of it. They crossed a railway line. By his map they were sixteen miles from the canal. They were entering a stretch where the wrecked equipment along the road was more or less continuous. Half a dozen twenty-five-pounder guns were piled beyond the ditch, as if swept up there by a heavy bulldozer. Up ahead where the land began to drop there was a junction with a back road and some kind of commotion was taking place. There was laughter from the soldiers on foot and raised voices at the roadside. As he came up, he saw a major from the Buffs, a pink-faced fellow of the old school, in his forties, shouting and pointing towards a wood that lay about a mile away across two fields. He was pulling men out of the column, or trying to. Most ignored him and kept going, some laughed at him, but a few were intimidated by his rank and had stopped, though he lacked any personal authority. They were gathered around him with their rifles, looking uncertain.

'You. Yes you. You'll do.'

The major's hand was on Turner's shoulder. He stopped and saluted before he knew what he was doing. The corporals were behind him.

The major had a little toothbrush moustache overhanging small, tight lips that clipped his words briskly. 'We've got Jerry trapped in the woods over there. He must be an advance party. But he's well dug in with a couple of machine guns. We're going to get in there and flush him out.'

Turner felt the horror chill and weaken his legs. He showed the major his empty palms.

'What with, sir?'

'With cunning and a bit of teamwork.'

How was the fool to be resisted? Turner was too tired to think, though he knew he wasn't going.

'Now, I've got the remains of two platoons halfway up the eastern . . .'

Remains was the word that told the story, and prompted Mace, with all his barrack-room skill, to interrupt.

'Beg pardon, sir. Permission to speak.'

'Not granted, corporal.'

'Thank you, sir. Orders is from GHQ. Proceed at haste and speed and celerity, without delay, diversion or divagation to Dunkirk for the purposes of immediate evacuation on account of being 'orribly and onerously overrun from all directions. Sir.'

The major turned and poked his forefinger into Mace's chest.

'Now look here you. This is our one last chance to show . . .'

Corporal Nettle said dreamily, 'It was Lord Gort what wrote out that order, sir, and sent it down personally.'

It seemed extraordinary to Turner that an officer should be addressed this way. And risky too. The major had not grasped that he was being mocked. He seemed to think that it was Turner who had spoken, for the little speech that followed was addressed to him.

'The retreat is a bloody shambles. For heaven's sake, man. This is your one last good chance to show what we can do when we're decisive and determined. What's more . . .'

He went on to say a good deal more, but it seemed to Turner that a muffling silence had descended on the bright late-morning scene. This time he wasn't asleep. He was looking past the major's shoulder towards the head of the column. Hanging there, a long way off, about thirty feet above the road, warped by the rising heat, was what looked like a plank of wood, suspended horizontally, with a bulge in its centre. The major's words were not reaching him, and nor were his own clear thoughts. The horizontal apparition hovered in the sky without growing larger, and though he was beginning to understand its meaning, it was, as in a dream, impossible to begin to respond or move his limbs. His only action had been to open his mouth, but he could make no sound, and would not have known what to say, even if he could.

Then, precisely at the moment when sound flooded back in, he was able to shout, 'Go!' He began to run directly towards the nearest cover. It was the vaguest, least soldierly form of advice, but he sensed the corporals not far behind. Dreamlike too was the way he could not move his legs fast enough. It was not pain he felt below his ribs, but something scraping against the bone. He let his greatcoat fall. Fifty yards ahead was a three-ton lorry on its side. That black greasy chassis, that bulbous differential was his only home. He didn't have long to get there. A fighter was strafing the length of the column. The broad spray of fire was advancing up the road at two hundred miles an hour, a rattling hail-storm din of cannon rounds hitting metal and glass. No one inside the near-stationary vehicles had started to react. Drivers were only just registering the spectacle through their windscreens. They were where he had been seconds before. Men in the backs of the lorries knew nothing. A sergeant stood in the centre of the road and raised his rifle. A woman screamed, and then fire was upon them just as Turner threw himself into the shadow of the upended lorry. The steel frame trembled as rounds hit it with the wild rapidity of a drum roll. Then the cannon fire swept on, hurtling down the column, chased by the fighter's roar and the flicker of its shadow. He pressed himself into the darkness of the chassis by the front wheel. Never had sump oil smelled sweeter. Waiting for another plane, he crouched foetally, his arms cradling his head and eyes tight shut, and thought only of survival.

But nothing came. Only the sounds of insects determined on their late-spring business, and birdsong resuming after a decent pause. And then, as if taking their cue from the birds, the wounded began to groan and call out, and terrified children began to cry. Someone, as usual, was cursing the RAF. Turner stood up and was dusting himself down when Nettle and Mace emerged and together they walked back towards the major who was sitting on the ground. All the colour had gone from his face, and he was nursing his right hand.

'Bullet went clean through it,' he said as they came up. 'Jolly lucky really.'

They helped him to his feet and offered to take him over to an ambulance where an RAMC captain and two orderlies were already seeing to the wounded. But he shook his head and stood there unaided. In shock he was talkative and his voice was softer.

'ME 109. Must have been his machine gun. The cannon would have blown my ruddy hand off. Twenty millimetre, you know. He must have strayed from his group. Spotted us on his way home and couldn't resist. Can't blame him, really. But it means there'll be more of them pretty soon.'

The half-dozen men he had gathered up before had picked themselves and their rifles out of the ditch and were wandering off. The sight of them recalled the major to himself.

'All right, chaps. Form up.'

They seemed quite unable to resist him and formed a line. Trembling a little now, he addressed Turner.

'And you three. At the double.'

'Actually, old boy, to tell the truth, I think we'd rather not.'

'Oh, I see.' He squinted at Turner's shoulder, seeming to see there the insignia of senior rank. He gave a good-natured salute with his left hand. 'In that case, sir, if you don't mind, we'll be off. Wish us luck.'

'Good luck, Major.'

They watched him march his reluctant detachment away towards the woods where the machine guns waited.

For half an hour the column did not move. Turner put himself at the disposal of the RAMC captain and helped on the stretcher parties bringing in the wounded. Afterwards he found places for them on the lorries. There was no sign of the corporals. He fetched and carried supplies from the back of an ambulance. Watching the captain at work, stitching a head wound, Turner felt the stirrings of his old ambitions. The quantity of blood obscured the textbook details he remembered. Along their stretch of road there were five injured and, surprisingly, no one dead, though the sergeant with the rifle was hit in the face and was not expected to live. Three vehicles had their front ends shot up and were pushed off the road. The petrol was siphoned off and, for good measure, bullets were fired through the tyres.

When all this was done in their section, there was still no movement up at the front of the column. Turner retrieved his greatcoat and walked on. He was too thirsty to wait about. An elderly Belgian lady shot in the knee had drunk the last of his water. His tongue was large in his mouth and all he could think of now was finding a drink. That, and keeping a watch on the sky. He passed sections like his own where vehicles were being disabled and the wounded were being lifted into lorries. He had been going for ten minutes when he saw Mace's head on the grass by a pile of dirt. It was about twenty-five yards away, in the deep green shadow of a stand of poplars. He went towards it, even though he suspected that it would be better for his state of mind to walk on. He found Mace and Nettle shoulder-deep in a hole. They were in the final stages of digging a grave. Lying face-down beyond the pile of earth was a boy of fifteen or so. A crimson stain on the back of his white shirt spread from neck to waist.

Mace leaned on his shovel and did a passable imitation. '"I think we'd rather not." Very good, Guv'nor. I'll remember that next time.'

'Divagation was nice. Where d'you get that one?'

'He swallowed a fucking dictionary,' Corporal Nettle said proudly.

'I used to like the crossword.'

'And 'orribly and onerously overrun?'

'That was a concert party they had in the sergeants' mess last Christmas.'

Still in the grave, he and Nettle sang tunelessly for Turner's benefit.

'Twas ostensibly ominous in the overview
To be 'orribly and onerously overrun.

Behind them the column was beginning to move.

'Better stick him in,' Corporal Mace said.

The three men lifted the boy down and set him on his back. Clipped to his shirt pocket was a row of fountain pens. The corporals didn't pause for ceremony. They began to shovel in the dirt and soon the boy had vanished.

Nettle said, 'Nice-looking kid.'

The corporals had bound two tent poles with twine to make a cross. Nettle banged it in with the back of his shovel. As soon as it was done they walked back to the road.

Mace said, 'He was with his grandparents. They didn't want him left in the ditch. I thought they'd come over and see him off like, but they're in a terrible state. We better tell them where he is.'

But the boy's grandparents were not to be seen. As they walked on, Turner took out the map and said, 'Keep watching the sky.' The major was right – after the Messerschmitt's casual pass, they would be back. They should have been back by now. The Bergues-Furnes canal was marked in thick bright blue on his map. Turner's impatience to reach it had become inseparable from his thirst. He would put his face in that blue and drink deeply. This thought put him in mind of childhood fevers, their wild and frightening logic, the search for the cool corner of the pillow, and his mother's hand upon his brow. Dear Grace. When he touched his own forehead the skin was papery and dry. The inflamation round his wound, he sensed, was growing, and the skin was becoming tighter, harder, with something, not blood, leaking out of it onto his shirt. He wanted to examine himself in private, but that was hardly possible here. The convoy was moving at its old inexorable pace. Their road ran straight to the coast – there would be no shortcuts now. As they drew closer, the black cloud, which surely came from a burning refinery in Dunkirk, was beginning to rule the northern sky. There was nothing to do but walk towards it. So he settled once more into silent head-down trudging.

The road no longer had the protection of the plane trees. Vulnerable to attack and without shade, it uncoiled across the undulating land in long shallow S shapes. He had wasted precious reserves in unnecessary talk and encounters. Tiredness had made him superficially elated and forthcoming. Now he reduced his progress to the rhythm of his boots – he walked across the land until he came to the sea. Everything that impeded him had to be outweighed, even if only by a fraction, by all that drove him on. In one pan of the scales, his wound, thirst, the blister, tiredness, the heat, the aching in his feet and legs, the Stukas, the distance, the Channel; in the other, *I'll wait for you*, and the memory of when she had said it, which he had come to treat like a sacred site. Also, the fear of capture. His most sensual memories – their few minutes in the library, the kiss in Whitehall – were bleached colourless through overuse. He knew by heart certain passages from her letters, he had revisited their tussle with the vase by the fountain, he remembered the warmth from her arm at the dinner when the twins went missing. These memories sustained him, but not so easily. Too often they reminded him of where he was when he last summoned them. They lay on the far side of a great divide in time, as significant as BC and AD. Before prison, before the war, before the sight of a corpse became a banality.

But these heresies died when he read her last letter. He touched his breast pocket. It was a kind of genuflection. Still there. Here was something new on the scales. That he could be cleared had all the simplicity of love. Merely tasting the possibility reminded him how much had narrowed and died. His taste for life, no less, all the old ambitions and pleasures. The prospect was of a rebirth, a triumphant return. He could become again the man who had once crossed a Surrey park at dusk in his best suit, swaggering on the promise of life, who had entered the house and with the clarity of passion made love to Cecilia – no, let him rescue the word from the corporals, they had fucked while others sipped their cocktails on the terrace. The story could resume, the one that he had been planning on that evening walk. He and Cecilia would no longer be isolated. Their love would have space and a society to grow in. He would not go about cap in hand to collect apologies from the friends who had shunned him. Nor would he sit back, proud and fierce, shunning them in return. He knew exactly how he would behave. He would simply resume. With his criminal record struck off, he could apply to medical college when the war was over, or even go for a commission now in the Medical Corps. If Cecilia made her peace with her family, he would keep his distance without seeming sour. He could never be on close terms with Emily or Jack. She had pursued his prosecution with a strange ferocity, while Jack turned away, vanished into his Ministry the moment he was needed.

None of that mattered. From here it looked simple. They were passing more bodies in the road, in the gutters and on the pavement, dozens of them, soldiers and civilians. The stench was cruel, insinuating itself into the folds of his clothes. The convoy had entered a bombed village, or perhaps the suburb of a small town – the place was rubble and it was impossible to tell. Who would care? Who could ever describe this confusion, and come up with the village names and the dates for the history books? And take the reasonable view and begin to assign the blame? No one would ever know what it was like to be here. Without the details there could be no larger picture. The abandoned stores, equipment and vehicles made an avenue of scrap that spilled across their path. With this, and the bodies, they were forced to walk in the centre of the road. That did not matter because the convoy was no longer moving. Soldiers were climbing out of troop carriers and continuing on foot, stumbling over brick and roof tiles. The wounded were left in the lorries to wait. There was a greater press of bodies in a narrower space, greater irritation. Turner kept his head down and followed the man in front, protectively folded in his thoughts.

He would be cleared. From the way it looked here, where you could hardly be bothered to lift your feet to step over a dead woman's arm, he did not think he would be needing apologies or tributes. To be cleared would be a pure state. He dreamed of it like a lover, with a simple longing. He dreamed of it in the way other soldiers dreamed of their hearths or allotments or old civilian jobs. If innocence seemed elemental here, there was no reason why it should not be so back in England. Let his name be cleared, then let everyone else adjust their thinking. He had put in time, now they must do the work. His business was simple. Find Cecilia and love her, marry her, and live without shame.

But there was one part in all this that he could not think through, one indistinct shape that the shambles twelve miles outside Dunkirk could not reduce to a simple outline. Briony. Here he came against the outer edge of what Cecilia called his generous spirit. And his rationality. If Cecilia were to be reunited with her family, if the sisters were close again, there would be no avoiding her. But could he accept her? Could he be in the same room? Here she was, offering a possibility of absolution. But it was not for him. He had done nothing wrong. It was for herself, for her own crime which her conscience could no longer bear. Was he supposed to feel grateful? And yes, of course, she was a child in nineteen thirty-five. He had told himself, he and Cecilia had told each other, over and again. Yes, she was just a child. But not every child sends a man to prison with a lie. Not every child is so purposeful and malign, so consistent over time, never wavering, never doubted. A child, but that had not stopped him daydreaming in his cell of her humiliation, of a dozen ways he might find revenge. In France once, in the bitterest week of winter, raging drunk on cognac, he had even conjured her onto the end of his bayonet. Briony and Danny Hardman. It was not reasonable or just to hate Briony, but it helped.

How to begin to understand this child's mind? Only one theory held up. There was a day in June 1932, all the more beautiful for coming suddenly, after a long spell of rain and wind. It was one of those rare mornings which declares itself, with a boastful extravagance of warmth and light and new leaves, as the true beginning, the grand portal to summer, and he was walking through it with Briony, past the Triton pond, down beyond the ha-ha and rhododendrons, through the iron kissing gate and onto the winding narrow woodland path. She was excited and talkative. She would have been about ten years old, just starting to write her little stories. Along with everyone else, he had received his own bound and illustrated tale of love, adversities overcome, reunion and a wedding. They were on their way down to the river for the swimming lesson he had promised her. As they left the house behind she may have been telling him about a story she had just finished or a book she was reading. She may have been holding his hand. She was a quiet, intense little girl, rather prim in her way, and this outpouring was unusual. He was happy to listen. These were exciting times for him too. He was nineteen, exams were almost over and he thought he'd done well. Soon he would cease to be a schoolboy. He had interviewed well at Cambridge and in two weeks he was leaving for France where he was to teach English at a religious school. There was a grandeur about the day, about the colossal, barely stirring beeches and oaks, and the light that dropped like jewels through the fresh foliage to make pools among last year's dead leaves. This magnificence, he sensed in his youthful self-importance, reflected the glorious momentum of his life.

She prattled on, and contentedly he half listened. The path emerged from the woods onto the broad grassy banks of the river. They walked upstream for half a mile and entered woods again. Here, on a bend in the river, below overhanging trees, was the pool, dug out in Briony's grandfather's time. A stone weir slowed the current and was a favourite diving and jumping-off place. Otherwise, it was not ideal for beginners. You went from the weir, or you jumped off the bank into nine feet of water. He dived in and trod water, waiting for her. They had started the lessons the year before, in late summer when the river was lower and the current sluggish. Now, even in the pool there was a steady rotating drift. She paused only for a moment, then jumped from the bank into his arms with a scream. She practised treading water until the current carried her against the weir, then he towed her across the pool so that she could start again. When she tried out her breast stroke after a winter of neglect, he had to support her, not easy when he was treading water himself. If he removed his hand from under her, she could only manage three or four strokes before sinking. She was amused by the fact that, going against the current, she swam to remain still. But she did not stay still. Instead, she was carried back each time to the weir, where she clung to a rusty iron ring, waiting for him, her white face vivid against the lurid mossy walls and greenish cement. Swimming uphill, she called it. She wanted to repeat the experience, but the water was cold and after fifteen minutes he'd had enough. He pulled her over to the bank and, ignoring her protests, helped her out.

He took his clothes from the basket and went a little way off into the woods to change. When he returned she was standing exactly where he had left her, on the bank, looking into the water, with her towel around her shoulders.

She said, 'If I fell in the river, would you save me?'

'Of course.'

He was bending over the basket as he said this and he heard, but did not see, her jump in. Her towel lay on the bank. Apart from the concentric ripples moving out across the pool, there was no sign of her. Then she bobbed up, snatched a breath and sank again. Desperate, he thought of running to the weir to fish her out from there, but the water was an opaque muddy green. He would only find her below the surface by touch. There was no choice – he stepped into the water, shoes, jacket and all. Almost immediately he found her arm, got his hand under her shoulder and heaved her up. To his surprise she was holding her breath. And then she was laughing joyously and clinging to his neck. He pushed her onto the bank and, with great difficulty in his sodden clothes, struggled out himself.

'Thank you,' she kept saying. 'Thank you, thank you.'

'That was a bloody stupid thing to do.'

'I wanted you to save me.'

'Don't you know how easily you could have drowned?'

'You saved me.'

Distress and relief were charging his anger. He was close to shouting. 'You stupid girl. You could have killed us both.'

She fell silent. He sat on the grass, emptying the water from his shoes. 'You went under the surface, I couldn't see you. My clothes were weighing me down. We could have drowned, both of us. Is it your idea of a joke? Well, is it?'

There was nothing more to say. She got dressed and they went back along the path, Briony first, and he squelching behind her. He wanted to get into the open sunlight of the park. Then he faced a long trudge back to the bungalow for a change of clothes. He had not yet spent his anger. She was not too young, he thought, to get her mind around an apology. She walked in silence, head lowered, possibly sulking, he could not see. When they came out of the woods and had gone through the kissing gate, she stopped and turned. Her tone was forthright, even defiant. Rather than sulk, she was squaring up to him.

'Do you know why I wanted you to save me?'

'No.'

'Isn't it obvious?'

'No, it isn't.'

'Because I love you.'

She said it bravely, with chin upraised, and she blinked rapidly as she spoke, dazzled by the momentous truth she had revealed.

He restrained an impulse to laugh. He was the object of a schoolgirl crush. 'What on earth do you mean by that?'

'I mean what everybody else means when they say it. I love you.'

This time the words were on a pathetic rising note. He realised that he should resist the temptation to mock. But it was difficult. He said, 'You love me, so you threw yourself in the river.'

'I wanted to know if you'd save me.'

'And now you know. I'd risk my life for yours. But that doesn't mean I love you.'

She drew herself up a little. 'I want to thank you for saving my life. I'll be eternally grateful to you.'

Lines, surely, from one of her books, one she had read lately, or one she had written.

He said, 'That's all right. But don't do it again, for me or anyone else. Promise?'

She nodded, and said in parting, 'I love you. Now you know.'

She walked away towards the house. Shivering in the sunlight, he watched her until she was out of sight, and then he set off for home. He did not see her on her own before he left for France, and by the time he came back in September, she was away at boarding school. Not long after, he went up to Cambridge, and in December spent Christmas with friends. He didn't see Briony until the following April, and by then the matter was forgotten.

Or was it?

He'd had plenty of time alone, too much time, to consider. He could remember no other unusual conversation with her, no strange behaviour, no meaningful looks or sulks to suggest that her schoolgirlish passion had lasted beyond that day in June. He had been back to Surrey almost every vacation and she had many opportunities to seek him out at the bungalow, or pass him a note. He was busy with his new life then, lost to the novelties of undergraduate life, and also intent at that time on putting a little distance between himself and the Tallis family. But there must have been signs which he had not noticed. For three years she must have nurtured a feeling for him, kept it hidden, nourished it with fantasy or embellished it in her stories. She was the sort of girl who lived in her thoughts. The drama by the river might have been enough to sustain her all that time.

This theory, or conviction, rested on the memory of a single encounter – the meeting at dusk on the bridge. For years he had dwelled on that walk across the park. She would have known he was invited to dinner. There she was, barefoot, in a dirty white frock. That was strange enough. She would have been waiting for him, perhaps preparing her little speech, even rehearsing it out loud as she sat on the stone parapet. When he finally arrived, she was tongue-tied. That was proof of a sort. Even at the time, he thought it odd that she did not speak to him. He gave her the letter and she ran off. Minutes later, she was opening it. She was shocked, and not only by a word. In her mind he had betrayed her love by favouring her sister. Then, in the library, confirmation of the worst, at which point, the whole fantasy crashed. First, disappointment and despair, then a rising bitterness. Finally, an extraordinary opportunity in the dark, during the search for the twins, to avenge herself. She named him – and no one but her sister and his mother doubted her. The impulse, the flash of malice, the infantile destructiveness he could understand. The wonder was the depth of the girl's rancour, her persistence with a story that saw him all the way to Wandsworth prison. Now he might be cleared, and that gave him joy. He acknowledged the courage it would require for her to go back to the law and deny the evidence she had given under oath. But he did not think his resentment of her could ever be erased. Yes, she was a child at the time, and he did not forgive her. He would never forgive her. That was the lasting damage.

There was more confusion ahead, more shouting. Incredibly, an armoured column was forcing its way against the forward press of traffic, soldiers and refugees. The crowd parted reluctantly. People squeezed into the gaps between abandoned vehicles or against shattered walls and doorways. It was a French column, hardly more than a detachment – three armoured cars, two half-tracks and two troop carriers. There was no show of common cause. Among the British troops the view was that the French had let them down. No will to fight for their own country. Irritated at being pushed aside, the tommies swore, and taunted their allies with shouts of 'Maginot!' For their part, the *poilus* must have heard rumours of an evacuation. And here they were, being sent to cover the rear. 'Cowards! To the boats! Go shit in your pants!' Then they were gone, and the crowd closed in again under a cloud of diesel smoke and walked on.

They were approaching the last houses in the village. In a field ahead, he saw a man and his collie dog walking behind a horse-drawn plough. Like the ladies in the shoe shop, the farmer did not seem aware of the convoy. These lives were lived in parallel – war was a hobby for the enthusiasts and no less serious for that. Like the deadly pursuit of a hunt to hounds, while over the next hedge a woman in the back seat of a passing motor car was absorbed in her knitting, and in the bare garden of a new house a man was teaching his son to kick a ball. Yes, the ploughing would still go on and there'd be a crop, someone to reap it and mill it, others to eat it, and not everyone would be dead . . .

Turner was thinking this when Nettle gripped his arm and pointed. The commotion of the passing French column had covered the sound, but they were easy enough to see. There were at least fifteen of them, at ten thousand feet, little dots in the blue, circling above the road. Turner and the corporals stopped to watch, and everyone nearby saw them too.

An exhausted voice murmured close to his ear, 'Fuck. Where's the RAF?'

Another said knowingly, 'They'll go for the Frogs.'

As if goaded into disproof, one of the specks peeled away and began its near-vertical dive, directly above their heads. For seconds the sound did not reach them. The silence was building like pressure in their ears. Even the wild shouts that went up and down the road did not relieve it. Take cover! Disperse! Disperse! At the double!

It was difficult to move. He could walk on at a steady trudge, and he could stop, but it was an effort, an effort of memory, to reach for the unfamiliar commands, to turn away from the road and run. They had stopped by the last house in the village. Beyond the house was a barn and flanking both was the field where the farmer had been ploughing. Now he was standing under a tree with his dog, as though sheltering from a shower of rain. His horse, still in harness, grazed along the unploughed strip. Soldiers and civilians were streaming away from the road in all directions. A woman brushed past him carrying a crying child, then she changed her mind and came back and stood, turning indecisively at the side of the road. Which way? The farmyard or the field? Her immobility delivered him from his own. As he pushed her by the shoulder towards the gate, the rising howl commenced. Nightmares had become a science. Someone, a mere human, had taken the time to dream up this satanic howling. And what success! It was the sound of panic itself, mounting and straining towards the extinction they all knew, individually, to be theirs. It was a sound you were obliged to take personally. Turner guided the woman through the gate. He wanted her to run with him into the centre of the field. He had touched her, and made her decision for her, so now he felt he could not abandon her. But the boy was at least six years old and heavy, and together they were making no progress at all.

He dragged the child from her arms. 'Come on,' he shouted.

A Stuka carried a single thousand-pound bomb. The idea on the ground was to get away from buildings, vehicles and other people. The pilot was not going to waste his precious load on a lone figure in a field. When he turned back to strafe it would be another matter. Turner had seen them hunt down a sprinting man for the sport of it. With a free hand he was pulling on the woman's arm. The boy was wetting his pants and screaming in Turner's ear. The mother seemed incapable of running. She was stretching out her hand and shouting. She wanted her son back. The child was wriggling towards her, across his shoulder. Now came the screech of the falling bomb. They said that if you heard the noise stop before the explosion, your time was up. As he dropped to the grass he pulled the woman with him and shoved her head down. He was half lying across the child as the ground shook to the unbelievable roar. The shock wave prised them from the earth. They covered their faces against the stinging spray of dirt. They heard the Stuka climb from its dive even as they heard the banshee wail of the next attack. The bomb had hit the road less than eighty yards away. He had the boy under his arm and he was trying to pull the woman to her feet.

'We've got to run again. We're too close to the road.'

The woman answered but he did not understand her. Again they were stumbling across the field. He felt the pain in his side like a flash of colour. The boy was in his arms, and again the woman seemed to be dragging back, and trying to get her son from him. There were hundreds in the field now, all making for the woods on the far side. At the shrill whine of the bomb everyone cowered on the ground. But the woman had no instinct for danger and he had to pull her down again. This time they were pressing their faces into freshly turned earth. As the screech grew louder the woman shouted what sounded like a prayer. He realised then that she wasn't speaking French. The explosion was on the far side of the road, more than a hundred and fifty yards away. But now the first Stuka was turning over the village and dropping for the strafe. The boy had gone silent with shock. His mother wouldn't stand. Turner pointed to the Stuka coming in over the rooftops. They were right in its path and there was no time for argument. She wouldn't move. He threw himself down into the furrow. The rippling thuds of machine-gun fire in the ploughed earth and the engine roar flashed past them. A wounded soldier was screaming. Turner was on his feet. But the woman would not take his hand. She sat on the ground and hugged the boy tightly to her. She was speaking Flemish to him, soothing him, surely telling him that everything was going to be all right. Mama would see to that. Turner didn't know a single word of the language. It would have made no difference. She paid him no attention. The boy was staring at him blankly over his mother's shoulder.

Turner took a step back. Then he ran. As he floundered across the furrows the attack was coming in. The rich soil was clinging to his boots. Only in nightmares were feet so heavy. A bomb fell on the road, way over in the centre of the village, where the lorries were. But one screech hid another, and it hit the field before he could go down. The blast lifted him forwards several feet and drove him face-first into the soil. When he came to, his mouth and nose and ears were filled with dirt. He was trying to clear his mouth, but he had no saliva. He used a finger, but that was worse. He was gagging on the dirt, then he was gagging on his filthy finger.

He blew the dirt from his nose. His snot was mud and it covered his mouth. But the woods were near, there would be streams and waterfalls and lakes in there. He imagined a paradise. When the rising howl of a diving Stuka sounded again, he struggled to place the sound. Was it the all-clear? His thoughts too were clogged. He could not spit or swallow, he could not easily breathe, and he could not think. Then, at the sight of the farmer with his dog still waiting patiently under the tree, it came back to him, he remembered everything and he turned to look back. Where the woman and her son had been was a crater. Even as he saw it, he thought he had always known. That was why he had to leave them. His business was to survive, though he had forgotten why. He kept on towards the woods.

He walked a few steps into the tree cover, and sat in the new undergrowth with his back to a birch sapling. His only thought was of water. There were more than two hundred people sheltering in the woods, including some wounded who had dragged themselves in. There was a man, a civilian, not far off, crying and shouting in pain. Turner got up and moved further away. All the new greenery spoke to him only of water. The attack continued on the road and over the village. He cleared away old leaves and used his helmet to dig. The soil was damp but no water oozed into the hole he had made, even when it was eighteen inches deep. So he sat and thought about water and tried to clean his tongue against his sleeve. When a Stuka dived, it was impossible not to tense and shrink, though each time he thought he didn't have the strength. Towards the end they came over to strafe the woods, but to no effect. Leaves and twigs tumbled from the canopy. Then the planes were gone, and in the huge silence that loomed over the fields and trees and the village, there was not even birdsong. After a while, from the direction of the road came blasts of a whistle for the all-clear. But no one moved. He remembered this from last time. They were too dazed, they were in shock from repeated episodes of terror.

Each dive brought every man, cornered and cowering, to face his execution. When it did not come, the trial had to be lived through all over again and the fear did not diminish. For the living, the end of a Stuka attack was the paralysis of shock, of repeated shocks. The sergeants and junior officers might come around shouting and kicking the men into standing. But they were drained and, for a good while, useless as troops.

So he sat there in a daze like everyone else, just as he had the first time, outside the village whose name he could not remember. These French villages with Belgian names. When he was separated from his unit and, what was worse for an infantryman, from his rifle. How many days ago? There could be no way of knowing. He examined his revolver which was clogged with dirt. He removed the ammunition and tossed the gun into the bushes. After a time there was a sound behind him and a hand was on his shoulder.

'Here you go. Courtesy of the Green Howards.'

Corporal Mace was passing him some dead man's water bottle. Since it was almost full he used the first swig to rinse out his mouth, but that was a waste. He drank the dirt with the rest.

'Mace, you're an angel.'

The corporal extended a hand to pull him up. 'Got to shift. There's a rumour the fucking Belgians have collapsed. We might get cut off from the east. Still miles to go.'

As they were walking back across the field, Nettle joined them. He had a bottle of wine and an Amo bar which they passed around.

'Nice bouquet,' Turner said when he had drunk deeply.

'Dead Frog.'

The peasant and his collie were back behind the plough. The three soldiers approached the crater where the smell of cordite was strong. The hole was a perfectly symmetrical inverted cone whose sides were smooth, as though finely sieved and raked. There were no human signs, not a shred of clothing or shoe leather. Mother and child had been vaporised. He paused to absorb this fact, but the corporals were in a hurry and pushed him on and soon they joined the stragglers on the road. It was easier now. There would be no traffic until the sappers took their bulldozers into the village. Ahead, the cloud of burning oil stood over the landscape like an angry father. High-flying bombers droned above, a steady two-way stream moving into and returning from their target. It occurred to Turner that he might be walking into a slaughter. But everyone was going that way, and he could think of no alternative. Their route was taking them well to the right of the cloud, to the east of Dunkirk, towards the Belgian border.

'Bray Dunes,' he said, remembering the name from the map.

Nettle said, 'I like the sound of those.'

They passed men who could barely walk for their blisters. Some were barefoot. A soldier with a bloody chest wound reclined in an ancient pram pushed by his mates. A sergeant was leading a carthorse over the back of which was draped an officer, unconscious or dead, his feet and wrists secured by ropes. Some troops were on bicycles, most walked in twos or threes. A dispatch rider from the Highland Light Infantry came by on a Norton. His bloodied legs dangled uselessly, and his pillion passenger, who had heavily bandaged arms, was working the foot pedals. All along the way were discarded greatcoats, left there by men too hot to carry them. Turner had already talked the corporals out of leaving theirs.

They had been going for an hour when they heard behind them a rhythmic thudding, like the ticking of a gigantic clock. They turned to look back. At first sight it seemed that an enormous horizontal door was flying up the road towards them. It was a platoon of Welsh Guards in good order, rifles at the slope, led by a second-lieutenant. They came by at a forced march, their gaze fixed forwards, their arms swinging high. The stragglers stood aside to let them through. These were cynical times, but no one risked a catcall. The show of discipline and cohesion was shaming. It was a relief when the Guards had pounded out of sight and the rest could resume their introspective trudging.

The sights were familiar, the inventory was the same, but now there was more of everything; vehicles, bomb craters, detritus. There were more bodies. He walked across the land until – he caught the taste of the sea, carried across the flat, marshy fields on a freshening breeze. The one-way flow of people with a single purpose, the constant self-important traffic in the air, the extravagant cloud advertising their destination, suggested to his tired but overactive mind some long-forgotten childhood treat, a carnival or sports event on which they were all converging. There was a memory that he could not place, of being carried on his father's shoulders, up a hill towards a great attraction, towards the source of a huge excitement. He would like those shoulders now. His missing father had left few memories. A knotted neck-scarf, a certain smell, the vaguest outline of a brooding, irritable presence. Did he avoid serving in the Great War, or did he die somewhere near here under another name? Perhaps he survived. Grace was certain he was too cowardly, too shifty, to join up, but she had her own reason to be bitter. Nearly every man here had a father who remembered northern France, or was buried in it. He wanted such a father, dead or alive. Long ago, before the war, before Wandsworth, he used to revel in his freedom to make his own life, devise his own story with only the distant help of Jack Tallis. Now he understood how conceited a delusion this was. Rootless, therefore futile. He wanted a father, and for the same reason, he wanted to be a father. It was common enough, to see so much death and want a child. Common, therefore human, and he wanted it all the more. When the wounded were screaming, you dreamed of sharing a little house somewhere, of an ordinary life, a family line, connection. All around him men were walking silently with their thoughts, reforming their lives, making resolutions. If I ever get out of this lot . . . They could never be counted, the dreamed-up children, mentally conceived on the walk into Dunkirk, and later made flesh. He would find Cecilia. Her address was on the letter in his pocket, next to the poem. *In the deserts of the heart/Let the healing fountain start*. He would find his father too. They were supposed to be good at tracking down missing persons, the Salvation Army. A perfect name. He would track down his father, or his dead father's story – either way, he would become his father's son.

They walked all afternoon until at last, a mile ahead, where grey and yellow smoke billowed up from surrounding fields, they saw the bridge across the Bergues-Furnes canal. All the way in now, not a farmhouse or barn was left standing. As well as smoke, a miasma of rotting meat drifted towards them – more slaughtered cavalry horses, hundreds of them, in a heap in a field. Not far from them was a smouldering mountain of uniforms and blankets. A beefy lance-corporal with a sledgehammer was smashing typewriters and mimeograph machines. Two ambulances were parked at the side of the road, their back doors open. From inside came the groans and shouts of wounded men. One of them was crying out, over and over, more in rage than pain, 'Water, I want water!' Like everyone else, Turner kept going.

The crowds were bunching up again. In front of the canal bridge was a junction, and from the Dunkirk direction, on the road that ran along the canal, came a convoy of three-ton lorries which the military police were trying to direct into a field beyond where the horses were. But troops swarming across the road forced the convoy to a halt. The drivers leaned on their horns and shouted insults. The crowd pressed on. Men tired of waiting, scrambled off the backs of the lorries. There was a shout of, Take cover! And before anyone could even glance round, the mountain of uniforms was detonated. It began to snow tiny pieces of dark green serge. Nearer, a detachment of artillery men were using hammers to smash up the dial sights and breech blocks of their guns. One of them, Turner noticed, was crying as he destroyed his howitzer. At the entrance to the same field, a chaplain and his clerk were dousing cases of prayer books and bibles with petrol. Men were crossing the field towards a NAAFI dump, looking for cigarettes and booze. When a shout went up, dozens more left the road to join them. One group sat by a farm gate, trying on new shoes. A soldier with crammed cheeks pushed past Turner with a box of pink and white marshmallows. A hundred yards away a dump of wellington boots, gas masks and capes was fired, and acrid smoke enveloped the line of men pushing forwards to the bridge. At last the lorries were on the move and turned into the biggest field, immediately south of the canal. Military police were organising the parking, lining up the rows, like stewards at a county show. The lorries were joining half-tracks, motorbikes, Bren-gun carriers and mobile kitchens. The disabling methods were, as always, simple – a bullet in the radiator, and the engine left running until it seized up.

The bridge was held by the Coldstream Guards. Two neatly sandbagged machine-gun posts covered the approach. The men were clean-shaven, stone-eyed, silently contemptuous of the filthy disorganised rabble trailing by. On the other side of the canal, evenly spaced, white-painted stones marked out a path to a hut being used as an orderly room. On the far bank, to the east and west, the Guards were well dug in along their section. Waterfront houses had been commandeered, roof tiles punched out, and windows sandbagged for machine-gun slits. A fierce sergeant was keeping order on the bridge. He was sending back a lieutenant on a motorbike. Absolutely no equipment or vehicles allowed. A man with a parrot in a cage was turned away. The sergeant was also pulling out men for perimeter defence duties, and doing it with far more authority than the poor major. A growing detachment stood unhappily at ease by the orderly room. Turner saw what was happening at the same time as the corporals, when they were still a good way back.

'They'll fucking have you, mate,' Mace said to Turner. 'Poor bloody infantry. If you want to go home to the crumpet, get between us and limp.'

Feeling dishonourable, but determined all the same, he put his arms round the corporals' shoulders and they staggered forwards.

'It's your left, remember, Guv'nor,' Nettle said. 'Would you like me to pop my bayonet through your foot?'

'Thanks awfully. I think I can manage.'

Turner let his head droop as they were crossing the bridge so he saw nothing of the duty sergeant's ferocious gaze, though he felt its heat. He heard the barked command, ''Ere, you!' Some unfortunate just behind him was pulled out to help hold off the onslaught which must surely come within two or three days, while the last of the BEF was piling into the boats. What he did see while his head was lowered was a long black barge slipping under the bridge in the direction of Furnes in Belgium. The boatman sat at his tiller smoking a pipe, looking stolidly ahead. Behind him, ten miles away, Dunkirk burned. Ahead, in the prow, two boys were bending over an upturned bike, mending a puncture perhaps. A line of washing which included women's smalls was hanging out to dry. The smell of cooking, of onions and garlic, rose from the boat. Turner and the corporals crossed the bridge and passed the whitewashed rocks, a reminder of training camp and all the bull. In the orderly hut a phone was ringing.

Mace murmured, 'You bloody well limp till we're out of sight.'

But the land was flat for miles and there was no telling which way the sergeant might be looking, and they didn't like to turn around to check. After half an hour they sat down on a rusty seed drill and watched the defeated army walk by. The idea was to get in among a completely fresh crowd, so that Turner's sudden recovery did not attract the attention of an officer. A lot of men who passed were irritated at not finding the beach just beyond the canal. They seemed to think it was a failure of planning. Turner knew from the map there were another seven miles, and once they were on the move again, they were the hardest, the dreariest they had walked that day. The wide featureless land denied all sense of progress. Though the late afternoon sun was slipping through the trailing edges of the oil cloud, it was warmer than ever. They saw planes high over the port dropping their bombs. Worse, there were Stuka attacks right over the beach they were heading towards. They passed the walking wounded who could go no further. They sat like beggars at the side of the road, calling out for help, or for a mouthful of water. Others just lay by the ditch, unconscious, or lost in hopelessness. Surely there would be ambulances coming up from the defence perimeter, making regular runs to the beach. If there was time to whitewash rocks, there must be time to organise that. There was no water. They had finished the wine and now their thirst was all the greater. They carried no medicines. What were they expected to do? Carry a dozen men on their backs when they could barely walk themselves?

In sudden petulance, Corporal Nettle sat down in the road, took off his boots and flung them into a field. He said he hated them, he fucking hated them more than all the fucking Germans put together. And his blisters were so bad he was better off with fuck all.

'It's a long way to England in your socks,' Turner said. He felt weirdly light-headed as he went into the field to search. The first boot was easy to find, but the second took him a while. At last he saw it lying in the grass near a black furry shape that seemed, as he approached, to be moving or pulsing. Suddenly a swarm of bluebottles rose into the air with an angry whining buzz, revealing the rotting corpse beneath. He held his breath, snatched the boot, and as he hurried away the flies settled back down and there was silence again.

After some coaxing, Nettle was persuaded to take back his

boots, tie them together and carry them round his neck. But
he did this, he said, only as a favour to Turner.

I t was in his clear moments he was troubled. It wasn't
the wound, though it hurt at every step, and it wasn't
the dive-bombers circling over the beach some miles to the
north. It was his mind. Periodically, something slipped. Some
everyday principle of continuity, the humdrum element that
told him where he was in his own story, faded from his
use, abandoning him to a waking dream in which there
were thoughts, but no sense of who was having them. No
responsibility, no memory of the hours before, no idea of what
he was about, where he was going, what his plan was. And
no curiosity about these matters. He would then find himself
in the grip of illogical certainties.

He was in this state as they came round the eastern edge
of the resort after three hours' walking. They went down
a street of shattered glass and broken tiles where children
were playing and watching the soldiers go by. Nettle had
put his boots back on, but he had left them loose, with the
laces trailing. Suddenly, like a jack-in-a-box, a lieutenant
from the Dorsets popped up from the cellar of a municipal
building that had been requisitioned for a headquarters. He
came towards them at a self-important clip with an attaché
case under his arm. When he stopped in front of them they
saluted. Scandalised, he ordered the corporal to tie his laces
immediately or face a charge.

While the corporal knelt to obey, the lieutenant – round-
shouldered, bony, with a desk-bound look and a wisp of
ginger moustache – said, 'You're a bloody disgrace, man.'

In the lucid freedom of his dream state, Turner intended

246

to shoot the officer through the chest. It would be better
for everybody. It was hardly worth discussing the matter
in advance. He reached for it, but his gun had gone – he
couldn't remember where – and the lieutenant was already
walking away.

After minutes of noisy crunching over glass, there was
sudden silence under their boots where the road ended in fine
sand. As they rose through a gap in the dunes, they heard the
sea and tasted a salty mouthful before they saw it. The taste
of holidays. They left the path and climbed through the dune
grass to a vantage point where they stood in silence for many
minutes. The fresh damp breeze off the Channel restored him
to clarity. Perhaps it was nothing more than his temperature
rising and falling in fits.

He thought he had no expectations – until he saw the beach.
He'd assumed that the cussed army spirit which whitewashed
rocks in the face of annihilation would prevail. He tried to
impose order now on the random movement before him,
and almost succeeded: marshalling centres, warrant officers
behind makeshift desks, rubber stamps and dockets, roped-off
lines towards the waiting boats; hectoring sergeants, tedious
queues around mobile canteens. In general, an end to all
private initiative. Without knowing it, that was the beach
he had been walking to for days. But the actual beach, the
one he and the corporals gazed on now, was no more than a
variation on all that had gone before: there was a rout, and
this was its terminus. It was obvious enough now they saw it
– this was what happened when a chaotic retreat could go no
further. It only took a moment to adjust. He saw thousands of
men, ten, twenty thousand, perhaps more, spread across the
vastness of the beach. In the distance they were like grains of
black sand. But there were no boats, apart from one upturned
whaler rolling in the distant surf. It was low tide and almost
a mile to the water's edge. There were no boats by the long
jetty. He blinked and looked again. That jetty was made of
men, a long file of them, six or eight deep, standing up to

their knees, their waists, their shoulders, stretching out for five hundred yards through the shallow waters. They waited, but there was nothing in sight, unless you counted in those smudges on the horizon – boats burning after an air attack. There was nothing that could reach the beach in hours. But the troops stood there, facing the horizon in their tin hats, rifles lifted above the waves. From this distance they looked as placid as cattle.

And these men were a small proportion of the total. The majority were on the beach, moving about aimlessly. Little clusters had formed around the wounded left by the last Stuka attack. As aimless as the men, half a dozen artillery horses galloped in a pack along the water's edge. A few troops were attempting to right the upturned whaler. Some had taken off their clothes to swim. Off to the east was a football game, and from the same direction came the feeble sound of a hymn being sung in unison, then fading. Beyond the football game was the only sign of official activity. On the shore, lorries were being lined up and lashed together to form a makeshift jetty. More lorries were driving down. Nearer, up the beach, individuals were scooping sand with their helmets to make foxholes. In the dunes, close to where Turner and the corporals stood, men had already dug themselves holes from which they peeped out, proprietorial and smug. Like marmots, he thought. But the majority of the army wandered about the sands without purpose, like citizens of an Italian town in the hour of the *passeggio*. They saw no immediate reason to join the enormous queue, but they were unwilling to come away from the beach in case a boat should suddenly appear.

To the left was the resort of Bray, a cheerful front of cafés and little shops that in a normal season would be renting out beach chairs and pedal bikes. In a circular park with a neatly mowed lawn was a bandstand, and a merry-go-round painted red, white and blue. In this setting, another, more insouciant company had hunkered down. Soldiers had opened up the cafés for themselves and were getting drunk at the tables outside, bawling and laughing. Men were larking about on the bikes along a pavement stained with vomit. A colony of drunks was spread out on the grass by the bandstand, sleeping it off. A solitary sunbather in his underpants, face-down on a towel, had patches of uneven sunburn on his shoulders and legs – pink and white like a strawberry and vanilla ice-cream.

It was not difficult to choose between these circles of suffering – the sea, the beach, the front. The corporals were already walking away. Thirst alone decided it. They found a path on the landward side of the dunes, then they were crossing a sandy lawn strewn with broken bottles. As they were making a way round the raucous tables Turner saw a naval party coming along the front and stopped to watch. There were five of them, two officers, three ratings, a gleaming group of fresh white, blue and gold. No concessions to camouflage. Straight-backed and severe, revolvers strapped to their belts, they moved with tranquil authority through the mass of sombre battledress and grimy faces, looking from side to side as if conducting a count. One of the officers made notes on a clipboard. They headed away towards the beach. With a childish feeling of abandonment, Turner watched them until they were out of sight.

He followed Mace and Nettle into the din and fumy stench of the first bar along the front. Two suitcases propped open on the bar were full of cigarettes – but there was nothing to drink. The shelves along the sandblasted mirror behind the bar were empty. When Nettle ducked behind the counter to rummage around, there were jeers. Everyone coming in had tried the same. The drink had long gone with the serious drinkers outside. Turner pushed through the crowd to a small kitchen at the back. The place was wrecked, the taps were dry. Outside was a pissoir and stacked crates of empties. A dog was trying to get its tongue inside an empty sardine can, pushing it across a patch of concrete. He turned and went back to the main room and its roar of voices. There was no electricity, only natural light which was stained brown, as though by the absent beer. Nothing to drink, but the bar remained full. Men came in, were disappointed and yet they stayed, held there by free cigarettes and the evidence of recent booze. The dispensers dangled empty on the wall where the inverted bottles had been wrenched away. The sweet smell of liquor rose from the sticky cement floor. The noise and press of bodies and damp tobacco air satisfied a homesick yearning for a Saturday night pub. This was the Mile End Road, and Sauchiehall Street, and everywhere in between.

He stood in the din, uncertain what to do. It would be such an effort, to fight his way out of the crowd. There were boats yesterday, he gathered from a snatch of conversation, and perhaps again tomorrow. Standing on tiptoe by the kitchen doorway, he gave a no-luck shrug across the crowd towards the corporals. Nettle cocked his head in the direction of the door and they began to converge on it. A drink would have been fine, but what interested them now was water. Progress through the press of bodies was slow, and then, just as they converged, their way to the door was blocked by a tight wall of backs forming around one man.

He must have been short – less than five foot six – and Turner could see nothing of him apart from a portion of the back of his head.

Someone said, 'You answer the fucking question, you little git.'

'Yeah, go on then.'

'Oi, Brylcreem job. Where was ya?'

'Where were you when they killed my mate?'

A globule of spittle hit the back of the man's head and fell behind his ear. Turner moved round to get a view. He saw first the grey-blue of a jacket, and then the mute apprehension in the man's face. He was a wiry little fellow with thick, unclean lenses in his glasses which magnified his frightened stare. He looked like a filing clerk, or a telephone operator, perhaps from a headquarters long-ago dispersed. But he was in the RAF and the tommies held him accountable. He turned slowly, gazing at the circle of his interrogators. He had no answers to their questions, and he made no attempt to deny his responsibility for the absence of Spitfires and Hurricanes over the beach. His right hand clutched his cap so hard his knuckles trembled. An artillery man standing by the door gave him a hard push in the back so that he stumbled across the ring into the chest of a soldier who sent him back with a casual punch to the head. There was a hum of approval. Everyone had suffered, and now someone was going to pay.

'So where's the RAF?'

A hand whipped out and slapped the man's face, knocking his glasses to the floor. The sound of the blow was precise as a whip-crack. It was a signal for a new stage, a new level of engagement. His naked eyes shrank to fluttering little dots as he went down to grope around his feet. That was a mistake. A kick from a steel-capped army boot caught him on the backside, lifting him an inch or two. There were chuckles all round. A sense of something tasty about to happen was spreading across the bar and drawing more soldiers in. As the crowd swelled around the circle, any remaining sense of individual responsibility fell away. A swaggering recklessness was taking hold. A cheer went up as someone stubbed his cigarette on the fellow's head. They laughed at his comic yelp. They hated him and he deserved everything that was coming his way. He was answerable for the Luftwaffe's freedom of the skies, for every Stuka attack, every dead friend. His slight frame contained every cause of an army's defeat. Turner assumed there was nothing he could do to help the man without risking a lynching himself. But it was impossible to do nothing. Joining in would be better than nothing. Unpleasantly excited, he strained forward. Now, a tripping Welsh accent proposed the question.

'Where's the RAF?'

It was eerie that the man had not shouted for help, or

pleaded, or protested his innocence. His silence seemed like collusion in his fate. Was he so dim that it had not occurred to him that he might be about to die? Sensibly, he had folded his glasses into his pocket. Without them his face was empty. Like a mole in bright light, he peered around at his tormentors, his lips parted, more in disbelief than in an attempt to form a word. Because he could not see it coming, he took a blow to the face full-on. It was a fist this time. As his head flipped back, another boot cracked into his shin and a little sporting cheer went up, with some uneven applause, as though for a decent catch in the slips on the village green. It was madness to go to the man's defence, it was loathsome not to. At the same time, Turner understood the exhilaration among the tormentors and the insidious way it could claim him. He himself could do something outrageous with his bowie knife and earn the love of a hundred men. To distance the thought he made himself count the two or three soldiers in the circle he reckoned bigger or stronger than himself. But the real danger came from the mob itself, its righteous state of mind. It would not be denied its pleasures.

A situation had now been reached in which whoever threw the next hit had to earn general approval by being ingenious or funny. There was an eagerness in the air to .please by being creative. No one wanted to strike a false note. For a few seconds these conditions imposed restraint. And at some point soon, Turner knew from his Wandsworth days, the single blow would become a cascade. Then there would be no turning back, and for the RAF man, only one end. A pink blotch had formed on the cheekbone under his right eye. He had drawn his fists up under his chin – he was still gripping his cap – and his shoulders were hunched. It may have been a protective stance, but it was also a gesture of weakness and submission which was bound to provoke greater violence. If he had said something, anything at all, the troops surrounding him might have remembered that he was a man, not a rabbit to be skinned. The Welshman who had spoken was a short, thickset fellow from the sappers. He now produced a belt of canvas webbing and held it up.

'What do you think, lads?'

His precise, insinuating delivery suggested horrors that Turner could not immediately grasp. Now was his last chance to act. As he looked around for the corporals, there was a roar from close by, like the bellowing of a speared bull. The crowd swayed and stumbled as Mace barged through them into the circle. With a wild hollering yodelling sound, like Johnny Weissmuller's Tarzan, he picked up the clerk from behind in a bear hug, lifting him eighteen inches clear of the ground and shook the terrified creature from side to side. There were cheers and whistles, foot-stamping and Wild West whoops.

'I know what I want to do with him,' Mace boomed. 'I want to drown him in the bloody sea!'

In response, there rose another storm of hooting and stamping. Nettle was suddenly at Turner's side and they exchanged a look. They guessed what Mace was about and they began to move towards the door, knowing they would have to be quick. Not everyone was in favour of the drowning idea. Even in the frenzy of the moment, some could still recall that the tide line was a mile away across the sands. The Welshman in particular felt cheated. He was holding up his webbing and shouting. There were catcalls and boos as well as cheers. Still holding his victim in his arms, Mace rushed for the door. Turner and Nettle were ahead of him, making a path through the crowd. When they reached the entrance – usefully, a single, not a double, door – they let Mace through, then they blocked the way, shoulder to shoulder, though they appeared not to, for they were shouting and shaking their fists like the rest. They felt against their backs a colossal and excited human weight which they could only resist for a matter of seconds. This was long enough for Mace to run, not towards the sea, but sharp left, and left again, up a narrow street that curved behind the shops and bars, away from the front.

The exultant crowd exploded from the bar like champagne,

hurling Turner and Nettle aside. Someone thought he saw Mace down on the sands, and for half a minute the crowd went that way. By the time the mistake was realised and the crowd began to turn back, there was no sign of Mace and his man. Turner and Nettle had melted away too.

The vast beach, the thousands waiting on it, and the sea empty of boats returned the tommies to their predicament. They emerged from a dream. Away to the east where the night was rising, the perimeter line was under heavy artillery fire. The enemy was closing in and England was a long way off. In the failing light not much time remained to find somewhere to bed down. A cold wind was coming in off the Channel, and the greatcoats lay on the roadsides far inland. The crowd began to break up. The RAF man was forgotten.

It seemed to Turner that he and Nettle had set out to look for Mace, and then forgot about him. They must have wandered the streets for a while, wanting to congratulate him on the rescue and share the joke of it. Turner did not know how he and Nettle came to be here, in this particular narrow street. He remembered no intervening time, no sore feet – but here he was, addressing in the politest terms an old lady who stood in the doorway of a flat-fronted terraced house. When he mentioned water, she looked at him suspiciously, as though she knew he wanted more than water. She was rather handsome, with dark skin, a proud look and a long straight nose, and a floral scarf was tied across her silver hair. He understood immediately she was a gypsy who was not fooled by his speaking French. She looked right into him and saw his faults, and knew he'd been in prison. Then she glanced with distaste at Nettle, and at last pointed along the street to where a pig was nosing around in the gutter.

'Bring her back,' she said, 'and I'll see what I have for you.'

'Fuck that,' Nettle said once Turner had translated. 'We're only asking for a cup of bloody water. We'll go in and take it.'

But Turner, feeling a familiar unreality taking hold, could not discount the possibility that the woman was possessed of certain powers. In the poor light the space above her head was pulsing to the rhythm of his own heart. He steadied himself against Nettle's shoulder. She was setting him a test he was too experienced, too wary, to refuse. He was an old hand. So close to home, he was not falling for any traps. Best to be cautious.

'We'll get the pig,' he said to Nettle. 'It'll only take a minute.'

Nettle was long used to following Turner's suggestions, for they were generally sound, but as they went up the street the corporal was muttering, 'There's something not right with you, Guv'nor.'

Their blisters made them slow. The sow was young and quick and fond of her freedom. And Nettle was frightened of her. When they had it cornered in a shop doorway, she ran at him and he leaped aside with a scream that was not all self-mockery. Turner went back to the lady for a length of rope, but no one came to the door and he wasn't certain that he had the right house. However, he was certain now that if they did not capture the pig, they would never get home. He was running a temperature again, he knew, but that did not make him wrong. The pig equalled success. As a child, Turner had once tried to persuade himself that preventing his mother's sudden death by avoiding the pavement cracks outside his school playground was a nonsense. But he had never trodden on them and she had not died.

As they advanced up the street, the pig remained just beyond their reach.

'Fuck it,' Nettle said. 'We can't be doing with this.'

But there was no choice. By a fallen telegraph pole Turner cut off a length of cable and made a noose. They were pursuing the sow along a road on the edge of the resort where bungalows were fronted by small patches of gardens surrounded by fences. They went along opening every front gate on both sides of the street. Then they took a detour down a side road in order to get round the pig and chase it back the way it had come. Sure enough, it soon stepped into a garden and began rooting it up. Turner closed the gate and, leaning over the fence, dropped the noose over the pig's head.

It took all their remaining strength to drag the squealing sow back home. Fortunately, Nettle knew where it lived. When it was finally secure in the tiny sty in her back garden, the old woman brought out two stone flagons of water. Watched by her they stood in bliss in her little yard by the kitchen door and drank. Even when their bellies seemed about to burst, their mouths craved more and they drank on. Then the woman brought them soap, flannels and two enamel bowls to wash in. Turner's hot face changed the water to rusty brown. Scabs of dried blood moulded to his upper lip came away satisfyingly whole. When he was done he felt a pleasing lightness in the air around him which slipped silkily over his skin and through his nostrils. They tipped the dirty water away onto the base of a clump of snapdragons which, Nettle said, made him homesick for his parents' back garden. The gypsy filled their canteens and brought them each a litre of red wine with the corks half pulled and a saucisson which they stowed in their haversacks. When they were about to take their leave she had another thought and went back inside. She returned with two small paper bags, each containing half a dozen sugared almonds.

Solemnly, they shook hands.

'For the rest of our lives we will remember your kindness,' Turner said.

She nodded, and he thought she said, 'My pig will always remind me of you.' The severity of her expression did not alter, and there was no telling whether there was insult or humour or a hidden message in her remark. Did she think they were not worthy of her kindness? He backed away awkwardly, and then they were walking down the street

and he was translating her words for Nettle. The corporal
had no doubts.

'She lives alone and she loves her pig. Stands to reason.
She's very grateful to us.' Then he added suspiciously, 'Are
you feeling all right, Guv'nor?'

'Extremely well, thank you.'

Troubled by their blisters, they limped back in the direction
of the beach with the idea of finding Mace and sharing the
food and drink. But having caught the pig, Nettle thought, it
was fair dos to crack open a bottle now. His faith in Turner's
judgment had been restored. They passed the wine between
them as they went along. Even in the late dusk, it was still
possible to make out the dark cloud over Dunkirk. In the other
direction, they could now see gun flashes. There was no let-up
along the defence perimeter.

'Those poor bastards,' Nettle said.

Turner knew he was talking about the men outside the
makeshift orderly room. He said, 'The line can't hold much
longer.'

'We'll be overrun.'

'So we'd better be on a boat tomorrow.'

Now they were no longer thirsty, dinner was on their
minds. Turner was thinking of a quiet room and a square
table covered with a green gingham cloth, with one of those
French ceramic oil lamps suspended from the ceiling on a
pulley. And the bread, wine, cheese and saucisson spread out
on a wooden board.

He said, 'I'm wondering if the beach would really be the
best place for dinner.'

'We could get robbed blind,' Nettle agreed.

'I think I know the kind of place we need.'

They were back in the street behind the bar. When they
glanced along the alley they had run down, they saw figures
moving in the half light outlined against the last gleam of the
sea, and far beyond them and to one side, a darker mass that
may have been troops on the beach or dune grass or even the

dunes themselves. It would be hard enough to find Mace by daylight, and impossible now. So they wandered on, looking for somewhere. In this part of the resort now there were hundreds of soldiers, many of them in loud gangs drifting through the streets, singing and shouting. Nettle slid the bottle back into his haversack. They felt more vulnerable without Mace.

They passed a hotel that had taken a hit. Turner wondered if it was a hotel room he had been thinking of. Nettle was seized by the idea of dragging out some bedding. They went in through a hole in the wall, and picked their way through the gloom, across rubble and fallen timbers, and found a staircase. But scores of men had the same idea. There was actually a queue forming up at the bottom of the stairs, and soldiers struggling down with heavy horsehair mattresses. On the landing above – Turner and Nettle could just see boots and lower legs moving stiffly from side to side – a fight was developing, with wrestling grunts and a smack of knuckles on flesh. Following a sudden shout, several men fell backwards down the stairs onto those waiting below. There was laughter as well as cursing, and people were getting to their feet and feeling their limbs. One man did not get up, but lay awkwardly across the stairs, his legs higher than his head, and screaming hoarsely, almost inaudibly, as though in a panicky dream. Someone held a lighter to his face and they saw his bared teeth and flecks of white in the corners of his mouth. He had broken his back, someone said, but there was nothing anyone could do, and now men were stepping over him with their blankets and bolsters, and others were jostling to go up.

They came away from the hotel and turned inland again, back towards the old lady and her pig. The electricity supply from Dunkirk must have been cut, but round the edges of some heavily curtained windows they saw the ochre glow of candlelight and oil lamps. On the other side of the road soldiers were knocking at doors, but no one would open up now. This was the moment Turner chose to describe to Nettle the kind of place that he had in mind for dinner. He embellished to make his point, adding French windows open onto a wrought-iron balcony through which an ancient wisteria threaded, and a gramophone on a round table covered by a green chenille cloth, and a Persian rug spread across a chaise longue. The more he described, the more certain he was that the room was close by. His words were bringing it into being.

Nettle, his front teeth resting on his lower lip in a look of kindly rodent bafflement, let him finish and said, 'I knew it. I fucking knew it.'

They were standing outside a bombed house whose cellar was half open to the sky and had the appearance of a gigantic cave. Grabbing him by his jacket, Nettle pulled him down a scree of broken bricks. Cautiously, he guided him across the cellar floor into the blackness. Turner knew this was not the place, but he could not resist Nettle's unusual determination. Ahead, there appeared a point of light, then another, and a third. The cigarettes of men already sheltering there.

A voice said, 'Geh. Bugger off. We're full.'

Nettle struck a match and held it up. All around the walls there were men, propped in a sitting position, most of them asleep. A few were lying in the centre of the floor, but there was still room, and when the match went out he pressed down on Turner's shoulders to make him sit. As he was pushing debris away from under his buttocks, Turner felt his soaked shirt. It may have been blood, or some other fluid, but for the moment there was no pain. Nettle arranged the greatcoat around Turner's shoulders. Now the weight was off his feet, an ecstasy of relief spread upwards through his knees and he knew he would not move again that night, however disappointed Nettle might be. The rocking motion of daylong walking transferred itself to the floor. Turner felt it tilt and buck beneath him as he sat in total darkness. The problem now was to eat without being set upon. To survive was to be selfish. But he did nothing for the moment and his mind emptied. After a while Nettle nudged him awake and slipped the bottle of wine into his hands. He got his mouth around the opening, tipped the bottle and drank. Someone heard him swallowing.

'What's that you got?'

'Sheep's milk,' Nettle said. 'Still warm. Have some.'

There was a hawking sound, and something tepid and jelly-like landed on the back of Turner's hand. 'You're filthy, you are.'

Another voice, more threatening, said, 'Shut up. I'm trying to sleep.'

Moving soundlessly, Nettle groped in his haversack for the saucisson, cut it into three and passed a piece to Turner with a chunk of bread. He stretched out full length on the concrete floor, pulled his greatcoat over his head to contain the smell of the meat as well as the sound of his chewing, and in the fug of his own breathing, and with pieces of brick and grit pressing into his cheek, began to eat the best meal of his life. There was a smell of scented soap on his face. He bit into the bread that tasted of army canvas, and tore and sucked at the sausage. As the food reached his stomach a bloom of warmth opened across his chest and throat. He had been walking these roads, he thought, all his life. When he closed his eyes he saw moving asphalt and his boots swinging in and out of view. Even as he chewed, he felt himself plunging into sleep for seconds on end. He entered another stretch of time, and now, lying snugly on his tongue, was a sugared almond, whose sweetness belonged to another world. He heard men complaining of the cold in the cellar and he was glad of the coat tucked around him, and felt a fatherly pride that he had stopped the corporals throwing theirs away.

A group of soldiers came in looking for shelter and striking matches, just as he and Nettle had. He felt unfriendly towards them and irritated by their West Country accents. Like everyone else in the cellar, he wanted them to go away.

But they found a place somewhere beyond his feet. He caught a whiff of brandy and resented them more. They were noisy organising their sleeping places, and when a voice from along the wall called out, 'Fucking yokels,' one of the newcomers lurched in that direction and for a moment it seemed there would be a rumble. But the darkness and the weary protests of the residents held the peace.

Soon there were only the sounds of steady breathing and snores. Beneath him the floor still seemed to list, then switch to the rhythm of a steady march, and once again Turner found himself too afflicted by impressions, too fevered, too exhausted to sleep. Through the material of his coat he felt for the bundle of her letters. *I'll wait for you. Come back.* The words were not meaningless, but they didn't touch him now. It was clear enough – one person waiting for another was like an arithmetical sum, and just as empty of emotion. Waiting. Simply one person doing nothing, over time, while another approached. Waiting was a heavy word. He felt it pressing down, heavy as a greatcoat. Everyone in the cellar was waiting, everyone on the beach. She was waiting, yes, but then what? He tried to make her voice say the words, but it was his own he heard, just below the tread of his heart. He could not even form her face. He forced his thoughts towards the new situation, the one that was supposed to make him happy. The intricacies were lost to him, the urgency had died. Briony would change her evidence, she would rewrite the past so that the guilty became the innocent. But what was guilt these days? It was cheap. Everyone was guilty, and no one was. No one would be redeemed by a change of evidence, for there weren't enough people, enough paper and pens, enough patience and peace, to take down the statements of all the witnesses and gather in the facts. The witnesses were guilty too. All day we've witnessed each other's crimes. You killed no one today? But how many did you leave to die? Down here in the cellar we'll keep quiet about it. We'll sleep it off, Briony. His sugared almond tasted of her name which seemed so quaintly improbable that he wondered if he had remembered it correctly. Cecilia's too. Had he always taken for granted the strangeness of these names? Even this question was hard to hold for long. He had so much unfinished business here in France that it seemed to him sensible to delay his departure for England, even though his bags were packed, his strange, heavy bags. No one would see them if he left them here and went back. Invisible baggage. He must go back and get the boy from the tree. He had done it before. He had gone back where no one else was and found the boys under a tree and carried Pierrot on his shoulders and Jackson in his arms, across the park. So heavy! He was in love, with Cecilia, with the twins, with success and the dawn and its curious glowing mist. And what a reception party! Now he was used to such things, a roadside commonplace, but back then, before the coarsening and general numbness, when it was a novelty and when everything was new, he felt it sharply. He cared when she ran out across the gravel and spoke to him by the open police car door. *Oh, when I was in love with you, Then I was clean and brave.* So he would go back the way he had come, walk back through the reverses of all they had achieved, across the drained and dreary marshes, past the fierce sergeant on the bridge, through the bombed-up village, and along the ribbon road that lay across the miles of undulating farmland, watching for the track on the left on the edge of the village, opposite the shoe shop, and two miles on, go over the barbed-wire fence and through the woods and fields to an overnight stop at the brothers' farm, and next day, in yellow morning light, on the swing of a compass needle, hurry through that glorious country of little valleys and streams and swarming bees, and take the rising footpath to the sad cottage by the railway. And the tree. Gather up from the mud the pieces of burned, striped cloth, the shreds of his pyjamas, then bring him down, the poor pale boy, and make a decent burial. A nice-looking kid. Let the guilty bury the innocent, and let no one change the evidence. And where was Mace to help with the digging? That brave bear, Corporal Mace. Here was more unfinished business and another reason why he could not leave. He must find Mace. But first he must cover the miles again, and go back north to the field where the farmer and his dog still walked behind the plough, and ask the Flemish lady and her son if they held him accountable for their deaths. For one can assume too much sometimes, in fits of conceited self-blame. She might say no – the Flemish for no. You tried to help us. You couldn't carry us across the field. You carried the twins, but not us, no. No, you are not guilty. No.

There was a whisper, and he felt the breath of it on his burning face. 'Too much noise, Guv'nor.'

Behind Corporal Nettle's head was a wide strip of deep blue sky and, etched against it, the ragged black edge of the cellar's ruined ceiling.

'Noise? What was I doing?'

'Shouting "no" and waking everyone up. Some of these lads was getting a bit peeved.'

He tried to lift his head and found that he couldn't. The corporal struck a match.

'Christ. You look fucking terrible. Come on. Drink.'

He raised Turner's head and put the canteen to his lips.

The water tasted metallic. When he was done, a long steady oceanic swell of exhaustion began to push him under. He walked across the land until he fell in the ocean. In order not to alarm Nettle, he tried to sound more reasonable than he really felt.

'Look, I've decided to stay on. There's some business I need to see to.'

With a dirty hand, Nettle was wiping Turner's forehead. He saw no reason why Nettle should think it necessary to put his face, his worried ratty face, so close to his own.

The corporal said, 'Guv'nor, can you hear me? Are you listening? About an hour ago I went out for a slash. Guess what I saw. There was the navy coming down the road, putting out the call for officers. They're getting organised on the beach. The boats are back. We're going home, mate. There's a lieutenant from the Buffs here who's marching us down at seven. So get some sleep and no more of your bloody shouting.'

He was falling now and sleep was all he wanted, a thousand hours of sleep. It was easier. The water was vile, but it helped and so did the news and Nettle's soothing whisper. They would be forming up in the road outside and marching to the beach. Squaring off to the right. Order would prevail. No one at Cambridge taught the benefits of good marching order. They revered the free, unruly spirits. The poets. But what did the poets know about survival? About surviving as a body of men. No breaking ranks, no rushing the boats, no first come first served, no devil take the hindmost. No sound of boots as they crossed the sand to the tide line. In the rolling surf, willing hands to steady the gunwale as their mates climbed in. But it was a tranquil sea, and now that he himself was calm, of course he saw how fine it really was that she was waiting. Arithmetic be damned. *I'll wait for you* was elemental. It was the reason he had survived. It was the ordinary way of saying she would refuse all other men. Only you. *Come back.* He remembered the feel of the gravel through his thin-soled shoes, he could feel it now, and the icy touch of the handcuffs on his wrists. He and the inspector stopped by the car and turned at the sound of her steps. How could he forget that green dress, how it clung to the curve of her hips and hampered her running and showed the beauty of her shoulders. Whiter than the mist. It didn't surprise him that the police let them talk. He didn't even think about it. He and Cecilia behaved as though they were alone. She would not let herself cry when she was telling him that she believed him, she trusted him, she loved him. He said to her simply that he would not forget this, by which he meant to tell her how grateful he was, especially then, especially now. Then she put a finger on the handcuffs and said she wasn't ashamed, there was nothing to be ashamed of. She took a corner of his lapel and gave it a little shake and this was when she said, 'I'll wait for you. Come back.' She meant it. Time would show she really meant it. After that they pushed him into the car, and she spoke hurriedly, before the crying began that she could no longer hold back, and she said that what had happened between them was theirs, only theirs. She meant the library, of course. It was theirs. No one could take it away. 'It's our secret,' she called out, in front of them all, just before the slam of the door.

'I won't say a word,' he said, though Nettle's head had long disappeared from his view. 'Wake me before seven. I promise, you won't hear another word from me.'

Part Three

The unease was not confined to the hospital. It seemed to rise with the turbulent brown river swollen by the April rains, and in the evenings lay across the blacked-out city like a mental dusk which the whole country could sense, a quiet and malign thickening, inseparable from the cool late spring, well concealed within its spreading beneficence. Something was coming to an end. The senior staff, conferring in self-important groups at the corridor intersections, were nursing a secret. Younger doctors were a little taller, their stride more aggressive, and the consultant was distracted on his round, and on one particular morning crossed to the window to gaze out across the river for minutes on end, while behind him the nurses stood to attention by the beds and waited. The elderly porters seemed depressed as they pushed the patients to and from the wards, and seemed to have forgotten their chirpy catch-phrases from the wireless comedy shows, and it might even have consoled Briony to hear again that line of theirs she so despised – Cheer up love, it might never happen.

But it was about to. The hospital had been emptying slowly, invisibly, for many days. It seemed purely chance at first, an epidemic of good health that the less intelligent of the trainees were tempted to put down to their own improving techniques. Only slowly did one detect a design. Empty beds spread across the ward, and through other wards, like deaths in the night. Briony imagined that retreating footsteps in the wide polished corridors had a muffled, apologetic sound, where once they had been bright and efficient. The workmen who came to install new drums of fire hose on the landings outside the lifts, and set out new buckets of fire-fighting sand, laboured all day, without a break, and spoke to no one before they left, not even the porters. In the ward, only eight beds out of twenty were occupied, and though the work was even harder than before, a certain disquiet, an almost superstitious dread, prevented the student nurses from complaining when they were alone together at tea. They were all generally calmer, more accepting. They no longer spread their hands to compare chilblains.

In addition, there was the constant and pervasive anxiety the trainees shared about making mistakes. They all lived in fear of Sister Marjorie Drummond, of the menacing meagre smile and softening of manner that preceded her fury. Briony knew she had recently accumulated a string of errors. Four days ago, despite careful instruction, a patient in her care had quaffed her carbolic gargle – according to the porter who saw it, down in one like a pint of Guinness – and was violently sick across her blankets. Briony was also aware that she had been observed by Sister Drummond carrying only three bedpans at a time, when by now they were expected to go the length of the ward reliably with a pile of six, like a busy waiter in La Coupole. There may have been other errors too, which she would have forgotten in her weariness, or never even known about. She was prone to errors of·deportment – in moments of abstraction she tended to shift her weight onto one foot in a way that particularly enraged her superior. Lapses and failures could carelessly accrue over several days: a broom improperly stowed, a blanket folded with its label facing up, a starched collar in infinitesimal disarray, the bed castors not lined up and pointing inwards, walking back down the ward empty-handed – all silently noted, until capacity was reached and then, if you had not read the signs, the wrath would come down as a shock. And just when you thought you were doing well.

But lately, the sister was not casting her mirthless smile in the direction of the probationers, nor speaking to them in the subdued voice that gave them such terrors. She hardly bothered with her charges at all. She was preoccupied, and often stood in the quadrangle by men's surgical, in long conferences with her counterpart, or she disappeared for two days at a time.

In another context, a different profession, she would have seemed motherly in her plumpness, or even sensual, for her unpainted lips were rich in natural colour and sweetly bowed, and her face with its rounded cheeks and doll's patches of healthy pink suggested a kindly nature. This impression was dispelled early on when a probationer in Briony's year, a large, kindly, slow-moving girl with a cow's harmless gaze, met the lacerating force of the ward sister's fury. Nurse Langland had been seconded to the men's surgical ward, and was asked to help prepare a young soldier for an appendectomy. Left alone with him for a minute or two, she chatted and made reassuring remarks about his operation. He must have asked the obvious question, and that was when she broke the hallowed rule. It was set out clearly in the handbook, though no one had guessed how important it was considered to be. Hours later, the soldier came round from his anaesthetic and muttered the student nurse's name while the surgical ward sister was standing close by. Nurse Langland was sent back to her own ward in disgrace. The others were made to gather round and take careful note. If poor Susan Langland had carelessly or cruelly killed two dozen patients, it could not have been worse for her. By the time Sister Drummond finished telling her that she was an abomination to the traditions of Nightingale nursing to which she aspired, and should consider herself lucky to be spending the next month sorting soiled linen, not only Langland, but half the girls present were weeping.

Briony was not among them, but that night in bed, still a little shivery, she went through the handbook again, to see if there were other points of etiquette she might have missed. She reread and committed to memory the commandment: in no circumstances should a nurse communicate to a patient her Christian name.

The wards emptied, but the work intensified. Every morning the beds were pushed into the centre so that the probationers could polish the floor with a heavy bumper that a girl on her own could barely swing from side to side. The floors were to be swept three times a day. Vacated lockers were scrubbed, mattresses fumigated, brass coat-hooks, doorknobs and keyholes were buffed. The woodwork – doors as well as skirting – was washed down with carbolic solution, and so were the beds themselves, the iron frames as well as springs. The students scoured, wiped and dried bedpans and bottles till they shone like dinner plates. Army three-ton lorries drew up at the loading bays, bringing yet more beds, filthy old ones that needed to be scrubbed down many times before they were carried into the ward and squeezed into the lines, and then carbolised. Between tasks, perhaps a dozen times a day, the students scrubbed their cracked and bleeding chilblained hands under freezing water. The war against germs never ceased. The probationers were initiated into the cult of hygiene. They learned that there was nothing so loathsome as a wisp of blanket fluff hiding under a bed, concealing within its form a battalion, a whole division, of bacteria. The everyday practice of boiling, scrubbing, buffing and wiping became the badge of the students' professional pride, to which all personal comfort must be sacrificed.

The porters brought up from the loading bays a great quantity of new supplies which had to be unpacked, inventoried and stowed – dressings, kidney bowls, hypodermics, three new autoclaves and many packages marked 'Bunyan Bags' whose use had not yet been explained. An extra medicine cupboard was installed and filled, once it had been scrubbed three times over. It was locked, and the key remained with Sister Drummond, but one morning Briony saw inside rows of bottles labelled morphine. When she was sent on errands, she saw other wards in similar states of preparation. One was already completely empty of patients, and gleamed in spacious silence, waiting. But it was not done to ask questions. The year before, just after war was declared, the wards on the top floor had been closed down completely as a protection against bombing. The operating theatres were now in the basement. The ground-floor windows had been sandbagged, and every skylight cemented over.

An army general made a tour of the hospital with half a dozen consultants at his side. There was no ceremony, or even silence when they came. Usually on such important visits, so it was said, the nose of every patient had to be in line with the centre creasing of the top sheet. But there was no time to prepare. The general and his party strode through the ward, murmuring and nodding, and then they were gone.

The unease grew, but there was little opportunity for speculation, which in any case was officially forbidden. When they were not on their shifts, the probationers were in lessons in their free time, or lectures, or at practical demonstrations or studying alone. Their meals and bedtimes were supervised as if they were new girls at Roedean. When Fiona, who slept in the bed next to Briony, pushed her plate away and announced to no one in particular that she was 'clinically incapable' of eating vegetables boiled with an Oxo cube, the Nightingale home sister stood over her until she had eaten the last scrap. Fiona was Briony's friend, by definition; in the dormitory, on the first night of preliminary training, she asked Briony to cut the fingernails of her right hand, explaining that her left hand couldn't make the scissors work and that her mother always did it for her. She was ginger-haired and freckled, which made Briony automatically wary. But unlike Lola, Fiona was loud and jolly, with dimples on the backs of her hands and an enormous bosom which caused the other girls to say that she was bound to be a ward sister one day. Her family lived in Chelsea. She whispered from her bed one night that her father was expecting to be asked to join Churchill's war cabinet. But when the cabinet was announced, the surnames didn't match up and nothing was said, and Briony thought it better not to enquire. In those first months after preliminary training, Fiona and Briony had little chance to find out if they actually liked each other. It was convenient for them to assume they did. They were among the few who had no medical background at all. Most of the other girls had done first-aid courses, and some had been VADs already and were familiar with blood and dead bodies, or at least, they said they were.

But friendships were not easy to cultivate. The probationers worked their shifts in the wards, studied three hours a day in their spare time, and slept. Their luxury was teatime, between four and five, when they took down from the wooden slatted shelves their miniature brown teapots inscribed with their names and sat together in a little day-room off the ward. Conversation was stilted. The home sister was there to supervise and ensure decorum. Besides, as soon as they sat down, tiredness came over them, heavy as three folded blankets. One girl fell asleep with a cup and saucer in her hand and scalded her thigh – a good opportunity, Sister Drummond said when she came in to see what the screaming was about, to practise the treatment of burns.

And she herself was a barrier to friendship. In those early months, Briony often thought that her only relationship was with Sister Drummond. She was always there, one moment at the end of a corridor, approaching with a terrible purpose, the next, at Briony's shoulder, murmuring in her ear that she had failed to pay attention during preliminary training to the correct procedures for blanket-bathing male patients: only after the *second* change of washing water should the freshly soaped back flannel and back towel be passed to the patient so that he could 'finish off for himself'. Briony's state of mind largely depended on how she stood that hour in the ward sister's opinion. She felt a coolness in her stomach whenever Sister Drummond's gaze fell on her. It was impossible to know whether you had done well. Briony dreaded her bad opinion. Praise was unheard of. The best one could hope for was indifference.

In the moments she had to herself, usually in the dark, minutes before falling asleep, Briony contemplated a ghostly parallel life in which she was at Girton, reading Milton. She could have been at her sister's college, rather than her sister's hospital. Briony had thought she was joining the war effort. In fact, she had narrowed her life to a relationship with a woman fifteen years older who assumed a power over her greater than that of a mother over an infant.

This narrowing, which was above all a stripping away of identity, began weeks before she had even heard of Sister Drummond. On her first day of the two months' preliminary training, Briony's humiliation in front of the class had been instructive. This was how it was going to be. She had gone up to the sister to point out courteously that a mistake had been made with her name badge. She was B. Tallis, not, as it said on the little rectangular brooch, N. Tallis.

The reply was calm. 'You are, and will remain, as you have been designated. Your Christian name is of no interest to me. Now kindly sit down, Nurse Tallis.'

The other girls would have laughed if they had dared, for they all had the same initial, but they correctly sensed that permission had not been granted. This was the time of hygiene lectures, and of practising blanket-baths on life-size models – Mrs Mackintosh, Lady Chase, and baby George whose blandly impaired physique allowed him to double as a baby girl. It was the time of adapting to unthinking obedience, of learning to carry bedpans in a stack, and remembering a fundamental rule: never walk up a ward without bringing something back. Physical discomfort helped close down Briony's mental horizons. The high starched collars rubbed her neck raw. Washing her hands a dozen times a day under stinging cold water with a block of soda brought on her first chilblains. The shoes she had to buy with her own money fiercely pinched her toes. The uniform, like all uniforms, eroded identity, and the daily attention required – ironing pleats, pinning hats, straightening seams, shoe polishing, especially the heels – began a process by which other concerns were slowly excluded. By the time the girls were ready to start their course as probationers, and to work in the wards (they were never to say 'on') under Sister Drummond, and to submit to the daily routine 'from bedpan to Bovril', their previous lives were becoming indistinct. Their minds had emptied to some extent, their defences were down, so that they were easily persuaded of the absolute authority of the ward sister. There could be no resistance as she filled their vacated minds.

It was never said, but the model behind this process was military. Miss Nightingale, who was never to be referred to as Florence, had been in the Crimea long enough to see the value of discipline, strong lines of command and well-trained troops. So when she lay in the dark listening to Fiona begin her nightlong snoring – she slept on her back – Briony already sensed that the parallel life, which she could imagine so easily from her visits to Cambridge as a child to see Leon and Cecilia, would soon begin to diverge from her own. This was her student life now, these four years, this enveloping regime, and she had no will, no freedom to leave. She was abandoning herself to a life of strictures, rules, obedience, housework, and a constant fear of disapproval. She was one of a batch of probationers – there was a new intake every few months – and she had no identity beyond her badge. There were no tutorials here, no one losing sleep over the precise course of her intellectual development. She emptied and sluiced the bedpans, swept and polished floors, made cocoa and Bovril, fetched and carried – and was delivered from introspection. At some point in the future, she knew from listening to the second-year students, she would begin to take pleasure in her competence. She had had a taste of it lately, having been entrusted with taking a pulse and temperature under supervision and marking the readings on a chart. In the way of medical treatments, she had already dabbed gentian violet on ringworm, aquaflavine emulsion on a cut, and painted lead lotion on a bruise. But mostly, she was a maid, a skivvy and, in her hours off, a crammer of simple facts. She was happy to have little time to think of anything else. But when she stood on her landing in her dressing gown, last thing at night, and she looked across the river at the unlit city, she remembered the unease that was out there in the streets as well as in the wards, and was like the darkness itself. Nothing in her routine, not even Sister Drummond, could protect her from it.

In the half hour before lights out, after cocoa, the girls would be in and out of each other's rooms, sitting on their beds writing letters home, or to sweethearts. Some still cried a little from homesickness, and there would be much comforting going on at this time, with arms around shoulders and soothing words. It seemed theatrical to Briony, and ridiculous, grown young women tearful for their mothers, or as one of the students put it through her sobs, for the smell of daddy's pipe. Those doing the consoling seemed to be enjoying themselves rather too much. In this cloying atmosphere Briony sometimes wrote her own concise letters home which conveyed little more than that she was not ill, not unhappy, not in need of her allowance and not about to change her mind in the way that her mother had predicted. Other girls proudly wrote out their exacting routines of work and study to astound their loving parents. Briony confided these matters only to her notebook, and even then, in no great detail. She did not want her mother to know about the lowly work she did. Part of the purpose of becoming a nurse was to work for her independence. It was important to her that her parents, especially her mother, knew as little about her life as possible.

Apart from a string of repeated questions which remained unanswered, Emily's letters were mostly about the evacuees. Three mothers with seven children, all from the Hackney area of London, had been billeted on the Tallis family. One of the mothers had disgraced herself in the village pub and was now banned. Another woman was a devout Catholic who walked four miles with her three children to the local town for mass on Sunday. But Betty, a Catholic herself, was not sensitive to these differences. She hated all the mothers and all their children. They told her on the first morning that they did not like her food. She claimed to have seen the church-goer spitting on the hallway floor. The oldest of the children, a thirteen-year-old boy who looked no bigger than eight, had got into the fountain, climbed onto the statue and snapped off the Triton's horn and his arm, right down to the elbow. Jack said that it could be fixed without too much trouble. But now the part, which had been carried into the house and left in the scullery, was missing. On information from old Hardman, Betty accused the boy of throwing it in the lake. The boy said he knew nothing. There was talk of draining the lake, but there was concern for the pair of mating swans. The mother was fierce in her son's defence, saying that it was dangerous to have a fountain when children were about, and that she was writing to the MP. Sir Arthur Ridley was Briony's godfather.

Still, Emily thought they should consider themselves lucky to have evacuees because at one point it had looked like the whole house was going to be requisitioned for use by the army. They settled instead on Hugh van Vliet's place because it had a snooker table. Her other news was that her sister Hermione was still in Paris but thinking of relocating to Nice, and the cows had been moved into three fields on the north side so that the park could be ploughed up for corn. A mile and a half of iron fencing dating from the 1750s had been taken away to be melted down to make Spitfires. Even the workmen who removed it said it was the wrong kind of metal. A cement and brick pillbox had been built down by the river, right on the bend, among the sedges, destroying the nests of the teal and the grey wagtails. Another pillbox was being built where the main road entered the village. They were storing all the fragile pieces in the cellars, including the harpsichord. Wretched Betty dropped Uncle Clem's vase carrying it down and it shattered on the steps. She said the pieces had simply come away in her hand, but that was hardly to be believed. Danny Hardman had joined the navy, but all the other boys in the village had gone into the East Surreys. Jack was working far too hard. He attended a special conference and when he came back he looked tired and thin, and wasn't allowed to tell her where he had been. He was furious about the vase and actually shouted at Betty, which was so unlike him. On top of it all, she had lost a ration book and they had to do without sugar for two weeks. The mother who was banned from the Red Lion had come without her gas mask and no replacement was to be had. The ARP warden, who was PC Vockins's brother, had been round a third time for a blackout inspection. He was turning out to be quite a little dictator. No one liked him.

Reading these letters at the end of an exhausting day, Briony felt a dreamy nostalgia, a vague yearning for a long-lost life. She could hardly feel sorry for herself. She was the one who had cut herself off from home. In the week's holiday after preliminary training, before the probationer year began, she had stayed with her uncle and aunt in Primrose Hill and had resisted her mother on the telephone. Why could Briony not visit, even for a day, when everyone would adore to see her and was desperate for her stories about her new life? And why did she write so infrequently? It was difficult to give a straight answer. For now it was necessary to stay away.

In the drawer of her bedside locker, she kept a foolscap notebook with marbled cardboard covers. Taped to the spine was a length of string on the end of which was a pencil. It was not permitted to use pen and ink in bed. She began her journal at the end of the first day of preliminary training, and managed at least ten minutes most nights before lights out. Her entries consisted of artistic manifestos, trivial complaints, character sketches and simple accounts of her day which increasingly shaded off into fantasy. She rarely read back over what she had written, but she liked to flip the filled pages. Here, behind the name badge and uniform, was her true self, secretly hoarded, quietly accumulating. She had never lost that childhood pleasure in seeing pages covered in her own handwriting. It almost didn't matter what she wrote. Since the drawer did not lock, she was careful to disguise her descriptions of Sister Drummond. She changed the names of the patients too. And having changed the names, it became easier to transform the circumstances and invent. She liked to write out what she imagined to be their rambling thoughts. She was under no obligation to the truth, she had promised no one a chronicle. This was the only place she could be free. She built little stories – not very convincing, somewhat overwritten – around the people on the ward. For a while she thought of herself as a kind of medical Chaucer, whose wards thronged with colourful types, coves, topers, old hats, nice dears with a sinister secret to tell. In later years she regretted not being more factual, not providing herself with a store of raw material. It would have been useful to know what happened, what it looked like, who was there, what was said. At the time, the journal preserved her dignity: she might look and behave like and live the life of a trainee nurse, but she was really an important writer in disguise. And at a time when she was cut off from everything she knew – family, home, friends – writing was the thread of continuity. It was what she had always done.

They were rare, the moments in the day when her mind

could wander freely. Sometimes she would be sent on an errand to the dispensary and would have to wait for the pharmacist to return. Then she would drift along the corridor to a stairwell where a window gave a view of the river. Imperceptibly, her weight would shift to her right foot as she stared across at the Houses of Parliament without seeing them, and thought not about her journal, but about the long story she had written and sent away to a magazine. During her stay in Primrose Hill she borrowed her uncle's typewriter, took over the dining room and typed out her final draft with her forefingers. She was at it all week for more than eight hours a day, until her back and neck ached, and ragged curls of unfurling ampersands swam across her vision. But she could hardly remember a greater pleasure than at the end, when she squared off the completed pile of pages – one hundred and three! – and felt at the tips of her raw fingers the weight of her creation. All her own. No one else could have written it. Keeping a carbon copy for herself, she wrapped her story (such an inadequate word) in brown paper, took the bus to Bloomsbury, walked to the address in Lansdowne Terrace, the office of the new magazine, *Horizon*, and delivered the package to a pleasant young woman who came to the door.

What excited her about her achievement was its design, the pure geometry and the defining uncertainty which reflected, she thought, a modern sensibility. The age of clear answers was over. So was the age of characters and plots. Despite her journal sketches, she no longer really believed in characters. They were quaint devices that belonged to the nineteenth century. The very concept of character was founded on errors that modern psychology had exposed. Plots too were like rusted machinery whose wheels would no longer turn. A modern novelist could no more write characters and plots than a modern composer could a Mozart symphony. It was thought, perception, sensations that interested her, the conscious mind as a river through time, and how to represent its onward roll, as well as all the tributaries that would swell it, and the obstacles that would divert it. If only she could reproduce the clear light of a summer's morning, the sensations of a child standing at a window, the curve and dip of a swallow's flight over a pool of water. The novel of the future would be unlike anything in the past. She had read Virginia Woolf's *The Waves* three times and thought that a great transformation was being worked in human nature itself, and that only fiction, a new kind of fiction, could capture the essence of the change. To enter a mind and show it at work, or being worked on, and to do this within a symmetrical design – this would be an artistic triumph. So thought Nurse Tallis as she lingered near the dispensary, waiting for the pharmacist to return, and gazing across the Thames, oblivious to the danger she was in, of being discovered standing on one leg by Sister Drummond.

Three months had passed, and Briony had heard nothing from *Horizon*.

A second piece of writing also brought no response. She had gone to the administration office and asked for Cecilia's address. In early May she had written to her sister. Now she was beginning to think that silence was Cecilia's answer.

Duringthe last days of May the deliveries of medical supplies increased. More non-urgent cases were sent home. Many wards would have been completely emptied had it not been for the admission of forty sailors – a rare type of jaundice was sweeping through the Royal Navy. Briony no longer had time to notice. New courses on hospital nursing and preliminary anatomy began. The first-year students hurried from their shifts to their lectures, to their meals and to private study. After three pages of reading, it would be difficult to stay awake. The chimes of Big Ben marked every change of the day, and there were times when the solemn single note of the quarter hour prompted moans of suppressed panic as the girls realised they were supposed to be elsewhere.

Total bed rest was considered a medical procedure in itself. Most patients, whatever their condition, were forbidden to walk the few steps to the lavatory. The days therefore began with bedpans. Sister did not approve of them being carried down the ward 'like tennis rackets'. They were to be carried 'to the glory of God', and emptied, sluiced, cleaned and stowed by half past seven, when it was time to start the morning drinks. All day long, bedpans, blanket-bathing, floor-cleaning. The girls complained of backache from bed-making, and fiery sensations in their feet from standing all day. An extra nursing duty was drawing the blackout over the huge ward windows. Towards the end of the day, more bedpans, the emptying of sputum mugs, the making of cocoa. There was barely time between the end of a shift and the beginning of a class to get back to the dormitory to collect papers and textbooks. Twice in one day, Briony had caught the disapproval of the ward sister for running in the corridor, and on each occasion the reprimand was delivered tonelessly. Only haemorrhages and fires were permissible reasons for a nurse to run.

But the principal domain of the junior probationers was the sluice room. There was talk of automatic bedpan- and bottle-washers being installed, but this was mere rumour of a promised land. For now, they must do as others had done before them. On the day she had been told off twice for running, Briony found herself sent to the sluice room for an extra turn. It may have been an accident of the unwritten roster, but she doubted it. She pulled the sluice room door behind her, and tied the heavy rubber apron around her waist. The trick of emptying, in fact the only way it was possible for her, was to close her eyes, hold her breath and avert her head. Then came the rinsing in a solution of carbolic. If she neglected to check that hollow bedpan handles were cleaned and dry she would be in deeper trouble with the sister.

From this task she went straight to tidying the near-empty ward at the end of the day – straightening lockers, emptying ash-trays, picking up the day's newspapers. Automatically, she glanced at a folded page of the *Sunday Graphic*. She had been following the news in unrelated scraps. There was never enough time to sit down and read a paper properly. She knew about the breaching of the Maginot Line, the bombing of Rotterdam, the surrender of the Dutch army, and some of the girls had been talking the night before about the imminent collapse of Belgium. The war was going badly, but it was bound to pick up. It was one anodyne sentence that caught her attention now – not for what it said, but for what it blandly tried to conceal. The British army in northern France was 'making strategic withdrawals to previously prepared positions'. Even she, who knew nothing of military strategy or journalistic convention, understood a euphemism for retreat. Perhaps she was the last person in the hospital to understand what was happening. The emptying wards, the flow of supplies, she had thought were simply part of general preparations for war. She had been too wrapped up in her own tiny concerns. Now she saw how the separate news items might connect, and understood what everyone else must know and what the hospital administration was planning for. The Germans had reached the Channel, the British army was in difficulties. It had all gone badly wrong in France, though no one knew on what kind of scale. This foreboding, this muted dread, was what she had sensed around her.

About this time, on the day the last patients were escorted from the ward, a letter came from her father. After a cursory greeting and enquiry after the course and her health, he passed on information picked up from a colleague and confirmed by the family: Paul Marshall and Lola Quincey were to be married a week Saturday in the Church of the Holy Trinity, Clapham Common. He gave no reason why he supposed she would want to know, and made no comment on the matter himself. He simply signed off in a scrawl down the page – 'love as always'.

All morning, as she went about her duties, she thought about the news. She had not seen Lola since that summer, so the figure she imagined at the altar was a spindly girl of fifteen. Briony helped a departing patient, an elderly lady from Lambeth, pack her suitcase, and tried to concentrate on her complaints. She had broken her toe and been promised twelve days' bedrest, and had had only seven. She was helped into a wheelchair and a porter took her away. On duty in the sluice room Briony did the sums. Lola was twenty, Marshall would be twenty-nine. It wasn't a surprise; the shock was in the confirmation. Briony was more than implicated in this union. She had made it possible.

Throughout the day, up and down the ward, along the corridors, Briony felt her familiar guilt pursue her with a novel vibrancy. She scrubbed down the vacated lockers, helped wash bedframes in carbolic, swept and polished the floors, ran errands to the dispensary and the almoner at double speed without actually running, was sent with another probationer to help dress a boil in men's general, and covered for Fiona who had to visit the dentist. On this first really fine day of May she sweated under her starchy uniform. All she wanted to do was work, then bathe and sleep until it was time to work again. But it was all useless, she knew. Whatever skivvying or humble nursing she did, and however well or hard she did it, whatever illumination in tutorial she had relinquished, or lifetime moment on a college lawn, she would never undo the damage. She was unforgivable.

For the first time in years she thought that she would like to talk to her father. She had always taken his remoteness for granted and expected nothing. She wondered whether in sending his letter with its specific information he was trying to tell her that he knew the truth. After tea, leaving herself too little time, she went to the phone box outside the hospital entrance near Westminster Bridge and attempted to call him at his work. The switchboard put her through to a helpful nasal voice, and then the connection was broken and she had to start again. The same happened, and on her third attempt the line went dead as soon as a voice said – Trying to connect you.

By this time she had run out of change and she was due back on the ward. She paused outside the phone box to admire the huge cumulus clouds piled against a pale blue sky. The river with its spring tide racing seaward reflected the colour with dashes of green and grey. Big Ben seemed to be endlessly toppling forwards against the restless sky. Despite the traffic fumes, there was a scent of fresh vegetation around, newly cut grass perhaps from the hospital gardens, or from young trees along the riverside. Though the light was brilliant, there was a delicious coolness in the air. She had seen or felt nothing so pleasing in days, perhaps weeks. She was indoors too much, breathing disinfectant. As she came away, two young army officers, medics from the military hospital on Millbank, gave her a friendly smile as they brushed past her. Automatically, she glanced down, then immediately regretted that she had not at least met their look. They walked away from her across the bridge, oblivious to everything but their own conversation. One of them mimed reaching up high, as though to grope for something on a shelf, and his companion laughed. Halfway across they stopped to admire a gunboat gliding under the bridge. She thought how lively and free the RAMC doctors looked, and wished she had returned their smiles. There were parts of herself she had completely forgotten. She was late and she had every reason to run, despite the shoes that pinched her toes. Here, on the stained, uncarbolised pavement, the writ of Sister Drummond did not apply. No haemorrhages or fires, but it was a surprising physical pleasure, a brief taste of freedom, to run as best she could in her starched apron to the hospital entrance.

N ow a languorous waiting settled over the hospital.
   Only the jaundiced seamen remained. There was much
fascination and amused talk about them among the nurses.
These tough ratings sat up in bed darning their socks, and
insisted on hand-washing their own smalls, which they dried
on washing lines improvised from string, suspended along
the radiators. Those who were still bed-bound would suffer
agonies rather than call for the bottle. It was said the able
seamen insisted on keeping the ward shipshape themselves
and had taken over the sweeping and the heavy bumper.
Such domesticity among men was unknown to the girls, and
Fiona said she would marry no man who had not served in
the Royal Navy.

For no apparent reason, the probationers were given a half
day off, free from study, though they were to remain in
uniform. After lunch Briony walked with Fiona across the
river past the Houses of Parliament and into St James's Park.
They strolled around the lake, bought tea at a stall, and rented
deckchairs to listen to elderly men of the Salvation Army
playing Elgar adapted for brass band. In those days of May,
before the story from France was fully understood, before the
bombing of the city in September, London had the outward
signs, but not yet the mentality, of war. Uniforms, posters
warning against fifth columnists, two big air-raid shelters dug
into the park lawns, and everywhere, surly officialdom. While
the girls were sitting on their deckchairs, a man in armband
and cap came over and demanded to see Fiona's gas mask –
it was partially obscured by her cape. Otherwise, it was still an
innocent time. The anxieties about the situation in France that
had been absorbing the country had for the moment dissipated
in the afternoon's sunshine. The dead were not yet present, the
absent were presumed alive. The scene was dreamlike in its
normality. Prams drifted along the paths, hoods down in full
sunlight, and white, soft-skulled babies gaped at the outdoor

world for the first time. Children who seemed to have escaped evacuation ran about on the grass shouting and laughing, the band struggled with music beyond its capabilities, and deckchairs still cost twopence. It was hard to believe that barely a hundred miles away was a military disaster.

Briony's thoughts remained fixed on her themes. Perhaps London would be overwhelmed by poisonous gas, or overrun by German parachutists aided on the ground by fifth columnists before Lola's wedding could take place. Briony had heard a know-all porter saying, with what sounded like satisfaction, that nothing now could stop the German army. They had the new tactics and we didn't, they had modernised, and we had not. The generals should have read Liddell Hart's book, or have come to the hospital porter's lodge and listened carefully during tea break.

At her side, Fiona talked of her adored little brother and the clever thing he had said at dinner, while Briony pretended to listen and thought about Robbie. If he had been fighting in France, he might already be captured. Or worse. How would Cecilia survive such news? As the music, enlivened by unscored dissonances, swelled to a raucous climax, she gripped the wooden sides of her chair, closed her eyes. If something happened to Robbie, if Cecilia and Robbie were never to be together . . . Her secret torment and the public upheaval of war had always seemed separate worlds, but now she understood how the war might compound her crime. The only conceivable solution would be for the past never to have happened. If he didn't come back . . . She longed to have someone else's past, to be someone else, like hearty Fiona with her unstained life stretching ahead, and her affectionate, sprawling family, whose dogs and cats had Latin names, whose home was a famous venue for artistic Chelsea people. All Fiona had to do was live her life, follow the road ahead and discover what was to happen. To Briony, it appeared that her life was going to be lived in one room, without a door.

'Briony, are you all right?'

'What? Yes, of course. I'm fine, thanks.'

'I don't believe you. Shall I get you some water?'

As the applause grew – no one seemed to mind how bad the band was – she watched Fiona go across the grass, past the musicians and the man in a brown coat renting out the deckchairs, to the little café among the trees. The Salvation Army was starting in on ''Bye 'Bye Blackbird' at which they were far more adept. People in their deckchairs were joining in, and some were clapping in time. Communal singalongs had a faintly coercive quality – that way strangers had of catching each other's eye as their voices rose – which she was determined to resist. Still, it lifted her spirits, and when Fiona returned with a teacup of water, and the band began a medley of old-time favourites with 'It's a Long Way to Tipperary', they began to talk about work. Fiona drew Briony into the gossip – about which pros they liked, and those that irritated them, about Sister Drummond whose voice Fiona could do, and the matron who was almost as grand and remote as a consultant. They remembered the eccentricities of various patients, and they shared grievances – Fiona was outraged that she wasn't allowed to keep things on her window-sill, Briony hated the eleven o'clock lights out – but they did so with self-conscious enjoyment and increasingly with a great deal of giggling, so that heads began to turn in their direction, and fingers were laid theatrically over lips. But these gestures were only half serious, and most of those who turned smiled indulgently from their deckchairs, for there was something about two young nurses – nurses in wartime – in their purple and white tunics, dark blue capes and spotless caps, that made them as irreproachable as nuns. The girls sensed their immunity and their laughter grew louder, into cackles of hilarity and derision. Fiona turned out to be a good mimic, and for all her merriness, there was a cruel touch to her humour that Briony liked. Fiona had her own version of Lambeth Cockney, and with heartless exaggeration caught the ignorance of some patients, and their pleading, whining voices. It's me 'art, Nurse. It's always been on the wrong side. Me mum was just the same. Is it true your baby comes out of your bottom, Nurse? 'Cos I don't know how mine's going to fit, seeing as 'ow I'm always blocked. I 'ad six nippers, then I goes and leaves one on a bus, the eighty-eight up from Brixton. Must've left 'im on the seat. Never saw 'im again, Nurse. Really upset, I was. Cried me eyes out.

As they walked back towards Parliament Square Briony was light-headed and still weak in the knees from laughing so hard. She wondered at herself, at how quickly her mood could be transformed. Her worries did not disappear, but slipped back, their emotional power temporarily exhausted. Arm in arm the girls walked across Westminster Bridge. The tide was out, and in such strong light there was a purple sheen on the mud-banks where thousands of worm-casts threw tiny sharp shadows. As Briony and Fiona turned right onto Lambeth Palace Road they saw a line of army lorries drawn up outside the main entrance. The girls groaned good-humouredly at the prospect of more supplies to be unpacked and stowed.

Then they saw the field ambulances among the lorries, and coming closer they saw the stretchers, scores of them, set down haphazardly on the ground, and an expanse of dirty green battledress and stained bandages. There were also soldiers standing in groups, dazed and immobile, and wrapped like the men on the ground in filthy bandages. A medical orderly was gathering rifles from the back of a lorry. A score of porters, nurses and doctors were moving through the crowd. Five or six trolleys had been brought out to the front of the hospital – clearly not enough. For a moment, Briony and Fiona stopped and looked, and then, at the same moment, they began to run.

In less than a minute they were down among the men. The brisk air of spring did not dispel the stench of engine oil and festering wounds. The soldiers' faces and hands were black, and with their stubble and matted black hair, and their tied-on labels from the casualty-receiving stations, they looked identical, a wild race of men from a terrible world. The ones who were standing appeared to be asleep. More nurses and doctors were pouring out of the entrance. A consultant was taking charge and a rough triage system was in place. Some of the urgent cases were being lifted onto the trolleys. For the first time in her training, Briony found herself addressed by a doctor, a registrar she had never seen before.

'You, get on the end of this stretcher.'

The doctor himself took the other end. She had never carried a stretcher before and the weight of it surprised her. They were through the entrance and ten yards down the corridor and she knew her left wrist could not hold up. She was at the feet end. The soldier had a sergeant's stripes. He was without his boots and his bluish toes stank. His head was wrapped in a bandage soaked to crimson and black. On his thigh his battledress was mangled into a wound. She thought she could see the white protuberance of bone. Each step they took gave him pain. His eyes were shut tight, but he opened and closed his mouth in silent agony. If her left hand failed, the stretcher would certainly tip. Her fingers were loosening as they reached the lift, stepped inside and set the stretcher down. While they slowly rose, the doctor felt the man's pulse, and breathed in sharply through his nose. He was oblivious to Briony's presence. As the second floor sank into their view, she thought only of the thirty yards of corridor to the ward, and whether she would make it. It was her duty to tell the doctor that she couldn't. But his back was to her as he slammed the lift gates apart, and told her to take her end. She willed more strength to her left arm, and she willed the doctor to go faster. She would not bear the disgrace if she were to fail. The black-faced man opened and closed his mouth in a kind of chewing action. His tongue was covered in white spots. His black Adam's apple rose and fell, and she made herself stare at that. They turned into the ward, and she was lucky that an emergency bed was ready by the door. Her fingers were already slipping. A sister and a qualified nurse were waiting. As the stretcher was manoeuvred into position alongside the bed, Briony's fingers went slack, she had no control over them, and she brought up her left knee in time to catch the weight. The wooden handle thumped against her leg. The stretcher wobbled, and it was the sister who leaned in to steady it. The wounded sergeant blew through his lips a sound of incredulity, as though he had never guessed that pain could be so vast.

'For God's sake, girl,' the doctor muttered. They eased their patient onto the bed.

Briony waited to find out if she was needed. But now the three were busy and ignored her. The nurse was removing the head bandage, and the sister was cutting away the soldier's trousers. The registrar turned away to the light to study the notes scribbled on the label he had pulled away from the man's shirt. Briony cleared her throat softly and the sister looked round and was annoyed to find her still there.

'Well don't just stand idle, Nurse Tallis. Get downstairs and help.'

She came away humiliated, and felt a hollow sensation spreading in her stomach. The moment the war touched her life, at the first moment of pressure, she had failed. If she was made to carry another stretcher, she would not make it halfway to the lift. But if she was told to, she would not dare refuse. If she dropped her end she would simply leave, gather her things from her room into her suitcase, and go to Scotland and work as a land-girl. It would be better for everyone. As she hurried along the ground-floor corridor she met Fiona coming the other way on the front of a stretcher. She was a stronger girl than Briony. The face of the man she was carrying was completely obliterated by dressings, with a dark oval hole for his mouth. The girls' eyes met and something passed between them, shock, or shame that they had been laughing in the park when there was this.

Briony went outside and saw with relief the last of the stretchers being lifted onto extra trolleys, and porters waiting to push them. A dozen qualified nurses were standing to one side with their suitcases. She recognised some from her own ward. There was no time to ask them where they were being sent. Something even worse was happening elsewhere. The priority now was the walking wounded. There were still more than two hundred of them. A sister told her to lead fifteen men up to Beatrice ward. They followed her in single file back down the corridor, like children in a school crocodile. Some had their arms in slings, others had head or chest wounds. Three men walked on crutches. No one spoke. There was a jam around the lifts with trolleys waiting to get to the operating theatres in the basement, and others still trying to get up to the wards. She found a place in an alcove for the men with crutches to sit, told them not to move, and took the rest up by the stairs. Progress was slow and they paused on each landing.

'Not far now,' she kept saying, but they did not seem to be aware of her.

When they reached the ward, etiquette required her to report to the sister. She was not in her office. Briony turned to her crocodile, which had bunched up behind her. They did not look at her. They were staring past her, into the grand Victorian space of the ward, the lofty pillars, the potted palms, the neatly ranged beds and their pure, turned-down sheets.

'You wait here,' she said. 'The sister will find you all a bed.'

She walked quickly to the far end where the sister and two nurses were attending a patient. There were shuffling footsteps behind Briony. The soldiers were coming down the ward.

Horrified, she flapped her hands at them. 'Go back, please go back and wait.'

But they were fanning out now across the ward. Each man had seen the bed that was his. Without being assigned, without removing their boots, without baths and delousing and hospital pyjamas, they were climbing onto the beds.

Their filthy hair, their blackened faces were on the pillows. The sister was coming at a sharp pace from her end of the ward, her heels resounding in the venerable space. Briony went to a bedside and plucked at the sleeve of a soldier who lay face-up, cradling his arm which had slipped its sling. As he kicked his legs out straight he made a scar of oil stain across his blanket. All her fault.

'You must get up,' she said as the sister was upon her. She added feebly, 'There's a procedure.'

'The men need to sleep. The procedures are for later.' The voice was Irish. The sister put a hand on Briony's shoulder and turned her so that her name badge could be read. 'You'll go back to your ward now, Nurse Tallis. You'll be needed there, I should think.'

With the gentlest of shoves, Briony was sent about her business. The ward could do without disciplinarians like her. The men around her were already asleep, and again she had been proved an idiot. Of course they should sleep. She had only wanted to do what she thought was expected. These weren't her rules, after all. They had been dinned into her these past few months, the thousand details of a new admission. How was she to know they meant nothing in fact? These indignant thoughts afflicted her until she was almost at her own ward when she remembered the men with crutches downstairs, waiting to be brought up in the lift. She hurried down the stairs. The alcove was empty, and there was no sign of the men in corridors. She did not want to expose her ineptitude by asking among the nurses or porters. Someone must have gathered the wounded men up. In the days that followed, she never saw them again.

Her own ward had been redesignated as an overflow to acute surgical, but the definitions meant nothing at first. It could have been a clearing station on the front line. Sisters and senior nurses had been drafted in to help, and five or six doctors were working on the most urgent cases. There were two padres, one sitting and talking to a man lying on his side, the other praying by a shape under a blanket. All the nurses wore masks, and they and the doctors had rolled up their sleeves. The sisters moved between the beds swiftly, giving injections – probably morphine – or administering the transfusion needles to connect the injured to the vacolitres of whole blood and the yellow flasks of plasma that hung like exotic fruits from the tall mobile stands. Probationers moved down the ward with piles of hot-water bottles. The soft echo of voices, medical voices, filled the ward, and was pierced regularly by groans and shouts of pain. Every bed was occupied, and new cases were left on the stretchers and laid between the beds to take advantage of the transfusion stands. Two orderlies were getting ready to take away the dead men. At many beds, nurses were removing dirty dressings. Always a decision, to be gentle and slow, or firm and quick and have it over with in one moment of pain. This ward favoured the latter, which accounted for some of the shouts. Everywhere, a soup of smells – the sticky sour odour of fresh blood, and also filthy clothes, sweat, oil, disinfectant, medical alcohol, and drifting above it all, the stink of gangrene. Two cases going down to the theatre turned out to be amputations.

With senior nurses seconded to casualty-receiving hospitals further out in the hospital's sector, and more cases coming in, the qualified nurses gave orders freely, and the probationers of Briony's set were given new responsibilities. A nurse sent Briony to remove the dressing and clean the leg wound of a corporal lying on a stretcher near the door. She was not to dress it again until one of the doctors had looked at it. The corporal was face-down, and grimaced when she knelt to speak in his ear.

'Don't mind me if I scream,' he murmured. 'Clean it up, Nurse. I don't want to lose it.'

The trouser leg had been cut clear. The outer bandaging looked relatively new. She began to unwind it, and when it was impossible to pass her hand under his leg, she used scissors to cut the dressing away.

'They did me up on the quayside at Dover.'

Now there was only gauze, black with congealed blood, along the length of the wound which ran from his knee to his ankle. The leg itself was hairless and black. She feared the worst and breathed through her mouth.

'Now how did you do a thing like that?' She made herself sound chirpy.

'Shell comes over, knocks me back onto this fence of corrugated tin.'

'That was bad luck. Now you know this dressing's got to come off.'

She gently lifted an edge and the corporal winced.

He said, 'Count me in, one two three like, and do it quick.'

The corporal clenched his fists. She took the edge she had freed, gripped it hard between forefinger and thumb, and pulled the dressing back in a sudden stroke. A memory came to her from childhood, of seeing at an afternoon birthday party the famous tablecloth trick. The dressing came away in one, with a gluey rasping sound.

The corporal said, 'I'm going to be sick.'

There was a kidney bowl to hand. He retched, but produced nothing. In the folds of skin at the back of his neck were beads of perspiration. The wound was eighteen inches long, perhaps more, and curved behind his knee. The stitches were clumsy and irregular. Here and there one edge of the ruptured skin rose over the other, revealing its fatty layers, and little obtrusions like miniature bunches of red grapes forced up from the fissure.

She said, 'Hold still. I'm going to clean round it, but I won't touch it.' She would not touch it yet. The leg was black and soft, like an overripe banana. She soaked cotton-wool in alcohol. Fearful that the skin would simply come away, she made a gentle pass, around his calf, two inches above the wound. Then she wiped again, with a little more pressure. The skin was firm, so she pressed the cotton-wool until he flinched. She took away her hand and saw the swathe of white skin she had revealed. The cotton-wool was black. Not gangrene. She couldn't help her gasp of relief. She even felt her throat constrict.

He said, 'What is it, Nurse? You can tell me.' He pushed up and was trying to look over his shoulder. There was fear in his voice.

She swallowed and said neutrally, 'I think it's healing well.'

She took more cotton-wool. It was oil, or grease, mixed in with beach sand, and it did not come away easily. She cleaned an area six inches back, working her way right round the wound.

She had been doing this for some minutes when a hand rested on her shoulder and a woman's voice said in her ear, 'That's good, Nurse Tallis, but you've got to work faster.'

She was on her knees, bent over the stretcher, squeezed against a bed, and it was not easy to turn round. By the time she did, she saw only the familiar form retreating. The corporal was asleep by the time Briony began to clean around the stitches. He flinched and stirred but did not quite wake. Exhaustion was his anaesthetic. As she straightened at last, and gathered her bowl and all the soiled cotton-wool, a doctor came and she was dismissed.

She scrubbed her hands and was set another task. Everything was different for her now she had achieved one small thing. She was set to taking water around to the soldiers who had collapsed with battle exhaustion. It was important that they did not dehydrate. Come on now, Private Carter. Drink this and you can go back to sleep. Sit up now . . . She held a little white enamel teapot and let them suck the water from its spout while she cradled their filthy heads against her apron, like giant babies. She scrubbed down again, and did a bedpan round. She had never minded it less. She was told to attend to a soldier with stomach wounds who had also lost a part of his nose. She could see through the bloody cartilage into his mouth, and onto the back of his lacerated tongue. Her job was to clean up his face. Again, it was oil, and sand which had been blasted into the skin. He was awake, she guessed, but he kept his eyes closed. Morphine had calmed him, and he swayed slightly from side to side, as though in time to music in his head. As his features began to appear from behind the mask of black, she thought of those books of glossy blank pages she had in childhood which she rubbed with a blunt pencil to make a picture appear. She thought too how one of these men might be Robbie, how she would dress his wounds without knowing who he was, and with cotton-wool tenderly rub his face until his familiar features emerged, and how he would turn to her with gratitude, realise who she was, and take her hand, and in silently squeezing it, forgive her. Then he would let her settle him down into sleep.

Her responsibilities increased. She was sent with forceps and a kidney bowl to an adjacent ward, to the bedside of an airman with shrapnel in his leg. He watched her warily as she set her equipment down.

'If I'm having them out, I'd rather have an operation.'

Her hands were trembling. But she was surprised how easily it came to her, the brisk voice of the no-nonsense nurse. She pulled the screen around his bed.

'Don't be silly. We'll have them out in a jiff. How did it happen?'

While he explained to her that his job was building runways in the fields of northern France, his eyes kept returning to the steel forceps she had collected from the autoclave. They lay dripping in the blue-edged kidney bowl.

'We'd get going on the job, then Jerry comes over and dumps his load. We drops back, starts all over in another field, then it's Jerry again and we're falling back again. Till we fell into the sea.'

She smiled and pulled back his bed covers. 'Let's have a look, shall we?'

The oil and grime had been washed from his legs to

reveal an area below his thigh where pieces of shrapnel were embedded in the flesh. He leaned forwards, watching her anxiously.

She said, 'Lie back so I can see what's there.'

'They're not bothering me or anything.'

'Just lie back.'

Several pieces were spread across a twelve-inch area. There was swelling and slight inflamation around each rupture in the skin.

'I don't mind them, Nurse. I'd be happy leaving them where they are.' He laughed without conviction. 'Something to show me grandchildren.'

'They're getting infected,' she said. 'And they could sink.'

'Sink?'

'Into your flesh. Into your bloodstream, and get carried to your heart. Or your brain.'

He seemed to believe her. He lay back and sighed at the distant ceiling. 'Bloody 'ell. I mean, excuse me, Nurse. I don't think I'm up to it today.'

'Let's count them up together, shall we?'

They did so, out loud. Eight. She pushed him gently in the chest.

'They've got to come out. Lie back now. I'll be as quick as I can. If it helps you, grip the bedhead behind you.'

His leg was tensed and trembling as she took the forceps.

'Don't hold your breath. Try and relax.'

He made a derisive, snorting sound. 'Relax!'

She steadied her right hand with her left. It would have been easier for her to sit on the edge of the bed, but that was unprofessional and strictly prohibited. When she placed her left hand on an unaffected part of his leg, he flinched. She chose the smallest piece she could find on the edge of the cluster. The protruding part was obliquely triangular. She gripped it, paused a second, then pulled it clear, firmly, but without jerking.

'Fuck!'

The escaped word ricocheted around the ward and seemed to repeat itself several times. There was silence, or at least a lowering of sound beyond the screens. Briony still held the bloody metal fragment between her forceps. It was three quarters of an inch long and narrowed to a point. Purposeful steps were approaching. She dropped the shrapnel into the kidney bowl as Sister Drummond whisked the screen aside. She was perfectly calm as she glanced at the foot of the bed to take in the man's name and, presumably, his condition, then she stood over him and gazed into his face.

'How dare you,' the sister said quietly. And then again, 'How dare you speak that way in front of one of my nurses.'

'I beg your pardon, Sister. It just came out.'

Sister Drummond looked with disdain into the bowl. 'Compared to what we've admitted these past few hours, Airman Young, your injuries are superficial. So you'll consider yourself lucky. And you'll show some courage worthy of your uniform. Carry on, Nurse Tallis.'

Into the silence that followed her departure, Briony said brightly, 'We'll get on, shall we? Only seven to go. When it's over, I'll bring you a measure of brandy.'

He sweated, his whole body shook, and his knuckles turned white round the iron bedhead, but he did not make a sound as she continued to pull the pieces clear.

'You know, you can shout, if you want.'

But he didn't want a second visit from Sister Drummond, and Briony understood. She was saving the largest until last. It did not come clear in one stroke. He bucked on the bed, and hissed through his clenched teeth. By the second attempt, the shrapnel stuck out two inches from his flesh. She tugged it clear on the third try, and held it up for him, a gory four-inch stiletto of irregular steel.

He stared at it in wonder. 'Run him under the tap, Nurse. I'll take him home.' Then he turned into the pillow and began to sob. It may have been the word home, as well as the pain.

She slipped away to get his brandy, and stopped in the sluice to be sick.

For a long time she undressed, washed and dressed the more superficial of the wounds. Then came the order she was dreading.

'I want you to go and dress Private Latimer's face.'

She had already tried to feed him earlier with a teaspoon into what remained of his mouth, trying to spare him the humiliation of dribbling. He had pushed her hand away. Swallowing was excruciating. Half his face had been shot away. What she dreaded, more than the removal of the dressing, was the look of reproach in his large brown eyes. *What have you done to me?* His form of communication was a soft aah sound from the back of his throat, a little moan of disappointment.

'We'll soon have you fixed,' she had kept repeating, and could think of nothing else.

And now, approaching his bed with her materials, she said cheerily, 'Hello, Private Latimer. It's me again.'

He looked at her without recognition. She said as she unpinned the bandage that was secured at the top of his head, 'It's going to be all right. You'll walk out of here in a week or two, you'll see. And that's more than we can say to a lot of them in here.'

That was one comfort. There was always someone worse. Half an hour earlier they had carried out a multiple amputation on a captain from the East Surreys – the regiment the boys in the village had joined. And then there were the dying.

Using a pair of surgical tongs, she began carefully pulling away the sodden, congealed lengths of ribbon gauze from the cavity in the side of his face. When the last was out, the resemblance to the cut-away model they used in anatomy classes was only faint. This was all ruin, crimson and raw. She could see through his missing cheek to his upper and lower molars, and the tongue glistening, and hideously long. Further up, where she hardly dared look, were the exposed muscles around his eye socket. So intimate, and never intended to be seen. Private Latimer had become a monster, and he must have guessed this was so. Did a girl love him before? Could she continue to?

'We'll soon have you fixed,' she lied again.

She began repacking his face with clean gauze soaked in eusol. As she was securing the pins he made his sad sound.

'Shall I bring you the bottle?'

He shook his head and made the sound again.

'You're uncomfortable?'

No.

'Water?'

A nod. Only a small corner of his lips remained. She inserted the little teapot spout and poured. With each swallow he winced, which in turn caused him agony around the missing muscles of his face. He could stand no more, but as she withdrew the water pot, he raised a hand towards her wrist. He had to have more. Rather pain than thirst. And so it went on for minutes – he couldn't bear the pain, he had to have the water.

She would have stayed with him, but there was always another job, always a sister demanding help or a soldier calling from his bed. She had a break from the wards when a man coming round from an anaesthetic was sick onto her lap and she had to find a clean apron. She was surprised to see from a corridor window that it was dark outside. Five hours had passed since they came back from the park. She was by the linen store tying her apron when Sister Drummond came up. It was hard to say what had changed – the manner was still quietly remote, the orders unchallengeable. Perhaps beneath the self-discipline, a touch of rapport in adversity.

'Nurse, you'll go and help apply the Bunyan bags to Corporal MacIntyre's arms and legs. You'll treat the rest of his body with tannic acid. If there are difficulties, you'll come straight to me.'

She turned away to give instructions to another nurse. Briony had seen them bring the corporal in. He was one of a number of men overwhelmed by burning oil on a sinking ferry off Dunkirk. He was picked out of the water by a destroyer. The viscous oil clung to the skin and seared through the tissue. It was the burned-out remains of a human they lifted onto the bed. She thought he could never survive. It was not easy to find a vein to give him morphine. Some time in the past two hours she had helped two other nurses lift him onto a bedpan and he had screamed at the first touch of their hands.

The Bunyan bags were big cellophane containers. The damaged limb floated inside, cushioned by saline solution that had to be at exactly the right temperature. A variation of one degree was not tolerated. As Briony came up, a probationer with a Primus stove on a trolley was already preparing the fresh solution. The bags had to be changed frequently. Corporal MacIntyre lay on his back under a bed cradle because he could not bear the touch of a sheet on his skin. He was whimpering pathetically for water. Burn cases were always badly dehydrated. His lips were too ruined, too swollen, and his tongue too blistered for him to be given fluid by mouth. His saline drip had come away. The needle would not hold in place in the damaged vein. A qualified nurse she had never seen before was attaching a new bag to the stand. Briony prepared the tannic acid in a bowl and took the roll of cotton-wool. She thought she would start with the corporal's legs in order to be out of the way of the nurse who was beginning to search his blackened arm, looking for a vein.

But the nurse said, 'Who sent you over here?'

'Sister Drummond.'

The nurse spoke tersely, and did not look up from her probing. 'He's suffering too much. I don't want him treated until I get him hydrated. Go and find something else to do.'

Briony did as she was told. She did not know how much later it was – perhaps it was in the small hours when she was sent to get fresh towels. She saw the nurse standing near the entrance to the duty room, unobtrusively crying. Corporal MacIntyre was dead. His bed was already taken by another case.

The probationers and the second-year students worked twelve hours without rest. The other trainees and the qualified nurses worked on, and no one could remember how long they were in the wards. All the training she had received, Briony felt later, had been useful preparation, especially in obedience, but everything she understood about nursing she learned that night. She had never seen men crying before. It shocked her at first, and within the hour she was used to it. On the other hand, the stoicism of some of the soldiers amazed and even appalled her. Men coming round from amputations seemed compelled to make terrible jokes. What am I going to kick the missus with now? Every secret of the body was rendered up – bone risen through flesh, sacrilegious glimpses of an intestine or an optic nerve. From this new and intimate perspective, she learned a simple, obvious thing she had always known, and everyone knew: that a person is, among all else, a material thing, easily torn, not easily mended. She came the closest she would ever be to the battlefield, for every case she helped with had some of its essential elements – blood, oil, sand, mud, sea water, bullets, shrapnel, engine grease, or the smell of cordite, or damp sweaty battledress whose pockets contained rancid food along with the sodden crumbs of Amo bars. Often, when she returned yet again to the sink with the high taps and the soda block, it was beach sand she scrubbed away from between her fingers. She and the other probationers of her set were aware of each other only as nurses, not as friends: she barely registered that one of the girls who had helped to move Corporal MacIntyre onto the bedpan was Fiona. Sometimes, when a soldier Briony was looking after was in great pain, she was touched by an impersonal tenderness that detached her from the suffering, so that she was able to do her work efficiently and without horror. That was when she saw what nursing might be, and she longed to qualify, to have that badge. She could imagine how she might abandon her ambitions of writing and dedicate her life in return for these moments of elated, generalised love.

Towards three thirty in the morning, she was told to go and see Sister Drummond. She was on her own, making up a bed. Earlier, Briony had seen her in the sluice room. She seemed to be everywhere, doing jobs at every level. Automatically, Briony began to help her.

The sister said, 'I seem to remember that you speak a bit of French.'

'It's only school French, Sister.'

She nodded towards the end of the ward. 'You see that soldier sitting up, at the end of the row? Acute surgical, but there's no need to wear a mask. Find a chair, go and sit with him. Hold his hand and talk to him.'

Briony could not help feeling offended. 'But I'm not tired, Sister. Honestly, I'm not.'

'You'll do as you're told.'

'Yes, Sister.'

He looked like a boy of fifteen, but she saw from his chart that he was her own age, eighteen. He was sitting, propped by several pillows, watching the commotion around him with a kind of abstracted childlike wonder. It was hard to think of him as a soldier. He had a fine, delicate face, with dark eyebrows and dark green eyes, and a soft full mouth. His face was white and had an unusual sheen, and the eyes were unhealthily radiant. His head was heavily bandaged. As she brought up her chair and sat down he smiled as though he had been expecting her, and when she took his hand he did not seem surprised.

'Te voilà enfin.' The French vowels had a musical twang, but she could just about understand him. His hand was cold and greasy to the touch.

She said, 'The sister told me to come and have a little chat with you.' Not knowing the word, she translated 'sister' literally.

'Your sister is very kind.' Then he cocked his head and added, 'But she always was. And is all going well for her? What does she do these days?'

There was such friendliness and charm in his eyes, such boyish eagerness to engage her, that she could only go along.

'She's a nurse too.'

'Of course. You told me before. Is she still happy? Did she get married to that man she loved so well? Do you know, I can't remember his name. I hope you'll forgive me. Since my injury my memory has been poor. But they tell me it will soon come back. What was his name?'

'Robbie. But . . .'

'And they're married now and happy?'

'Er, I hope they will be soon.'

'I'm so happy for her.'

'You haven't told me your name.'

'Luc. Luc Cornet. And yours?'

She hesitated. 'Tallis.'

'Tallis. That's very pretty.' The way he pronounced it, it was.

He looked away from her face and gazed at the ward, turning his head slowly, quietly amazed. Then he closed his eyes and began to ramble, speaking softly under his breath. Her vocabulary was not good enough to follow him easily. She caught, 'You count them slowly, in your hand, on your fingers . . . my mother's scarf . . . you choose the colour and you have to live with it.'

He fell silent for some minutes. His hand tightened its grip on hers. When he spoke again, his eyes were still closed.

'Do you want to know something odd? This is my first time in Paris.'

'Luc, you're in London. Soon we'll be sending you home.'

'They said that the people would be cold and unfriendly,

but the opposite is true. They're very kind. And you're very kind, coming to see me again.'

For a while she thought he might have fallen asleep. Sitting for the first time in hours, she felt her own fatigue gathering behind her eyes.

Then he was looking about him with that same slow turn of the head, and then he looked at her and said, 'Of course, you're the girl with the English accent.'

She said, 'Tell me what you did before the war? Where did you live? Can you remember?'

'Do you remember that Easter, when you came to Millau.' Feebly, he swung her hand from side to side as he spoke, as though to stir her memory, and his dark green eyes scanned her face in anticipation.

She thought it wasn't right to lead him on. 'I've never been to Millau . . .'

'Do you remember the first time you came in our shop?'

She pulled her chair nearer the bed. His pale, oily face gleamed and bobbed in front of her eyes. 'Luc, I want you to listen to me.'

'I think it was my mother who served you. Or perhaps it was one of my sisters. I was working with my father on the ovens at the back. I heard your accent and came to take a look at you . . .'

'I want to tell you where you are. You're not in Paris . . .'

'Then you were back the next day, and this time I was there and you said . . .'

'Soon you can sleep. I'll come and see you tomorrow, I promise.'

Luc raised his hand to his head and frowned. He said in a lower voice, 'I want to ask you a little favour, Tallis.'

'Of course.'

'These bandages are so tight. Will you loosen them for me a little?'

She stood and peered down at his head. The gauze bows were tied for easy release. As she gently pulled the ends away he said, 'My youngest sister, Anne, do you remember her? She's the prettiest girl in Millau. She passed her grade exam with a tiny piece by Debussy, so full of light and fun. Anyway, that's what Anne says. It keeps running through my mind. Perhaps you know it.'

He hummed a few random notes. She was uncoiling the layer of gauze.

'No one knows where she got her gift from. The rest of our family is completely hopeless. When she plays her back is so straight. She never smiles till she reaches the end. That's beginning to feel better. I think it was Anne who served you that first time you came into the shop.'

She was not intending to remove the gauze, but as she loosened it, the heavy sterile towel beneath it slid away, taking a part of the bloodied dressing with it. The side of Luc's head was missing. The hair was shaved well back from the missing portion of skull. Below the jagged line of bone was a spongy crimson mess of brain, several inches across, reaching from the crown almost to the tip of his ear. She caught the towel before it slipped to the floor, and she held it while she waited for her nausea to pass. Only now did it occur to her what a foolish and unprofessional thing she had done. Luc sat quietly, waiting for her. She glanced down the ward. No one was paying attention. She replaced the sterile towel, fixed the gauze and retied the bows. When she sat down again, she found his hand, and tried to steady herself in its cold moist grip.

Luc was rambling again. 'I don't smoke. I promised my ration to Jeannot . . . Look, it's all over the table . . . under the flowers now . . . the rabbit can't hear you, stupid . . .' Then words came in a torrent, and she lost him. Later she caught a reference to a schoolmaster who was too strict, or perhaps it was an army officer. Finally he was quiet. She wiped his sweating face with a damp towel and waited.

When he opened his eyes, he resumed their conversation as though there had been no interlude.

'What did you think of our baguettes and ficelles?'

'Delicious.'

'That was why you came every day.'

'Yes.'

He paused to consider this. Then he said cautiously, raising a delicate matter, 'And our croissants?'

'The best in Millau.'

He smiled. When he spoke, there was a grating sound at the back of his throat which they both ignored.

'It's my father's special recipe. It all depends on the quality of butter.'

He was gazing at her in rapture. He brought his free hand to cover hers.

He said, 'You know that my mother is very fond of you.'

'Is she?'

'She talks about you all the time. She thinks we should be married in the summer.'

She held his gaze. She knew now why she had been sent. He was having difficulty swallowing, and drops of sweat were forming on his brow, along the edge of the dressing and along his upper lip. She wiped them away, and was about to reach the water for him, but he said,

'Do you love me?'

She hesitated. 'Yes.' No other reply was possible. Besides, for that moment, she did. He was a lovely boy who was a long way from his family and he was about to die.

She gave him some water. While she was wiping his face again he said, 'Have you ever been on the Causse de Larzac?'

'No. I've never been there.'

But he did not offer to take her. Instead he turned his head away into the pillow, and soon he was murmuring his unintelligible scraps. His grip on her hand remained tight as though he were aware of her presence.

When he became lucid again, he turned his head towards her.

'You won't leave just yet.'

'Of course not. I'll stay with you.'

'Tallis . . .'

Still smiling, he half closed his eyes. Suddenly, he jerked upright as if an electric current had been applied to his limbs. He was gazing at her in surprise, with his lips parted. Then he tipped forwards, and seemed to lunge at her. She jumped up from her chair to prevent him toppling to the floor. His hand still held hers, and his free arm was around her neck. His forehead was pressed into her shoulder, his cheek was against hers. She was afraid the sterile towel would slip from his head. She thought she could not support his weight or bear to see his wound again. The grating sound from deep in his throat resounded in her ear. Staggering, she eased him onto the bed and settled him back on the pillows.

'It's Briony,' she said, so only he would hear.

His eyes had a wide-open look of astonishment and his waxy skin gleamed in the electric light. She moved closer and put her lips to his ear. Behind her was a presence, and then a hand resting on her shoulder.

'It's not Tallis. You should call me Briony,' she whispered, as the hand reached over to touch hers, and loosened her fingers from the boy's.

'Stand up now, Nurse Tallis.'

Sister Drummond took her elbow and helped her to her feet. The sister's cheek patches were bright, and across the cheek-bones the pink skin met the white in a precise straight line.

On the other side of the bed, a nurse drew the sheet over Luc Cornet's face.

Pursing her lips, the sister straightened Briony's collar. 'There's a good girl. Now go and wash the blood from your face. We don't want the other patients upset.'

She did as she was told and went to the lavatories and washed her face in cold water, and minutes later returned to her duties in the ward.

At four thirty in the morning the probationers were sent to their lodgings to sleep, and told to report back at eleven.

Briony walked with Fiona. Neither girl spoke, and when they linked arms it seemed they were resuming, after a lifetime of experience, their walk across Westminster Bridge. They could not have begun to describe their time in the wards, or how it had changed them. It was enough to be able to keep walking down the empty corridors behind the other girls.

When she had said her goodnights and entered her tiny room, Briony found a letter on the floor. The handwriting on the envelope was unfamiliar. One of the girls must have picked it up at the porter's lodge and pushed it under her door. Rather than open it straight away, she undressed and prepared herself for sleep. She sat on her bed in her nightdress with the letter in her lap and thought about the boy. The corner of sky in her window was already white. She could still hear his voice, the way he said Tallis, turning it into a girl's name. She imagined the unavailable future – the boulangerie in a narrow shady street swarming with skinny cats, piano music from an upstairs window, her giggling sisters-in-law teasing her about her accent, and Luc Cornet loving her in his eager way. She would have liked to cry for him, and for his family in Millau who would be waiting to hear news from him. But she couldn't feel a thing. She was empty. She sat for almost half an hour, in a daze, and then at last, exhausted but still not sleepy, she tied her hair back with the ribbon she always used, got into bed and opened the letter.

Dear Miss Tallis,

Thank you for sending us *Two Figures by a Fountain*, and please accept our apologies for this dilatory response. As you must know, it would be unusual for us to publish a complete novella by an unknown writer, or for that matter a well-established one. However, we did read with an eye to an extract we might take. Unfortunately we are not able to take any of it. I am returning the typescript under separate cover.

That said, we found ourselves (initially against our better

judgment, for there is much to do in this office) reading the whole with great interest. Though we cannot offer to publish any part of it, we thought you should know that in this quarter there are others as well as myself who would take an interest in what you might write in the future. We are not complacent about the average age of our contributors and are keen to publish promising young writers. We would like to see whatever you do, especially if you were to write a short story or two.

We found *Two Figures by a Fountain* arresting enough to read with dedicated attention. I do not say this lightly. We cast aside a great deal of material, some of it by writers of reputation. There are some good images – I liked 'the long grass stalked by the leonine yellow of high summer' – and you both capture a flow of thought, and represent it with subtle differences in order to make attempts at characterisation. Something unique and unexplained is caught. However, we wondered whether it owed a little too much to the techniques of Mrs Woolf. The crystalline present moment is of course a worthy subject in itself, especially for poetry; it allows a writer to show his gifts, delve into mysteries of perception, present a stylised version of thought processes, permit the vagaries and unpredictability of the private self to be explored and so on. Who can doubt the value of this experimentation? However, such writing can become precious when there is no sense of forward movement. Put the other way round, our attention would have been held even more effectively had there been an underlying pull of simple narrative. Development is required.

So, for example, the child at the window whose account we read first – her fundamental lack of grasp of the situation is nicely caught. So too is the resolve in her that follows, and the sense of initiation into grown-up mysteries. We catch this young girl at the dawn of her selfhood. One is intrigued by her resolve to abandon the fairy stories and home-made folk tales and plays she has been writing (how much nicer if we had the flavour of one) but she may have thrown the baby of fictional technique out with the folk-tale water. For all the fine rhythms and nice observations, nothing much happens after a beginning that has such promise. A young man and woman by a fountain, who clearly have a great deal of unresolved feeling between them, tussle over a Ming vase and break it. (More than one of us here thought Ming rather too priceless to take outdoors? Wouldn't Sèvres or Nymphenburg suit your purpose?) The woman goes fully dressed into the fountain to retrieve the pieces. Wouldn't it help you if the watching girl did not actually realise that the vase had broken? It would be all the more of a mystery to her that the woman submerges herself. So much might unfold from what you have – but you dedicate scores of pages to the quality of light and shade, and to random impressions. Then we have matters from the man's view, then the woman's – though we don't really learn much that is fresh. Just more about the look and feel of things, and some irrelevant memories. The man and woman part, leaving a damp patch on the ground which rapidly evaporates – and there we have reached the end. This static quality does not serve your evident talent well.

If this girl has so fully misunderstood or been so wholly baffled by the strange little scene that has unfolded before her, how might it affect the lives of the two adults? Might she come between them in some disastrous fashion? Or bring them closer, either by design or accident? Might she innocently expose them somehow, to the young woman's parents perhaps? They surely would not approve of a liaison between their eldest daughter and their charlady's son. Might the young couple come to use her as a messenger?

In other words, rather than dwell for quite so long on the perceptions of each of the three figures, would it not be possible to set them before us with greater economy, still keeping some of the vivid writing about light and stone and water which you do so well – but then move on to create some tension, some light and shade within the narrative itself. Your most sophisticated readers might be well up on the latest Bergsonian theories of consciousness, but I'm sure they retain a childlike desire to be told a story, to be held in suspense, to know what happens. Incidentally, from your description, the Bernini you refer to is the one in the Piazza Barberini, not the Piazza Navona.

Simply put, you need the backbone of a story. It may interest you to know that one of your avid readers was Mrs Elizabeth Bowen. She picked up the bundle of typescript in an idle moment while passing through this office on her way to luncheon, asked to take it home to read, and finished it that afternoon. Initially, she thought the prose 'too full, too cloying' but with 'redeeming shades of *Dusty Answer*' (which I wouldn't have thought of at all). Then she was 'hooked for a while' and finally she gave us some notes, which are, as it were, mulched into the above. You may feel perfectly satisfied with your pages as they stand, or our reservations may fill you with dismissive anger, or such despair you never want to look at the thing again. We sincerely hope not. Our wish is that you will take our remarks – which are given with sincere enthusiasm – as a basis for another draft.

Your covering letter was admirably reticent, but you did hint that you had almost no free time at present. If that should change, and you are passing this way, we would be more than happy to see you over a glass of wine and discuss this further. We hope you will not be discouraged. It may help you to know that our letters of rejection are usually no more than three sentences long.

You apologise, in passing, for not writing about the war. We will be sending you a copy of our most recent issue, with a relevant editorial. As you will see, we do not believe that artists have an obligation to strike up attitudes to the war. Indeed, they are wise and right to ignore it and devote themselves to other subjects. Since artists are politically impotent, they must use this time to develop at deeper emotional levels. Your work, your war work, is to cultivate your talent, and go in the direction it demands. Warfare, as we remarked, is the enemy of creative activity.

Your address suggests you may be either a doctor or suffering from a long illness. If the latter, then all of us wish you a speedy and successful recovery.

Finally, one of us here wonders whether you have an older sister who was at Girton six or seven years ago.

Yours sincerely,
CC

In the days that followed, the reversion to a strict shift system dispelled the sense of floating timelessness of those first twenty-four hours. She counted herself lucky to be on days, seven till eight with half hours for meals. When her alarm sounded at five forty-five, she drifted upwards from a soft pit of exhaustion, and in the several seconds of no-man's-land, between sleep and full consciousness, she became aware of some excitement in store, a treat, or a momentous change. Waking as a child on Christmas day was like this – the sleepy thrill, before remembering its source. With her eyes still closed against the summer-morning brightness in the room, she fumbled for the button on her clock and sank back into her pillow, and then it came back to her. The very opposite of Christmas in fact. The opposite of everything. The Germans were about to invade. Everybody said it was so, from the porters who were forming their own hospital Local Defence Volunteers unit, to Churchill himself who conjured an image of the country subjugated and starving with only the

Royal Navy still at large. Briony knew it would be dreadful, that there would be hand-to-hand fighting in the streets and public hangings, a descent into slavery and the destruction of everything decent. But as she sat on the edge of her rumpled, still-warm bed, pulling on her stockings, she could not prevent or deny her horrible exhilaration. As everyone kept saying, the country stood alone now, and it was better that way.

Already, things looked different – the fleur-de-lys pattern on her wash-bag, the chipped plaster frame of the mirror, her face in it as she brushed her hair, all looked brighter, in sharper focus. The doorknob in her hand as she turned it felt obtrusively cool and hard. When she stepped into the corridor and heard distant heavy footsteps in the stairwell, she thought of German jackboots, and her stomach lurched. Before breakfast she had a minute or two to herself along the walkway by the river. Even at this hour, under a clear sky, there was a ferocious sparkle in its tidal freshness as it slid past the hospital. Was it really possible that the Germans could own the Thames?

The clarity of everything she saw or touched or heard was certainly not prompted by the fresh beginnings and abundance of early summer; it was an inflamed awareness of an approaching conclusion, of events converging on an end point. These were the last days, she felt, and they would shine in the memory in a particular way. This brightness, this long spell of sunny days, was history's last fling before another stretch of time began. The early-morning duties, the sluice room, the taking round of tea, the changing of dressings, and the renewed contact with all the irreparable damage did not dim this heightened perception. It conditioned everything she did and was a constant background. And it gave an urgency to her plans. She felt she did not have much time. If she delayed, she thought, the Germans might arrive and she might never have another chance.

Fresh cases arrived each day, but no longer in a deluge. The system was taking hold, and there was a bed for everyone. The surgical cases were prepared for the basement operating theatres. Afterwards, most patients were sent off to outlying hospitals to convalesce. The turnover among the dead was high, and for the probationers there was no drama now, only routine: the screens drawn round the padre's bedside murmur, the sheet pulled up, the porters called, the bed stripped and remade. How quickly the dead faded into each other, so that Sergeant Mooney's face became Private Lowell's, and both exchanged their fatal wounds with those of other men whose names they could no longer recall.

Now France had fallen it was assumed that the bombing of London, the softening-up, must soon begin. No one was to stay in the city unnecessarily. The sandbagging on the ground-floor windows was reinforced, and civilian contractors were on the roofs checking the firmness of the chimney stacks and the concreted skylights. There were various rehearsals for evacuating the wards, with much stern shouting and blowing of whistles. There were fire drills too, and assembly-point procedures, and fitting gas masks on incapable or unconscious patients. The nurses were reminded to put their own masks on first. They were no longer terrorised by Sister Drummond. Now they had been blooded, she did not speak to them like schoolgirls. Her tone when she gave instructions was cool, professionally neutral, and they were flattered. In this new environment it was relatively easy for Briony to arrange to swap her day off with Fiona who generously gave up her Saturday for a Monday.

Because of an administrative bungle, some soldiers were left to convalesce in the hospital. Once they had slept off their exhaustion, and got used to regular meals again and regained some weight, the mood was sour or surly, even among those without permanent disabilities. They were infantrymen mostly. They lay on their beds smoking, silently staring at the ceiling, brooding over their recent memories. Or they gathered to talk in mutinous little groups. They were disgusted with themselves. A few of them told Briony they had never even fired a shot. But mostly they were angry with the 'brass', and with their own officers for abandoning them in the retreat, and with the French for collapsing without a fight. They were bitter about the newspaper celebrations of the miracle evacuation and the heroism of the little boats.

'A fucking shambles,' she heard them mutter. 'Fucking RAF.'

Some men were even unfriendly, and unco-operative about their medicines, having managed to blur the distinction between the generals and the nurses. All mindless authority, as far as they were concerned. It took a visit from Sister Drummond to set them straight.

On Saturday morning Briony left the hospital at eight without eating breakfast and walked with the river on her right, upstream. As she passed the gates of Lambeth Palace, three buses went by. All the destination boards were blank now. Confusion to the invader. It did not matter because she had already decided to walk. It was of no help that she had memorised a few street names. All the signs had been taken down or blacked out. Her vague idea was to go along the river a couple of miles and then head off to the left, which should be south. Most plans and maps of the city had been confiscated by order. Finally she had managed to borrow a crumbling bus route map dated 1926. It was torn along its folds, right along the line of the way she wanted to take. Opening it was to risk breaking it in pieces. And she was nervous of the kind of impression she would make. There were stories in the paper of German parachutists disguised as nurses and nuns, spreading out through the cities and infiltrating the population. They were to be identified by the maps they might sometimes consult and, on questioning, by their too-perfect English and their ignorance of common nursery rhymes. Once the idea was in her mind, she could not stop thinking about how suspicious she looked. She had thought her uniform would protect her as she crossed unknown territory. Instead, she looked like a spy.

As she walked against the flow of morning traffic, she ran through the nursery rhymes she remembered. There were very few she could have recited all the way through. Ahead of her, a milkman had got down from his cart to tighten the girth straps of his horse. He was murmuring to the animal as she came up. Briefly there came back to her, as she stood behind him and politely cleared her throat, a memory of old Hardman and his trap. Anyone who was, say, seventy now, would have been her age in eighteen eighty-eight. Still the age of the horse, at least on the streets, and the old men hated to let it go.

When she asked him the way the milkman was friendly enough and gave a long indistinct account of the route. He was a large fellow with a tobacco-stained white beard. He suffered from an adenoidal problem that made his words bleed into each other through a humming sound in his nostrils. He waved her towards a road forking to the left, under a railway bridge. She thought it might be too soon to be leaving the river, but as she walked on, she sensed him watching her and thought it would be impolite to disregard his directions. Perhaps the left fork was a shortcut.

She was surprised by how clumsy and self-conscious she was, after all she had learned and seen. She felt inept, unnerved by being out on her own, and no longer part of her group. For months she had lived a closed life whose every hour was marked on a timetable. She knew her humble place in the ward. As she became more proficient in the work, so she became better at taking orders and following procedures and ceasing to think for herself. It was a long time since she had done anything on her own. Not since her week in Primrose Hill, typing out the novella, and what a foolish excitement that seemed now.

She was walking under the bridge as a train passed overhead. The thunderous, rhythmic rumble reached right into her bones. Steel gliding and thumping over steel, the great bolted sheets of it high above her in the gloom, an inexplicable door sunk into the brickwork, mighty cast-iron pipework clamped in rusting brackets and carrying no one knew what – such brutal invention belonged to a race of supermen. She herself mopped floors and tied bandages. Did she really have the strength for this journey?

When she stepped out from under the bridge, crossing a wedge of dusty morning sunlight, the train was making a harmless clicking suburban sound as it receded. What she needed, Briony told herself yet again, was backbone. She passed a tiny municipal park with a tennis court on which two men in flannels were hitting a ball back and forwards, warming up for a game with lazy confidence. There were two girls in khaki shorts on a bench nearby reading a letter. She thought of her letter, her sugar-coated rejection slip. She had been carrying it in her pocket during her shift and the second page had acquired a crab-like stain of carbolic. She had come to see that, without intending to, it delivered a significant personal indictment. *Might she come between them in some disastrous fashion?* Yes, indeed. And having done so, might she obscure the fact by concocting a slight, barely clever fiction and satisfy her vanity by sending it off to a magazine? The interminable pages about light and stone and water, a narrative split between three different points of view, the hovering stillness of nothing much seeming to happen – none of this could conceal her cowardice. Did she really think she could hide behind some borrowed notions of modern writing, and drown her guilt in a stream – three streams! – of consciousness? The evasions of her little novel were exactly those of her life. Everything she did not wish to confront was also missing from her novella – and was necessary to it. What was she to do now? It was not the backbone of a story that she lacked. It was backbone.

She left the little park behind, and passed a small factory whose thrumming machinery made the pavement vibrate. There was no telling what was being made behind those high filthy windows, or why yellow and black smoke poured from a single slender aluminium stack. Opposite, set in a diagonal across a street corner, the wide-open double doors of a pub suggested a theatre stage. Inside, where a boy with an attractive, pensive look was emptying ash-trays into a bucket, last night's air still had a bluish look. Two men in leather aprons were unloading beer barrels down a ramp from the dray cart. She had never seen so many horses on the streets. The military must have requisitioned all the lorries. Someone was pushing open the cellar trap doors from inside. They banged against the pavement, sending up the dust, and a man with a tonsure, whose legs were still below street level, paused and turned to watch her go by. He appeared to her like a giant chess piece. The draymen were watching her too, and one of them wolf-whistled.

'All right, darling?'

She didn't mind, but she never knew how to reply. Yes, thank you? She smiled at them all, glad of the folds of her cape. Everyone, she assumed, was thinking about the invasion, but there was nothing to do but keep on. Even if the Germans came, people would still play tennis, or gossip, or drink beer. Perhaps the wolf-whistling would stop. As the street curved and narrowed, the steady traffic along it sounded louder and the warm fumes blew into her face. A Victorian terrace of bright red brick faced right onto the pavement. A woman in a paisley apron was sweeping with demented vigour in front of her house through whose open door came the smell of fried breakfast. She stood back to let Briony pass, for the way was narrow here, but she looked away sharply at Briony's good morning. Approaching her were a woman and four jug-eared boys with suitcases and knapsacks. The kids were jostling and shouting and kicking along an old shoe. They ignored their mother's exhausted cry as Briony was forced to stand aside and let them pass.

'Leave off, will ya! Let the nursey through.'

As she passed, the woman gave a lopsided smile of rueful apology. Two of her front teeth were missing. She was wearing

321

a strong perfume and between her fingers she carried an unlit cigarette.

'They's so excited about going in the countryside. Never been before, would you believe.'

Briony said, 'Good luck. I hope you get a nice family.'

The woman, whose ears also protruded, but were partially obscured by her hair cut in a bob, gave a gay shout of a laugh. 'They dunno what they're in for with this lot!'

She came at last to a confluence of shabby streets which she assumed from the detached quarter of her map was Stockwell. Commanding the route south was a pillbox and standing by it, with only one rifle between them, was a handful of bored Home Guards. An elderly fellow in a trilby, overalls and arm-band, with drooping jowls like a bulldog's, detached himself and demanded to see her identity card. Self-importantly, he waved her on. She thought better of asking him directions. As she understood it, her way lay straight along the Clapham Road for almost two miles. There were fewer people here and less traffic, and the street was broader than the one she had come up. The only sound was the rumble of a departing tram. By a line of smart Edwardian flats set well back from the road, she allowed herself to sit for half a minute on a low parapet wall, in the shade of a plane tree, and remove her shoe to examine a blister on her heel. A convoy of three-ton lorries went by, heading south, out of town. Automatically, she glanced at their backs half expecting to see wounded men. But there were only wooden crates.

Forty minutes later she reached Clapham Common tube station. A squat church of rumpled stone turned out to be locked. She took out her father's letter and read it over again. A woman in a shoe shop pointed her towards the Common. Even when Briony had crossed the road and walked onto the grass she did not see the church at first. It was half concealed among trees in leaf, and was not what she expected. She had been imagining the scene of a crime, a gothic cathedral, whose flamboyant vaulting would be flooded with brazen

light of scarlet and indigo from a stained-glass backdrop of
lurid suffering. What appeared among the cool trees as she
approached was a brick barn of elegant dimensions, like a
Greek temple, with a black-tiled roof, windows of plain glass,
and a low portico with white columns beneath a clocktower of
harmonious proportions. Parked outside, close to the portico,
was a polished black Rolls-Royce. The driver's door was ajar,
but there was no chauffeur in sight. As she passed the car she
felt the warmth of its radiator, as intimate as body heat, and
heard the click of contracting metal. She went up the steps
and pushed on the heavy, studded door.

The sweet waxy smell of wood, the watery smell of stone,
were of churches everywhere. Even as she turned her back to
close the door discreetly, she was aware that the church was
almost empty. The vicar's words were in counterpoint with
their echoes. She stood by the door, partly screened by the font,
waiting for her eyes and ears to adjust. Then she advanced to
the rear pew and slid along to the end where she still had a
view of the altar. She had been to various family weddings,
though she was too young to have been at the grand affair
in Liverpool Cathedral of Uncle Cecil and Aunt Hermione,
whose form and elaborate hat she could now distinguish
in the front row. Next to her were Pierrot and Jackson,
lankier by five or six inches, wedged between the outlines
of their estranged parents. On the other side of the aisle were
three members of the Marshall family. This was the entire
congregation. A private ceremony. No society journalists.
Briony was not meant to be there. She was familiar enough
with the form of words to know that she had not missed the
moment itself.

'Secondly, it was ordained for a remedy against sin, and
to avoid fornication, that such persons as have not the gift
of continency might marry and keep themselves undefiled
members of Christ's body.'

Facing the altar, framed by the elevated white-sheeted
shape of the vicar, stood the couple. She was in white, the

full traditional wear, and, as far as Briony could tell from the rear, was heavily veiled. Her hair was gathered into a single childish plait that fell from under the froth of tulle and organdie and lay along the length of her spine. Marshall stood erect, the lines of his padded morning-suit shoulders etched sharply against the vicar's surplice.

'Thirdly, it was ordained for the mutual society, help and comfort, that the one ought to have of the other . . .'

She felt the memories, the needling details, like a rash, like dirt on her skin: Lola coming to her room in tears, her chafed and bruised wrists, and the scratches on Lola's shoulder and down Marshall's face; Lola's silence in the darkness at the lakeside as she let her earnest, ridiculous, oh so prim younger cousin, who couldn't tell real life from the stories in her head, deliver the attacker into safety. Poor vain and vulnerable Lola with the pearl-studded choker and the rose-water scent, who longed to throw off the last restraints of childhood, who saved herself from humiliation by falling in love, or persuading herself she had, and who could not believe her luck when Briony insisted on doing the talking and blaming. And what luck that was for Lola – barely more than a child, prised open and taken – to marry her rapist.

'. . . Therefore if any man can show any just cause, why they may not be lawfully joined together, let him now speak, or else hereafter for ever hold his peace.'

Was it really happening? Was she really rising now, with weak legs and empty contracting stomach and stuttering heart, and moving along the pew to take her position in the centre of the aisle, and setting out her reasons, her just causes, in a defiant untrembling voice as she advanced in her cape and headdress, like a bride of Christ, towards the altar, towards the open-mouthed vicar who had never before in his long career been interrupted, towards the congregation of twisted necks, and the half-turned white-faced couple? She had not planned it, but the question, which she had quite forgotten, from the *Book of Common Prayer*, was a provocation. And what were the impediments exactly? Now was her chance to proclaim in public all the private anguish and purge herself of all that she had done wrong. Before the altar of this most rational of churches.

But the scratches and bruises were long healed, and all her own statements at the time were to the contrary. Nor did the bride appear to be a victim, and she had her parents' consent. More than that, surely; a chocolate magnate, the creator of Amo. Aunt Hermione would be rubbing her hands. That Paul Marshall, Lola Quincey and she, Briony Tallis, had conspired with silence and falsehoods to send an innocent man to jail? But the words that had convicted him had been her very own, read out loud on her behalf in the Assize Court. The sentence had already been served. The debt was paid. The verdict stood.

She remained in her seat with her accelerating heart and sweating palms, and humbly inclined her head.

'I require and charge you both, as ye will answer at the dreadful day of judgment when the secrets of all hearts will be disclosed, that if either of you know of any impediment, why ye may not be lawfully joined together in matrimony, ye do now confess it.'

By any estimate, it was a very long time until judgment day, and until then the truth that only Marshall and his bride knew at first hand, was steadily being walled up within the mausoleum of their marriage. There it would lie secure in the darkness, long after anyone who cared was dead. Every word in the ceremony was another brick in place.

'Who giveth this woman to be married to this man?'

Birdlike Uncle Cecil stepped up smartly, no doubt anxious to be done with his duty before hurrying back to the sanctuary of All Souls, Oxford. Straining to hear any wavering doubt in their voices, Briony listened to Marshall, then Lola, repeating the words after the vicar. She was sweet and sure, while Marshall boomed, as though in defiance. How flagrantly, sensually, it reverberated before the altar, when she said, 'With my body I thee worship.'

'Let us pray.'

Then the seven outlined heads in the front pews drooped and the vicar removed his tortoiseshell glasses, lifted his chin and with eyes closed addressed the heavenly powers in his weary, sorrowful singsong.

'O Eternal God, Creator and Preserver of all mankind, Giver of all spiritual grace, the Author of everlasting life; Send thy blessing upon these thy servants, this man and this woman . . .'

The last brick was set in place as the vicar, having put his glasses back on, made the celebrated pronouncement – man and wife together – and invoked the Trinity after which his church was named. There were more prayers, a psalm, the Lord's Prayer and another long one in which the falling tones of valediction gathered into a melancholy finality.

'. . . Pour upon you the riches of his grace, sanctify and bless you, that ye may please him both in body and soul, and live together in holy love unto your lives' end.'

Immediately, there cascaded from the fluting organ confetti of skittering triplets as the vicar turned to lead the couple down the aisle and the six family members fell in behind. Briony, who had been on her knees in a pretence of prayer, stood and turned to face the procession as it reached her. The vicar seemed a little pressed for time, and was many feet ahead of the rest. When he glanced to his left and saw the young nurse, his kindly look and tilt of the head expressed both welcome and curiosity. Then he strode on to pull one of the big doors wide open. A slanting tongue of sunlight reached all the way to where she stood and illuminated her face and headdress. She wanted to be seen, but not quite so clearly. There would be no missing her now. Lola, who was on Briony's side, drew level and their eyes met. Her veil was already parted. The freckles had vanished, but otherwise she was not much changed. Only slightly taller perhaps, and prettier, softer and rounder in the face, and the eyebrows severely plucked. Briony simply stared. All she wanted was for Lola to know she was there and to wonder why. The sunlight made it harder for Briony to see, but for a fraction of a moment, a tiny frown of displeasure may have registered in the bride's face. Then she pursed her lips and looked to the front, and then she was gone. Paul Marshall had seen her too, but had not recognised her, and nor had Aunt Hermione or Uncle Cecil who had not met her in years. But the twins, bringing up the rear in school uniform trousers at half mast, were delighted to see her, and mimed mock-horror at her costume, and did clownish eye-rolling yawns, with hands flapping on their mouths.

Then she was alone in the church with the unseen organist who went on playing for his own pleasure. It was over too quickly, and nothing for certain was achieved. She remained standing in place, beginning to feel a little foolish, reluctant to go outside. Daylight, and the banality of family small-talk, would dispel whatever impact she had made as a ghostly illuminated apparition. She also lacked courage for a confrontation. And how would she explain herself, the uninvited guest, to her uncle and aunt? They might be offended, or worse, they might not be, and want to take her off to some excruciating breakfast in a hotel, with Mr and Mrs Paul Marshall oily with hatred, and Hermione failing to conceal her contempt for Cecil. Briony lingered another minute or two, as though held there by the music, then, annoyed with her own cowardice, hurried out onto the portico. The vicar was a hundred yards off at least, walking quickly away across the common with arms swinging freely. The newly-weds were in the Rolls, Marshall at the wheel, reversing in order to turn round. She was certain they saw her. There was a metallic screech as he changed gear – a good sign perhaps. The car moved away, and through a side window she saw Lola's white shape huddled against the driver's arm. As for the congregation, it had vanished completely among the trees.

She knew from her map that Balham lay at the far end of the Common, in the direction the vicar was walking. It was not very far, and this fact alone made her reluctant to continue. She would arrive too soon. She had eaten nothing, she was thirsty, and her heel was throbbing and had glued itself to the back of her shoe. It was warm now, and she would be crossing a shadeless expanse of grass, broken by straight asphalt paths and public shelters. In the distance was a bandstand where men in dark blue uniforms were milling about. She thought of Fiona whose day off she had taken, and of their afternoon in St James's Park. It seemed a far-off, innocent time, but it was no more than ten days ago. Fiona would be doing the second bedpan round by now. Briony remained in the shade of the portico and thought about the little present she would buy her friend – something delicious to eat, a banana, oranges, Swiss chocolate. The porters knew how to get these things. She had heard them say that anything, everything, was available, if you had the right money. She watched the file of traffic moving round the Common, along her route, and she thought about food. Slabs of ham, poached eggs, the leg of a roast chicken, thick Irish stew, lemon meringue. A cup of tea. She became aware of the nervy, fidgeting music behind her the moment it ceased, and in the sudden new measure of silence, which seemed to confer freedom, she decided she must eat breakfast. There were no shops that she could see in the direction she had to walk, only dull mansion blocks of flats in deep orange brick.

Some minutes passed, and the organist came out holding his hat in one hand and a heavy set of keys in the other. She would have asked him the way to the nearest café, but he was a jittery-looking man at one with his music, who seemed determined to ignore her as he slammed the church door shut and stooped over to lock it. He rammed his hat on and hurried away.

Perhaps this was the first step in the undoing of her plans, but she was already walking back, retracing her steps, in the direction of Clapham High Street. She would have breakfast, and she would reconsider. Near the tube station she passed a stone drinking trough and could happily have sunk her face in it. She found a drab little place with smeared windows, and cigarette butts all over the floor, but the food could be no worse than what she was used to. She ordered tea, and three pieces of toast and margarine, and strawberry jam of palest pink. She heaped sugar into the tea, having diagnosed herself as suffering from hypoglycaemia. The sweetness did not quite conceal a taste of disinfectant.

She drank a second cup, glad that it was lukewarm so she could gulp it down, then she made use of a reeking seatless lavatory across a cobbled courtyard behind the café. But there was no stench that could impress a trainee nurse. She wedged lavatory paper into the heel of her shoe. It would see her another mile or two. A handbasin with a single tap was bolted to a brick wall. There was a grey-veined lozenge of soap she preferred not to touch. When she ran the water, the waste fell straight out onto her shins. She dried them with her sleeves, and combed her hair, trying to imagine her face in the brickwork. However, she couldn't reapply her lipstick without a mirror. She dabbed her face with a soaked handkerchief, and patted her cheeks to bring up the colour. A decision had been made – without her, it seemed. This was an interview she was preparing for, the post of beloved younger sister.

She left the café, and as she walked along the Common she felt the distance widen between her and another self, no less real, who was walking back towards the hospital. Perhaps the Briony who was walking in the direction of Balham was the imagined or ghostly persona. This unreal feeling was heightened when, after half an hour, she reached another High Street, more or less the same as the one she had left behind. That was all London was beyond its centre, an agglomeration of dull little towns. She made a resolution never to live in any of them.

The street she was looking for was three turnings past the tube station, itself another replica. The Edwardian terraces, net-curtained and seedy, ran straight for half a mile. 43 Dudley Villas was halfway down, with nothing to distinguish it from the others except for an old Ford 8, without wheels, supported on brick piles, which took up the whole of the front garden. If there was no one in, she could go away, telling herself she had tried. The doorbell did not work. She let the knocker fall twice and stood back. She heard a woman's angry voice, then the slam of a door and the thud of footsteps. Briony took another pace back. It was not too late to retreat up the street. There was a fumbling with the catch and an irritable sigh, and the door was opened by a tall, sharp-faced woman in her thirties who was out of breath from some terrible exertion. She was in a fury. She had been interrupted in a row, and was unable to adjust her expression – the mouth open, the upper lip slightly curled – as she took Briony in.

'What do you want?'

'I'm looking for a Miss Cecilia Tallis.'

Her shoulders sagged, and she turned her head back, as though recoiling from an insult. She looked Briony up and down.

'You look like her.'

Bewildered, Briony simply stared at her.

The woman gave another sigh that was almost like a spitting sound, and went along the hallway to the foot of the stairs.

'Tallis!' she yelled. 'Door!'

She came halfway back along the corridor to the entrance to her sitting room, flashed Briony a look of contempt, then disappeared, pulling the door violently behind her.

The house was silent. Briony's view past the open front door was of a stretch of floral lino, and the first seven or eight stairs which were covered in deep red carpet. The brass rod on the third step was missing. Halfway along

the hall was a semicircular table against the wall, and on it
was a polished wooden stand, like a toast rack, for holding
letters. It was empty. The lino extended past the stairs to a
door with a frosted-glass window which probably opened
onto the kitchen out the back. The wallpaper was floral too
– a posy of three roses alternating with a snowflake design.
From the threshold to the beginning of the stairs she counted
fifteen roses, sixteen snowflakes. Inauspicious.

At last, she heard a door opening upstairs, possibly the
one she had heard slammed when she had knocked. Then
the creak of a stair, and feet wearing thick socks came into
view, and a flash of bare skin, and a blue silk dressing gown
that she recognised. Finally, Cecilia's face tilting sideways as
she leaned down to make out who was at the front door and
spare herself the trouble of descending further, improperly
dressed. It took her some moments to recognise her sister.
She came down slowly another three steps.

'Oh my God.'

She sat down and folded her arms.

Briony remained standing with one foot still on the garden
path, the other on the front step. A wireless in the landlady's sitting room came on, and the laughter of an audience
swelled as the valves warmed. There followed a comedian's
wheedling monologue, broken at last by applause, and a jolly
band striking up. Briony took a step into the hallway.

She murmured, 'I have to talk to you.'

Cecilia was about to get up, then changed her mind. 'Why
didn't you tell me you were coming?'

'You didn't answer my letter, so I came.'

She drew her dressing gown around her, and patted its
pocket, probably in the hope of a cigarette. She was much
darker in complexion, and her hands too were brown. She
had not found what she wanted, but for the moment she did
not make to rise.

Marking time rather than changing the subject she said,
'You're a probationer.'

'Yes.'

'Whose ward?'

'Sister Drummond's.'

There was no telling whether Cecilia was familiar with this name, or whether she was displeased that her younger sister was training at the same hospital. There was another obvious difference – Cecilia had always spoken to her in a motherly or condescending way. Little Sis! No room for that now. There was a hardness in her tone that warned Briony off asking about Robbie. She took another step further into the hallway, conscious of the front door open behind her.

'And where are you?'

'Near Morden. It's an EMS.'

An Emergency Medical Services hospital, a commandeered place, most likely dealing with the brunt, the real brunt of the evacuation. There was too much that couldn't be said, or asked. The two sisters looked at each other. Even though Cecilia had the rumpled look of someone who had just got out of bed, she was more beautiful than Briony remembered her. That long face always looked odd, and vulnerable, horsey everyone said, even in the best of lights. Now it looked boldly sensual, with an accentuated bow of the full purplish lips. The eyes were dark and enlarged, by fatigue perhaps. Or sorrow. The long fine nose, the dainty flare of the nostrils – there was something mask-like and carved about the face, and very still. And hard to read. Her sister's appearance added to Briony's unease, and made her feel clumsy. She barely knew this woman whom she hadn't seen in five years. Briony could take nothing for granted. She was searching for another neutral topic, but there was nothing that did not lead back to the sensitive subjects – the subjects she was going to have to confront in any case – and it was because she could no longer bear the silence and the staring that she said at last,

'Have you heard from the Old Man?'

'No, I haven't.'

The downward tone implied she didn't want to, and wouldn't care or reply if she did.

Cecilia said, 'Have you?'

'I had a scribbled note a couple of weeks ago.'

'Good.'

So there was no more to be said on that. After another pause, Briony tried again.

'What about from home?'

'No. I'm not in touch. And you?'

'She writes now and then.'

'And what's her news, Briony?'

The question and the use of her name was sardonic. As she forced her memory back, she felt she was being exposed as a traitor to her sister's cause.

'They've taken in evacuees and Betty hates them. The park's been ploughed up for corn.' She trailed away. It was inane to be standing there listing these details.

But Cecilia said coldly, 'Go on. What else?'

'Well, most of the lads in the village have joined the East Surreys, except for . . .'

'Except for Danny Hardman. Yes, I know all about that.' She smiled in a bright, artificial way, waiting for Briony to continue.

'They've built a pillbox by the post office, and they've taken up all the old railings. Um. Aunt Hermione's living in Nice, and oh yes, Betty broke Uncle Clem's vase.'

Only now was Cecilia roused from her coolness. She uncrossed her arms and pressed a hand against her cheek.

'Broke?'

'She dropped it on a step.'

'You mean properly broken, in lots of pieces?'

'Yes.'

Cecilia considered this. Finally she said, 'That's terrible.'

'Yes,' Briony said. 'Poor Uncle Clem.' At least her sister was no longer derisive. The interrogation continued.

'Did they keep the pieces?'

'I don't know. Emily said the Old Man shouted at Betty.'

At that moment, the door snapped open and the landlady stood right in front of Briony, so close to her that she could smell peppermint on the woman's breath. She pointed at the front door.

'This isn't a railway station. Either you're in, young lady, or you're out.'

Cecilia was getting to her feet without any particular hurry, and was retying the silk cord of her dressing gown. She said languidly, 'This is my sister, Briony, Mrs Jarvis. Try and remember your manners when you speak to her.'

'In my own home I'll speak as I please,' Mrs Jarvis said. She turned back to Briony. 'Stay if you're staying, otherwise leave now and close the door behind you.'

Briony looked at her sister, guessing that she was unlikely to let her go now. Mrs Jarvis had turned out to be an unwitting ally.

Cecilia spoke as though they were alone. 'Don't mind the landlady. I'm leaving at the end of the week. Close the door and come up.'

Watched by Mrs Jarvis, Briony began to follow her sister up the stairs.

'And as for you, Lady Muck,' the landlady called up.

But Cecilia turned sharply and cut her off. 'Enough, Mrs Jarvis. Now that's quite enough.'

Briony recognised the tone. Pure Nightingale, for use on difficult patients or tearful students. It took years to perfect. Cecilia had surely been promoted to ward sister.

On the first-floor landing, as she was about to open her door, she gave Briony a look, a cool glance to let her know that nothing had changed, nothing had softened. From the bathroom across the way, through its half-open door, drifted a humid scented air and a hollow dripping sound. Cecilia had been about to take a bath. She led Briony into her flat. Some of the tidiest nurses on the ward lived in stews in their own rooms, and she would not have been surprised to see a new version of Cecilia's old chaos. But the impression here was of a simple and lonely life. A medium-sized room had been divided to make a narrow strip of a kitchen and, presumably, a bedroom next door. The walls were papered with a design of pale vertical strips, like a boy's pyjamas, which heightened the sense of confinement. The lino was irregular offcuts from downstairs, and in places, grey floorboards showed. Under the single sash window was a sink with one tap and a one-ring gas cooker. Against the wall, leaving little room to squeeze by, was a table covered with a yellow gingham cloth. On it was a jam jar of blue flowers, harebells perhaps, and a full ash-tray, and a pile of books. At the bottom were *Gray's Anatomy* and a collected Shakespeare, and above them, on slenderer spines, names in faded silver and gold – she saw Housman and Crabbe. By the books were two bottles of stout. In the corner furthest from the window was the door to the bedroom on which was tacked a map of northern Europe.

Cecilia took a cigarette from a packet by the cooker, and then, remembering that her sister was no longer a child, offered one to her. There were two kitchen chairs by the table, but Cecilia, who leaned with her back to the sink, did not invite Briony to sit down. The two women smoked and waited, so it seemed to Briony, for the air to clear of the landlady's presence.

Cecilia said in a quiet level voice, 'When I got your letter I went to see a solicitor. It's not straightforward, unless there's hard new evidence. Your change of heart won't be enough. Lola will go on saying she doesn't know. Our only hope was Old Hardman and now he's dead.'

'Hardman?' The contending elements – the fact of his death, his relevance to the case – confused Briony and she struggled with her memory. Was Hardman out that night looking for the twins? Did he see something? Was something said in court that she didn't know about?

'Didn't you know he was dead?'

'No. But . . .'

'Unbelievable.'

Cecilia's attempts at a neutral, factual tone were coming apart. Agitated, she came away from the cooking area, squeezed past the table and went to the other end of the room and stood by the bedroom door. Her voice was breathy as she tried to control her anger.

'How odd that Emily didn't include that in her news along with the corn and the evacuees. He had cancer. Perhaps with the fear of God in him he was saying something in his last days that was rather too inconvenient for everyone at this stage.'

'But Cee . . .'

She snapped, 'Don't call me that!' She repeated in a softer voice, 'Please don't call me that.' Her fingers were on the handle of the bedroom door and it looked like the interview was coming to an end. She was about to disappear.

With an implausible display of calm, she summarised for Briony.

'What I paid two guineas to discover is this. There isn't going to be an appeal just because five years on you've decided to tell the truth.'

'I don't understand what you're saying . . .' Briony wanted to get back to Hardman, but Cecilia needed to tell her what must have gone through her head many times lately.

'It isn't difficult. If you were lying then, why should a court believe you now? There are no new facts, and you're an unreliable witness.'

Briony carried her half-smoked cigarette to the sink. She was feeling sick. She took a saucer for an ash-tray from the plate rack. Her sister's confirmation of her crime was terrible to hear. But the perspective was unfamiliar. Weak, stupid, confused, cowardly, evasive – she had hated herself for everything she had been, but she had never thought of herself as a liar. How strange, and how clear it must seem to Cecilia. It was obvious, and irrefutable. And yet, for a moment she even thought of defending herself. She hadn't intended to mislead, she hadn't acted out of malice. But who would believe that?

She stood where Cecilia had stood, with her back to the sink and, unable to meet her sister's eye, said, 'What I did was terrible. I don't expect you to forgive me.'

'Don't worry about that,' she said soothingly, and in the second or two during which she drew deeply on her cigarette, Briony flinched as her hopes lifted unreally. 'Don't worry,' her sister resumed. 'I won't ever forgive you.'

'And if I can't go to court, that won't stop me telling everyone what I did.'

As her sister gave a wild little laugh, Briony realised how frightened she was of Cecilia. Her derision was even harder to confront than her anger. This narrow room with its stripes like bars contained a history of feeling that no one could imagine. Briony pressed on. She was, after all, in a part of the conversation she had rehearsed.

'I'll go to Surrey and speak to Emily and the Old Man. I'll tell them everything.'

'Yes, you said that in your letter. What's stopping you? You've had five years. Why haven't you been?'

'I wanted to see you first.'

Cecilia came away from the bedroom door and stood by the table. She dropped her stub into the neck of a stout bottle. There was a brief hiss and a thin line of smoke rose from the black glass. Her sister's action made Briony feel nauseous again. She had thought the bottles were full. She wondered if she had ingested something unclean with her breakfast.

Cecilia said, 'I know why you haven't been. Because your guess is the same as mine. They don't want to hear anything more about it. That unpleasantness is all in the past, thank you very much. What's done is done. Why stir things up now? And you know very well they believed Hardman's story.'

Briony came away from the sink and stood right across the table from her sister. It was not easy to look into that beautiful mask.

She said very deliberately, 'I don't understand what you're

talking about. What's he got to do with this? I'm sorry he's dead, I'm sorry I didn't know . . .'

At a sound, she started. The bedroom door was opening and Robbie stood before them. He wore army trousers and shirt and polished boots, and his braces hung free at his waist. He was unshaven and tousled, and his gaze was on Cecilia only. She had turned to face him, but she did not go towards him. In the seconds during which they looked at each other in silence, Briony, partly obscured by her sister, shrank into her uniform.

He spoke to Cecilia quietly, as though they were alone, 'I heard voices and I guessed it was something to do with the hospital.'

'That's all right.'

He looked at his watch. 'Better get moving.'

As he crossed the room, just before he went out onto the landing, he made a brief nod in Briony's direction. 'Excuse me.'

They heard the bathroom door close. Into the silence Cecilia said, as if there were nothing between her and her sister, 'He sleeps so deeply. I didn't want to wake him.' Then she added, 'I thought it would be better if you didn't meet.'

Briony's knees were actually beginning to tremble. Supporting herself with one hand on the table, she moved away from the kitchen area so that Cecilia could fill the kettle. Briony longed to sit down. She would not do so until invited, and she would never ask. So she stood by the wall, pretending not to lean against it, and watched her sister. What was surprising was the speed with which her relief that Robbie was alive was supplanted by her dread of confronting him. Now she had seen him walk across the room, the other possibility, that he could have been killed, seemed outlandish, against all the odds. It would have made no sense. She was staring at her sister's back as she moved about the tiny kitchen. Briony wanted to tell her how wonderful it was that Robbie had come back safely. What deliverance. But how banal that would have sounded. And she had no business saying it. She feared her sister, and her scorn.

Still feeling nauseous, and now hot, Briony pressed her cheek against the wall. It was no cooler than her face. She longed for a glass of water, but she did not want to ask her sister for anything. Briskly, Cecilia moved about her tasks, mixing milk and water to egg powder, and setting out a pot of jam and three plates and cups on the table. Briony registered this, but it gave her no comfort. It only increased her foreboding of the meeting that lay ahead. Did Cecilia really think that in this situation they could sit together and still have an appetite for scrambled eggs? Or was she soothing herself by being busy? Briony was listening out for footsteps on the landing, and it was to distract herself that she attempted a conversational tone. She had seen the cape hanging on the back of the door.

'Cecilia, are you a ward sister now?'

'Yes, I am.'

She said it with a downward finality, closing off the subject. Their shared profession was not going to be a bond. Nothing was, and there was nothing to talk about until Robbie came back.

At last she heard the click of the lock on the bathroom door. He was whistling as he crossed the landing. Briony moved away from the door, further down towards the darker end of the room. But she was in his sightline as he came in. He had half raised his right hand in order to shake hers, and his left trailed, about to close the door behind him. If it was a double take, it was undramatic. As soon as their eyes met, his hands dropped to his sides and he gave a little winded sigh as he continued to look at her hard. However intimidated, she felt she could not look away. She smelled the faint perfume of his shaving soap. The shock was how much older he looked, especially round the eyes. Did everything have to be her fault? she wondered stupidly. Couldn't it also be the war's?

'So it was you,' he said finally. He pushed the door closed

behind him with his foot. Cecilia had come to stand by his side and he looked at her.

She gave an exact summary, but even if she had wanted, she would not have been able to withhold her sarcasm.

'Briony's going to tell everybody the truth. She wanted to see me first.'

He turned back to Briony. 'Did you think I might be here?'

Her immediate concern was not to cry. At that moment, nothing would have been more humiliating. Relief, shame, self-pity, she didn't know which it was, but it was coming. The smooth wave rose, tightening her throat, making it impossible to speak, and then, as she held on, tensing her lips, it fell away and she was safe. No tears, but her voice was a miserable whisper.

'I didn't know if you were alive.'

Cecilia said, 'If we're going to talk we should sit down.'

'I don't know that I can.' He moved away impatiently to the adjacent wall, a distance of seven feet or so, and leaned against it, arms crossed, looking from Briony to Cecilia. Almost immediately he moved again, down the room to the bedroom door where he turned to come back, changed his mind and stood there, hands in pockets. He was a large man, and the room seemed to have shrunk. In the confined space he was desperate in his movements, as though suffocating. He took his hands from his pockets and smoothed the hair at the back of his neck. Then he rested his hands on his hips. Then he let them drop. It took all this time, all this movement, for Briony to realise that he was angry, very angry, and just as she did, he said,

'What are you doing here? Don't talk to me about Surrey. No one's stopping you going. Why are you here?'

She said, 'I had to talk to Cecilia.'

'Oh yes. And what about?'

'The terrible thing that I did.'

Cecilia was going towards him. 'Robbie,' she whispered. 'Darling.' She put her hand on his arm, but he pulled it clear.

'I don't know why you let her in.' Then to Briony, 'I'll be quite honest with you. I'm torn between breaking your stupid neck here and taking you outside and throwing you down the stairs.'

If it had not been for her recent experience, she would have been terrified. Sometimes she heard soldiers on the ward raging against their helplessness. At the height of their passion, it was foolish to reason with them or try to reassure them. It had to come out, and it was best to stand and listen. She knew that even offering to leave now could be provocative. So she faced Robbie and waited for the rest, her due. But she was not frightened of him, not physically.

He did not raise his voice, though it was straining with contempt. 'Have you any idea at all what it's like inside?'

She imagined small high windows in a cliff face of brick, and thought perhaps she did, the way people imagined the different torments of hell. She shook her head faintly. To steady herself she was trying to concentrate on the details of his transformation. The impression of added height was due to his parade-ground posture. No Cambridge student ever stood so straight. Even in his distraction his shoulders were well back, and his chin was raised like an old-fashioned boxer.

'No, of course you don't. And when I was inside, did that give you pleasure?'

'No.'

'But you did nothing.'

She had thought about this conversation many times, like a child anticipating a beating. Now it was happening at last, and it was as if she wasn't quite here. She was watching from far away and she was numb. But she knew his words would hurt her later.

Cecilia had stood back. Now she put her hand again on Robbie's arm. He had lost weight, though he looked stronger, with a lean and stringy muscular ferocity. He half turned to her.

'Remember,' Cecilia was starting to say, but he spoke over her.

'Do you think I assaulted your cousin?'

'No.'

'Did you think it then?'

She fumbled her words. 'Yes, yes and no. I wasn't certain.'

'And what's made you so certain now?'

She hesitated, conscious that in answering she would be offering a form of defence, a rationale, and that it might enrage him further.

'Growing up.'

He stared at her, lips slightly parted. He really had changed in five years. The hardness in his gaze was new, and the eyes were smaller and narrower, and in the corners were the firm prints of crows' feet. His face was thinner than she remembered, the cheeks were sunken, like an Indian brave's. He had grown a little toothbrush moustache in the military style. He was startlingly handsome, and there came back to her from years ago, when she was ten or eleven, the memory of a passion she'd had for him, a real crush that had lasted days. Then she confessed it to him one morning in the garden and immediately forgot about it.

She had been right to be wary. He was gripped by the kind of anger that passes itself off as wonderment.

'Growing up,' he echoed. When he raised his voice she jumped. 'Godamnit! You're eighteen. How much growing up do you need to do? There are soldiers dying in the field at eighteen. Old enough to be left to die on the roads. Did you know that?'

'Yes.'

It was a pathetic source of comfort, that he could not know what she had seen. Strange, that for all her guilt, she should feel the need to withstand him. It was that, or be annihilated.

She barely nodded. She did not dare speak. At the mention of dying, a surge of feeling had engulfed him, pushing him

beyond anger into an extremity of bewilderment and disgust.
His breathing was irregular and heavy, he clenched and
unclenched his right fist. And still he stared at her, into
her, with a rigidity, a savagery in his look. His eyes were
bright, and he swallowed hard several times. The muscles
in his throat tensed and knotted. He too was fighting off an
emotion he did not want witnessed. She had learned the little
she knew, the tiny, next-to-nothing scraps that came the way
of a trainee nurse, in the safety of the ward and the bedside.
She knew enough to recognise that memories were crowding
in, and there was nothing he could do. They wouldn't let him
speak. She would never know what scenes were driving this
turmoil. He took a step towards her and she shrank back, no
longer certain of his harmlessness – if he couldn't talk, he
might have to act. Another step, and he could have reached
her with his sinewy arm. But Cecilia slid between them. With
her back to Briony, she faced Robbie and placed her hands on
his shoulders. He turned his face away from her.

'Look at me,' she murmured. 'Robbie. Look at me.'

The reply he made was lost to Briony. She heard his dissent
or denial. Perhaps it was an obscenity. As Cecilia gripped him
tighter, he twisted his whole body away from her, and they
seemed like wrestlers as she reached up and tried to turn
his head towards her. But his face was tilted back, his lips
retracted and teeth bared in a ghoulish parody of a smile.
Now with two hands she was gripping his cheeks tightly,
and with an effort she turned his face and drew it towards
her own. At last he was looking into her eyes, but still she
kept her grip on his cheeks. She pulled him closer, drawing
him into her gaze, until their faces met and she kissed him
lightly, lingeringly on the lips. With a tenderness that Briony
remembered from years ago, waking in the night, Cecilia said,
'Come back . . . Robbie, come back.'

He nodded faintly, and took a deep breath which he released
slowly as she relaxed her grip and withdrew her hands from
his face. In the silence, the room appeared to shrink even

smaller. He put his arms around her, lowered his head and kissed her, a deep, sustained and private kiss. Briony moved away quietly to the other end of the room, towards the window. While she drank a glass of water from the kitchen tap, the kiss continued, binding the couple into their solitude. She felt obliterated, expunged from the room, and was relieved.

She turned her back and looked out at the quiet terraced houses in full sunlight, at the way she had come from the High Street. She was surprised to discover that she had no wish to leave yet, even though she was embarrassed by the long kiss, and dreaded what more there was to come. She watched an old woman dressed in a heavy overcoat, despite the heat. She was on the far pavement walking an ailing swag-bellied dachshund on a lead. Cecilia and Robbie were talking in low voices now, and Briony decided that to respect their privacy she would not turn from the window until she was spoken to. It was soothing to watch the woman unfasten her front gate, close it carefully behind her with fussy exactitude, and then, halfway to her front door, bend with difficulty to pull up a weed from the narrow bed that ran the length of her front path. As she did so, the dog waddled forwards and licked her wrist. The lady and her dog went indoors, and the street was empty again. A blackbird dropped down onto a privet hedge and, finding no satisfactory foothold, flew away. The shadow of a cloud came and swiftly dimmed the light, and passed on. It could be any Saturday afternoon. There was little evidence of a war in this suburban street. A glimpse of blackout blinds in a window across the way, the Ford 8 on its blocks, perhaps.

Briony heard her sister say her name and turned round.

'There isn't much time. Robbie has to report for duty at six tonight and he's got a train to catch. So sit down. There are some things you're going to do for us.'

It was the ward sister's voice. Not even bossy. She simply described the inevitable. Briony took the chair nearest her, Robbie brought over a stool, and Cecilia sat between them. The breakfast she had prepared was forgotten. The three empty cups stood in the centre of the table. He lifted the pile of books to the floor. As Cecilia moved the jam jar of harebells to one side where it could not be knocked over, she exchanged a look with Robbie.

He was staring at the flowers as he cleared his throat. When he began to speak, his voice was purged of emotion. He could have been reading from a set of standing orders. He was looking at her now. His eyes were steady, and he had everything under control. But there were drops of sweat on his forehead, above his eyebrows.

'The most important thing you've already agreed to. You're to go to your parents as soon as you can and tell them everything they need to know to be convinced that your evidence was false. When's your day off?'

'Sunday week.'

'That's when you'll go. You'll take our addresses and you'll tell Jack and Emily that Cecilia is waiting to hear from them. The second thing you'll do tomorrow. Cecilia says you'll have an hour at some point. You'll go to a solicitor, a commissioner for oaths, and make a statement which will be signed and witnessed. In it you'll say what you did wrong, and how you're retracting your evidence. You'll send copies to both of us. Is that clear?'

'Yes.'

'Then you'll write to me in much greater detail. In this letter you'll put in absolutely everything you think is relevant. Everything that led up to you saying you saw me by the lake. And why, even though you were uncertain, you stuck to your story in the months leading up to my trial. If there were pressures on you, from the police or your parents, I want to know. Have you got that? It needs to be a long letter.'

'Yes.'

He met Cecilia's look and nodded. 'And if you can remember anything at all about Danny Hardman, where he was, what he was doing, at what time, who else saw him – anything that might put his alibi in question, then we want to hear it.'

Cecilia was writing out the addresses. Briony was shaking her head and starting to speak, but Robbie ignored her and spoke over her. He had got to his feet and was looking at his watch.

'There's very little time. We're going to walk you to the tube. Cecilia and I want the last hour together alone before I have to leave. And you'll need to spend the rest of today writing your statement, and letting your parents know you're coming. And you could start thinking about this letter you're sending me.'

With this brittle précis of her obligations he left the table and went towards the bedroom.

Briony stood too and said, 'Old Hardman was probably telling the truth. Danny was with him all that night.'

Cecilia was about to pass the folded sheet of paper she had been writing on. Robbie had stopped in the bedroom doorway.

Cecilia said, 'What do you mean by that? What are you saying?'

'It was Paul Marshall.'

During the silence that followed, Briony tried to imagine the adjustments that each would be making. Years of seeing it a certain way. And yet, however startling, it was only a detail. Nothing essential was changed by it. Nothing in her own role.

Robbie came back to the table. 'Marshall?'

'Yes.'

'You saw him?'

'I saw a man his height.'

'My height.'

'Yes.'

Cecilia now stood and looked around her – a hunt for the cigarettes was about to start. Robbie found them and tossed the packet across the room. Cecilia lit up and said as she exhaled, 'I find it difficult to believe. He's a fool, I know . . .'

'He's a greedy fool,' Robbie said. 'But I can't imagine him with Lola Quincey, even for the five minutes it took . . .'

Given all that had happened, and all its terrible consequences, it was frivolous, she knew, but Briony took calm pleasure in delivering her clinching news.

'I've just come from their wedding.'

Again, the amazed adjustments, the incredulous repetition. Wedding? This morning? Clapham? Then reflective silence, broken by single remarks.

'I want to find him.'

'You'll do no such thing.'

'I want to kill him.'

And then, 'It's time to go.'

There was so much more that could have been said. But they seemed exhausted, by her presence, or by the subject. Or they simply longed to be alone. Either way, it was clear they felt their meeting was at an end. All curiosity was spent. Everything could wait until she wrote her letter. Robbie fetched his jacket and cap from the bedroom. Briony noted the corporal's single stripe.

Cecilia was saying to him, 'He's immune. She'll always cover for him.'

Minutes were lost while she searched for her ration book. Finally, she gave up and said to Robbie, 'I'm sure it's in Wiltshire, in the cottage.'

As they were about to leave, and he was holding the door open for the sisters, Robbie said, 'I suppose we owe an apology to Able Seaman Hardman.'

Downstairs, Mrs Jarvis did not appear from her sitting room as they went by. They heard clarinets playing on her wireless. Once through the front door, it seemed to Briony that she was stepping into another day. There was a strong, gritty breeze blowing, and the street was in harsh relief, with even more sunlight, fewer shadows than before. There was not enough room on the pavement to go three abreast. Robbie and Cecilia walked behind her, hand in hand. Briony felt her blistered heel rubbing against her shoe, but she was determined they should not see her limp. She had the impression of being seen off the premises. At one point she turned and told them she would be happy to walk to the tube on her own. But they insisted. They had purchases to make for Robbie's journey. They walked on in silence. Small-talk was not an option. She knew that she did not have the right to ask her sister about her new address, or Robbie where the train was taking him, or about the cottage in Wiltshire. Was that where the harebells came from? Surely there had been an idyll. Nor could she ask when the two of them would see each other again. Together, she and her sister and Robbie had only one subject, and it was fixed in the unchangeable past.

They stood outside Balham tube station, which in three months' time would achieve its terrible form of fame in the Blitz. A thin stream of Saturday shoppers moved around them, causing them, against their will, to stand closer. They made a cool farewell. Robbie reminded her to have money with her when she saw the commissioner for oaths. Cecilia told her she was not to forget to take the addresses with her to Surrey. Then it was over. They stared at her, waiting for her to leave. But there was one thing she had not said.

She spoke slowly. 'I'm very very sorry. I've caused you such terrible distress.' They continued to stare at her, and she repeated herself. 'I'm very sorry.'

It sounded so foolish and inadequate, as though she had knocked over a favourite houseplant, or forgotten a birthday.

Robbie said softly, 'Just do all the things we've asked.'

It was almost conciliatory, that 'just', but not quite, not yet.

She said, 'Of course,' and then turned and walked away, conscious of them watching her as she entered the ticket hall and crossed it. She paid her fare to Waterloo. When she reached the barrier, she looked back and they had gone.

She showed her ticket and went through into the dirty yellow light, to the head of the clanking, creaking escalator, and it began to take her down, into the man-made breeze rising from the blackness, the breath of a million Londoners cooling her face and tugging at her cape. She stood still and let herself be carried down, grateful to be moving without scouring her heel. She was surprised at how serene she felt, and just a little sad. Was it disappointment? She had hardly expected to be forgiven. What she felt was more like homesickness, though there was no source for it, no home. But she was sad to leave her sister. It was her sister she missed – or more precisely, it was her sister with Robbie. Their love. Neither Briony nor the war had destroyed it. This was what soothed her as she sank deeper under the city. How Cecilia had drawn him to her with her eyes. That tenderness in her voice when she called him back from his memories, from Dunkirk, or from the roads that led to it. She used to speak like that to her sometimes, when Cecilia was sixteen and she was a child of six and things went impossibly wrong. Or in the night, when Cecilia came to rescue her from a nightmare and take her into her own bed. Those were the words she used. *Come back. It was only a bad dream. Briony, come back.* How easily this unthinking family love was forgotten. She was gliding down now, through the soupy brown light, almost to the bottom. There were no other passengers in sight, and the air was suddenly still. She was calm as she considered what she had to do. Together, the note to her parents and the formal statement would take no time at all. Then she would be free for the rest of the day. She knew what was required of her. Not simply a letter, but a new draft, an atonement, and she was ready to begin.

BT
London 1999

Edition 1999

London, 1999

What a strange time this has been. Today, on the morning of my seventy-seventh birthday, I decided to make one last visit to the Imperial War Museum library in Lambeth. It suited my peculiar state of mind. The reading room, housed right up in the dome of the building, was formerly the chapel of the Royal Bethlehem Hospital – the old Bedlam. Where the unhinged once came to offer their prayers, scholars now gather to research the collective insanity of war. The car the family was sending was not due until after lunch, so I thought I would distract myself, checking final details, and saying my farewells to the Keeper of Documents, and to the cheerful porters who have been escorting me up and down in the lift during these wintry weeks. I also intended to donate to the archives my dozen long letters from old Mr Nettle. It was a birthday present to myself, I suppose, to pass an hour or two in a half-pretence of seeming busy, fussing about with those little tasks of housekeeping that come at the end, and are part of the reluctant process of letting go. In the same mood, I was busy in my study yesterday afternoon; now the drafts are in order and dated, the photocopied sources labelled, the borrowed books ready for return, and everything is in the right box file. I've always liked to make a tidy finish.

It was too cold and wet, and I was feeling too troubled

to go by public transport. I took a taxi from Regent's Park, and in the long crawl through central London I thought of those sad inmates of Bedlam who were once a source of general entertainment, and I reflected in a self-pitying way on how I was soon to join their ranks. The results of my scan have come through and I went to see my doctor about them yesterday morning. It was not good news. This was the way he put it as soon as I sat down. My headaches, the sensation of tightness around the temples, have a particular and sinister cause. He pointed out some granular smears across a section of the scan. I noticed how the pencil tip quivered in his hand, and I wondered if he too was suffering some neural disorder. In the spirit of shoot the messenger, I rather hoped he was. I was experiencing, he said, a series of tiny, nearly imperceptible strokes. The process will be slow, but my brain, my mind, is closing down. The little failures of memory that dog us all beyond a certain point will become more noticeable, more debilitating, until the time will come when I won't notice them because I will have lost the ability to comprehend anything at all. The days of the week, the events of the morning, or even ten minutes ago, will be beyond my reach. My phone number, my address, my name and what I did with my life will be gone. In two, three or four years' time, I will not recognise my remaining oldest friends, and when I wake in the morning, I will not recognise that I am in my own room. And soon I won't be, because I will need continuous care.

I have vascular dementia, the doctor told me, and there was some comfort to be had. There's the slowness of the undoing, which he must have mentioned a dozen times. Also, it's not as bad as Alzheimer's, with its mood swings and aggression. If I'm lucky, it might turn out to be somewhat benign. I might not be unhappy – just a dim old biddy in a chair, knowing nothing, expecting nothing. I had asked him to be frank, so I could not complain. Now he was hurrying me out. There were twelve people in his waiting room wanting their turn. In summary, as he helped me into my coat, he gave me the route map: loss of memory, short- and long-term, the disappearance of single words – simple nouns might be the first to go – then language itself, along with balance, and soon after, all motor control, and finally the autonomous nervous system. Bon voyage!

I wasn't distressed, not at first. On the contrary, I was elated and urgently wanted to tell my closest friends. I spent an hour on the phone breaking my news. Perhaps I was already losing my grip. It seemed so momentous. All afternoon I pottered about in my study with my housekeeping chores, and by the time I finished, there were six new box files on the shelves. Stella and John came over in the evening and we ordered in some Chinese food. Between them they drank two bottles of Morgon. I drank green tea. My charming friends were devastated by my description of my future. They're both in their sixties, old enough to start fooling themselves that seventy-seven is still young. Today, in the taxi, as I crossed London at walking pace in the freezing rain, I thought of little else. I'm going mad, I told myself. Let me not be mad. But I couldn't really believe it. Perhaps I was nothing more than a victim of modern diagnostics; in another century it would have been said of me that I was old and therefore losing my mind. What else would I expect? I'm only dying then, I'm fading into unknowing.

My taxi was cutting through the back streets of Bloomsbury, past the house where my father lived after his second marriage, and past the basement flat where I lived and worked all through the fifties. Beyond a certain age, a journey across the city becomes uncomfortably reflective. The addresses of the dead pile up. We crossed the square where Leon heroically nursed his wife, and then raised his boisterous children with a devotion that amazed us all. One day I too will prompt a moment's reflection in the passenger of a passing cab. It's a popular shortcut, the Inner Circle of Regent's Park.

We crossed the river at Waterloo Bridge. I sat forward on the edge of my seat to take in my favourite view of the city, and as I turned my neck, downstream to St Paul's, upstream to Big Ben, the full panoply of tourist London in between, I felt myself to be physically well and mentally intact, give or take the headaches and a little tiredness. However withered, I still feel myself to be exactly the same person I've always been. Hard to explain that to the young. We may look truly reptilian, but we're not a separate tribe. In the next year or two, however, I will be losing my claim to this familiar protestation. The seriously ill, the deranged, are another race, an inferior race. I won't let anyone persuade me otherwise.

My cabbie was cursing. Over the river, roadworks were forcing us on a detour towards the old County Hall. As we swung off the roundabout there, towards Lambeth, I had a glimpse of St Thomas's Hospital. It took a clobbering in the Blitz – I wasn't there, thank God – and the replacement buildings and the tower block are a national disgrace. I worked in three hospitals in the duration – Alder Hey and the Royal East Sussex as well as St Thomas's – and I merged them in my description to concentrate all my experiences into one place. A convenient distortion, and the least of my offences against veracity.

It was raining less heavily as the driver made a neat U-turn in the middle of the road to bring us outside the main gates of the museum. With the business of gathering up my bag, finding a twenty-pound note and unfolding my umbrella, I did not notice the car parked immediately in front until my cab pulled away. It was a black Rolls. For a moment I thought it was unattended. In fact, the chauffeur was a diminutive fellow almost lost behind the front wheel. I'm not sure that what I am about to describe really rates as a startling coincidence. I occasionally think of the Marshalls whenever I see a parked Rolls without a driver. It's become a habit over the years. They often pass through my mind, usually without generating any particular feeling. I've grown used to the idea of them. They still appear in the newspapers occasionally, in connection with their Foundation and all its good work for medical research, or the collection they've donated to the

Tate, or their generous funding of agricultural projects in sub-Saharan Africa. And her parties, and their vigorous libel actions against national newspapers. It was not remarkable that Lord and Lady Marshall passed through my thoughts as I approached those massive twin guns in front of the museum, but it was a shock to see them coming down the steps towards me.

A posse of officials – I recognised the museum's director – and a single photographer made up a farewell party. Two young men held umbrellas over the Marshalls' heads as they descended the steps by the columns. I held back, slowing my pace rather than stopping and drawing attention to myself. There was a round of handshakes, and a chorus of genial laughter at something Lord Marshall said. He leaned on a walking stick, the lacquered cane that I think has become something of a trademark. He and his wife and the director posed for the camera, then the Marshalls came away, accompanied by the suited young men with the umbrellas. The museum officials remained on the steps. My concern was to see which way the Marshalls would go so that I could avoid a head-on encounter. They chose to pass the guns on their left, so I did the same.

Concealed partly by the raised barrels and their concrete emplacements, partly by my tilted umbrella, I kept hidden, but still managed a good look. They went by in silence. He was familiar from his photographs. Despite the liver spots and the purplish swags under his eyes, he at last appeared the cruelly handsome plutocrat, though somewhat reduced. Age had shrunk his face and delivered the look he had always fallen short of by a fraction. It was his jaw that had scaled itself down – bone-loss had been kind. He was a little doddery and flat-footed, but he walked reasonably well for a man of eighty-eight. One becomes a judge of these things. But his hand was firmly on her arm and the stick was not just for show. It has often been remarked upon, how much good he did in the world. Perhaps he's spent a lifetime making amends. Or perhaps he just swept onwards without a thought, to live the life that was always his.

As for Lola – my high-living, chain-smoking cousin – here she was, still as lean and fit as a racing dog, and still faithful. Who would have dreamed it? This, as they used to say, was the side on which her bread was buttered. That may sound sour, but it went through my mind as I glanced across at her. She wore a sable coat and a scarlet wide-brimmed fedora. Bold rather than vulgar. Near-on eighty years old, and still wearing high heels. They clicked on the pavement with the sound of a younger woman's stride. There was no sign of a cigarette. In fact, there was an air of the health farm about her, and an indoor tan. She was taller than her husband now, and there was no doubting her vigour. But there was also something comic about her – or was I clutching at straws? She was heavy on the make-up, quite garish around the mouth and liberal with the smoothing cream and powder. I've always been a puritan in this, so I count myself an unreliable witness. I thought there was a touch of the stage villain here – the gaunt figure, the black coat, the lurid lips. A cigarette holder, a lapdog tucked under one arm and she could have been Cruella de Vil.

We passed by each other in a matter of seconds. I went on up the steps, then stopped under the pediment, out of the rain, to watch the group make its way to the car. He was helped in first, and I saw then how frail he was. He couldn't bend at the waist, nor could he take his own weight on one foot. They had to lift him into his seat. The far door was held open for Lady Lola who folded herself in with a terrible agility. I watched the Rolls pull away into the traffic, then I went in. Seeing them laid something heavy on my heart, and I was trying not to think about it, or feel it now. I already had enough to deal with today. But Lola's health was on my mind as I gave my bag in at the cloakroom, and exchanged cheery good mornings with the porters. The rule here is that one must be escorted up to the reading room in a lift, whose cramped space makes small-talk compulsory as far as I'm concerned. As I made it – shocking weather, but improvements were due by the weekend – I couldn't resist thinking about my encounter outside in the fundamental terms of health: I might outlive Paul Marshall, but Lola would certainly outlive me. The consequences of this are clear. The issue has been with us for years. As my editor put it once, publication equals litigation. But I could hardly face that now. There was already enough that I didn't want to be thinking about. I had come here to be busy.

I spent a while chatting with the Keeper of Documents. I handed over the bundle of letters Mr Nettle wrote me about Dunkirk – most gratefully received. They'll be stored with all the others I've given. The Keeper had found me an obliging old colonel of the Buffs, something of an amateur historian himself, who had read the relevant pages of my typescript and faxed through his suggestions. His notes were handed to me now – irascible, helpful. I was completely absorbed by them, thank God.

'Absolutely no (underlined twice) soldier serving with the British army would say "On the double". Only an American would give such an order. The correct term is "At the double".'

I love these little things, this pointillist approach to verisimilitude, the correction of detail that cumulatively gives such satisfaction.

'No one would ever think of saying "twenty-five-pound guns". The term was either "twenty-five pounders" or "twenty-five-pounder guns". Your usage would sound distinctly bizarre, even to a man who was not with the Royal Artillery.'

Like policemen in a search team, we go on hands and knees and crawl our way towards the truth.

'You have your RAF chappie wearing a beret. I really don't think so. Outside the Tank Corps, even the army didn't have them in 1940. I think you'd better give the man a forage cap.'

Finally, the colonel, who began his letter by addressing me as 'Miss Tallis', allowed some impatience with my sex to show through. What was our kind doing anyway, meddling in these affairs?

'Madame (underlined three times) – a Stuka does not carry "a single thousand-ton bomb". Are you aware that a navy frigate hardly weighs that much? I suggest you look into the matter further.'

Merely a typo. I meant to type 'pound'. I made a note of these corrections, and wrote a letter of thanks to the colonel. I paid for some photocopies of documents which I arranged into orderly piles for my own archives. I returned the books I had been using to the front desk, and threw away various scraps of paper. The workspace was cleared of all traces of me. As I said my goodbyes to the Keeper, I learned that the Marshall Foundation was about to make a grant to the museum. After a round of handshaking with the other librarians, and my promise to acknowledge the department's help, a porter was called to see me down. Very kindly, the girl in the cloakroom called a taxi, and one of the younger members of the door staff carried my bag all the way out to the pavement.

During the ride back north, I thought about the colonel's letter, or rather, about my own pleasure in these trivial alterations. If I really cared so much about facts, I should have written a different kind of book. But my work was done. There would be no further drafts. These were the thoughts I had as we entered the old tram tunnel under the Aldwych, just before I fell asleep. When I was woken by the driver, the cab was outside my flat in Regent's Park.

I filed away the papers I had brought from the library, made a sandwich, then packed an overnight case. I was conscious as I moved about my flat, from one familiar room to another, that the years of my independence could soon be over. On my desk was a framed photograph of my husband, Thierry, taken in Marseilles two years before he died. One day I would be asking who he was. I soothed myself by spending time choosing a dress to wear for my birthday dinner. The process was actually rejuvenating. I'm thinner than I was a year ago. As I trailed my fingers along the racks I forgot about the diagnosis for minutes on end. I decided on a shirtwaisted cashmere dress in dove grey. Everything followed easily then: a white satin scarf held by Emily's cameo brooch, patent court shoes – low-heeled, of course – a black dévoré shawl. I closed the case and was surprised by how light it seemed as I carried it into the hallway.

My secretary would be coming in tomorrow, before I returned. I left her a note, setting out the work I wanted her to do, then I took a book and a cup of tea and sat in an armchair at a window with a view over the park. I've always been good at not thinking about the things that are really troubling me. But I was not able to read. I felt excited. A journey into the country, a dinner in my honour, a renewal of family bonds. And yet I'd had one of those classic conversations with a doctor. I should have been depressed. Was it possible that I was, in the modern term, in denial? Thinking this changed nothing. The car was not due for another half hour and I was restless. I got out of the chair, and went up and down the room a few times. My knees hurt if I sit too long. I was haunted by the thought of Lola, the severity of that gaunt old painted face, her boldness of stride in the perilous high heels, her vitality, ducking into the Rolls. Was I competing with her as I trod the carpet between the fireplace and the Chesterfield? I always thought the high life, the cigarettes, would see her off. Even in our fifties I thought that. But at eighty she has a voracious, knowing look. She was always the superior older girl, one step ahead of me. But in that final important matter, I will be ahead of her, while she'll live on to be a hundred. I will not be able to publish in my lifetime.

The Rolls must have turned my head, because the car when it came – fifteen minutes late – was a disappointment. Such things do not usually trouble me. It was a dusty minicab, whose rear seat was covered in nylon fur with a zebra pattern.

But the driver, Michael, was a cheerful West Indian lad who took my case and made a fuss of sliding the front passenger seat forwards for me. Once it was established that I would not tolerate the thumping music at any volume from the speakers on the ledge behind my head, and he had recovered from a little sulkiness, we got along well and talked about families. He had never known his father, and his mother was a doctor at the Middlesex Hospital. He himself graduated in law from Leicester University, and now he was going to the LSE to write a doctoral thesis on law and poverty in the third world. As we headed out of London by the dismal Westway, he gave me his condensed version: no property law, therefore no capital, therefore no wealth.

'There's a lawyer talking,' I said. 'Drumming up business for yourself.'

He laughed politely, though he must have thought me profoundly stupid. It is quite impossible these days to assume anything about people's educational level from the way they talk or dress or from their taste in music. Safest to treat everyone you meet as a distinguished intellectual.

After twenty minutes we had spoken enough, and as the car reached a motorway and the engine settled into an unvarying drone, I fell asleep again and when I woke we were on a country road, and a painful tightness was around my forehead. I took from my handbag three aspirins which I chewed and swallowed with distaste. Which portion of my mind, of my memory, had I lost to a minuscule stroke while I was asleep? I would never know. It was then, in the back of that tinny little car, that I experienced for the first time something like desperation. Panic would be too strong a word. Claustrophobia was part of it, helpless confinement within a process of decay, and a sensation of shrinking. I tapped Michael's shoulder and asked him to turn on his music. He assumed I was indulging him because we were close to our destination, and he refused. But I insisted, and so the thumping twangy bass noise resumed, and over it, a light baritone chanting in Caribbean patois to the rhythms of a nursery rhyme, or a playground skipping-rope jingle. It helped me. It amused me. It sounded so childish, though I had a suspicion that some terrible sentiments were being expressed. I didn't ask for a translation.

The music was still playing as we turned into the drive of Tilney's Hotel . More than twenty-five years had passed since I came this way, for Emily's funeral. I noticed first the absence of parkland trees, the giant elms lost to disease I supposed, and the remaining oaks cleared to make way for a golf course. We were slowing now to let some golfers and their caddies cross. I couldn't help thinking of them as trespassers. The woods that surrounded Grace Turner's old bungalow were still there, and as the drive cleared a last stand of beeches, the main house came into view. There was no need to be nostalgic – it was always an ugly place. But from a distance it had a stark and unprotected look. The ivy which used to soften the effect of that bright red façade had been stripped away, perhaps to preserve the brickwork. Soon we were approaching the first bridge, and already I could see that the lake was no longer there. On the bridge we were suspended above an area of perfect lawn, such as you sometimes see in an old moat. It was not unpleasant in itself, if you did not know what had once been there – the sedge, the ducks, and the giant carp that two tramps had roasted and feasted on by the island temple. Which had also gone. Where it stood was a wooden bench, and a litter basket. The island, which of course was no longer that, was a long mound of smooth grass, like an immense ancient barrow, where rhododendrons and other shrubbery were growing. There was a gravel path looping round, with more benches here and there, and spherical garden lights. I did not have time to try and estimate the spot where I once sat and comforted the young Lady Lola Marshall, for we were already crossing the second bridge and then slowing to turn into the asphalted car park that ran the length of the house.

Michael carried my case into the reception area in the old

hall. How odd that they should have taken the trouble to lay needlecord carpet over those black and white tiles. I supposed that the acoustic was always troublesome, though I never minded it. A Vivaldi Season was burbling through concealed speakers. There was a decent rosewood desk with a computer screen and a vase of flowers, and standing guard on each side were two suits of armour; mounted on the panelling, crossed halberds and a coat of arms; above them, the portrait that used to be in the dining room which my grandfather imported to give the family some lineage. I tipped Michael and earnestly wished him luck with property rights and poverty. I was trying to unsay my foolish remark about lawyers. He wished me happy birthday and shook my hand – how feathery and unassertive his grip was – and left. From behind the desk a grave-faced girl in a business suit gave me my key and told me that the old library had been booked for the exclusive use of our party. The few who had already arrived had gone out for a stroll. The plan was to gather for drinks at six. A porter would bring my case up. There was a lift for my convenience.

No one to greet me then, but I was relieved. I preferred to take it in alone, the interest of so much change, before I was obliged to become the guest of honour. I took the lift to the second floor, went through a set of glass fire doors, and walked along the corridor whose polished boards creaked in a familiar way. It was bizarre, to see the bedrooms numbered and locked. Of course, my room number – seven – told me nothing, but I think I'd already guessed where I would be sleeping. At least, when I stopped outside the door, I wasn't surprised. Not my old room, but Auntie Venus's, always considered to have the best view in the house, over the lake, the driveway, the woods and the hills beyond. Charles, Pierrot's grandson and the organising spirit, would have reserved it for me.

It was a pleasant surprise, stepping in. Rooms on either side had been incorporated to make a grand suite. On a low glass table stood a giant spray of hothouse flowers. The huge high bed Auntie Venus had occupied for so long without complaint had gone, and so had the carved trousseau chest and the green silk sofa. They were now the property of the eldest son by Leon's second marriage and installed in a castle somewhere in the Scottish Highlands. But the new furnishings were fine, and I liked my room. My case arrived, I ordered a pot of tea and hung my dress. I explored my sitting room which had a writing desk and a good lamp, and was impressed by the vastness of the bathroom with its pot-pourri and stacks of towels on a heated rack. It was a relief not to see everything in terms of tasteless decline – it easily becomes a habit of age. I stood at the window to admire the sunlight slanting over the golf course, and burnishing the bare trees on the distant hills. I could not quite accept the absence of the lake, but it could be restored one day perhaps, and the building itself surely embraced more human happiness now, as a hotel, than it did when I lived here.

Charles phoned an hour later, just as I was beginning to think about getting dressed. He suggested that he came to get me at six fifteen, after everyone else was gathered, and bring me down so that I could make an entrance. And so it was that I entered that enormous L-shaped room, on his arm, in my cashmere finery, to the applause, and then the raised glasses of fifty relatives. My immediate impression as I came in was of recognising no one. Not a familiar face! I wondered if this was a foretaste of the incomprehension I had been promised. Then slowly people came into focus. One must make allowances for the years, and the speed with which babes-in-arms become boisterous ten-year-olds. There was no mistaking my brother, curled and slumped to one side in his wheelchair, a napkin at his throat to catch the spills of champagne that someone held to his lips. As I leaned over to kiss Leon, he managed a smile in the half of his face still under his control. And nor did I mistake for long Pierrot, much shrivelled and with a shining pate I wanted to put my hand on, but still twinkly as ever and very much the paterfamilias. It's accepted that we never mention his sister.

I made a progress round the room, with Charles at my side, prompting me with the names. How delightful to be at the heart of such a good-willed reunion. I reacquainted myself with the children, grandchildren and great-grandchildren of Jackson who died fifteen years ago. In fact, between them the twins had fairly peopled the room. And Leon had not done so badly either, with his four marriages and dedicated fathering. We ranged in age from three months to his eighty-nine years. And what a din of voices, from gruff to shrill, as the waiters came round with more champagne and lemonade. The ageing children of distant cousins greeted me like long-lost friends. Every second person wanted to tell me something kind about my books. A group of enchanting teenagers told me how they were studying my books at school. I promised to read the typescript novel of someone's absent son. Notes and cards were pressed into my hands. Piled on a table in the corner of the room were presents which I would have to open, several children told me, before, not after, their bedtime. I made my promises, I shook hands, kissed cheeks and lips, admired and tickled babies, and just as I was beginning to think how much I wanted to sit down somewhere, I noticed that chairs were being set out, facing one way. Then Charles clapped his hands and, shouting over the noise that barely subsided, announced that before dinner there was to be an entertainment in my honour. Would we all take our seats.

I was led to an armchair in the front row. Next to me was old Pierrot, who was in conversation with a cousin on his left. A fidgety near-silence descended on the room. From a corner came the agitated whispers of children, which I thought it tactful to ignore. While we waited, while I had, as it were, some seconds to myself, I looked about me, and only now properly absorbed the fact that all the books were gone from the library, and all the shelves too. That was why the room had seemed so much bigger than I remembered. The only reading matter was the country magazines in racks by the fireplace. At the sound of shushing, and the scrape of a chair, there stood before us a boy with a black cloak over his shoulders. He was pale, freckled and ginger-haired – no mistaking a Quincey child. I guessed him to be about nine or ten years old. His body was frail, which made his head seem large and gave him an ethereal look. But he looked confident as he gazed around the room, waiting for his audience to settle. Then at last he raised his elfin chin, filled his lungs, and spoke out in a clear pure treble. I'd been expecting a magic trick, but what I heard had the ring of the supernatural.

> This is the tale of spontaneous Arabella
> Who ran off with an extrinsic fellow.
> It grieved her parents to see their first born
> Evanesce from her home to go to Eastbourne
> Without permission, to get ill and find indigence
> Until she was down to her last sixpence.

Suddenly, she was right there before me, that busy, priggish, conceited little girl, and she was not dead either, for when people tittered appreciatively at 'evanesce' my feeble heart – ridiculous vanity! – made a little leap. The boy recited with a thrilling clarity, and a jarring touch of what my generation would call Cockney, though I have no idea these days what the significance is of a glottal 't'. I knew the words were mine, but I barely remembered them, and it was hard to concentrate, with so many questions, so much feeling, crowding in. Where had they found the copy, and was this unearthly confidence a symptom of a different age? I glanced at my neighbour, Pierrot. He had his handkerchief out and was dabbing at his eyes, and I don't think it was only great-grandfatherly pride. I also suspected that this was all his idea. The prologue rose to its reasonable climax:

> For that fortuitous girl the sweet day dawned
> To wed her gorgeous prince. But be warned,

> Because Arabella almost learned too late,
> That before we love, we must cogitate!

We made a rowdy applause. There was even some vulgar whistling. That dictionary, that *Oxford Concise*. Where was it now? North-west Scotland? I wanted it back. The boy made a bow and retreated a couple of yards and was joined by four other children who had come up, unnoticed by me, and were waiting in what would have been the wings.

And so *The Trials of Arabella* began, with a leave-taking from the anxious, saddened parents. I recognised the heroine immediately as Leon's great-granddaughter, Chloe. What a lovely solemn girl she is, with her rich low voice and her mother's Spanish blood. I remember being at her first birthday party, and it seemed only months ago. I watched her fall convincingly into poverty and despair, once abandoned by the wicked count – who was the prologue speaker in his black cloak. In less than ten minutes it was over. In memory, distorted by a child's sense of time, it had always seemed the length of a Shakespeare play. I had completely forgotten that after the wedding ceremony Arabella and the medical prince link arms and, speaking in unison, step forwards to address to the audience a final couplet.

> Here's the beginning of love at the end of our travail.
> So farewell, kind friends, as into the sunset we sail!

Not my best, I thought. But the whole room, except for Leon, Pierrot and myself, rose for the applause. How practised these children were, right down to the curtain call. Hand in hand, they stood in line abreast, taking their cue from Chloe, stepped back two paces, came forwards, bowed again. In the uproar, no one noticed that poor Pierrot was completely overcome and put his face in his hands. Was he reliving that lonely, terrifying time here after his parents' divorce? They'd so much wanted to be in the play, the twins, for that evening in the library, and here it was at last, sixty-four years late, and his brother long dead.

I was helped out of my comfortable chair and made a little speech of thanks. Competing with a wailing baby at the back of the room, I tried to evoke that hot summer of nineteen thirty-five, when the cousins came down from the north. I turned to the cast and told them that our production would have been no match for theirs. Pierrot was nodding emphatically. I explained that it was entirely my fault the rehearsals fell apart, because halfway through I had decided to become a novelist. There was indulgent laughter, more applause, then Charles announced that it was dinner. And so the pleasant evening unravelled – the noisy meal at which I even drank a little wine, the presents, bedtime for the younger children, while their bigger brothers and sisters went off to watch television. Then speeches over coffee and much good-natured laughter, and by ten o'clock I was beginning to think of my splendid room upstairs, not because I was tired, but because I was tired of being in company and the object of so much attention, however kindly. Another half hour passed in goodnights and farewells before Charles and his wife Annie escorted me to my room.

Now it is five in the morning and I am still at the writing desk, thinking over my strange two days. It's true about the old not needing sleep – at least, not in the night. I still have so much to consider, and soon, within the year perhaps, I'll have far less of a mind to do it with. I've been thinking about my last novel, the one that should have been my first. The earliest version, January 1940, the latest, March 1999, and in between, half a dozen different drafts. The second draft, June 1947, the third . . . who cares to know? My fifty-nine-year assignment is over. There was our crime – Lola's, Marshall's, mine – and from the second version onwards, I set out to describe it. I've regarded it as my duty to disguise nothing – the names, the places, the exact circumstances – I put it all there as a matter of historical record. But as a matter of legal reality, so various editors have told me over the years, my forensic memoir could never be published while my fellow criminals were alive. You may only libel yourself and the dead. The Marshalls have been active about the courts since the late forties, defending their good names with a most expensive ferocity. They could ruin a publishing house with ease from their current accounts. One might almost think they had something to hide. Think, yes, but not write. The obvious suggestions have been made – displace, transmute, dissemble. Bring down the fogs of the imagination! What are novelists for? Go just so far as is necessary, set up camp inches beyond the reach, the fingertips of the law. But no one knows these precise distances until a judgment is handed down. To be safe, one would have to be bland and obscure. I know I cannot publish until they are dead. And as of this morning, I accept that will not be until I am. No good, just one of them going. Even with Lord Marshall's bone-shrunk mug on the obituary pages at last, my cousin from the north would not tolerate an accusation of criminal conspiracy.

There was a crime. But there were also the lovers. Lovers and their happy ends have been on my mind all night long. As into the sunset we sail. An unhappy inversion. It occurs to me that I have not travelled so very far after all, since I wrote my little play. Or rather, I've made a huge digression and doubled back to my starting place. It is only in this last version that my lovers end well, standing side by side on a South London pavement as I walk away. All the preceding drafts were pitiless. But now I can no longer think what purpose would be served if, say, I tried to persuade my reader, by direct or indirect means, that Robbie Turner died of septicaemia at Bray Dunes on 1 June 1940, or that Cecilia was killed in September of the same year by the bomb that destroyed Balham Underground station. That I never saw them in that year. That my walk across London ended at the church on Clapham Common, and that a cowardly Briony limped back to the hospital, unable to confront her recently bereaved sister. That the letters the lovers wrote are in the archives of the War Museum. How could that constitute an ending? What sense or hope or satisfaction could a reader draw from such an account? Who would want to believe that they never met again, never fulfilled their love? Who would want to believe that, except in the service of the bleakest realism? I couldn't do it to them. I'm too old, too frightened, too much in love with the shred of life I have remaining. I face an incoming tide of forgetting, and then oblivion. I no longer possess the courage of my pessimism. When I am dead, and the Marshalls are dead, and the novel is finally published, we will only exist as my inventions. Briony will be as much of a fantasy as the lovers who shared a bed in Balham and enraged their landlady. No one will care what events and which individuals were misrepresented to make a novel. I know there's always a certain kind of reader who will be compelled to ask, But what *really* happened? The answer is simple: the lovers survive and flourish. As long as there is a single copy, a solitary typescript of my final draft, then my spontaneous, fortuitous sister and her medical prince survive to love.

The problem these fifty-nine years has been this: how can a novelist achieve atonement when, with her absolute power of deciding outcomes, she is also God? There is no one, no entity or higher form that she can appeal to, or be reconciled with, or that can forgive her. There is nothing outside her. In her imagination she has set the limits and the terms. No atonement for God, or novelists, even if they are atheists. It was always an impossible task, and that was precisely the point. The attempt was all.

I've been standing at the window, feeling waves of tiredness beat the remaining strength from my body. The floor seems to be undulating beneath my feet. I've been watching the first grey light bring into view the park and the bridges over the vanished lake. And the long narrow driveway down which they drove Robbie away, into the whiteness. I like to think that it isn't weakness or evasion, but a final act of kindness, a stand against oblivion and despair, to let my lovers live and to unite them at the end. I gave them happiness, but I was not so self-serving as to let them forgive me. Not quite, not yet. If I had the power to conjure them at my birthday celebration . . . Robbie and Cecilia, still alive, still in love, sitting side by side in the library, smiling at *The Trials of Arabella*? It's not impossible.

But now I must sleep.

Acknowledgements

I am indebted to the staff of the Department of Documents in the Imperial War Museum for allowing me to see unpublished letters, journals and reminiscences of soldiers and nurses serving in 1940. I am also indebted to the following authors and books: Gregory Blaxland, *Destination Dunkirk*; Walter Lord, *The Miracle of Dunkirk*; Lucilla Andrews, *No Time for Romance*. I am grateful to Claire Tomalin, and to Craig Raine and Tim Garton-Ash for their incisive and helpful comments, and above all to my wife, Annalena McAfee, for all her encouragement and formidable close reading.

IM